Last Man Standing

Catalyst Trilogy Book Three

TIMOTHY DIAMOND

Last Man Standing
Author: Timothy Diamond

National Library of Australia Cataloguing-in-Publication entry

Creator: Diamond, Timothy author.

Creator: Diamond, Timothy, author.

Title: Last Man Standing / Timothy Diamond.

ISBN: 9780994263148 (paperback)

Series: Diamond, Timothy. Catalyst Trilogy ; bk. 3.

Subjects: Undercover operations--Fiction.

Organized crime--Fiction.

Dewey Number: A823.4

Published with the assistance of www.loveofbooks.com.au

"Catalyst"
By Timothy Diamond

"Catalyst":

/'katalist/n – 1. A chemical agent that causes catalysis

2. A substance (e g an enzyme) that changes especially increases, the rate of a chemical reaction, but itself remains chemically unchanged.

3. Somebody or something whose action inspires further and usually more important events.

As defined by: The Longman Pocket English Dictionary

First published   1986

Third Impression 1987

ABOUT THE AUTHOR

"Timothy Diamond" is a pseudonym for my real name.

I grew up in the provincial town of Rockhampton in Central Queensland, and the exploits of my hero, "Tom Davis," are loosely based on actual events in my own life. (Hence the pseudonym)

My story is original and exciting; it contains elements of young love, teenage rebellion, family conflict, corruption, war time experiences, and espionage, a book that could rival the works of Clive Cussler and Ken Follett.

The Catalyst Trilogy is my first full length work of fiction. However, between 1988 and 1994, I wrote multiple articles and reports on recreational diving that were published in *Scuba Diver Magazine* and the *Gold Coast Bulletin*. I also wrote the feature article 'The Round Trip' for *Yachting Australia* magazine in 2009.

The first book in the "Catalyst" trilogy, "Playing with Fire" was written and published in 2014, and is selling well. After taking a break, I started writing this second book of the trilogy, "Divine Retribution", and completed it in April 2015. After it was completed, I started work on the final book of the trilogy, "Last Man Standing" which I completed in October.

ACKNOWLEDGEMENTS

To Diane, without your insistence, patience, putting up with my all night sessions, first draft editing, and cover design. This book could not have been written. Thank you, I love you.

Ralf B: for 30 odd years, you gained snippets that hinted at some of the things I had been involved in, you suggested that I write a book, well now it's all out there; I hope you enjoy the full story in the right sequence. To change Spock's dialogue a little, "You have been, and always will be, my best friend".

Diana Mason: for keeping an eye on my health, and helping me function.

Martin Devereaux: for keeping my hands working to pound the keyboard.

Chris Hannon: for keeping me looking good, and cutting out the bad bits.

Tennille: for keeping the hair out of my eyes and from pulling it out.

Julie McGregor, my Publisher: for her patience and all the help.

GLOSSARY OF TERMS & ABBREVIATIONS

Military or 24 hour time is used in this book, expressed in hundreds. 3pm+12hrs would be 1500 hundred. Each time zone is given a designation in the phonetic alphabet GMT is expressed as Zulu time.

Distance is measured in both old imperial measure, and also metric. Even though we changed to the metric system in 1964, some people and places still use the imperial system.

ASIS – Australian Secret Intelligence Service (the more militarized spy agency, much more competent that its civillian counterpart)

DFRDB – Defence Force Retirement and Death Benefit

ASIO – Australian Secret Intelligence Organization

AFP – Australian Federal Police

ASAP – As Soon As Possible

CC TV – Closed Circuit Cameras

FEDS – AFP

DEA – Drug Enforcement Agency (US)

M.I.5 – British internal Security

CIA – Central Intelligence Agency (US)

M.I.6 – British overseas Security

Mossad – Israeli Intelligence

CIB – Criminal Investigation Branch

TAC – Abbreviation for tactical

ETA – Estimated time of Arrival

RPG - Rocket Propelled Grenade

SAS – Special Air Service

TAG – Tactical Assault Group

Regulator – SCUBA Mouthpiece

BCD – Bouyancy Compensation device

ETA – Estimated Time of Arrival

SCUBA – Self Contained Underwater Breathing Apparatus

BRA – Bougainville Revolutionary Army

Helo – Helicopter

GPS – Global Positioning System

RIBs – Rigid Inflatable Boat

FO – Foreign Office

GLOSSARY OF
TERMS & ABBREVIATIONS

How to work out boat speed from knots to kilometres per hour:

1 knot (kt) is equal to 6 kilometres, so multiply by six, and then divide by 2.7 to bring it into metric as opposed to imperial, i.e. a boat doing 10kt:

10 x 6 = 60 divide x 2.7 = 22.22kph

LZ – Landing zone	Click – Kilometre
2IC – 2nd in charge	Sitrep – Situation Report

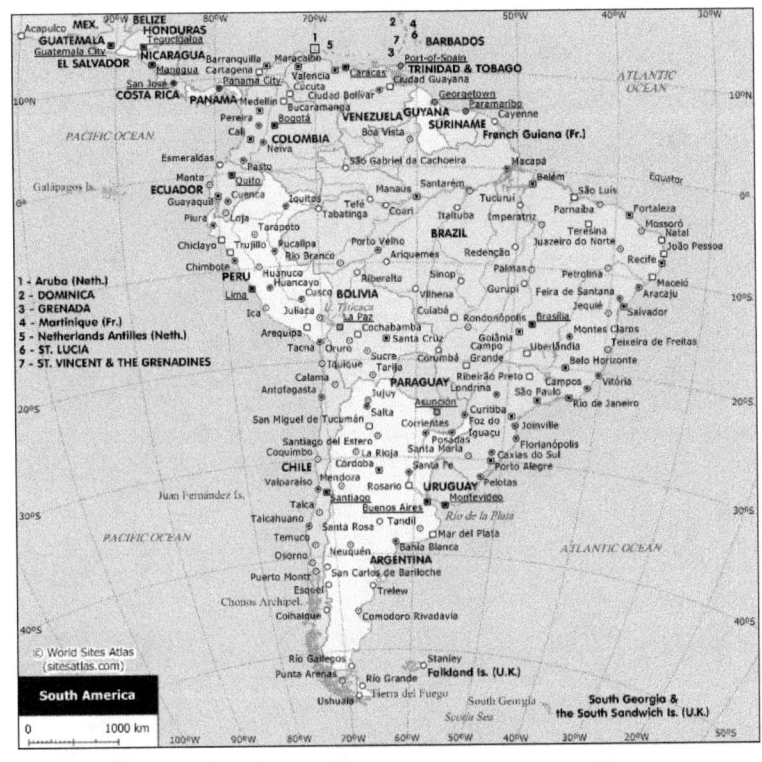

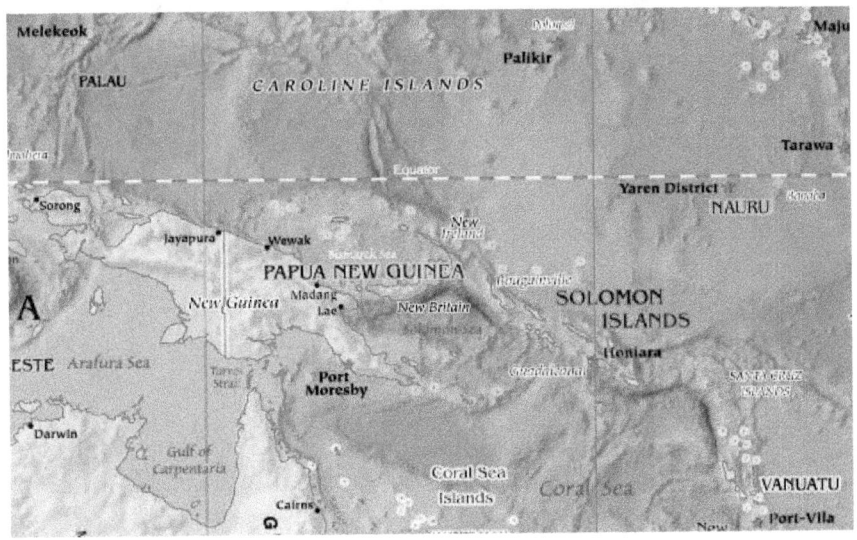

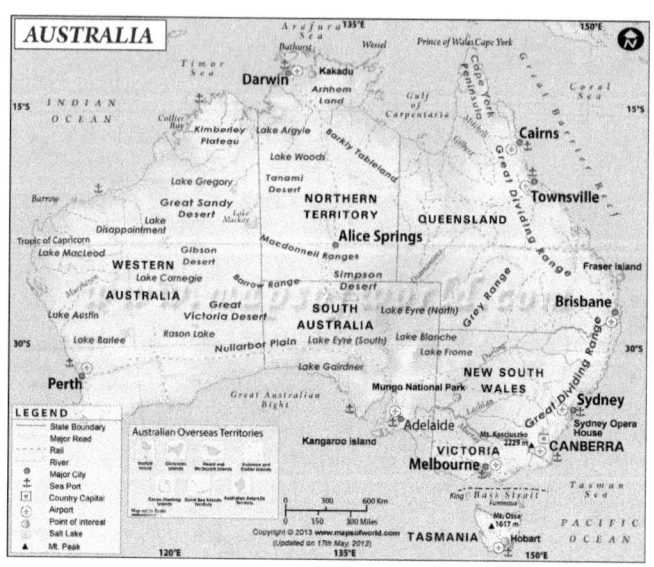

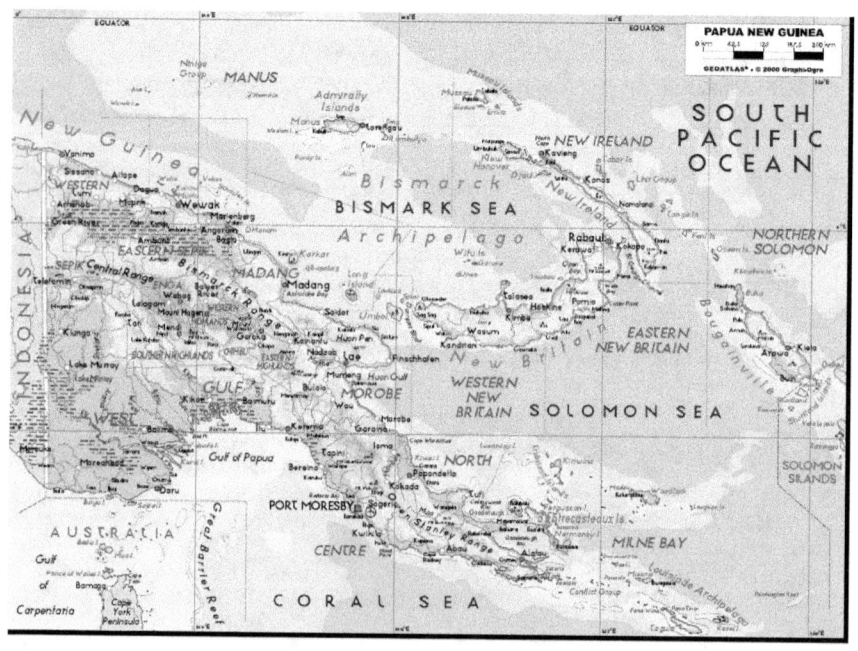

CHAPTER 1

Each morning of that first week after breakfast, the pain would begin, the repeated laser bursts seemed to go on for hours, and at times I felt like yelling out through the high threshold pain barrier I had built up over the years. The only way I was able to withstand that amount of torture, and pain was to mentally remind myself constantly, 'why I'd agreed to this' and 'how I'd got here.'

After Callaway had left my office, I did nothing but mull over his offer in my head, as I tried to weigh up the pros and cons, and then compared it to what Joseph had offered. Both offers ran along the same sort of lines, the only difference between them being, in Israel I'd be a large fish in a medium sized bowl, whereas here I'd be only a small fish in a large bowl, but here the job wouldn't be based on constant warfare either. I figured that if I did decide to have a go at this that Joseph's offer would still be on the back burner, if I needed it.

That night over a couple of drinks I talked with Lisa about the offer, and she laughed, as she said, "Tiger why are you beating about the bush, you already know you're champing at the bit to have a go." That comment made me laugh also, and replied "Yeah I suppose you're right, but I'll need to speak to Callaway more about this." The next morning at work, I phoned the number Callaway had given me, and when he answered, I said "Davis here John, I need to talk further with you is that possible?" He answered "Yeah, what I'll do is phone your CO, tell him I need you for the rest of the week. Then I'll pick you up at ten, and we'll go for a drive." Fifteen minutes later, Colonel Lewis phoned to tell me I'd be required by the Foreign Affairs officer, and to make myself available to him for the rest of the week. I smiled as I hung up the phone, and then went to change into a set of civvies I had in my locker.

At ten, as Callaway drove up to my office, I was dressed in a pair of jeans and a golf shirt, out of his car window he said "Drive your car home, I'll follow, and we'll go on from there." I left my car in the driveway, got into his car, and as he reversed out, said "Whereto?" So we went out to the Samford country club, he ordered drinks while I got a table away from anybody else toward the back of the room. As he joined me he passed a pot of beer, and said "Cheers," as we sat. He looked at me waiting for me to ask what I wanted and he didn't have to wait long, I asked "If I accept the offer, what happens next?"

Callaway explained the steps that would then be taken, as I was inducted as an ASIS agent. Once you leave the Defence Force your background is investigated, and if you're found not to be a foreign spy, we induct you into the service. I stopped him there and asked, "Do I go in as any sort of rank, or what?" He thought for a minute, and replied "Oh I see what you mean, seniority or grading?" I nodded, and he smiled, "Yes, normally freshly inducted agents are classified with a level two security grading, and therefore only have clearance to view level two classified documents. Nothing above level two, but you however are a different kettle of fish. Because of your previous background, you will be given a level eight security grading, and there's only two more grading levels after that, nine and ten."

I looked at him, and said, "Ok I get a level eight security clearance, what does that mean exactly?" He Laughed, and said "Ah yes, I see what you're getting at, well you would be one of a few, a dozen in all with that grading, and therefore are considered in the upper echelons of the service. You have clearance for any document s up to Top Secret Eyes Only, to arrest people within this country and certain other countries, also the authority to kill here and overseas if required, and you'll be privy to so much information, you'll not want to know." "Right, and what level are you, before we go on." I answered. He laughed, and replied "Same as you eight, our boss at the FO, Colin Gorman is a nine, and there's only one ten, that's the present Prime Minister at the time."

I let him go on with what happens then. I'd be flown to the service headquarters which is in Sydney, where all the paperwork would be gone through and signed. Then my ID would be entered into the system and counter verified with palm prints. I would be given three ID's one as a Foreign Affairs Diplomatic Attaché, one as a high level ASIS agent, and one as an AFP Officer. Each had a different use, and I would be told that during the induction. After the induction, I would be taken on a tour of all the inter-state headquarters buildings, and a couple of sub branches. Then in my case, sent to the US for Reconstructive Surgery to remove any distinguishing features, once that was completed I would be able to take up my position as a station chief.

After this information, we took a break for lunch, and he asked if this place had a reasonable course, and then we talked golf for a while until we'd finished lunch, and then I said, "Ok back to it, what if I needed something done, what happens then?" He thought for a minute, and replied "As a level eight any request you have supersedes any request lower than your grading, why?"

I looked at him, and then said "Well I wish to keep tabs on four people, and it would be an ongoing thing," he replied "Well considering that would be a permanent request, you'd have to ask the boss's permission for that, perhaps you may wish to ask him when you meet him."

Then I asked, "If I decide to accept the offer, could I start getting things under way before my discharge was official?" He smiled, and replied "Normally no, but in your case we may have a little leeway, let me make some calls, and I'll pick you up in the morning from your place at nine o'clock." I nodded in agreement, and then we left the country club, he dropped me at my place, and then continued on, after I put my car away, and closed the garage, I went upstairs, and Lisa was coming down, and told me she was going to have a soak in the spa, and asked if I was going to join her, so I turned back down, and grabbed two towels out of the cupboard, and then stripped off and went in naked, seeing this she shrugged her shoulders and stripped off the swimming costume she was wearing, and got in naked as well.

While we were in there soaking, I told her what had been going on, and she warned me that I would be better off switching or taking my DFRDB (Defence Force Retirement and Death Benefit), and warned if I took it lump sum, I'd probably lose some, but it may be worth it in the long run. So I put that on my mental to do list.

The following morning John arrived, and I invited him in for a coffee before we left, and while we were having it, I asked "What about weaponry?" He answered "Well if you don't have your own, we can supply you with a pistol when required." I laughed and was shaking my head, and as he finished his coffee I took him downstairs to the barroom and opened the cupboard that had my weapons hanging up in it. He exclaimed "Holy shit! You should have them in a safe. You wouldn't need those assault weapons, but your pistol yes. Oh you've got a silencer for it too huh, ok if you wanted to. These could be put into the safe at the office, speaking of which that's where we're going now. Oh and your query about getting things under way, no problem, all you have to do is let me know that you are accepting the job."

We drove into the city, and as we pulled into the carpark of a certain government building near the middle of the city and got out, we walked to a door that couldn't be seen from the carpark. It had 'No Entry' written on it and no door handle, he put a key into a panel beside the door and it slid open.

Then it slid shut as we entered into what I assumed was an empty area, there was another panel near the door, it had three buttons but without any keyhole. Curious I watched Callaway as he placed his hand on the glass panel, and pressed the bottom button. While his hand was on the panel a red beam of light scrolled across it much like a photocopier, he saw me watching and said "Biometric palm and fingerprint scanner, we own the building and this was put in during the building of the tower. It goes down five floors under the carparks deepest level which is three. So effectively we're eight stories below ground level. The top button takes you to hard copy filing, of maps and reference material, and closed operations. The second to radio, television, and computer communication, and the third where we are going, is office planning rooms, conference rooms, eating area, and a fully outfitted operations room with direct satellite feed.

If you join, I'll show you your office, even though you'd be third in charge, as a level eight you would effectively be the station chief because you have the right to veto or countermand any order." I thought to myself, *'huh, that sounds a bit weird, until I realised that the two people above me in station management didn't have the high clearance I would have, interesting to see how that played out.'*

John showed me my office, it was actually three rooms, a bathroom with toilet and shower, a room that had a double bed in it, and wardrobes, that joined to the bathroom with a connecting door, and the office itself which included the desk and seats, a leather lounge a couple of casual seats, a safe, and had a bar and hot drink making and food heating facilities.

John sat at the desk, and I sat opposite as leaned forward with his hands outstretched together, looked at me and said with a smile "Well what do you think?" I replied "I like," looking a little exasperated he asked "And, what are you going to do?" I smiled and thought *Gotcha!* Then I said "Ok, I'm in." He smiled and gave a sigh of relief, as he said "ok tomo…" that was as far as he got before I interrupted, and said "Tomorrow, first thing I'll go into work, resign, and ask for my discharge, so if you want me make it after ten, because I should be home by then." He nodded with a smile, opened a drawer of the desk and put a box and what looked like the same satellite phone I had in Israel on top of the desk, and passed them to me, saying "It's a sat phone, it has one number stored in it, mine, keep that and in the box is the charger, the number for it is also in the box, now tomorrow I'll pick you up after ten, if you're held up ring me, otherwise I'll see you just after ten, pack for a few days."

As he was about to continue, a woman with brownish blonde hair, about five six with grey eyes, a slim figure and roughly in her late twenties came in, and asked "Would you like coffee Mr Callaway?" John replied "Ah Janice, come in and let me introduce you, Janice Small this is Tom or Tiger Davis, he will be joining you here, Tiger, Janice will be your secretary and yes to coffee Janice for both of us thank you." She asked how I liked my coffee, I told her, and then she left. Then Callaway said "As I was about to say we'll be making a few trips to different places, but first we'll be going to headquarters in Sydney, where you'll meet the boss."

Five minutes after he finished talking, Janice came back carrying the drinks on a tray with a plate of biscuits, placed them on the desk, and left. While we were enjoying the drinks, I looked at my watch, it was only ten thirty, and I thought *if this was going to be all for today, if we get away soon I could probably change into uniform and resign today, and that way we can get away south earlier, yeah let's see what Callaway has to say.* So I asked John, and he thought it was a good idea, we finished our coffees and left the office, on the way out, Janice was at her desk, and I said "Janice, we have to go, sorry we left the mugs in there, but could you clean up for us please?" She replied "Certainly Mr Davis, no problems," I smiled, and said "Janice do me a favour please, call me Sir, Tom, or Tiger, Mr Davis is my father," she smiled and replied "Yes Tiger," I smiled and thanked her, and then Callaway and I left. Up in the carpark he showed me all the spaces that were for our exclusive use, and then drove me home.

Back at the transport compound, the first thing I did was get on the blower to the DFRDB office, and made arrangements to take all monies in my account as a lump sum payment, and I went through the figures with them on the phone, and all the paperwork and I'd have to go and sign them all, but this could be done at the same time I picked up my check, by taking lump sum it worked out that I'd be losing nearly thirty six thousand dollars, but I'd be receiving just over two million one hundred and forty one thousand, and thought, that'll really boost the bank balance! The next thing I did, after getting off the phone, was to make my way to the admin building, and asked to see the boss.

Colonel Lewis was taken back when I asked for my discharge, and after explaining the reason behind my quitting, was go into another branch of government, he was mollified and became really helpful, he too advised me to pull out my DFRDB, and with a smile I told him I'd already made the arrangements, he nodded and asked "So your mind's made up is it Tiger?"

I looked him in the eye as I replied, "Yes sir it is," he smiled and said "In that case I'll get this underway, and approved ASAP. Until it's approved and we know for sure, consider yourself on leave for as long as you want. I'll let you know one way or the other, all I can do is wish you luck, and thank you for your service." He stood up and shook my hand, and then I saluted before leaving his office. I then went back to my office and cleared everything of mine into the car, and then drove over to the DFRDB office, and after half an hour, left with a cheque for over two mill burning a hole in my pocket, so I drove straight to the nearest bank branch, and divided it up into ten differently timed term deposits.

Later at home, I used the sat phone to call Callaway, and told him everything had been done, and we could leave when he wished, and he told me he'd call me back. While I waited for his call, I packed my go bag, with enough gear for a week, plus going out clothes, and put my pistol and holster in, so when he called back and asked if I could be ready to leave at midnight, I was able to answer yes.

We landed at Mascot just after three am, and after grabbing a cab, John gave the driver a George street building address, and because we were still in the small hours the trip only took half an hour. As we walked into the building and down a corridor behind the lift bank, we came to another door with no handle, and no exit written on it, and just the now familiar keyhole, as we entered the lift to go down, john explained that this was the largest office in the country, and as such had a twenty-four hour operating kitchen, so we'd go to the dining room and have breakfast before everyone started arriving. When we'd finished a leisurely and extremely good breakfast, and finished our coffees, John took me for a tour of the complex, while he showed me the operations room, he told me the one in the other branches were mirror images of this one, only slightly smaller, there were huge video screens on each wall just above the oval table height, down the far end of the room was the communications desks that faced the table. The table itself had room for twelve to be seated, and each seating area had a phone handset, two built in speakers each side, and also a flexible microphone placed further in from behind the desk blotting pad at each chair.

Behind the main table the room wall were ringed with what looked to be comfortable desk chairs, but fixed into place, as I looked around I thought, *now this is nice, if the one in Bris is like this I'm definitely going to enjoy using it.* After the rest of the tour we went to John's office, which was much like the one I'd be using in Brisbane, and I learned that he was the Sydney office station chief.

As we entered the anteroom of his office his secretary Charlie, (Charlene) whom I was introduced to, was already at her desk, and as we went through into the office, she brought in a tray with coffee and tea supplies, and replenished the office supplies while she prepared drinks for us and then left. While we drank, John said "Ok, because I will be doing your induction, we'll start getting into the paperwork soon. We will go and get your ID's made up, your palm scanned and entered into the system with your level eight security grading, so you have access to the offices and so on. Almost everything you need is by palm print verification, so that's a must. Then we'll get together with one of our security fabrication tech's, and make up a new background legend for you, also a failsafe backstop identity and documents should you ever need it, that by the way stays in your office safe and never used, except in case of emergency."

Then we started on the mound of paperwork, filling in some signing others, one of the pieces of paperwork was an issue or indemnity form, so John crossed out issue and initialled it, then wrote in my pistol details including the silencer, and asked "Do you have it with you?" I nodded yes, and he said "Good, carry it and the silencer with you when we leave the office." When I signed the indemnity, he placed it aside from the other forms previously completed, and when we came to the last one he said with a laugh, "This one you probably know backward, but you'll have to sign the Official Secrets Act again while I witness it,", which I did, and he continued "Right let's get going, get the other stuff out of the way, and then you'll meet the boss and he'll swear you in."

First we had my ID's made, the ASIS ID, I was to wear whenever in any of the offices, or Government Buildings away from public view. The Foreign Office ID was to be carried with my passport, and the most important one the AFP ID was to be secreted where I could get it fast if I needed. It would allow me to arrest people in foreign countries, and get on commercial aircraft carrying a gun amongst other things. I looked at the ASIS ID, it had my photo, thumbprint and name, and an eight beside my photo. I clipped it to my belt, as we passed a laboratory, on the way to get my palm print done, John quickly turned into it and I followed. He spoke to one of the tech's, who came over and asked for my gun and silencer while holding the indemnity form. He took my gun, and went into a soundproof room, and as I watched, he fired one round into a water tank, and then screwed on the silencer and fired another round into another tank. Then he came back out and said "All done thank you, nice feel by the way," I smiled and nodded as John and I continued onto another room.

Another tech in a white coat was sitting at a desk, John gave him all my paperwork, including a copy of my service record. He started entering it all into a computer where everything about me would be recorded, and after an hour of typing and questions for me, he finished and stood up. He took me to a glass panel and had me place first one hand, and the other onto the panel while a red beam scrolled across the screen. After some typing onto a keyboard attached to the panel, he said with a smile "Right, that's you all done, you're now recorded into the system, you'll be able to use the palm readers as of now anywhere," "Thank you," I replied.

Then we moved onto another where after retrieving my records, the technician I sat across from passed me pad and pen, and asked me to fill as much about I had done prior to joining the army, starting as far back as I could remember, and to give dates of events, while he asked probing questions. We then discussed what sort of background would be required with Callaway, and turned to me and said, "With your backstop alter identity, I'll try to keep as close to your own as history, that way you'll get used to it quicker, now with your working background, I'll be changing everything, so you'll need to learn it thoroughly. Then they'll be recorded to your information, I should have this ready in an hour or so, if you want to go and have lunch while you're waiting that's ok with me." So John and I went off to the cafeteria and had lunch.

As we ate, I asked what would be in my new background legend, and he explained that because I would only go under-cover on aspects I was familiar with being to do with guns and drugs, my new legend would accommodate a criminal aspect to the background. Therefore, it will include petty to serious crimes like stealing, assault, where you've been caught, and the suspected involvement in other more serious crimes like robbery, extortion, and arms dealing, as of now forget you were ever in the army, because that won't exist in your new background.

When we returned to the backgrounds office the tech smiled, and said "Come in and take a seat gents, I've just finished planting your new background into the relevant police agencies, two main points to remember, early in your life you did time in jail for misdemeanour types offences, and that was served close to your hometown, so I made that Etna Creek Jail, I hope you know it, (I nodded), and you've also spent time in maximum security for assault and demanding money with menaces, also suspected of murder, but not enough evidence to prove it, maximum security jail in Brisbane is Boggo Road, don't forget that."

As I listened to him rabbit on, I thought, *Christ what's this turkey doing to me, if anybody I know hears this I'll be treated like a criminal, which I guess is what they wanted.* The tech was looking and waiting for an answer from me, and I said "Sorry can you repeat that please?" So he said "Because this is one of our manufactured backgrounds, the minute someone looks into it because it's tagged someone here will know immediately, but I asked you if you wanted to be informed also?" I nodded, and said "Yes, by all means," he nodded and made a note on the computer, and said "A text message will be sent to your sat phone," and I thanked him. He also told me that it would be at least an hour before he had all the documents ready to go with my emergency ID, and that he would send them to Callaway's office as soon as it was ready.

Now it was time to meet the boss, Colin Gorman, was just a shade over six foot, had salt and pepper hair, brown eyes, and was dressed conservatively, a vast improvement on his predecessor, he was straight forward and called a spade a spade, had a no nonsense attitude that I liked. After administering the oath of service, he asked if he could do anything further for me, and I asked him about keeping tabs on the surviving SRT team members, while he looked at me on the opposite side of his desk thinking, he nodded, and said "Ok your reasoning is understandable, and as long as we don't tie up too much man hours, I'll approve the request, but once we locate this Dumper fellow, we'll only look in on him only now and again, fair enough?" I smiled and nodded, as I said "Fair enough, and thank you, by the way what do I call you?" He stood up as did we, and he said "Call me Colin; welcome to ASIS Tom, we'll get to see more of each other later.

On the way out, I picked up my emergency ID from Callaway's office, and for the next four days, we racked up the air miles visiting all the countries offices. When we finally got back to the Brisbane office, he took a plastic card out of the desk draw saying "This is good for any yellow cab in the country, put it in your wallet, just show this to the driver, sign the docket and that's all there is to it, the government picks up the tab. The car we have been driving around in is yours, there's a Caltex fuel card on top of the visor, SOP's for all our vehicles. Now I'll drop you home, and you pack for a few weeks, you'll be heading to the states in a week, until I contact you, your time is your own."

He contacted me four days later, to tell me to meet the jet at the airport the following night at six pm, where I'd be on my way to the states. I'd be met at the other end, and taken to the reconstruction facility.

Now I was going to get a break from the pain of the laser treatment, because the doctor wanted to wait a few days, to see how much of the tattoos had disappeared, however I wasn't going to get off that lightly at all. I was told while I was outside my room enjoying a smoke, that the following morning I'd be having work start on the rest of my scars and marks.

The following morning, I was sedated and taken to the operating room, that day the doctors went to work on me while I was out to it, and I found out later when I woke up that every mark scar and wound, had been removed or fixed so there were no distinguishing marks on the back of my body at all, even a chain mark that I used to have on my right calf was gone, I saw. Two days later the front of my body was done. After I had recovered from that, I had a couple more days of the laser again before being pronounced distinguishing mark free. Three days later I boarded the jet for home, and arrived in the Brisbane office, seated across the desk from John two days after leaving the states.

Readers Note: I apologise if you have gotten bored with the time spent on my induction process, however going to work for this agency, is definitely not like any normal job interview, and under normal circumstances you don't get to approach them, it's the other way round, also intelligence agencies are a closed community. However, I've endeavoured to give you an idea of an abridged and broad, cross section of some of the things required.

CHAPTER 2

A week after I'd returned to Australia, and started work at ASIS, Colonel Lewis contacted me at my home number, and Lisa relayed by phoning the sat phone. My discharge had come through and the papers were ready for signing. After going out to five trucks, in what was officially my car. I signed the papers, and there was a list of issue equipment that was required to be returned to the closest Q store, and Lewis gave me the form to be signed off by the quartermaster, so my discharge would be effective. I took the list home with me and Lisa helped me fulfil the items required, by reading off the list as I threw said items into a pile on the floor of my bedroom.

The list was rather ridiculous actually, and one item that wasn't on it was my foot locker. I decided to put everything into it for return, also my rifle wasn't included on the list, and that surely was a surprise. Anyway after all the listed items made their way into the foot locker, it made its way to the boot of the car, and back at the Q store everything was signed for as being received. I took the form to Colonel Lewis, and he countersigned it. We shook hands as I left the Defence Force for good, but in a way I was serving the country in another aspect of its defence.

Back at the office, I was slowly learning my way through the role I would be taking on as an agent with high security grading. One of the tasks was taking my seat at the routine heads of department meetings. This consisted of discussing the direction of current operations being carried on within the state, and what was required to bring them to a conclusion. To prepare me for this, Janice would bring me case files of ongoing operations to peruse, and I would make notations in regard to each case. I was working my way through the pile one by one, I came to one marked as pending, opened it and started reading. It was a query from the

AFP, into the possible link between a known, but never caught drug importer, and the theft of a shipment of arms from the main container yard at Fisherman's Island. One of the things that had been on CCTV (closed circuit security cameras) was the partial registration number of a car very like one used by the suspected drug importer, but included was a list of all vehicles that matched the make and model of the suspect vehicle all within the partial plate range, and the number of vehicles that fell into that criteria was over three thousand, one reason to relegate the file to pending, as I delved deeper into the file, there were a numerous amount of photos of people known to visit the suspect, that were unknown to the policing authorities.

So I divided the photos that were known with names and addresses written on the backs of the photos as notes, and made two piles one for known, and one for unknown, naturally the unknowns outnumbered the known, therefore another reason to relegate to the back burner, *for those of you that don't already know, I hate unanswered questions and dead ends, they always get me guessing, and I want to solve the mystery,* so leaving the photos face down in their piles I continued to read through the rest of the material, which in itself had me starting to wonder. While my mind was still occupied on the file notes, I absently started to turn over first the known photos, and then the unknowns, and after glancing at them I'd leave them face up. As I glanced at them I was leaning back in my chair, I reached for one and reached for the next. I came upright in my chair as I grabbed back the previous photo, I KNEW THAT FACE!

I grabbed up the file, and tidied everything on the desk, and then started going over all the unknown photos, grabbed a red Nikko marker, and went over them slowly and thoroughly. Marked each with an x in the corner of photos that had photos of people I'd met. There were over forty photos of unknowns, but sixteen of them showed people I'd met before! I called to Janice. As she rushed into my office, I was walking toward her, grabbed her hand, and guided her to the desk to show her the file, as I asked "How long has this file been here?" She looked and replied, "It came in while you and Mr Callaway were touring the other offices Tom, and it was only a routine enquiry we get from time to time, why?" I smiled, and answered "I know some of the people in the photos of the unknown persons, so what do I do now?" She looked at me, and said "Well you have a choice, Tom you can leave it until the weekly meeting, and bring it up then, or I can get the other two department heads to join you, and you sort out what needs to be done." I nodded and smiled as I thought, then said "Get them for me please," she nodded and went back to her desk, meanwhile I tidied up the folder, keeping out the crossed photos, and wracked my brain to put names to the faces.

When the other two department heads, John Lime from Communications, and Harry Callan from Tech Services joined me and Janice had shut the door. I passed them the file, and as they looked it over, I said "I know this file has been here a while, but after going through it, I've been able to identify some of the unknown people so my question is this, what do we do now, ignore it, or start to further investigate and see if there is a link, and if so shut it down, or hand it back to the feds with what we know. I think we should at least do something about it."

John said "I think that we deal with this now, and see how things are going at our weekly meeting, and then devise our strategy. If you can supply the names you know Tiger, I'll get some agents tracking them down, and see what we come up with," I nodded my head and passed him the photos I'd written names on, and we agreed to review it as a priority during the weekly meeting, that gave agents at least five days to come up with leads to addresses and so on. I replied "I think I might have to call Callaway as well, because I think I may know a way in to infiltrate the group, it's a long shot, but it might pay dividends, I think it may be worthwhile talking to him about it, and see what he has to say, and unless it's urgent I'll let you know what he says on Monday at the meeting." Soon after the meeting broke up, and I was free to call Callaway in Sydney.

After talking to Charlie, she put me through to Callaway, and we discussed the request. The way the group could be infiltrated to find out what we needed to know, and at what I had in mind, he said "Yeah, that's feasible, but I'll leave the decision in your hands, it's your operation. Now on another subject, have you done anything about getting a job yet as a cover?" So I replied "Hell give me a chance, I only just left the army. Besides what would I apply for, I really don't have a trade or anything." I heard him laughing on the phone, as he replied "Well you've hopefully learned the background we made up for you, remember you're good in sales, or trucking, so my advice would be to try one of those, something that will give freedom to move about, and look as if you have a normal job that pays." I nodded to myself as he said this, knowing he was right, I couldn't very well answer any query from people about my job, as being a secret government agent could I? So I told him that I would get onto it, and find one. He was happy with that, and after he asked me to keep him informed about the case, we hung up from each other.

The next morning while I was in the office having a morning coffee that Janice had brought in with the paper, I looked at the classifieds. One ad caught my attention, AMP was advertising for sales consultants, so I rang the number, and was given an interview time for that day, after hanging up, I called for Janice and asked her if she could make up a job resume for me, and smiled as she said "There's half a dozen already typed up in the filing cabinet from your background legend, I'll just grab one for you to look at, and I'll make any changes you need." She came back a few minutes later with a complete work resume, and handed it to me to read. It was perfect, and should do the job nicely, so a couple of hours later I left the office.

I didn't have all that far to go, it was only a few blocks downtown. I arrived before the scheduled appointment time, and had to wait for a while. The person that interviewed me was Rick Welsh, and he was the office manager at a little regional office in Newmarket. After explaining the job, and what it required, I was starting to be more interested. It was paid on a commission only basis, and therefore the more work I did the more I'd be paid, but I didn't need to go into an office all the time and I'd more or less be my own boss. Now this really would suit my circumstances, so I said I was interested, and Rick started all the necessary paperwork. After telling me that if I worked out of his office he'd make sure I got all the help I needed to start with, I agreed. He booked my place in the next training school that started the following Monday for two weeks. I was fine with that, it just meant I'd have to change a few things when I was back at the office, to accommodate the training school time.

Because the other two department heads weren't field agents and didn't need a cover occupation, John and Harry would stay later in the office on Monday so we could have our weekly meeting after the training school commitment I now had. I have a tendency to believe that they were a little relieved that I wouldn't be spending as much time in the office as I had been, nothing concrete, but just a feeling I had. I arranged with Janice that I'd come in early most mornings before going to the training school, and also come into the office after I was finished for the day, and that anything urgent that came in could be left on my desk for me to read and answer, or leave instructions for her.

On Monday I was in the office by six am, and was going through some of the reports that had come in, in regard to chasing down some of the names I'd been able to supply for the AFP inquiry, and it included the address and phone number of the main contender that I wanted to meet up with. It also listed an itinerary of some of the places she frequented, and that surveillance was ongoing. *Great* I thought, *if the surveillance is kept up, after I'm done with this course, I could frequent the places she goes, and I would eventually meet up with her, then we start an undercover operation, so that I was introduced into the suspected group, learn what we needed to know, and either pass it on, or shut them down ourselves.* After leaving a note for Janice telling her I'd be in briefly at lunchtime, and should be in the office by four that afternoon, I got myself ready to walk downtown to the office building preparing myself to go back to school. To my surprise what we were learning, I found quite interesting, during the day the group of students doing the course was reduced.

From the initial twenty that started the first day, five left after finding out that the initial four hundred dollars a week we were being paid while doing the course, would be taken out of the commission of the first sale that any of us made. That was a little detrimental I thought, because what if none of the students on the course were able to produce sales, where did that leave them? So, the so called retainer wasn't a retainer after all! Hmm that made me determined to learn all I could, because I wanted to be off the retainer system as soon as possible, otherwise it could turn into a financial drain.

Some of you may think this was a sort of con game, and I'll not disagree with you, but in those days the commissions that could be made selling Insurance were astronomical, if you knew what you were talking about, and could explain the reason for a policy properly, in other words sell it, there was a lot of money to be made, I know, I made stacks, the only drawback was the amount of tax I was paying.

Anyway back to the story, that first afternoon we were out of the building by three, and I was back in my proper office ten minutes later. As I went in I asked Janice to get John and Harry to meet me in the operations room for our meeting, and after gathering up what I wanted from my desk, headed there. I thought that I'd be the first in the room, but Harry was waiting as I walked in, closely followed by John. We dispensed with all the current operations and investigations after half an hour, before moving on to the new business, the only new business being the AFP request, whether we moved ahead with it, or turned it down.

I was convinced that we should go ahead with the investigation, and told the other two why. I knew one of the targets, and could go undercover properly and get introduced around to members that we'd been asked about. I would renew my acquaintance with the target, and start moving in her circles to get what we wanted. The three of us decided that if nothing could be produced by the investigation within three months, that we'd call a halt to it, if however, we did get some results, then we'd have to make up our minds whether we continued with it, or passed it on to the feds. It was decided that I'd finish the insurance course first, and then armed with surveillance data, I could start making my way into the group, by turning up and being seen by them in different places that they hung out in, before I actually made contact with my target. We agreed that the plan was sound, and that I could get started as soon as I was finished the course.

Naturally with my mental ability to soak up information, I was fast becoming the top of the course, and the final two days of the course were reserved for role playing and product examinations, and I graduated with honourable high scores. Rick Welsh was at the graduation ceremony, and after shaking my hand in congratulations, he gave me the address of the Newmarket office, and said he looked forward to seeing me on Monday sometime during the afternoon, because he had a couple of appointments lined up for Monday night for me to get started with.

I was back in my office by two, and John, Harry, and I had a short discussion over the best way for me to start making the rounds of the places that the target gang hung around, considering most of the venues were pubs, stopping in for a drink would suffice, if it was a closed venue, then I'd have to rely on something else. John passed me the list of hang outs, and I told them I'd make a start over the weekend, and see them for our usual Monday meeting at ten. After our meeting broke up, I told Janice to have an early day, and that I was going home.

When I arrived home, Lisa had some news for me from the real estate agent with a query, so after I settled in, we went into the bar for a drink. We had our usual afternoon debrief and drinks time, where we went over the days' events. I could see there was something that she really wanted to talk to me about, apart from the rest of the days' events, so I said "Alright Lisa, your dying to talk to me about something, so forget all the other stuff for now, let's just talk about what you want to discuss first."

She weakly half smiled, and answered "I keep forgetting about your ability to see through people, I hope this doesn't upset you, but here goes, a couple of weeks ago I met a man down at the shopping centre, and we had sort of an instant connection, anyway we had a coffee and talked for ages, and since then we've met up just about every other day, he's widowed and is just a year older than me. I like him and I'm interested in seeing him, but now he wants to see more of me, and has even suggested spending the night together, but I also like the arrangement that we have, so I'm in a quandary about what to do."

Half smiling, I replied "Lisa, you've said you like him, so give it a go, I'd be happy if you found someone you like, sure I'd miss what we have together, but don't let that get in the way of your happiness, it doesn't mean to have to stop living here, this is your home as long as you wish, but don't close yourself off to what could make you happy."

Before continuing I had a sip of my drink, and said "However if he hurts you in any way, I'll want to know about it quick start, understood?" She nodded with a weak smile, and I asked "Ok, what else has happened?"

With a relieved sigh, she told me that the real estate agent had rung, and the people that had been renting the Stafford house were going to be moving south in two weeks, and he wanted to know if I wanted the house rented out again. As I thought over what she'd told me I sipped on my drink, and then said with a smile "Bingo, this could be the answer to your problem Lisa, how about we move you into the Stafford house when it's vacant, and that way you'll be able to have the privacy you need with your new boyfriend, but also if it doesn't work out with the new guy, we still have our own arrangement, and we talk to each other each night on the phone, how's that sound?"

While I'd been explaining it to her, she was smiling and nodding, and said "Oh Tom that sounds wonderful, but what if something needs doing here?" I replied "Well you'd still keep this place clean, and if I need to at any stage I could move into there so keep the master bedroom free for me, ok?" She agreed to this, so I made a mental note to ring the real estate agent in the morning to cancel renting the house once the present occupants left.

After having an early game of golf the following morning, I returned home and started to get ready to troll through some of the haunts frequented by the target group. After checking the list I'd been given, I decided to make the Story Bridge Hotel my first port of call. When I got there I casually strolled through each of the bar areas, and only noticed one of the known faces. So I left soon after and moved on to the next location in the valley, there I had better luck and found three of the people on the unknowns list sitting in a group watching the football game on the TV while they were having their drinks. While I pondered how to get noticed by them, one of them made his way to the bar beside me, and I casually said "So who do you think will win the game?" He looked at me and said "Manly of course"; I replied "No I don't think so, even though Parra are behind, I reckon they'll end up winning, my name's Tom by the way." He shook my hand and introduced himself as Brian, and said "Well if you think that, why not come over to the table and join us," so I nodded to him and followed him to the table where he announced, "Hey guys, this bloke Tom reckons that Parra's going to get up and win, Tom this is Denny and Joe," I shook hands and then sat down with them, and spent most of the second half with them, I smiled as Parramatta won by a try, and I was asked how I knew.

So I proceeded to tell them that I used to play 'A' grade footy before I busted up one of my knees, but still keep up with the insiders' game news that I heard from time to time. Joe asked "So what did you do after the football?" I leaned my head down as a slight smile played across my face, and then went into a part of my cover legend, with my head still down, I slowly rose it up as I was saying "Well I got into a few scrapes with the law, and ended up doing some jail time, then moved into a lot of things, I'm in sales right now, and flogging insurance, but I have a few side lines. Anyway it was nice to meet you, but I've got some people to meet, so I best get going, maybe we'll up again sometime around the ridges." They all stood up and shook hands goodbye, and I moved out of the bar.

Back in the car, I smiled as I thought to myself, *well, that went rather well and it left them wanting more info, now I'll just keep moving through the list of haunts and see who else I can find, I may have to use different approaches but the cover story seems to work well enough, ok where to next let's see, yeah ok up to Newfarm first then back down here to the clubs after something to eat.* I started the car and headed up into the Newfarm area. I went into the pub on my lists and did as before and drifted through all the bar areas, and in the back bar as I was drinking, I watched a woman come from the toilets and head to a table with another girl, luckily she didn't glance in my direction, and I was able to leave without being seen, she was the one person I didn't want to meet up with just yet.

After I had dinner in one of the cafes in the valley, the rest of the night I spent trolling a couple of the nightclubs, and making acquaintances with different faces on the target list, and after what I considered a successful day and night, I finally drove towards home just after one am.

Monday morning, I arrived at the office around eight, and while I was having coffee with Janice at my desk, we were discussing the days' events, and what had come in over the weekend, and what had to be done during the rest of the week. Then it was time for the weekly department head meeting with John and Harry, so after gathering up all my paperwork that had to be addressed, I set off to the conference room, and started to make a cuppa. Harry joined me, and was telling me about a new microphone and recorder he'd got in as we were joined by John, and then we all got down to business. I reported on my weekend effort and after advising them all of some of the snippets of conversation I'd picked up, we decided that it was an operation worth pursuing, and investigating.

We would worry at a later stage whether to pass on the information to the feds or take it down ourselves. The rest of the meeting concerned ongoing operations and general office details, and Harry told us about the new recording device, and I asked to have one to trial, so after our meeting broke up I went with Harry to the second floor to pick it up. After showing me how to work it, which was like a normal recording machine, the difference being mainly in the microphone it had no lead to plug into the recorder, and was in the shape of a pen. The pen was a micro transmitter with a range of five hundred yards, but the drawback was that it operated on a battery that only lasted twelve hours, but the recorder could tape for the same amount of time, and was voice activated, eventually Harry finished his briefing on the device, and I asked "So does the pen write or is it just a fake casing?" Harry laughed, and smilingly said "Yes it works like an ordinary pen, medium black in case you're wondering, now they've both been charged and ready to go just remember to bring them to me for charging after you use them."

That afternoon I went to the Newmarket insurance office, and Rick Welsh introduced me around to the other sales agents, and then assigned me a cubicle that I'd use before I started making sales, if I did, he'd then think of assigning me a proper office. We sat in my cubicle and he explained the procedure. Normally I'd be given a list of current clients to phone and see if they were requiring upgrades to their insurance, make appointments, and then see them and try to sell more insurance, after that I was to make appointments out of the phone book, or a list of people that I knew. I didn't have to make the calls myself, I could have someone make them for me, but I would have to pay them for doing it. The appointments that Rick had for us tonight had been made by his own secretary so were confirmed and wouldn't fall over, the name given to an appointment that cancels. Considering they had come from his sources, if I made a sale it was expected that he would get some of the commission, but he told me that wouldn't be the case this time, as I was still in training he was paid as my trainer, I was considered to be in training until I'd made four sales, so he would have to be present at each set appointment until that had happened.

That night during the first appointment, he had to interrupt to correct a mistake I'd made, but in the end I did make a sale. When we were in his car he held out his hand to congratulate me before starting off to the next appointment, again another sale, as we drove back to the office to retrieve my car, he told me that I'd made close to six thousand dollars in commission from the two sales.

I thought to myself, *hmm not bad for three hour's work, I could really make some serious money with this lark,* as he dropped me he said he set up another appointment for me and then I'd be on my own to make them after he gave me a client list, and that he'd see me the following afternoon.

The next morning, I stopped on the second level of the office to see Harry before continuing down to my office, we went over the trial recording I'd made the previous night, and after a few technical questions in regard to range from transmitter to recorder and so on. He told me he'd wipe the recording and have the units charged, then they'd be ready for me any time I needed them.

That evening Rick and I finished the appointment with another sale, and as he dropped me off at my car, he told me to let him know when I had another appointment as he passed me the client list and said "You can use these if you wish or use another method, your choice, another sale and you'll be on your own."

Considering it was still early I decided to drive into Newfarm, as I entered the pub, I saw Brian, Denny, and Joe seated at a table with someone with their back to me, as Brian saw me walk in, he motioned me across to them, and as I got to the table, he said "Tom I'd like you to meet a friend of ours," as he was saying this the person in front of me rose and turned around, I was looking straight into the face of Darlene Smith!

CHAPTER 3

I smiled and said "That's ok Brian, Darlene and I already know each other, so if you'll just give us a couple of minutes to catch up, we'll re-join you," as I took Darlene's' hand and guided her off to a corner where we could talk without being overheard by anyone.

She spoke first, and said "My god Tiger! I had no idea, I thought you were in the army, I didn't have any idea you were the one the boys were talking about, what are you, a spy or something, do you still carry a gun?" I thought, *ok this is where my legend is about to get a proper workout, I've got to convince her that I wasn't who she really thought I was,* and I replied "Christ, I've finally found you, yeah I was in the army, but after that last mission I had a real barney with an officer, and I told him what I thought of him, and after a court martial I was dishonourably discharged, when I got back to Brisbane I called and looked for you, but you'd gone, since then I've done a few things, but have ended up selling insurance, I'll tell you about the other things later, but right now let's get back to Brian and the others, they may be able to put me onto someone I've been looking for, who can shift a lot of weapons that I've got hold of, and it means very big money, but keep quiet about that ok?"

After meeting Darlene, I sensed that everything changed in regard to certain aspects of the conversation we were all having, without showing it, my instincts for self-preservation kicked into high gear, but either I had been alarmed for nothing, or something else was to follow, I'm not sure which, but after the guys left Darlene and I stayed on to talk with each other. I knew that asking her back to my place would be a little difficult, but she made it easier by asking me to take her home, and suggested that we spend the night together. I smiled at the suggestion, but as we entered the carpark, my senses were on full alert, and so thought that the attempt to mug us was an audition of some sort. A person wearing a ski mask tried to hold us up at knifepoint, until that is, I produced my gun, and went about giving him a pistol whipping before Darlene and I got into the car and drove off, and as we went, she asked "Aren't you going to call the cops?" To which I replied "You're kidding, they'd probably try to arrest me for having a firearm, besides no damage was done except to him, so let's just leave it, I don't think he'll come looking for evens, but if he does, I'll be able to manage him any time, now how do we get to your place?" She gave me the directions to one of the new high rise apartments that had been built recently, and her flat was on the ninth floor, below the two penthouses.

As I looked around the apartment, checking things out, I asked "Are you still going to Uni, or did you graduate, and are making a shitload of money working somewhere?" She laughed, and replied "No I'm still doing my course, but this place is owned by a friend of mine, and he's letting me stay here rent free to look after it." I looked at her and enquired "Does he sleep here also?" Again she laughed and answered "What, with me do you mean, no, he's out of the country at the moment, and that's why I'm looking after the place." I nodded my head in acknowledgement.

Later after an intense lovemaking session, we talked, and she told me what had brought about the move from the gap, after a massive fight with Linda, her flatmate, and that she had drifted around the suburbs a bit before being offered the flat we were in. I told her about coming back to Brisbane and trying to find her, and that I'd even gone to her old place, but Linda had moved out also and there was someone else living there that didn't know where either of them had gone. When she asked me what I was doing now, I acted a little cagey, so that she would have to seem to be digging hard for the information, and eventually in pieces so that she had to ask about, I let the details of my cover come out. In that I was only using the insurance job as a means of making money and appear to have a legal job, while in actual fact I'd become a middleman dealer in drugs and guns both in Australia and overseas, and that I was looking for a buyer for a shipment of weapons that had come into my possession.

She seemed to be thinking about what I'd told her, and told me that she'd also done a few what was considered to be illegal things like smoking pot and also selling it in small quantities, but that it was a means to an end, which was allowing her to complete her studies to get qualified, and asked me if it was the same for me, to which I told her that I had no intention to keep doing the illegal stuff for the rest of my life, but long enough to retire early and never want for anything because I'd have a shitload of money to fund whatever I wanted to do. She laughed and asked if I was ever afraid of getting caught by the police, and I told her that I had a secret get out of jail free card if ever I needed to use it, and laughed, saying "I don't know if it'll work, but I'd give it a good shot." As I got dressed in the morning she asked if she could make me dinner that night, and I told her that I wasn't sure whether I'd have an appointment to go to, but that I'd give her a ring, and then asked for her numbers. Readers Note: during that particular time, there was no such thing as a small mobile phone, except one of the satellite phones I had, and most people still had pagers or a fixed phone.

After promising to call in regard to dinner, I left and drove to the office. As I was settling down with a cuppa and the overnight reports, John ducked his head in and asked if we could talk, so I motioned for him to come in and he closed the door before sitting opposite me at the desk. He asked how things were progressing with the operation, and I told him that I'd already taken things to a deeper level, and I was holding back to see how things were going that night, and then as he asked how I was going with my cover, I knew he was hedging about something, so after telling him things were going well, I said "Alright John, stop beating about the bush and ask me what you really came in here to ask!"

He stared at me before smiling, and said "I'm sorry Tiger, I asked about your cover because I'd like to talk to someone about insurance, because I want to insure my wife Debbie and our son Paul, can you recommend anyone?" I looked at him in disbelief, and replied "Are you serious? Of course I can recommend someone, me you dummy, just because insurance is my cover, that doesn't mean I don't know anything about it, in fact I know a lot about it, so here's what we're going to do, give me your address, and at six tomorrow evening I'll call in with an associate, and we'll go through everything you need, but between now and then, I want you to write down anybody that you think of that may require insurance with their name address and phone number and I'll ask you for that list tomorrow night, how's that sound?" He nodded agreement and wrote down his address, which I wrote into my diary as an appointment, and as he left my office, I smiled in bewilderment, and said to myself "Could I recommend anyone, shit, idiots!"

Next I rang home, and asked Lisa if anything urgent needed doing, and after receiving a negative answer, I told her I'd probably be home later to change, but would most possibly be out all night again, and I also asked her to remind me that I wanted to talk to her about something I had in mind, when we had some talking time together. Then I rang Darlene, and told her I'd be right for dinner that night, and asked what time to be there, and she told me she hoped that I wasn't figuring to go home, as she'd like me to spend the night again, I laughed and told her I would stay the night, but only under protest, and that made her laugh, and then we ended the call because she had to get ready to go to a lecture. My next call wasn't until after lunch, it was to Rick Welsh to tell him about the appointment the following night, he was pleased and arranged to meet me at John's address after I told him that I wouldn't be into the office before.

Leaving the office shortly after two, I headed home to change and get ready for the night with Darlene, but I had plenty of time to sit down with Lisa and offer her another job, I explained to her that I needed someone who would make phone calls and make appointments for, and told her that she could make the calls from home, or go into the Newmarket office and make them. She opted for making them from home, whether from here or the Stafford house. That way she could do the cleaning then spend two or three hours on the phone, she reminded me that we were shifting her stuff to the Stafford house the coming weekend, and then asked whether she would be paid for making the calls on my behalf.

I laughed and said "Sorry we sort of moved over that topic didn't we? Ok I get paid by commission and so will you, for every appointment you make, I'll pay you one hundred dollars, and if I make a sale from that appointment, you'll get an extra hundred, how's that sound?" She replied "Sounds good to me but what would I say?" I told her I had some phone making cheat sheets at the office along with a list to start on of current clients that I would get for her, and that she could start making calls from Monday if she wished because I'd have given her the paperwork by then, and she said that would be fine.

Later that night after having a terrific dinner, and a very intense prolonged bout of lovemaking, I was unobtrusively asking Darlene how she moved into the drug trade, and seeing how far I could push the limits with questions, and I had to make up how I became involved with criminal activities, starting with small things and then more serious crime, but I told her that mostly I stuck to the illegal weapons trade, but did do the odd drug run, and also that my main thing was obtaining what was required, and then getting it smuggled into different countries.

She made the comment, "Some of the people I know could maybe have a use for that kind of thing. I'll ask around, you never know, what's the biggest thing you've smuggled into this country?" I laughed and then told her what we'd prearranged in the office, saying "Well I've got a container full of weapons sitting in a transport yard waiting to go somewhere," her eyes went wide, and she said "Wow." The container was real, Customs had intercepted it a month earlier coming off a Columbian registered ship, it was full of an assortment of guns and ammunition, and even two anti-tank missile launchers.

Then after another bout of lovemaking, as she was drifting off to sleep, I asked a couple more questions, which she dreamily answered.

However, she wasn't too forthcoming with any names, but she said I'd probably meet them one day, if we stick together. That morning she had an early lecture and I told her that I probably wouldn't see her that night due to an appointment, so we decided that I'd ring, or page her when I was free, and we'd get together. We left at the same time, she to catch a bus and I headed for the office, once I was in the building I stopped on John's floor, and made sure that evening was still a go, he told me it was definitely on, and I told him I'd see him then, as I was going to leave early, and then I continued to my office, where Janice was just making coffee for our morning catch up session.

We got the urgent stuff out of the way first and that was easy as there wasn't any, and so we went straight to the routine stuff. After we'd finished I asked her to go up and grab the recorder for me and if possible, a couple of spare tapes and the charging gear. Fifteen minutes later she knocked on my door and brought in everything I'd asked for, and I told her I'd be leaving the office at lunch time, and that she could have an early day if she wished. I got home about one o'clock, and got showered and into a fresh set of clothes. After that I drove into the Newmarket insurance office, but because I was meeting Rick at John's address, instead of driving the work sedan, I was in the Mustang. While I was sitting in my cubicle sorting things out, and putting policy forms into my briefcase, Noel one of the other agents sat down for a natter. So I asked him about the office routine, and it was just as well I did, because he told me that if Rick assigned me an office, I'd be paying rent on the space, and that any blank forms that I got, I'd be paying for them, and that the money was deducted from my commission account before I even got a cheque. I asked him if there was another way around it, and he suggested that if my house was big enough, to convert a room into an office, and I would save two ways, not having to pay office rental space, plus I could then claim office expenses from my tax. He also suggested that I open a separate bank account and put thirty percent of my commissions into it, because we were responsible for paying our own tax, and he said that if I worked on thirty cents in the dollar, I should be able to cover my tax bill from that account.

Going into the office, had given me a better insight into the way things were done when being paid on commission, the one piece of information that I was really grateful for was that our commission was paid monthly, but the society would advance us money against our commissions, but again at a cost. So obviously he'd given me things to think about.

However, I wasn't just blindly going to follow his advice, first I'd check the information he'd given me with Rick, and if what Noel had told me was true, I might start to reappraise a few things. Rick Welsh came into the office as I was about to leave, and I asked to speak with him. In his office he told me that he was set for the appointment at John's, but he'd be seeing a client beforehand, and that was why he'd meet me there. Then asked me what I wanted, so I questioned him in regard to what Noel had told me, and he confirmed it. So then I asked what happened, should I decide to have my house as my office, and he told me that it was quite acceptable, but there were times when I'd have to be in the Newmarket office, and that one of those occasions was every Friday at two there was a sales meeting that lasted at least an hour, and that it was mandatory for everyone to attend.

That evening at John's Rick sat silent as I controlled the conversation, and suggested policies that could cover all of the things that John and Debbie required. After an hour they had taken out five different policies, and while each of them was filling in the paperwork John passed me a list of close to thirty people that they knew that would benefit from talking to me. I asked if I could use their names as being the referrers when my secretary called them, and Debbie had commented "Do so by all means, and I'll even tell them all to expect a call, you've helped us out immensely Tiger, thank you," I smiled and said "Well you'll have to let me know when your home and contents insurance is due, because we do that also, so please let me know and I'll see if we can give you a better quote.

Outside in the car Rick was in seventh heaven and couldn't heap enough praise on me, I'd walked out with five signed policies from one household, as he stated, "Well you can consider yourself out of training, and if you keep this up you'll be the best salesman of the year by Christmas, congratulations Tom you've done well, if I don't see you before I'll see you on Friday."

Back to Darlene's I went that night and we ended up meeting a lot of the Uni crowd at the Newfarm pub. I was able to account for all but two of the unknowns, as yet I hadn't met them at any stage. Along with the unknowns there was a sprinkling of known criminals. Darlene noticed that I was on a high and asked me about it, and I told her after waiting for a Qld buyer for my merchandise, I'd got sick of waiting and had contacted someone in Victoria that I knew, and because they knew my reputation they'd bought the whole load of weapons sight unseen, and the container was already on its way south.

The look of amazement I received was something to behold, as she enquired how much money I'd made on the deal, and when I told her I'd got three and a half million for the entire container. She was dumbfounded as I continued telling her that after expenses I'd made over a million, and she asked "What are you going to do with that?" and I told her I'd go looking for more guns to buy, because I could sell them in Africa at ten times their normal value due to the arms embargoes, but I knew how to get around them, and I said "So if you know anybody that can supply me, now is the time I need to speak with them."

Having thrown that bone out for chewing, I shut up and let her move around the room, and on more than one occasion I saw eyes directed towards me, as I assumed she was passing along the news. Soon I was joined by one of the known people in their group, and he introduced himself as Kevin, and said "You're Tom right? Word has it that you're looking to buy some weapons, and I might be able to help you there, but instead of talking here let's meet tomorrow somewhere with a bit more privacy." I looked at him, and glanced at the table he'd moved to me from, the three others sitting there were watching intently, as I took up a coaster, I replied "Sure, write down where you want to meet, and the time, and I'll be there, but I'll want to see a sample of what you have to offer." After he wrote down an address and time on the coaster we nodded to each other and he moved back to his table.

I started thinking to myself, *that was almost too easy, and I bet that all of those four will be there, ok I can fix that, I'll make sure I will have close backup, and I'll have my gun if needed, and I better take along the recorder, at least it looks like it will be a business address instead of a private house, but really lovely, a wrecking yard of all places.* Soon after Darlene returned to the table and with her she brought me a pint of Guinness, and a drink for herself. We stayed on 'til closing time mixing with the group, and by now they were all used to seeing me, and so I was no longer treated like an outsider. I was included in the conversations and joking around, I put it down to the fact that I was dating Darlene that had led to my integration into the group quicker than I had hoped.

Next morning, I was in the office early, and I left word with John's and Harry's secretaries that I needed to see them urgently on my way through. Half an hour later they both entered my office, and I filled them in on what had happened at the pub the previous night, and that I'd need some backup for the meeting. I also gave the recorder to Harry for charging, and he said "It'll take nearly four hours before this I'll be charged again so I'll give you the spare Tiger."

As for surveillance of the yard, we went to the operations room and shortly after Harry had the aerial view of the yard, there was a tall building next to the yard, so we'd have one of the field agents up there with a camera, and a rifle just in case I got into trouble, and John would have a car with four agents placed outside the yard prior to my arriving, also we'd have a surveillance team in place ready to follow anyone leaving the yard after I left. Harry told me that the microphone in the pen would also transmit everything as well as the recorder, so all other agents would be able to hear what was taking place, and also John and Harry back here in the operations room. I told Janice that she would take my place in the operations room, but it would be John and Harry that made any operational decision. An hour later as I was preparing to leave, the operations room staff assembled in the room.

I pulled up the mustang in front of the yard, and as I got out one of Kevin's mates from the previous night was leaning with his back against the wall and from his position he'd be able to see who turned up, and into the office, he nodded as I walked up near him, and said "He's inside," I nodded as I passed him and went into the counter area. Kevin came forward to the counter, holding out his hand, and I shook it, as he said "Tom, let's talk some business," and I shook my head, and replied "No, let's have a look at the merchandise first, and then we'll talk business," he thought on this a moment, and then said "Ok, but my boys will have to make sure you're not bugged or anything." I sighed and started to undo my shirt, and pulled my gun, as I said "Sure, I can understand that, but I'm keeping my gun," as I held my arms out with my finger through the trigger guard of my gun while it hung from my finger, one of his mates opened my shirt, and then raised the back of it looking for any tell-tale wires taped to me, and shook his head to Kevin, who smiled, and said "That's cool, keep your gun by all means, but holster it, you won't need it here, we're all mates."

After holstering my pistol, and doing up my shirt, I looked at Kevin, who in turn looked towards the door guard and received a nod. So he stooped and started producing weapons from below the counter, the array on the counter was quite extensive, and included M16s, SLRs, Browning Pistols, Grenades, M60s, and even a Mortar tube. I looked at the assortment of weapons, and said "Do you have any RPGs and mines as well?" Kevin opened his arms in a sweeping motion over the weapons, and replied "This is all I've got, but I can get hold of the other stuff, if you've got the right amount of cash inducement that is."

I nodded, and replied "You could say that I have, now what about ammo?" Kevin smiled, and replied "All that you need, now how many would you like?" looking over the haul of weapons, I said "Ok, a thousand M16s, six hundred SLRs..." "Whoa, whoa" Kevin said "I haven't got that many man, the best I could do is a couple of the rifles, and maybe five or six of the pistols, that's all." I looked at him coldly, and the chill could be heard in my voice, as I said "I don't like having my time wasted, you say you have arms to sell, and really all you've got is a pittance, now unless you have access to what I want, you're wasting my time, our business is done!"

As I turned from him and started to leave, he said "Hey wait a moment man, just because I don't have many, doesn't mean that I can't get them from another source man." I turned with a cold sneer on my face, and said "You are nothing but a penny ante crim, who are you going to know that deals in hundreds and thousands of weapons and ammunition," he shrugged with his arms out-stretched, and said weakly "I just know a guy, that's all, I can get them for you." I coldly laughed disbelievingly, and replied "Well here's what we'll do, you'll introduce me to this guy, and if he's genuine and can deal in the massive numbers I want, I may give you a finders' fee, but if he is penny ante like you, I will shoot you for wasting my time again, we clear?" He was nodding his head vigorously, and replied "Yeah, yeah we're sure man," As I turned to leave, I said over my shoulder "You know where to get hold of me, don't make it too long!"

As I fired up the car, and left I breathed out a sigh of relief, and said openly "Ok stand down everyone, it's up to the dogs now, everyone heads back to base and thank you all, just as well they were cowards and took the abuse I piled on them, otherwise we could have had a firefight on our hands." As I drove into the carpark another two cars had followed me in, after making sure it was clear the men started to cross to the carpark to the passageway where they wouldn't be seen by anyone, we all travelled down to the field operatives floor which was mine, and as we all left the lift we were greeted with applause from John, Harry, Janice, and the office staff that were in on the operation. We all smiled and nodded in acknowledgement, because we knew everyone wanted to celebrate the first operation that had taken place in the capital city since the office opened. On the way to my office with John and Harry in tow, I passed the recorder to Harry, who passed it to Janice and asked that she take it upstairs to his secretary, he'd deal with it later, but to also bring down the charged unit.

As we passed into my office, Janice started to make the coffees, and when finished left closing the door behind her. As I sipped appreciatively on the coffee, I started to debrief the situation. The mirth and joking started soon after Harry had said that he nearly had a heart attack at the arrogant way that I talked to them, and my reply was that because my legend made me out to be a hardnosed asshole, that was the way I had to play it, and I finished with "Believe me, I started to have kittens, and was apprehensive as all shit, just waiting for the first gun to lift, I guarantee that if Kevin had picked up any of those weapons laid out there, I would have shot him I was that jumpy!"

After we had finished laughing, Janice knocked on the door and came in carrying the second recorder, which she gave to Harry, and I said to her "Janice pull up a seat please, you were in the ops room, and do you have anything to say, or offer any suggestions?" She looked rather sternly at me as she sat, and said "Sir perhaps I could suggest that you don't try to appear as aggressive as you did, during your next encounter, I nearly had heart failure when you told that person he was only penny ante." Shortly after that we all decided that we had to inform the main office of the operation, in case we needed any further backup. So I would do that the following day, but now it was time to head back and see Darlene, and tell her what I thought of the mob of pussies she mixed with, making sure I had the recorder, I headed out and told everyone that I'd see them in the morning.

CHAPTER 4

At the unit that night I told Darlene of the wasted day I'd had, and she told me that she didn't think anyone of her usual gang would have anywhere near access to the people I really needed, but she did know a friend or two that may have the connections I needed, and asked "Why did I need such big numbers?" Then I quietly replied, "Well what I really wish to do is make a couple big shipments, and the money I get from them should be enough for me to get a large boat, and buy a house up in the Islands and retire real early and live comfortably for the rest of my life."

She looked at me, and laughed saying "What would you do? Shack up with some native bird?" I laughed at her comment, and replied "Well no, I'd try to find someone who I like and get along with, and if they were willing, take them with me." "Hmm, sounds good," she replied and continued while looking me in the face to show her sincerity, "Remember how we lived together the last time we were together, and were thinking of getting married? Well how about we go ahead and get married, because we both really like each other, and again we're now practically living together anyway. We're both good in bed together, and I could help you with the contacts, then we could take off and live happily for the rest of our lives, because I do love you Tiger, and I think you love me too. You've still got the Keperra house; if Terry comes home, we just move out of here and go back out there, plus when we leave the country it'll give us more money by you selling it, what do you think?"

Well alarm bells were ringing in my head, as I thought, this bloody bird was trying to run roughshod over me, well she wasn't going to be a happy camper when I put her in her place, who the hell did she think she was? No one was going to control my life like that, my mother tried it and that didn't work, this bird had no chance, besides not that she knows it, but she's on the wrong side of the law. The bugger of it is that I can't shut her down yet, she's got info I need! So I said to her, "Darlene, this is a pretty big deal, yes we get on, but will we be able to do that years' from now, besides I've still got to find a supplier, who knows how long that'll take. How about you let me think this over for a couple of days, but don't keep asking me if I've made my mind up, otherwise I'll really get pissed off, and say no regardless."

She laughed, and said "Yeah, I remember how you are, but one of the people I know has mob connections, so we'll be able to get what we need."

She took a drink before continuing, "Even better, I could invite him to the wedding, and if we get married in the registry office it will only take a month before we're married, and he could be one of the witnesses. So yeah honey think about it, I know you'll let me know when you're ready, but at the moment I think I've got an even better idea, how about we go to bed early and celebrate our engagement." As she said this she started slowly taking off her top and bra, and started to undo my trousers, and when they were off, along with my jocks, her mouth quickly drew in my penis, and I started to get aroused.

The next morning, I told her that I had a few things to do at the house that night, along with a couple of appointments, so we agreed for me to ring her when I was free, and we'd get together again. In the office I gave the recording to Harry for transcribing and deletion from the tape, the recorder and microphone for charging. Told him I'd need a copy of the transcription from the tape ASAP, and he told me that he'd get on it straight away, and that I should have a copy within the hour. As I entered my office I warned Janice that it was coming down, and that it took priority, and to bring it into me as soon as it arrived. While I was on the phone to Lisa, Janice came in with a cuppa for me, she entered as Lisa was telling me about a couple of the phone calls she'd made, and exited as I nodded to her, before I had to speak, and after asking Lisa where she'd be in a couple of hours, I told her I'd pick her up, and we'd take a trip over to the Stafford house, and maybe even take some of her stuff with us.

The transcription finally arrived, and as soon as Janice gave it to me, I asked her to get John Callaway on the phone for me, and as he came on the line my phone buzzed, and I picked it up. I started to fill him in with developments with the operation, and then read him the transcription, and as I finished he laughed, and said "At least you've got one female yearning after you," and I replied with, "Yeah hah har, seriously John this could be a problem, any ideas?" His voice was quiet for a minute or so, and then he said "Hmm yes, I see the problem, and you're going to have to make a choice, to tell her no deal, and run the risk of making an enemy out of her, which would mean she could blow you're cover, or for the sake of the op, you marry her and get in deeper than you right now, we can always get you divorced afterward, but the choice is down to you. Now what are you thinking about doing with the crew from the wreckers?"

Somehow I knew he was going to ask that at some point in our conversation, and so my answer was already prepared, I said "I've already introduced myself to the AFP head honcho, and I was going to pass it onto them…"

After a cough, I continued "So they could organise a raid on them, but tell me when it was going to happen, and I'd make sure I was with them, so I could be arrested at the same time. That way they wouldn't think that I was to blame, and of course I could be bailed with no charge. Which could put me in deeper with Darlene, because I'd have her come to collect me, but nothing will happen 'til after the usual Monday meeting." He chuckled, and said "Sounds like a plan Stan, let me know which way you go with your decision, so if we have to, we put it on record how far you were going for the sake of the operation, talk later, see ya." And he hung up, I pressed the intercom button and Janice picked up, and I said "Janice can you please go and get a copy of that last conversation, I want to keep it in your office filed away thanks."

Readers Note: all communication from and to all offices were automatically recorded for security reasons, and copies of any call made in a ten-year period were available to those with a high enough clearance.

When Janice came in to let me know she had the copy, she passed me the charged recorder and mic, because she had to go past Harry's office either way to get to the communications floor, and to paraphrase one of the latest comedy shows. I said "Good thinking ninety-nine," and she smiled, and as she was about to leave my office, I said "Oh Janice, I'll be calling it a day soon, it's up to you if you want to leave early, I'll leave that up to you, and thanks," as I held up the recorder.

Lisa and I pulled into the driveway at Stafford, and went inside the house, the tenants had already left, but had left the house in good repair and clean. After checking out all the rooms, Lisa decided on the next largest room across from the master bedroom, it had an adjoining toilet, but no shower. Lisa helped me unload the car, and we put her stuff into her room to sort out later, and then we went downstairs. After throwing ideas back and forth, we decided that we could convert the games room into an office, as it had a pair of sliding doors that faced the front of the house. All we'd have to do was build-in a couple of walls for an office, and get some desks, while we were there, I had Lisa phone the builder and he said he'd come and give me a quote at two, to which I agreed because we only had to wait for just over an hour. So we took a quick trip down to the shopping centre, where we found a couple of desks and chairs that we liked, and arranged for them to be delivered within the hour, (after I paid extra for the service) and we got back to the house just as the builder arrived. He suggested that I use a commercial grade concertina type partition for the walls.

After he explained the advantages, which were easy to install and quicker, solid panelling and soundproof, and could be opened up easily. All we really needed to do was agree which colour the panels would be, so he went out to his vehicle to bring in a colour book of the panels, and after choosing a colour, I told him to go ahead, and he said he could get the job done in a few hours, if someone would be there the next day. I looked at Lisa, and she nodded her head, so it was arranged that he'd be there the next day at ten, and he left. I told Lisa that if she wanted we'd load the work sedan with more of her stuff when we got home, and she could use it to take some more to the house the next day. Luckily there was a couple of phone jacks close to where we'd designed the office s layout, and then after the desks had arrived, we went to a telecom shop on the way home, and bought a couple more handsets for the downstairs office.

That night I went to an appointment Lisa had made with one of the people off John's list, after seeing them I left with another list of names, and three more policies sold. The next day being Friday, I was supposed to be at the sales meeting at Newmarket that afternoon. I decided that I'd lodge the policy paperwork when I went in for the meeting, instead of dropping it off on the way through to the city. When I got home Lisa was still up so I told her that I'd made a sale from her appointment, and that I'd get to the bank and draw out the two hundred that I owed her the next day, plus I gave her the new list of referral names.

Next morning after spending a couple of hours checking all the overnight reports, and sorting out things that had to be done with Janice I left the office after telling her what I'd be up to for the rest of the day, and wished her a good weekend. My first stop was at the wreckers where Kevin hung out. I was intending to stay on a friendly basis, and for them to be used to me dropping in, that way they wouldn't be suspicious when I was there when the feds turned up to search and arrest them. After setting the recorder I left the car and walked in. The heavy was in his usual position and we nodded to each other as I walked toward the counter, and Kevin got up from his seat, and greeted me saying "Hey man, how you going," putting a smile on my dial, I replied "Fine Kev hope you are too, just thought I'd call in as I was passing to see if you've had any word yet." He smiled in return, and answered "Nah not yet Tiger, I've left a couple of messages for him, but he hasn't got back to me yet, but I'll let you know as soon as I hear from him," I laughed, and replied "Yeah that's cool, but I pass this way sometimes, so I might drop in now and again as I go past."

Kevin smiled, and answered, "Yeah that's cool, you never know you may need something for your mustang," I exclaimed "I better bloody not, it's only a few years old!" and we both laughed, and as I turned to leave, I said "Catch ya later Kev," and I left. After buying a counter lunch at the Newmarket pub, I left my car in the pub carpark, and after getting all the stuff I'd need, and the paperwork from the previous night, I walked next door into the office building.

I handed over the paperwork to one of the secretaries, and because it was in before the close of business, they were eligible to be included in my weekly figures. At the sales meeting it was announced that even before I had made a further two sales the previous night, I was the states rookie salesman, and with the other two written, I was also the leading salesman in the office sales team with ten sales in a week since leaving the training school. Along with the kudos went a bonus of one thousand dollars from AMP into my commission account and vouchers for ten sets of free replacement policy paperwork sets, and select brochures, and ten policy document folders.

After the meeting, Rick told me he wanted a word with me before I went, and then I went to a quiet cubicle where I put in a call to Darlene. We arranged to meet up as soon as I was through at the office, and then I went back to the celebration party. I grabbed one of the beers that I was told was supplied by Rick had for all the sales meetings, and stubby in hand went up to Rick to see what he wanted me for. He asked if I'd decided what I was doing in regard to office space, so I told him that I had an office at home that I was going to use, and it was also convenient for the secretary I'd hired. He laughed, and said "Good for you, now we have some signage that you can put up on your house, if you like I can show you a couple of sample signs that can be made up, the society would get them made up, and you can pay for them from your commission account. I think the most that they'd be is a couple of hundred," so I nodded my head and we went into his office. I chose two with the same design, one large one that would be attached to the fence, and a smaller one that could go on the wall near the office door. He said he'd get them made up during the coming week and I should be able to collect them at the next sales meeting, and then asked me about the information I wished on my business cards. The first five hundred were free, and then could be purchased from the AMP store for twenty bucks per hundred after that, and then he gave me a store catalogue to have a look at in case I wanted any other merchandise at a later date. All I'd do was drop in the order form to the office and the girls would take care of it.

I smiled and nodded, and he told me that he should have both the cards and the signs by the following week's sales meeting, but if it looked as if there was going to be a hold up, he'd let me know. I thanked him, and then told him that I had to make a call, but would probably make tracks after the phone call, he smiled, and said "You do whatever you wish, as long as you keep making sales, we'll get along fine."

I made a call to Lisa to check how things had gone with the builder, and then I told her I was on my way home, but would be going straight out again after getting changed. I would be home in the morning to shift the rest of her stuff. Then I left the office, but before retrieving the car, I went to the bank and withdrew some cash, before driving home. After having a shower and changing, and giving Lisa the two hundred that I owed her, I was back in the car heading to the Newfarm apartment.

When I let myself into the apartment, I found Darlene waiting for me on the bed naked, and as she started undoing my trousers and taking them down along with my jocks, she said "I know it's been a few nights, so I thought I would be ready for you to have me once I arouse your interest," and then she started licking and sucking my penis, guiding it into her mouth with her tongue. Needless to say, I soon had my shirt off, and my shoulder holster followed it to the floor, and as I joined her on the bed, Darlene took my engorged penis and guided it into her as she straddled me, and after I gave two deep thrusts up into her, she yelled as her orgasm took her. I brought her to six more before I rolled her onto her back, and just as she was going again, I gave a final couple of very deep thrusts into her vagina, and she screamed, "Now!" As I shot my load of warm semen deep into her, she rocked, shuddered, and mumbled incoherently with the intense orgasm it produced.

After we had been recovering for a while, she asked "I don't feel like cooking after that magnificent entrée, can we just go up to the pub for dinner, and a few drinks?" I nodded, and replied "Yeah sure honey, oh and by the way you know that proposal you made the other night? Well I agree with you, so we may as well go ahead and get married." She sat up quickly, looked at me with a smile, and then squirmed into my arms and kissed me, and said "Oh thank you, thank you darling, we'll be so good together I promise." As she was talking I rolled onto my side and once I reached my trousers, I searched in the pockets for what I wanted, and having found it, I gave it to her.

Then I said "Seeing we're going out, you'd better wear this," she opened the box to find a half karat solitaire diamond engagement ring." She shrieked with joy when she saw it, and said "It's beautiful, can I try it on?" I laughed and nodded my head, as she put it on, she said "Oh it fits perfectly, I love it, thank you," and she moved closer and kissed me. After her kiss I reached for my pants and pulled out another ring, and said with a smile "Oh so it should fit, by the way here's that ring you've been looking for, sorry I needed it and couldn't tell you 'til now," she replied with "You, crafty bastard, come on let's get dressed and go to the pub, I can't wait to show this off,"

I had picked the ring out a couple of days earlier when Lisa had gone to the toilet in the shopping centre, and gave them the other ring for sizing. I had picked it up on the way through to the unit. I could have made it cheaper on myself and given her the engagement ring part of the wedding set I'd bought for Shari some years back now because I had kept them, but somehow thought that giving them to Darlene would be doing a discourtesy to Shari, and it was if I was being told to keep them for someone worthy.

Down at the pub that night, I finally got to meet the last two unknowns on our list, as Darlene dashed about showing off her ring. After we'd finished dinner. The best thing that happened that night, was the ones in the group that were the more reserved about me being around had finally lost their reserve and openly welcomed me into the fold. One of them even bought me a beer, as he picked my brains about shipping drugs from up here to the southern states by using motorbikes and long haul truckies. Thankfully he was being recorded, because everything he had to say sounded feasible, and if this wasn't looked into, it had the potential to create a very lucrative way of shipping quantities of drugs all over the country.

Later that night, while Darlene and I were in bed talking, I told her I had things to do during the day, but I could most likely spend my nights with her, or if she wanted she could come out to my place and spend a few nights out there, but she opted to stay in the unit, after we sorted that out she moved and curled up in my arms after giving me a kiss, and then we went to sleep.

Next morning, I was quiet as I could be as I showered, and dressed in casual clothes, before heading to the carpark in the basement where I fired up the mustang and headed for my house. Lisa cooked us both a nice breakfast before we got started, and after that we loaded up both of our cars.

By the time, her car and the office sedan were loaded, there wasn't any of her stuff left, so it would only be the one trip for me, and Lisa was going to spend her time in this house from then, and only go to the Keperra house every three days or so, or unless I needed her for something else. When we arrived at the house, Lisa wanted to show me the renovation job that the builder had done in the bar area, which was still pretty much that for half the room. The other half now being our work offices, and he'd done a terrific job, and Lisa told me she'd got his labourers to put the desks into the right positions as well. Which I laughed at after she told me, as I knew she could get anyone to help her if she needed, if she flashed the promising smile she had.

A four-wheel drive pulled into the driveway as we were heading to the cars to unload, and a spry silver headed guy about five nine got out, and asked "Do you still need a hand my lovely Mona Lisa?" When I heard that, I couldn't help but burst out laughing, and Lisa got all flustered and jittery as she tried to introduce us to each other, so I took over saying "Hi, I'm Tiger, Lisa's boss, and you are?" He smiled, and said "My name's Reg, and I guess I'm Lisa's boyfriend, I guess that would be the best description, though at our age I'm not too sure," and we shook hands. With three hands the work went much faster, and then we all sat down as the jug boiled, and while having a cuppa we got to know each other. Reg asked how I was Lisa's boss after she told him she was on a pension, so Lisa stepped in, and explained that even though she was on a pension, she still had bills to pay off, and so on, and that she did housework for cash in hand sometimes. Then she had met me as she was about to be evicted from her house, and that I had given her a place to live rent free in exchange for the housework.

Reg was keeping up so far, and then he asked "But haven't you just moved into here, won't you be paying rent to someone?" Half way through his question, I could see where he was leading to, and started chuckling, and when he'd finished Lisa started laughing, and as he looked from her to me and back again, so Lisa kept explaining telling him that I owned this place as well, and that she had decided to move into here for more privacy, but would still be doing the housework over at Keperra a couple of times a week, plus now that I'd renovated downstairs into an office, she would be acting as my secretary for which she'd be paid extremely well on a performance basis, and cash in hand, so it didn't need to be

47

declared, by the time she finished explaining, he was chuckling too, and nodding his head, as he said "You two seem to have a good deal going between you both, just hang on a minute while I clear my throat."

After having a good cough, he continued "Sorry, a bit of a hangover from a cold recently, as I was saying, I hope me going out with Lisa doesn't present any problem with your arrangement." We both told him that it wouldn't be a problem at all, and I told him that I was grateful that he'd be staying over from time to time now that I was working longer hours and that it had been my suggestion that Lisa move into here. To give the both of you more privacy when you were together, he was nodding and thanked both of us for clearing that up for him, and then said, "There is one thing that still puzzles me, and that is that from what I've seen, Lisa isn't moving into the master bedroom." Lisa laughed, and I told him that after all it was still my house, and if I needed to sleep here for any reason, or occasionally, I still had my own room with an on-suite. So I didn't need to disturb them in any way. After that he was quite at ease with my presence while we finished sorting things out, and at one o'clock I was on the way home again, and now that Lisa's car wasn't in the way I could put both cars in the garage. I got some clothes together in my go bag along with a couple of business suits, and drove back to Newfarm where Darlene drove me nuts, wanting to wait on me the rest of the weekend.

I did however get to peruse the catalogue that Rick had given me, and wrote a list of the things and the item numbers that I wished to purchase. Which included some Top Flite golf balls with the company logo, a pre-tied tie on a plastic expandable loop and some marble pens to give away as freebies, I left the list on the bedside table, and on Monday morning put it into the jacket I was wearing, and after saying hooray to Darlene, I headed for the office.

During our usual meeting, after we'd discussed the ongoing investigations, leaving the one I was working to last, we all listened to the recordings again. Harry had dated each recording, and the subject matter, splicing it all into one continuous recording to date. I asked him for a copy, and he had already anticipated my request, and passed across a flat box containing another reel tape. Then I filled them into what had happened over the intervening week between meetings, and they had a quiet laugh as I explained the situation with Darlene, and Harry commented "Well you have to give the girl A for effort, she wants to get married, and I guess it's you she's set her sights on." This drew another bit of laughter and I joined in, and then I said "Well now we know that there's two different areas to this op, and it looks like it may split into two different fields, so I'm proposing that we continue running the Darlene angle." I stopped to let them think it over, and had a sip of coffee.

Then I continued, "…and because Kevin and his crew fit the brief that the feds asked for, we throw them a bone, and let them have them, that's why a need a copy of the tape, I'll take it upstairs with me to see Jack McCord and make sure that he arrests me with them because I'll set it up for him. I have a hunch that we'll get deeper into a far reaching organization if we do, Kevin and his bunch are just small time crims, and we won't get far pursuing them. So what do you guys think?"

After a few minutes, Harry said "I think you may be right, so I'm with you and vote yes." As we both looked at John, he said "Well Tiger you have a reputation for good hunches, so I'm in, but what do you think we should call it Operation Marry Me?" His comment received a chuckle from Harry, and a scowl from me. Looking at them both, I said "We know a few things about it already, that it's deep seated, but no one knows much about it, not us, ASIO, or the feds, and it's kept real quiet in on the other side of the law, so let's call it Deep Silence." John was nodding his head, and Harry said "Operation Deep Silence it is then, so what do we do now?"

I told them that after I'd made up an operational folder for it, and that I'd write up a detailed brief, of how it came about, and what we were aiming to do, and where we were to date and after that was done. I'd go upstairs and see Jack McCord to get them rolling on Kevin, and then I'd get on the blower to John Callaway in Sydney, and bring him up to date. The next thing I did was to tell them the names of the remaining unknowns, and that I'd made contact with them, and then told them and played the recording I'd made on Friday night, and we agreed that because it really didn't have anything to do with us, but the feds may as well have it to look into. Shortly afterward the meeting ended, and we all went about our normal business and after writing up the operation report, I asked Janice to get onto the feds office and see if Jack McCord was available to see me.

CHAPTER 5

After going up to the carpark in the lift, I walked across to the normal lifts, and went up to the eighth floor offices of the AFP, when I was seated in Jack's office, I told him that while investigating a query that they'd sent us. I also picked up some other information that may be of interest to him, and before playing the recording I told him where, when and by who it was made. After hearing it he was definitely interested, and asked for a copy of the tape, and as I passed across a copy, he wrote all the relevant details on the tape cover. Then we discussed the operation we'd been running for them, and after he listened to the tape, I asked what he wanted to do about what I was giving them.

He sat back, and asked what my opinion was, and I told him that yes they definitely dealt in drugs, but if they were dealing in guns, after talking with them and seeing what they had available. I didn't think they were doing it in a big way, they may be just on selling ordinance that may have been stolen from army bases, but I didn't think they had any international connections. It may pay dividends to have a joint operation with the state cops and arrest them, and see what sort of information could be sweated out of them, if there was anything of use to us, I'd expect that the AFP would pass it on to me. Then I told him that if they were going to arrest them, I needed to know, so that it would throw away any suspicion of me being the informant, and also it would boost my criminal credentials.

He was nodding and smiling, as he said "Ok Tom, leave it with me and I'll arrange something, but I'd say that you'd be looking at Wednesday at an earliest, but I'll keep you in the loop, and thanks for the help." I nodded and then left him with the information, and then returned to my sub level offices, and thought with a laugh, He'd have kittens if he knew where our offices were! When I got to my desk, I phoned Lisa to see how things were and she told me that she'd made another three appointments for me, two that evening and one for the following night, and after making note of the times addresses and names in my diary, and talked for a while before hanging up.

My next call was to Darlene, luckily she had just walked in, and I told her that if I did come over that night it would be late due to the scheduled appointments I had, so I'd stay at my place, and I warned her of already having another one the following night, and she told me that, that was ok, as most of her lectures that week were going to be after five most nights, so she'd be getting in late as well.

I smiled and thought to myself, *well that could work out perfectly, if the feds were going to arrest Kevin and crew during the daylight hours, that means she'll be home to come and pick me up from the cop shop, things were working out well.* As I looked at my watch the time was moving on toward two, so I decided that it was time to leave, and that way I had time to call in at the AMP office before heading home to get ready for the evening.

On my way out, I said my goodbyes to Janice and smiled as she passed me the recorder. Making my way to the car, I pulled out of the building and headed for Newmarket, where I dropped the catalogue back onto Rick's desk, and gave the order form to the girls. Shirley who processed it for me asked if the payment was coming out of my commission account, and also if I wanted the latest catalogue. After telling her yes to both, she went to the fax machine and sent it, and then said "That's it all done Tom, here's your original, and that will be out here maybe by Friday, but if not I'll let you know when." I smiled and thanked her, and then headed for home.

That night I made three more sales, with another one pending a call back the following afternoon. In the morning, while I was going over the reports from overnight, Janice Buzzed to say that McCord was on the line, so I got her to transfer him through. He told me that the wrecking yard was going to be raided at nine the following day, and that it would involve the state police as well as the AFP, and he would arrange that only his officers grabbed me for questioning back at the valley CIB where everyone would be taken, and of course they would nothing to hold me on, so I would be the only one released. I thanked him and told him I'd be in place the following day waiting to be arrested. As soon as he was off the line, I asked Janice to get hold of Harry and John to meet in my office and when they arrived she was to join us.

Five minutes later we were all seated around my desk, and I told them that the AFP and the state cops were going to take down Kevin and his crew and what part I'd be playing, so I needed them to, one, John was get hold of the radio channel they were going to use, two, Harry was to make sure we had a satellite available so the raid could be seen from overhead, three, they all needed to be in the tactical room following and recording the bust, and four, they had to relay information to me via the earpiece I'd be wearing, that would be supplied by Harry. Then I informed them of the most salient point of why I required the coverage, because I didn't want to lay myself open to a charge of carrying a concealed weapon, or for my gun to be confiscated, I would be going unarmed!

That piece of news created a small furore, as I thought it would, but a let them voice their concerns before I told them that my mind was made up and that I wasn't about to change my decision. Eventually they had to agree with my decision and shortly afterwards our meeting broke up, after that I rang Callaway in Sydney, and brought him up to date, and after listening and hearing his laughter, I explained the action scheduled for the next day, and told him that we'd made the decision to split the investigation so that we could concentrate on the main issue and give any off shoots to the AFP to deal with. After all it was them that wanted the information in the first place, but what had been uncovered so far was just superficial, but I wanted to find who had been behind the theft of the weapons container that had been intercepted, and he agreed to let me run with it.

Later in the morning I rang Lisa, and she told me that I had an appointment the following afternoon at the office, the people concerned lived in Stafford and the husband worked shifts, but they were happy to come to our office at two, after I agreed to the appointment I also told her not to make any more appointments until I let her know, but told her I had made sales from both appointments the previous evening, so I owed her four hundred to start with, and if I went ok that night it would probably climb to six hundred, which pleased her no end, and after telling her I'd see her the next day, we hung up.

My next call was to the last clients of the previous night, just to check that the call back appointment was still on, and didn't fall over, and the wife answered and said they'd been talking it over and had definitely decided to go ahead, and that if the husband hadn't made it home on time. She still wanted to go ahead signing up paperwork, after letting her know that I would be there at three as arranged I rung off, and thought to myself, hah, that made four, with another possible tonight and tomorrow, it could be six or more for the week, yeah!

Then after a late lunch in the cafeteria, I got ready to head out once I'd got back to my office, I had decided that seeing the insurance office didn't shut till five I had enough time to get the fourth policy paperwork signed, and then lodge them at the office before heading home to get ready for that nights' appointment. Everything went according to plan, and I got the policy paperwork back and lodged all four together, and ended up leaving the office just before four thirty, and then made my way home. That night I wrote another three policies, and the best part was that I was also getting a heap of referral business, by having the clients write out a list of people they knew that may benefit by my advice.

Next morning, I had a sleep in because I wasn't going into the office first up, but instead I was going to go straight to the wrecking yard to wait getting arrested along with everyone else, and if things went to plan Darlene would pick me up, I would go onto the insurance office, lodge the three policy sales written the previous night, and then have ample time to get to my own office at Stafford.

As soon as I was in my car, I put my gun and holster in the secret compartment, that I'd had installed under the driver's seat, placed the earphone into my ear, and after looking in the rear view mirror saw that it wasn't noticeable, then activated it after looking at my watch, knowing John he would have his tactical team already in the operations room. I asked if anyone could hear me, and I received a low volume affirmative, so I started the car and drove toward the wrecking yard arriving at five to nine. When I pulled into the parking area I informed base that the usual guard wasn't in his normal place, and walked into the counter sales area, all four of the boys were sitting behind the counter drinking coffee, so I said "Hey guys how about making me one, black no sugar thanks." They were all smiling, and Rodger the door guard went to the urn and made me the coffee I requested and rested it on the counter. I walked through the counter gate, and sat with my back intentionally toward the door on the counter beside the preferred mug, and as I took a sip, the earpiece said "They're about ready to come in," Kevin was smiling and about to say something, when police stormed the office wearing vests and pointing rifles and shotguns at us yelling, "Hands up, get down on your knees,"

I saw Kevin glance at the M16 that he'd had sitting on the desk, and I looked at him, and shook my head he nodded and raised his eyebrows before complying with the barked orders. AFP officers came in behind the counter, and started handcuffing us, and the lead detective looked at me, and said "Well, well, well, if it isn't Tiger Davis international arms dealer, so you're behind this little set up? What I can't understand is that you're reputed to allegedly deal with enough weapons to supply whole armies, why would you be only interested in stealing one container load? Then he looked at the assortment of weapons that had been found and placed on the counter, and then he looked at me. And continued "Oh I get it, you're here on a buying trip," I smiled and replied

"I'm not saying anything until I have my lawyer present, so when we get to wherever you're taking us, you'll have to contact him first before speaking to me."

We were all pulled to our feet, and taken outside; Kevin and his mates were placed into two marked police cars, while I was put in an unmarked one.

The AFP detective hopped into the back seat and two others got into the front, the boss turned to me holding up a key, saying "Let's get you un-cuffed, and on your way," I replied "Don't be silly, take me to where you're going with the others before we all get split up, and then you can let me go," he looked puzzled and said "But what about your car and so on," and I shook my head saying "Don't worry about that it's all covered." We were taken to the valley CIB yard, and the others were being taken out of the cars as we drove in, and then we were all placed into a holding cell with the cuffs still on, and I said to Kevin, "Thanks a bloody lot Kevin, now the damned feds know I'm in the country, just tell them you don't know me, I was only there trying to sell you my mustang, before having to leave the country quickly for work purposes, got it!" They all nodded as I looked at each of them in turn, a couple minutes after that a cop came to the cell, called my name, and roughly dragged me out, and then took me by the arm toward the hallway and then closed the door to the holding cell area.

As soon as he'd done that he took me to an interview room where Jack McCord was waiting with the lead detective, after the state cop left the room, I turned and the cuffs were taken off, as I asked "Ok so how did it go?" Jack laughed, and replied "Well along with what was found at the yard, we recovered forty-two rifles, ten handguns, a dozen grenades, and ten kilos of heroin, all in all not a bad haul, now we'll be into them about the rest of the guns, and who supplies the drugs, you'd best make tracks, Dave will show you out, and thanks Tom I owe you one." We shook hands as I got up to leave, and once we were outside I turned to

Dave and shook his hand also.

Once I was alone, I said "Well I hope you were able to get all that, now it's time for me to put part two into play, I won't be in till tomorrow morning, and then we'll have a briefing, say at nine in the conference room." The earpiece came alive in my ear, saying "Yeah we got everything and it's recorded, we'll all be ready tomorrow, see you then, we're disconnecting now, cheers." I turned off the earpiece after taking it out, and put it back in its small case returning it to my pocket, and pulled out the sat phone, brought up the number for Darlene, and rang it.

She answered on the fourth ring, and I said "Hi sweetheart it's me, can you do me a favour? I need you to come and pick me up from the valley CIB, don't worry no problems and I'll explain as you drive me to my car." She replied hesitantly "Yeah sure honey, I'll be there in ten minutes, will we have to go far, because I'm low on fuel." "No, I'll see you when you get here" I replied.

When she arrived the first thing she asked as I got in was, "You got arrested? How and why? So I proceeded to tell her the story that I was visiting Kevin and having a coffee with the boys when the cops burst in, everything would have been sweet, but they found the sample weapons of what he was selling, so they nabbed the lot of us, and because I wasn't suspected of being involved, and Kev told them that I was just a customer they let me go after I was interviewed. Ok head for the wrecking yard, and pull into the first servo along the way and I'll fill your tank for you."

As we drove off, I thought to myself, *interesting, she hasn't asked where it was or for an address, but she's heading straight for it*. When we reached the yard I thanked her and kissed her goodbye after telling her I'd see her that night after she got home, and then got into my car, and drove to the Newmarket office and lodged the three sales from the previous night before heading to my own office.

I drove into the driveway at eleven thirty, and as I walked into the office, Lisa was sitting at her desk I put my briefcase down and sat in a chair in front of her, and with a smile I said to her

"I owe you six hundred so far this week, seven if these people turn up, and eight if I make a sale. Now I need you to tell me something, when you're making the phone calls, how many on average do you make before you get an appointment?" She smiled and replied "Well so far with each call the people have wanted the appointment, so it's been a case of each call has been an appointment, and I think the reason for that is, because you get their names from someone they know." I nodded my head and replied with a smile "That's why I said not to make any appointments, if that ends up being the case, only make appointments for Monday, Tuesday and Wednesday nights, but also if anyone wants to see me through the day that's ok as well, except Monday mornings and Friday afternoons, but if you can get them to come here that's even better."

The couple arrived a little before the appointment time, but was fine by me and I was able to take them through to my office. After a bit of a question and answer session, during which I jotted down some notes, after which we made a bit of small talk, and then once they were at ease, I dealt with each policy that I was recommending to them one by one, explaining them in detail, and the pros and cons of having them, and after they'd agreed or disagreed to each of my suggestions, then I would get the paperwork for each out one they agreed to purchase, and so by the time we were finished, and the paperwork completed, I had made another five sales.

After they had left, I told Lisa that I now owed her eight hundred, and she smiled and told me she'd never made that much money in a week before, and I reminded her that it was only half way through jokingly, and then we talked for a while, and I told her I'd go to the bank either on the way, or back from the office, and that way we'd be up to date, and I'd see her when I returned. Then I went over to the insurance office at Newmarket, and Rick was there when I walked in, and called out "How's my gun salesman going this week?" So I walked into his office, and replied "Going well actually, I'm just in to lodge these, and then taking the rest of the week off." He looked at me questioningly and said, "Why are taking time off, you need to be out there selling, you'll make more money that way, you can't just take time off after a couple of sales and rest on your laurels, you need to be out there! How many sales have you made this week? One or two maybe three, it's not always going to be as easy as your first week."

Until then I had been in a fairly good mood, having had the arrests made, and having sold another five policies, but the way Rick spoke to me, especially mouthing off without checking on facts first, instantly soured my mood and made me angry, so I replied "Well firstly Mr Welsh, when I first started this job, you told me because I'm on commission, I'm my own boss and could work when I wanted, secondly if I were you I'd be checking facts before making any assumptions, why don't you pick up your phone and ask the office girls how many proposals I have in at present, and then with these five, I figure I've done enough this week, I not going to exhaust myself for you, or anybody else. I am taking the rest of the week off, however I will be here for the sales meeting on Friday, but if you ever talk to me like that again, you'll not see me for dust, now instead of making that call, why don't you just follow me to the service desk."

He was shaken by my retort, but tried to make light of it and told me he'd only been joking, but the best way to make myself a success, was by getting out there, and by the time we'd reached the counter he'd finished, as I passed across the proposals to Shirley, she remarked "Hey boss, Tom's going to make you famous if he keeps this up, another five on top of the seven already lodged and its only Wednesday!" Rick was really amazed, and said "Twelve! In only three days my god you're going to beat everyone again, disregard anything I was saying to you, you just keep going the way you want to, and I promise never to get on your case again, I should have known better, I'm sorry Tom, and I hope there's no hard feelings." And he held out his hand, and I shook it.

After his apology and congratulations, I refilled my supply of proposal forms and brochures before leaving the office, telling them all I'd see them on Friday. Then went across the road to the bank and withdrew one thousand dollars in cash, eight hundred was to cover what I owed Lisa, which I gave to her as soon as I arrived back at the Stafford office. She was over the moon, thanking and hugging me, and when she settled down a bit, I told her she could go ahead and make appointments for me for next week, but no more that week.

During the next few weeks, things and events settled into a more routine pace, I was still averaging between seven and ten sales a week, my bank balance had grown considerably after I received my monthly commission cheque. A couple of the operations we'd been monitoring had concluded, but as is always the case others took their place in short time. Darlene and I still lived at the apartment, and I was getting deeper into the criminal side of her group of friends, and had been included in on a couple of robberies, they'd pulled on jewellery shops, but I complained to Darlene that this really wasn't getting us what we wanted, and she had placated me by informing me that the top man would be attending our wedding that was only a week away.

Apart from marrying someone that I had no wish to, everything to do with the investigation was going well, some of the information that I was able to record and bring back as I worked my way up the hierarchy chain, was able to be linked to others crimes that no one focused on being part of a bigger picture, or being part of larger organization, until we were able to put it altogether, but it looked as if this ring were responsible for many gun thefts and looked like branching into the drug trade distribution, and sale.

We had now identified all but two of the major players, and their addresses, and because the wedding was on Wednesday, at our usual Monday meeting it was decided that we'd have two agents that would pass as friends, or business associates there as a backup to me with the best video and small cameras that Harry could get hold of. It would be their job to get images of the so called top man, after Darlene had confirmed to me he was turning up. This could be a good opportunity considering he would be signing the paperwork as one of the witnesses; therefore, he'd be included in the wedding party. As our planning was going ahead, we were interrupted by the arrival of John Calloway, who would be overseeing the operation while I was in the field, one of the ideas he had was to have someone staying nearby in the Maldives to be able to replace and charge the recorder for the week I would be there having my honeymoon.

Once we'd made all the final operational arrangements, John and I went to my office where we talked over the whole operation, and one of the things I told him was that I was relying on him to get me out of this sham of a marriage once the whole lot was busted, but I agreed that that wouldn't be able to happen until we had all the evidence to convict every member of the group, but trying to be fair, I asked that Darlene wasn't arrested, because she would have enough on her plate wondering what had happened when the time for the takedown came. *However, as they say the best laid plans of mice and men are always likely to go awry, no matter how meticulously they are planned, which you will see as we continue.*

In most things I try to be as fair as possible, and even though I really didn't wish to be lumbered with a wife that I didn't want, I still tried to maintain true to my ideals, so considering Darlene had planned the wedding, because I thought it only fair, I took care to arrange some sort of honeymoon, and I had booked a suite at the five star hotel in the Maldives, where each suite was located over the water, and the ambient lowest temperature was twenty two degrees at night, and a very pleasant twenty eight during the day, with the sea temperature of twenty one, which would make swimming and diving excellent. Our flight would leave at thirteen hundred the day after the wedding, so I arranged a car to pick us up at the Park Royal where we were going to have a small reception, and stay the night.

The registry office was in the treasury building in the city, so Darlene had arranged that everyone was to meet in the park behind the building, and in between the next government building along in George street. The first to arrive were my two fellow agents, that were providing any backup should it be required, so I introduced them as

Ted and Terry, two old friends from up north. Slowly in dribs and drabs people that had been invited for the four o'clock wedding turned up, just as I was looking at the time on my watch, four men in suits got out of a limo in George Street, and made their way to us. The one leading was roughly six foot with close cropped black hair, and a moustache, and walked as if he owned the world, the next one was about five eight, with long brown hair, and was sporting a wide grin. The other two I dismissed as bodyguards, they were built, but they weren't wearing tailored clothing and the slight bulges of wearing shoulder holsters was discernible to the trained eye. I looked around at my two agents, and received an almost imperceptible nod that told me that the faces had been caught on still cameras, as well as video.

When they were within ten feet of us Darlene rushed forward, and hugged the leader of the group, and then pulled him forward to meet me, and as I shook the hand of the person I was after, he was introduced to me as Trevor Dyson. As he shook my hand, he said "Tom, it's good to finally meet you, I've heard a lot of good things about you, and I look forward to us getting together and talking business with you that could benefit both of us." I smiled and replied "So do I Trevor, but I'm afraid that's not going to be for a while, after all you're here for a wedding, and I hope you'll take the place of my best man, unfortunately he wasn't able to make it at the last minute, so considering that you're a good friend of Darlene's, I'd be honoured if you would take his place?"

Dyson was slightly taken back, but it took a trained eye to notice it, as he answered "I'd be honoured, now let me introduce my second in command Lyle Thomas, perhaps we may get the chance to get together for a quick chat at the reception." I shook hands with Thomas, and replied to Dyson "I'd like that very much if we have time, but right now I think it's time we made our way into the building."

Then everyone started making their way across the road, and Darlene and I led the way upstairs to the registry office ceremony room, where we were married twenty minutes later.

CHAPTER 6

Well, from what I could gather from different sources, things went okay while I was away enjoying myself on my honeymoon, during my time there I went diving almost twice a day, but because Darlene was scared of the water, I would take time out now and again to spend time with her during the day, by now she had gotten used to the room being built over the water, but she still had trouble going anywhere near the chest high railing, she really should have informed me of her fear of water before I booked the honeymoon, but when we were up at the main guest areas onshore she was fine, and believe it or not she actually went swimming in the hotel pool, but over the water, she was like a cat waiting to pounce. At least I enjoyed my time there, but I think she went along with it just to please me, so I give her an A for that.

Once we landed back in Brisbane we took a cab back to the apartment building at Newfarm, and we relaxed, she had time to get over her jetlag before I went into the office early on the Monday. During the time I was away everything from the wedding had been disseminated, and as I walked into my office, there were complete dossiers pertaining to, our main target Trevor Dyson, and his 2IC, Lyle Thomas. As I walked past the situation board, I grabbed both of the dossiers, and sat down at my desk to read them, soon after Janice came in to welcome me back, and congratulate me, and passed me a cuppa, and then left as I continued to read.

An hour later, I was joined by John Callaway as he walked into my office, he was closely followed by Janice with another mug of coffee for him, and as he sat opposite me, said "Well how did the honeymoon go, it shouldn't have been too bad, after all she is quite a looker." I glared at him, and replied "That maybe so, but I still want out of this relationship after the job is done, oh, and while we're on that, she gets away from this with no charges, she's to be free to go wherever she wants, but she has to get out of Brisbane."

He nodded in agreement, and then he filled me in on what had been discovered about our two main targets, apart from what was in the files. That took us up to the time of the weekly meeting, so we both headed to the conference room. John and Harry welcomed me back with looks of relieve, and inwardly I smiled, as assumed that they weren't too happy working with Callaway in my place, and I wondered what he'd would have done to put them both offside, unless he'd been demanding a more intense workload from them.

Considering the amount of information that had been uncovered during the week I was away, I assumed this to be the case, plus I knew that they weren't ever pleased whenever they had to deal with the head office types, and that could explain their warmness in greeting me back. Having dealt with the state of affairs to date, it was time to move onto new business, and I told them that during the reception I'd been given Dyson's contact number, and he'd told me to get in touch as soon as I was back from my honeymoon. So I was well placed to keep going with our investigation, so we decided that I wait a couple of days, and then contact him, and set up a meeting. The only other item was brought up by John, and it concerned a communique that had been passed along from Sydney, apparently someone in the US DEA was trying to determine my whereabouts, and a direct line number, had been passed along for return calling.

This was usually unprecedented, and a discussion ensued as to how anyone would know our operatives by name, but Callaway said "At times we share our information with other intelligence agencies around the world, and yes will at times divulge our agent's identity, but the only ones we've been talking to of late has been the CIA, about our targets, and that was only for requesting any data that could help with our inquiry, how the DEA has got involved, is beyond me. I slapped my hand onto the table, to get their attention because each of them had started to talk over each other, and when I had their attention, I said "I might know something about this, and it's the only thing that makes sense."

I explained to them "Some years back now while I was in Vietnam, I was seconded to a DEA operation that had CIA backing, and it was against the renegade Air America group, my mission had involved going into Laos, and destroying the source of the drugs that Air America supplied. During that op, I worked closely with the senior agents on the ground at that time, and afterwards they were to be pulling out and heading back to Washington, I later learned that the most senior agent, had been promoted to director in their organisation, but at the time I knew them, they were working very closely with the CIA. I would suggest that you make a call back to them John, and set up a time to have a conference call with them, and all of us can find out what this is all about at the same time."

John looked at his watch, and said "If I get on the phone within the next hour, I'll still be able to get an answer." I replied "Good, we're done here anyway, you go make the call, and let me know the result," and I looked at each of the faces at the table, and they were all nodding in the affirmative.

Back in my office, John and I sat opposite each other, and after glaring at him for a minute or two, I said "Ok do you know if anyone has passed along the info that I now work with you guys?" He was looking me in the eye, as he replied "No, not that I'm aware of, but don't forget the intelligence community is small, so it could have filtered out." I looked at him and scoffed, saying "Listen to yourself John, Christ, you of all people should know that's just bullshit! I've only been with ASIS just short of three months, and have yet to have an overseas assignment, for Christ's sake you can't tell me that's enough time for that to find its way to the CIA. We have strict security protocols, so there's no way that could happen without a leak somewhere in the agency, and now it's been passed to the DEA, shit how many more people are going to know!"

He looked at me, and then around the room, and I could tell that he was mulling over what I'd just said, and after a few minutes, he said, "You may be right, and if that is the case, for now it has to stay between you and me, tell no one, but we have to find a way to confirm it first, and once that's been established, I'll carry out my own internal investigation." Just then the phone buzzed, it was Janice telling me that John was on the line, she patched him through, and he informed me that the conference call was set for four am our time tomorrow, I thanked him, and asked that he inform Harry, and told him I'd see him then if not before, and rang off.

I looked at Callaway as I hung up, and said "The call is arranged for four am in the morning, so I'm going to finish up here soon, and get going, but I want to make a couple of calls first, so by the time you finish lunch, you'll be able to use my office, but don't forget it's an early morning tomorrow." After I'd finished he nodded his head, and left me alone in the office, as I reached for the phone and called Lisa, and while we were talking business, she told me she had three couples that would like day time appointments this coming week, and I told her to ring them, and arrange two for that afternoon and the other for the following arvo, and try to get another if she could for tonight, and I'd see her in half an hour at the office. My next call was to Darlene, and I told her I'd be sleeping at my place that night, due to an evening appointment, she was ok with that piece of news, and told me she had an early lecture the next morning, so she'd by out most of that morning.

When I arrived at the office, Lisa asked "So how's married life?" I smiled and replied "Actually it's no different to what I've been doing, mind you I'd still prefer to be single, and I can see this becoming a problem though."

She smiled, and told me not to let it get me down too much, and that there was one couple due into the office in half an hour, another would be waiting for me at three o'clock, and I also had a six o'clock at Gaythorne. I laughed and kissed her on the cheek, and as she brushed it off she told me to get my head in the right place, and make some sales because she'd missed the money I made for her during the last week while I was away. We both laughed, and I headed into my office, and ten minutes later Lisa brought in my first clients in over a week.

Out of the three clients I saw that day, I made ten sales, so that night I was on a high as I drove into my house at Keperra, I'd made the equivalent of a week's sales in the one day, I just hoped that would keep up the following day. Instead of driving the mustang the next morning I opted for the sedan, and arrived in the conference room with a mug of coffee in hand at five to four, the only person missing was Callaway who virtually followed me in the door, with nods of meeting to everyone we sat, and Harry informed us that he'd set everything up so the call could be recorded.

Precisely on time the phone rang and I initiated the answering button, and said "ASIS Brisbane here, agent Tom Davis speaking, who've I got on the line please?" The speakers crackled into life "Tiger? Thank Christ for that, its Alex Stein here do you remember me from Australia and Vietnam? I've been trying to get hold of you everywhere, after Stockton had told me that after reaching out to a friend of his at the CIA he found out you had moved into the spy game, and you were passing yourself off as an arms dealer." I shot a quick glance at John Callaway, and he was sitting back in his chair drawing in breath, as I pursed my lips, and replied "Yeah Alex I remember all too well, where are you these days, and what can I do for you?"

The answer that came back from Alex was, "Before we get into that Tom, I don't need you worrying too much the only other person that knows about this call is the director, and he is listening as well." Stockton spoke up, saying "Hi Tiger, you and I need to talk after this call, so please don't hang up after Alex does." I smiled and answered him, saying "Hi John, hope you're not getting a shiny bum from all that desk work, Roger that I'll hang on after Alex hangs up, and speaking of Alex, ok let's hear it buddy."

Alex came back on the line, saying "Hey Tiger I'm in LA and

headed up the office here so I guess I have to do a fair bit of desk driving as well, anyway Mose is my number two man, and he's the reason I've been trying to get you."

I interrupted him, by saying "Well I was wondering why I've been pulled into the picture, I hope this is not another search and destroy mission you're trying to talk me into." His laugh came through the speakers, as he continued "No, not another of those, unless you're volunteering? Anyway back to where we were, at the moment Mose is up to his neck in an undercover operation against the Morales cartel in Columbia, he's infiltrated to a fairly high position as one of Jose's lieutenants, and he found out Jose was after weapons, so because we already knew you were using that as a cover, and aren't connected to us in anyway, Mose suggested he try to contact you, to get you to come to Columbia and meet him and Jose, but what we really need is for you to get him onto neutral ground, where we can arrest him, do you think you can assist me on this?"

Thinking quickly, I answered "Alex, I can help you, but the request would have to come through official channels, so I'll explain to John what I need after we're finished, but back to the case in point Alex, I think the best way to handle this would be to go ahead and meet him, make a deal and then he will have to come to a place of my choosing for delivery, let's say somewhere like Panama, can you make an arrest there?" Alex answered "Yeah we sure can." "Good" I replied "Now I'll need a number where I can get hold of Mose, for when I get to Bogota, what alias is he using, and your direct line number so I can contact you."

Alex gave the number for Mose, who was using the alias of John Wheeler, and also his direct line, I wrote both of them down even though the conversation was being taped, and after telling him I'd be in contact with him later, he hung up, and John Stockton the DEA director came on the line, before we started speaking I asked him to hold for a moment, and flipped the hold call switch. Then I asked John and Harry to leave the room because I had a few issues to take care of with Stockton that really didn't involve them, but they could listen to the tape later if they wished.

As I flipped the hold switch to open the line, I said "Now then Hammer, what can I do for you?" Using his old call sign and I heard him chuckling over the speakers, as he asked "Who else is in the room with you, broadsword?" Now it was my turn to laugh, and replied "I've got the second in charge of our agency and his name is John Callaway, it's him that you'll be talking to in regard to the request for our agencies assistance in the form of me, and as soon as we get it, I can start moving on Alex's request, but first what were you going to say?"

Stockton answered, "Well your boss has the right first name, and I use his golf clubs," and he started laughing and John chuckled. Then Stockton said, "Now back to serious Tiger, I think you may have a mole in your agency, and I'll tell you why, when Alex proposed this operation, I reached out to a friend of mine in the CIA, and he asked me if I knew you, and I told him about our thing in Laos. He told me that you had gone across to intelligence, and that you were going to use a cover as a drug and arms dealer, now that was three months ago, way before this idea about getting you to help us came up, so what do you think?"

I looked at Callaway, and he answered "John Callaway here Director, this was something that Tiger and I having been discussing recently, and we both have to agree with your assessment of the situation, don't worry too much about it, because I'll be doing some mole hunting, at least no one will be aware of this operation, and as soon as I give you what I need to come from you, Tiger can be away by the end of the week." They both spoke together at length going over what was required, and that the DEA would cover all expenses, provide ample weapons as required for inspection, and indemnify me should I find I have to discharge my weapon and shoot someone to defend myself. They seemed to be getting on like a house on fire, so I motioned to Callaway that I was going back to my office, and left them to finish their conversation.

When Callaway came back into my office some fifteen minutes later, I was staring into space with two things going around in my head, one the operation that Mose had taken on in Columbia, and the second was the fact that secrets were coming from within ASIS, and that the leak had to be found and stopped. As John sat across from me, I said "Well I think that what Stockton had to say has just confirmed what you wanted to hear?" He nodded his head, and said with a sigh "Yeah, so that means I have some work to do, hopefully I'll have got to the bottom of it by the time you get back, and yes I'm approving the request, and later I'll have Ross and Bob bring up the jet from Sydney, look towards leaving by Friday, knowing you, you've already started planning it in your head so I'll call a meeting tomorrow at ten, and you can brief us all, will that give you enough time?"

I nodded my head, and replied "Yeah plenty, as you said I'm already working on it, and by tonight I'll be ready with a full plan of how to go about this operation, anyway, right now I have cover business to take care of so I'll get going as soon as I clean up my mug, so I'll see you in the morning.

My next stop was to call in at the bank and withdraw one thousand dollars, six hundred dollars of which was owed to Lisa, and then I drove into the insurance office parking lot, and went upstairs, and as I handed my proposal paperwork to Shirley, she exclaimed "Jesus, first day back and you bring ten, you wrote ten in one day, Rick's going to love you." Smiling at her I went to a cubicle and made a call to Darlene, and once she came on the line I asked her about coming over to the Keperra house for the night, as I would be late when I got in, and I had something to discuss with her, but because she had an early lecture she couldn't, so I said I'd call when I was free, and hung up.

After leaving the insurance office I carried onto the Stafford office, and paid Lisa her six hundred, and she was rapt, and then reminded me that she'd lined up four appointments for that day.

Then we sat down to talk, and I warned her that I might be taking more time off, and that it would be best if she only made appointments on a day to day basis, but to leave Friday free, but I would work Thursday if I could, and I'd let her know. During that afternoon and evening I sold fifteen policies, and was fairly shagged when I got home at ten, I hoped I wouldn't get many early morning calls like that. At nine the next morning I handed over my paperwork to Shirley with a wide grin on my face, and question turned to a shriek, as she said "What are you so happy about? Holy shit you've got another fifteen here, that's twenty-five in two days, Christ!" While Shirley was getting my paperwork supplies refurbished, I went to look at the sales board and my name was up the top with ten without the additional fifteen, the closest to my tally was a salesman that had been selling insurance for over ten years, and his tally for the week we were in was two.

I drove into the carpark of the office and went down to my level, and stopped by my office, before I went into the conference room, and asked Janice to get me a couple of maps, one of north, and the other south America. She left quickly to find the maps, knowing there was a briefing scheduled, and she came back with what I wanted and I smiled as I thanked her. As I walked into the conference room, I saw two new faces that belonged to Ross Higgins and Bob Walsh the pilots that had taken my team to Africa, as I saw them I smiled and thought to myself, *Good going John, Ross may have another flight route that could be better, so I'll leave a gap in my briefing to accommodate any input from him.*

Without sitting down, I said "Good morning gentlemen, I hope you've all met Ross and Bob, they're agency pilots for those that don't know, and I've worked well with them before, and I'm glad that John was able to get them up here."

I hung the maps, and then turned to face them, and said "While Ross and Bob weren't here for our call yesterday, they're smart enough to follow the briefing without that need to be caught up." I smiled as they both nodded their heads, and continued "The plan is to fly to Hawaii, and from there go direct to Bogota, find a good hotel, and contact Mose, who will I'm sure will arrange a meeting with Jose Morales, and then in my inimitable style. I'll propose the arms deal after finding out what he requires. Now if he requires a viewing of samples of the merchandise, I'll offer to fly him to Panama, and take him to a prearranged container yard where the DEA will have a container already stocked with the weapons that should hold his interest long enough for them to get into position and arrest him. Then we come on home after the jobs finished, now if there's any problems, I may have to fly to LA and sort through them with Alex, now I'm going to pass to Ross, to see if he has a better travel route in mind."

Ross suggested that we fly to LA from Hawaii and sort out any foreseeable problems with the DEA while we're there refuelling, and then fly down to Columbia, but the rest of my plan he was happy with, and we all agreed that we'd do it that way. Ross suggested a departure time of zero four hundred hours on Friday morning, which was agreed to. Shortly after our conference briefing ended, and I went to my office and rang Alex's direct line in LA, and surprisingly enough he was in his office, one of the first things I arranged with him was the meeting at LAX where we would be refuelling, and he said he'd have it all arranged for us, the next item on my list was to get him to arrange the container and yard in Panama, after his assurance that it would be done, he asked me what weapon samples I'd need, so I rattled off a list of ordinance, and also told him that I'd call him from Columbia if I needed to change some items, and after telling him I looked forward to seeing him in the next few days, we both hung up.

While I was having a cuppa and chat after the briefing with Callaway, my Sat phone rang, it was Lisa, so I told her I'd ring her back in a couple of minutes. He took the mugs out to clean them while I phoned Lisa back, she told me that I only had one appointment that afternoon at three, and asked if I wanted her to make any more appointments, and after telling her no, I told her I'd be out to see her soon. I left the office soon after that telling everyone I'd see them in the morning, on my way to Stafford I stopped into the bank and withdrew another thousand, and when I got to the house I saw that the fence sign had been fixed on, and also the smaller one by the office door, and I smiled.

Lisa opened the office door while I was admiring both of the signs, and told me that they'd arrived at eight and only took an hour to put them in the right places, and we both smiled, when we were back in the office she gave me the address of where the appointment was, and I thought that the address was in an industrial area, saying as much to Lisa, and she told me that the client had asked for me to meet there and his name, so I shrugged my shoulders and said okay. We were sitting down at her desk having a cuppa, as I told her that I was going away for a couple of weeks on Friday and that was why I had asked for no more appointments to be made. She made a shrewd guess as to why, and told me to look after myself, and then I gave her the eight hundred I owed her from the appointments made and sold the previous day.

The address Lisa had been given was indeed in the industrial area of Stafford, and I arrived five minutes before I was due, and went into see the client. He told me that he'd talked with the person that had referred his name, and that he wanted me to speak to his workers about superannuation and other policies available to them, and that once I had done that for him, he would like to see me at a later date. When I could review his family's financial state, and give some recommendations, I was happy enough to comply with this, but told him that it would probably be at least two weeks or so before I could get around to seeing him and his family, and he nodded saying that was fine by him. Then he asked about how to set up a superannuation scheme, and I told that the easiest way, was for me to have our super team make an appointment with him to come out and talk to him, after that we went to the staff lunch room where everyone had gathered.

That afternoon I made twenty six sales and twelve more red

hot appointments, after explaining that I would be away for a couple of weeks, and before going back to the office I went to the bank again, and drew out a further fifteen hundred dollars because I'd figured out that was going to get at least ten thousand odd in commission, and so thought it only fair that considering Lisa made the appointment instead of giving her the hundred for the sale, I' d give fifty of each sale, so when I arrived back there and told her what I'd do she was over the moon, as I counted out a further fourteen hundred into her hand, and also gave her the list of red hots, telling her they'd be the first to ring when I got back from my trip. Then I headed to my place and while I was pulling out clothes to take that would go into my go bag, I phoned Darlene, and I told her I'd be over that night, but had an early start the next day.

When I got the apartment Darlene was looking after, she told me that Trevor had wanted to get hold of me, and she wanted to know if I'd meet him the coming Friday night. So I told her to tell him to contact me when I was back from overseas, and then told her I'd been contacted by a friend in Columbia that was looking to buy arms, so I was going to see him, and so I was flying out early Friday morning, and would be gone for a week or two.

Next morning at the office, I rang Rick Welsh at home at nine, asking him to meet me at the office at eleven, and he said he would, and then I rang the super team office, and spoke to the team leader, telling him what I'd got from the client so far and what he was looking to do, the leader then told me that I couldn't claim all of the commission from the super scheme that they may sell him, and that I'd only get half, which was fine by me because I'd probably pickup other policy sales from him anyway.

Rick and I arrived in the carpark at the same time, and he asked why I wanted to see him, after showing him the proposals and telling him about the super scheme that I'd set in motion he whistled, and asked me how many proposals I had, by this time

74

we'd reached the office and Shirley piped up saying "Tigers got twenty five in so far this week boss," I was smiling as I handed her the bundle, and her eyes went wide as I told her she had another twenty six to process, and she exclaimed "Shit fifty one sales in one week, Christ Tiger!"

I think that Rick was a little distracted as I told him I wouldn't be at the Friday meeting, and that I was taking another three weeks off, because his answer was quiet and without real thought, as he said "Sure, sure fine take as long as you wish, I think you've made enough sales to cover yourself."

I arrived at the old terminal building at the airport the next morning at three thirty, this was where all the private jets left from, and I was met by Bob, who showed me where to garage my car. Twenty minutes later we were wheels up bound for Columbia, via the US.

CHAPTER 7

We landed at LAX just after nine local time, and were escorted to the private jet hangers, and as Ross and Bob shutdown the engines, and opened the front door, a set of stairs were wheeled into place, and as I reached the tarmac, a refuelling truck was pulling to a stop under the starboard (Right) wing. A limo was parked near the hanger door, and Alex Stein got out and made his way toward me, and as he got closer he put a smile on his face and held his hand out, as we shook hands I looked him over, and said "Jesus Alex, you're starting to go grey," he replied with "Well you're not getting any younger either, must be the jobs we're in I guess, it certainly isn't our ages." We both started laughing as we headed toward the hanger office, where we each took a seat, after closing the door on the outside noise.

As we both brought each other up to date with our lives since last seeing each other, there were laughs and commiserations as we caught up before we got down to business. Alex told me that he'd had a container filled with empty munition crates, and had placed all the types I'd asked for on some crates with only a few weapons in them, for all intense and purposes the container would like to genuine article, and then he passed me the name of the container yard and address in Panama, and said that from now on he would have it under surveillance twenty four seven, and that there was a full team of agents that would pose as workers as well, ready for whenever could get Morales there. He passed across another piece of paper and was telling me, that is the best hotel in Bogota, would be in fashion with an international arms dealer, I've booked you a suite in your name there, also John knows that's where you'll be staying and he'll get in contact.

I gave my Sat phone number to Alex telling him that if he needed me to contact me on it unless he wanted any of our information to go to the other side, he grinned and told me I was becoming more cynical and less trusting of others than I used to be, and I countered that with telling him that's how come I was still around, and we both laughed as he sighed, "Ah, the lurks of the spy game." We kept going through the finer details of the operation as much as we could, Then, after about an hour, Ross came and knocked on the door, and stuck his head in to tell us that everything had been completed, and they were ready for take-off whenever I was, I answered him saying "Righto get us listed for the flight to Bogota, and I'll be there shortly," I turned to Alex and we wished each other well, and hoped that the operation would be a success.

As I boarded the jet the stairs were withdrawn, and I helped Bob secure the door, and then went to sit ready for that exhilarating burst of speed down the runway prior to the wheels leaving the ground, as we made for Bogota. When we landed, arrangements had already been made for the jet to be placed in a private hangar, and after we taxied to the hangar, we waited for the immigration and customs officers to board, and after we were cleared Ross arranged for refuelling while I rang the hotel, and had them send a limo for myself and staff, after being assured that my staff rooms were also ready, then after the hangar was locked up we were taken to the main terminal where the limo was already waiting for us.

When I checked in, Ross and Bob were given the keys to their rooms, and as I given the key card to my suite, before leaving the reception desk, I asked if there were any messages for me. After looking the senior receptionist passed across a box, telling me that it had been left by a senor Wheeler, and in the lift I slit open the box to find another Sat phone inside. After turning it on I checked the memory, and there was only one stored number, so according to Moses' note to ring from outside my suite when I arrived, closing the door of the suite I went out onto the balcony, closing the door behind me, and pressed the call button and when it was answered by Mose. I said "Wheeler old buddy, obviously the law hasn't caught up with you yet, I've arrived in Bogota, and thought I'd let you know I was here, how about we get together soon old friend?" He told me to wait for his call, and to be careful when saying anything inside the room. I caught on immediately to the idea that the room was possibly bugged, and filed the information.

Back inside, I toured the suite before going down to the restaurant for some dinner, and then made my way across the road to the casino, where I wandered around the card tables while I sipped my scotch from the bar, taking a seat at a Blackjack table that had a minimum bet limit of ten thousand pesos, which equated to ten dollars Australian, I had a wandering cashier change some of my money for me, and she brought me back one hundred thousand pesos and another scotch, and I lit up and joined the game, it didn't take long before I started to accumulate a huge pile of chips, and after separating my original stake, I played for the next few hours on winnings, and eventually left the table four million pesos in front, I kept the hundred thousand pesos in my pocket, but had the four million converted into US Dollars, which equated to one hundred and sixty five thousand.

Hmm, not a bad profit for a couple hours of relaxation, I thought to myself as I walked back across the road to the hotel, and went up to my suite, and after having a shower, I slipped my gun under one of the pillows on the bed, and slept. While I was having breakfast in the restaurant the next morning, a house phone was brought to the table, and told that the concierge desk was trying to call me, so after finishing a mouthful of toast. I picked it up and asked for the concierge, and after being connected I was told that there was a person waiting to see me, so I told them I'd be with them as soon as I had finished my breakfast.

As I approached the concierge desk, he held out his hand pointing to two men sitting in armchairs in the foyer, and as I walked over to them they both started to rise, as I said "I'm Tiger Davis, can I help you?" I ran my eye over both of them as I asked my question, they were both dressed in suits, but without ties, and I also made out the slight bulges under their jackets, which told me they were both armed, they were both the same height and both had black hair with dark eyes, and they both had very visible scars one with a scar running across his throat, and the one that spoke had one running from his left eye down his cheek to his neck, and he said "Senor, my name is Jesus Montoya, and I've been sent here to ask you to visit the home of my master, for a couple of days by Senor Wheeler." I nodded my head, and said "Very well Jesus, I'd be glad to come, if you'll give me a few minutes I'll go pack some things, and then join you," he replied, "Gracias Senor Davis, we will wait here for you to return."

In my room I gathered my toiletries and placed them in my go bag, which I hadn't really unpacked, and grabbing my jacket out of the closet it put it on over my shirt, and instead of replacing my gun and holster to outside my shirt, I left it under my shirt. I joined Jesus and his partner in the foyer, and they took me to a black BMW that looked more like a four wheel drive, and from the back seat I was able to discern that it wasn't a four wheel drive, but one of the new type all-wheel drive models that were becoming popular in the states, *give me a good old four by four anytime, instead of these newfangled things, but I suppose they'll by everywhere in a few years, I just hope they don't replace four wheel drives for the likes of these things,* I thought to myself. Soon we were out of the city, and moving higher up into the mountains, but in a south easterly direction and soon came to a road sign showing the next town as Villavicencio, and settled back to inspect the scenery. I noticed that we'd levelled off and must have been on a ridge, but the bush was much like the jungles of Vietnam.

Glancing at my watch, the altimeter was reading sixteen thousand feet, and then realised that instead of jungle the bush was part of the lush tropical rain forest that covered the entire northern region of South America which included Peru, Columbia, Brazil, and the entire Amazon basin. Ten minutes after driving through Villavicencio, we turned left into a side road that ended at a large walled estate, and as we pulled up to the main house I saw Mose walking out the front door to greet me. As I got out of the vehicle

Mose and I shook hands embraced and slapped each other on the backs, all the while smiling as long parted friends would do, but while we were turning in our embrace, I realised that he was showing me the positions of armed guards, and I softly said "Ah huh, got them," into his ear. He remarked the house is bugged too.

As we let go of each other he said "Ah Tiger it's good to see you, it's been a while, c'mon let's get you bunked down, the boss isn't here at the moment but will be back by cocktail hour, say in forty minutes." I smiled and said as we went into the house with Jesus behind us carrying my bag, "Yeah well I haven't seen you since you got arrested in Mexico, glad to see you made it out, I must say I was surprised when I heard from you, Oh and here's your Sat phone too by the way, these things cost a bundle, I've put the number into mine, hope you don't mind, and tough if you did." We both burst out laughing as I handed him the Sat phone that had been left at the hotel.

Jesus placed my bag on the bed and left as Mose showed me the rooms, in the huge bathroom, he started running water into the spa bath, saying "I always enjoy a spa after that trip up from Bogota, try it yourself, you'll love it." Then we had a whispered conversation close to the running tap, finally I nodded, and we made our way silently into the main room, and he said "Just come down to the main room when you're ready, and we'll catch up over some drinks, see you soon Tiger." In the bathtub I pushed the button for the jets, and as they did their work on sore muscles, that I hadn't thought were sore, I saw what John meant. Later dressed in a pair of jeans with a shirt hanging outside them plus my gun, and in sneakers I made my way down to the main room, and as I entered Mose came across and led me to the other man in the room, and as I approached I took in his looks.

He was close to six foot, with salt and pepper coloured hair, with more grey than black, with a Zapata style moustache, he was pudgy but at one stage would have been very fit, his eyes were steel grey, and cold and deadly. I imagined he could easily order a killing, as offhand as he would brush off a fly.

Everything about him screamed out to the senses danger, danger. As I smiled Mose made the introductions eagerly putting my hand out, and as we shook hands, I was reminded of handling snakes, and when Morales said to me, "Mr Davis please let me pour you a drink, Wheeler tells me that you usually only drink very expensive malt scotch, a man after my own heart, but please give me your opinion of this one, you may find it to your taste, ice?" It seemed as if he was talking through a filtering cloth, and as I inwardly shuddered I thought, *this guy is more dangerous than a platoon of VC, I hope he doesn't have any idea who Mose is, or we could be in for the fight of our lives here, with this snake.*

I tasted the malt after an ice cube had been placed in it and swirling the tumbler, as I sipped I smiled, and said "Glenmorangie black, almost as hard to get as the Johnny Walker Blue Label, both are very smooth Jose, but I do prefer the Blue label it has a tad more peat blending." He stared at me with cold dead eyes, and then started laughing, as he said "Bravo senor Davis, maybe it's just as well I ordered in a case of the Blue Label then." Then he ordered one of the servants to take the decanter away and replace it with a decanter of Blue Label in Spanish, however I didn't let on that I knew everything he was saying, and I remarked to him, "Jose, make it Tiger, as I tell everyone Mr Davis was my father, so how come you have this old reprobate Wheeler working for you, mind you, you've done well to get him there's not many people John would work for." Morales started laughing, and he said "Well done Tiger, there's not many that would get away with saying that in his presence, and live, you must be a special kind of man." Mose piped in by saying, "Tiger and I go back a long way Jose."

After about an hour of small talk, and getting to know each other, I decided to get down to business, and said "This get to know session has been nice Jose, but I've travelled thousands of miles for this meeting, so let's cut the crap, I have put other deals on hold for this, and there's no way I would have done it for anyone else other than Wheeler, so tell me why am I here, and what do you want?"

He looked at me coldly with expressionless eyes as I lit up a cigarette, and looked at him, and the tension that had entered the room could almost be seen, and then he laughed, saying "Tiger, my friend, I like you, you don't mess around with how is it you say, bullshit. You're a businessman and I like that, so if you like we can get down to business, and then we'll have dinner, where we'll be joined by some lovely ladies for your enjoyment."

I looked him in the eye without wavering, and said "Ok Jose you tell me what you're having a problem with, and I'll see if I can accommodate a solution for you, is that fair enough?" After refilling our glasses, he suggested "Let's move out to the balcony with our drinks, I wish to show you something." So as we moved out onto the balcony, we went over to the stone railing, and as I took in the view of the valleys surrounding the complex, I noticed something odd and voiced my curiosity. Jose laughed and said "You're right Tiger there is as you said abnormal about the valleys, what you are seeing is only the camouflage netting, we had to string them as close together as possible, and that's why as you say all the valleys are the same depth, underneath the netting that fools any air surveillance are my fields and factories, tomorrow we'll take you on a tour, and you can see for yourself how extensive my operation is."

He waved his arm over the vista, and said "Under all that, and here I have roughly six hundred men, and at present only one in ten are armed with pistolas only, we have very few long range weapons, and that is where you come in, as they say." I nodded my head, saying "Yeah ok Jose, now I can provide you with anything from handguns and rifles to surface to air missiles and anti-tank weapons, how about you tell me what you'd like to have, or I can give you my recommendations." He chuckled, and replied "You are a businessman that I do admire Tiger, you are very much like me, you do not beat around the bush, I like that, let's go and sit in comfort while we have our discussion, and you can tell me what you would recommend."

As we moved into the lounge I had been thinking quickly, because I was as they say, playing this off the cuff, I needed to sound genuine, and as I sat down, I pulled a notebook out of my pocket and a pen, and opened it, and said with a smile, "This way I don't forget anything, now Jose what do you prefer in the way of rifles, M16's or AK47's?" He asked the difference, and I told him that M16s are far more accurate, but the AK's were mainly for spraying bullets and hoping some to hit the target, and he wanted to go with some of each, so as I took a sip of scotch, and gave him my recommendations, he declined to take the surface to air missiles and hand grenades, but liked the idea of the RPG's, M60 machine guns, and automatic pistols. When the list was complete, I showed him, and he agreed, and asked for a price, so as he refilled my tumbler, and added ice, I looked to be playing with figures crossing things out and putting new stuff in, and eventually after taking a sip of my refreshed drink, said "Jose the price I'm giving you includes a thousand rounds of ammunition also."

He leaned forward, as I sat back in my seat taking another sip of my drink, before continuing "All up including landing them in Panama, which could be done within a week, will cost you nine and a half million US Dollars cash or ten million through wire transfer, and that's cutting my profit right down, because Wheeler is a friend, which also makes you a friend."

Now the best way to make the sale was to sit back and not say anything else, the minute he said something I knew that I would have a deal, so I watched silently as he sat back, and thought things over, I glanced at Mose, and as he caught it, he imperceptibly raised his eyebrows, I smiled and took another sip of my drink, and turned my attention back to Morales.

As I was taking another sip of scotch, he looked at me, and said "I always pay in cash, I don't trust bank transfers, my answer is yes, we have a deal, but on one condition, I get to see a sample of what you are selling, and to show good faith I will have your money for you when I see them."

I smiled, and said "Deal, and if I could make a couple of calls, I can fly you and John up to my Panama yard and back day after tomorrow, and then that night you can be my guests in Bogota." He smiled and said "Agreed, tomorrow I show you my plantation, and then we go down to Bogota in the afternoon, and then you fly me to Panama the day after," We both leaned forward and shook hands, and then he passed me a cigar box, and after taking one passed it to John, and then we all lit up smiling, and as we enjoyed our drinks and cigars, Morales said to me, "My wife Julianna has arranged for you to have a very nice woman as your companion tonight and for dinner, so feel free to indulge yourself, but you must tell me what you think of her tomorrow." And then he sat back laughing. I lifted the phone and dialled the hotel number that Mose gave me, and once connected I asked for Ross's room, when he answered, I told where I was and that we'd be back the next evening, but I wanted him to make sure the jet was refuelled for a trip to Panama and back, because he knew the plans, I knew from our conversation he'd contact Alex and tell him we were coming, and when.

A little later we were joined by Julianna and two other women, and after Morales made the introduction to his wife, she in turn introduced Carmelita, who was to be my companion. She was about five two, with jet black long hair and hazel eyes, and she was dressed in a very shape hugging dress and was very pretty, but she didn't speak English, and not wanting Jose to know I spoke Spanish, I had to get Moses' girl Juanita to interpret for me.

Carmelita did however stay close to me, and that night, showed no hesitation in striping naked to crawl into bed beside me, and try to interest me in having sex with her, but after I feigned sleepiness, she just wrapped her body in mine and went to sleep. Readers Note: I won't say I wasn't tempted, I was, but I remained true to my morals and what was off limits due to being married, even if it was a marriage for convenience sake.

Next morning, I woke early, and after I disentangled myself from Carmelita, had a long shower, when I went back into the bedroom, Carmelita had gone, but soon returned with a pot of coffee and some croissants, and we both had breakfast sitting on the balcony in the sun. After that I dressed, but this time I wore my gun outside my shirt, as I was about to put my jacket on when there came a knock at the door, and Mose stood there, and asked if I was ready to go, apparently everyone had risen early and Jose was in the AWD waiting for us, I got into the back with Jose, while Mose got in beside the driver. The car moved off as we were saying our good mornings to each other, we drove along a ridge for a while and then when we dropped underneath the camouflage nets the light dulled but the sun still shone through.

As we drove through the opium fields going downhill, Morales kept up a constant flow of conversation, informing me that there were six valley's under the one lot of nets here, and that there were four such hidden areas near the bottom of the main valley was a group of sheds, and these were used for the drug refining process and as we walked through the different rooms with the face masks supplied, I took the time to have a good look at the process, and asked what they were making in this hut, and was told that this building was used to manufacture cocaine, and through the window Jose pointed to another shed, and told me that in that one because of extra refinement was needed it that was where his heroin was processed. Then we passed into what could only be described as a storeroom, but in this particular storeroom was pallets of cocaine, Jose told me each package weighted one kilo and each pallet held one thousand individual packages, Christ! A ton of cocaine on each pallet, and there was, easily forty odd pallets that I could see, incredulously I asked if the heroin was treated the same way, and was told that at present there was eighty pallets in that storeroom ready to be shipped, while we were in the storeroom, Morales looked at me and asked "Are you sure you want cash, I can give you the equivalent in product if you wish?"

I smiled, and replied shaking my head, "No, I'll take the cash thanks, but I know who to come to if I move into drugs."

When we got back to the house, we all had lunch together, and then arranged to leave an hour later, so making sure I had packed everything into my go bag, I went downstairs and waited in the main lounge, I saw Mose out on the balcony, so after pouring a drink, made my way out to join him. Even though we were out of the house, we still kept our conversation low, as I joined him I told him that once Morales was under lock and key, that this whole set up needed to be destroyed, he nodded his head and told me that he'd been thinking the same, but it would probably have to be done by the DEA themselves, there was too much temptation here to pass it on to the Columbian Federales to destroy, so it would probably be up to him to take care of it, knowing that he'd already been here and knew where everything was.

Morales called out and asked if we were ready, and we both turned and headed back inside the lounge, and as I joined him he passed me a wide attach case, and it was very weighty, so I enquired what was in it and he told me that it was my money. I opened the case on the coffee table and it was stacked with US currency in bundles of fifty thousand, randomly I rifled through the stacks and made sure it was all genuine, and as I closed the case, Jose told me that I was free to count it, and I replied "Jose, I don't need to count it, I know you are an honourable man, and also a friend, and I trust my friends."

After that we made our way to the car, and made the journey down to Bogota, where after I booked Mose and Morales in, we spent the night. Ross came over to see us during dinner and informed me that the plane was ready, but if we were to make it up and back accounting for time on the ground, we'd need to be airborne by nine in the morning, and so we decided on an eight o'clock depart time from the hotel in the morning, as Ross moved away out of Morales' sight he gave us a nod, and both Mose and I saw it, and we knew it was to confirm that everything would be in place. After dinner we went into the bar, and watched and listened to the entertainment, as we decided to call it a night Mose and Morales got up to head to their rooms, and before going up to my suite, as I passed the desk, I made sure that the hotel limo would be available at eight to take us to the airport, and after that was confirmed I went up to bed.

As we boarded the plane the next morning, I placed the case of money in the overhead locker above Morales' seat, and said "Jose this will stay there until after you have seen the merchandise and approved the deal, and then I'll transfer it to my office, but right now I need to have a word with my pilot, and then I'll be back to join you both."

While I was in the cockpit where we couldn't be overheard, Ross told me the full extent of his call to Alex, Alex would arrange a limo to pick us up at the airport and the driver would also be a DEA agent, who would pass me a key to the container lock, the arrest in the yard would take place the minute I picked up a weapon inside the container, and Alex would arrest all of us, to maintain our covers, and once we were in the DEA building, that's when we would be split up.

After I was back in the main cabin, Ross started to taxi out to the main runway, and after take-off, I suggested that we have a game of cards during the flight to while away the time, also hinting to Mose in a roundabout way about sign language, and while we played I passed on to him, what to expect when we got to Panama and the container yard. He acknowledged the information with an imperceptible nod and replied in sign that he'd be ready.

When we landed, the limo pulled up at the bottom of the stairway, and as I reached the tarmac, the driver came forward to shake my hand saying "Hola! Senor Davis it's good to see you back again." As we shook hands the agent pressed the key into my palm, and as I stepped toward the door and waited for Jose and Mose to enter the limo, I slipped the key into my pocket.

CHAPTER 8

During the drive to the yard, I looked at Morales and explained that the yard we were going to was the same one where his weapons would be available for pickup, and enquired whether he would have them shipped by a transport company, or picked up by his own men. He looked at Mose, and Mose answered realising that I was trying to keep Morales distracted, asked whether the weapons would be in a normal twenty-foot container or larger. I told him that they would, and then Mose looked at Morales and told him that in that case they'd either need a semi-trailer and move the container on it, or time would be needed to unload the containers contents into smaller trucks. I looked at Morales, and suggested that I could have the shipment delivered to his hacienda from here at a reasonable price, and Jose laughed. Just then the driver's partition slide down and the driver asked "Will I take you to the office Senor Davis?" I replied "Yes thank you Juan."

He opened the door for us after stopping in front of the office building, and I said to both of them, "If you wait here a sec, I'll go get the key." Once inside the office I moved to a desk, and Alex was lying there, and he told me which container I was looking for, and after telling him that both Mose and I would be waiting, I moved outside, and strode toward the container that Alex directed me to, with Mose and Morales following a couple of steps behind. I bent to unlock the doors, opened them wide and then turned to see Morales with a grin on his face as he took a couple of steps closer, and I beckoned them inside the container, looking out I noticed some movement outside, and so picked up the empty Vulcan revolving cannon, saying to Morales "How'd you like one of these Jose?"

He had a wide grin on his face, and was nodding his head but stiffened as we heard the command, to "Freeze, put the weapon down! Hold your hands in the air, and come out of the container, get down on your knees! Each command was spaced as we complied with each direction, while on our knees in a line facing the container, I looked around as we were confronted by men holding shotguns and rifles levelled at us dressed in dark blue flak jackets, jeans and wearing combat helmets, the jackets had DEA emblazoned on them. Then from behind our arms were grabbed and we were handcuffed with our hand behind us, they all seemed to be waiting for something, I was shaking my head, Jose was swearing in Spanish, and Mose, acting out the Wheeler persona, was swearing at them, and then I yelled out "You can't arrest us, we're not in the US!"

Then from behind us came Alex's voice, saying "True but the Panamanian Government has signed a charter agreement with the US and therefore we are allowed to operate here, now let's have a look at who we have here." As he walked around in front to see us, and he continued "Well, well, well, Tom Tiger Davis, suspected arms dealer, I guess we can drop the suspected now, Jonathon Wheeler, wanted for drug importation, unfortunately our Mexican cousins have a prior claim on you for murder and escaping jail, they're going to love getting hands on you again, and look who we got here boys, number one on our hit parade, Jose Morales head of the Morales Columbian crime cartel wanted for the murder of three DEA agents, drug trafficking, and drug supply and importation." I interrupted him playing the part by saying "Yeah well there are no drugs anywhere near here, so you better let us go."

Alex laughed and with an evil smile, answered "I'm a fair man Mr Davis, so I'll tell you what I'm going to do, these two already come under our jurisdiction, but you don't, so eventually I'll be letting you go, and handing you over to my colleagues in the ATF, you see we all tend to help our sister agencies, and you seem to have been on their radar for quite some time, ok get them up and put them in separate vehicles." The agents pulled us onto our feet, and the first person bundled away in a car with three agents was

Morales, and as a second vehicle drew up, the first one was out of eyesight, so everyone relaxed and started laughing as the cuffs were removed from John and me. After embracing Mose, Alex turned to me and told me that our conversation was a damned good piece of acting as far as he was concerned, now I've got us all booked into the plaza for the night, including your pilots Tiger, so let's go do some celebrating.

Ross and Bob joined us at the Plaza, and as we were going up in the lift to our rooms, Ross having brought my go bag, told me that the jet had been refuelled and we would have enough fuel to fly into Guam, so Alex told us to fly into the airbase and by the time we got there he'd have arranged for our refuelling and stopover, so we thanked him and we decided to all meet in the bar after a half hour to freshen up, so an hour later we seated around a table enjoying ourselves, as Alex said "Ok Tiger, John's told me about what you said about destroying Morales' setup, and I agree, especially knowing the amount of dope that's sitting there waiting for someone to put his grubby hands on. How do you suggest we accomplish it?" I laughed, and asked "Do you have access to fighter jets? That's the best way, but you'd need more besides them a ground team as well, but now would be the best time to strike, while Morales isn't there."

Alex replied that they did have the availability to get the fighters at short notice if there was a viable target, which it would be, and asked again what I would propose doing. So I told them what I would do if I was in their position, the first thing I'd do would be to send John back in with an assault team back up, he head back to the hacienda with the excuse that Jose was parting with me in Panama, the assault team would then sever all power and communication lines, now we know that back-up generators kick in with power loss but the phones wouldn't be usable, then the assault team would take over the hacienda and John would guide the fighters to their targets, after the air strike, it would be up to John and the assault team to assess and finish the destruction, and then hotfoot it out of the country. I looked at John and asked whether he knew how to open Jose's safe and he nodded his head, and I said then clearing it would also be on the job list, because you never know when you may have to fund your own operation, you keep it and use it for running expenses.

Next morning, Alex took us to the airport, and Ross and Bob went to get the plane ready for the journey home as Alex and I shook hands and said our good byes, and he told me John and his team had already flown back to Columbia to complete the destruction of the Morales cartel, I asked Alex to wish him luck for me, and then said our final goodbyes, and parted. When I got abroad I told Ross and Bob that I was ready whenever they were, and five minutes later we started to taxi, and then get airborne, when we levelled off at cruising height. I opened the overhead locker and retrieved the case of money and counted out five hundred thousand which I placed in my go bag, and put both bags together on the seat, going to the tape library I selected the latest Clint Eastwood video release of Sudden Impact, placed it into the player, and watched it as we made our way to Guam.

We left there early the next morning, after a very enjoyable night, sleep in what were comfortable beds, and arrived in Brisbane at fourteen thirty, and before leaving the plane, I offered both Bob and Ross a lift into the office, but told me they'd make use of the agencies safe house not far from the airport, and said they'd see me the next morning at the office. I left my go bag in the car as I climbed out in the carpark but took the case with me, as I made my way to my office, Janice smiled as soon as I entered and told me she was glad to see me back, and that Mr Callaway had left for the day, I nodded and asked her to join me, and we went into my office, and I opened the safe, and then asked her to count the money that I was going to put in there, as I gave her the case.

As she opened it she gasped, and asked "How much is supposed to be in here?" Her eyes went wide as I answered nonchalantly, "Nine million," she gasped again, and said "My god." I laughed as I answered, "Yeah ok I'll answer to that," and she laughed as she looked at me, and then started pulling the bundles out of the case. The counting took quite a deal of time, and it was after four as she watched me close and lock up the safe, giving the tumbler a spin.

Janice left the office as I said I had a couple of calls to make and then I'd be gone for the night, and told her to go if she wanted because I wouldn't need her, and then I made a call to Lisa, and as she answered, I told her I was back, and that if she had nothing to do over the weekend, she could go ahead and make appointments for me, but only from the red hot list, after she asked when did I want the appointments I said I'd be available from Monday morning onwards, and after telling her I'd see her Monday, I hung up. I called for Janice, and thankfully she was still there, so I asked her to arrange with John and Harry to bring our Monday meeting forward to one o'clock the next day which was Friday, and after she said she'd handle it, I made my next call which was to Darlene.

She answered on the second ring, and as I told her I was back, she asked where I'd been, so I told her I'd had some business to take care of in Columbia and Panama, she thought I was kidding, intimating that if I wasn't too sure about our marriage, that she had been good while I'd been away, and I had better have been if I knew what was good for me, I shrugged off her implied threat and asked if she'd heard from Dyson, and she told me that he'd been in contact with her just about every second day since I'd been gone, wanting to arrange a meeting, I smiled and thought, *hah, leave them wanting more,* as I said that I was at the airport and that I'd be home soon, and we could have dinner out if she wanted, that cheered her up and she said she'd be waiting for me to get home.

When I walked in the door at the apartment, Darlene was waiting and had poured me a drink, and after I had put my go bag away, I joined her in the lounge, and after picking up my drink, I then tossed her my passport, and said "Seeing you doubt, where I've been, have a look in there, and then you'll apologise to me, and after that should you ever doubt what I say, you and I will be through, and take that warning as gospel, do you understand? She nodded looking shocked, and was about to say something, but I overrode her asking, "Now what's happening with your mate Trevor Dyson?"

Looking rather taken back and ashamed, she answered quietly "Well because he's been so insistent about talking to you, I phone him after you called, and said that we would be at the pub tonight for dinner and drinks." I nodded my head and asked "So how did you get his number?" She replied "He gave it to me to call him when you were around, after the third time he asked me to get hold of you, but I told him I couldn't because I didn't know where you were, I told him all I knew was that you were overseas making a deal." After nodding my head, and asking for the number, and she passed me a piece of paper with it on, and then I remained silent as I thought things over, and while I was doing that, I watched her checking all the stamps in my passport, and then she asked "This Panama stamp, does that mean you've been to the Panama Canal?" I looked at her and laughed, sarcastically saying "Well it bloody cuts the country in two, so yes, I've been to the Panama Canal, now did you book a table for tonight, or are we just going to rock up, and hope for the best?"

She replied that she'd booked our usual table for seven, and that there was going to be an Irish band there that night so it should be good to stay and listen to the music as well. After a couple more drinks, I had a quick shower and changed, and we left the apartment building at six thirty to walk up to the pub. As we walked we held hands, and she told me that she'd heard from Peter the guy that owned the apartment, and that he would be returning in a fortnight, so she asked me if we could start moving her stuff out to my house, and that soon we'd have to start living there together. So I told her that we could start moving her stuff on the weekend which was only a day away, and that way we'd get all her stuff moved in the one hit, which would leave the apartment empty, so it could be cleaned. She told me that she'd have most afternoons the following week to clean it, because all her lectures the following week were in the morning.

I told her that would be good, just as we arrived at the pub, and as we made our way inside the staff, knowing us by sigh escorted us straight to our usual table that had a reserved sign on it, I looked enquiringly at the waitress, and she told me that they were expecting a big crowd, and so it would be wise to order early, and then she asked if she should get us our usual drinks, and said yes. As I sat down I filled Darlene in on what I'd been told, and she nodded and picked up the menu to decide what she was going to have, I quickly perused the menu, and decided what I was going to have, and when the waitress came back with our drinks, a scotch and soda for Darlene and my usual pint of Guinness.

I thanked her, and told her we were ready to order, so saying she'd be right back she went off to get her order book, and then came back and took our order. Half way through our meal I looked around to see Trevor Dyson and his mate heading for our table, and he reached us Dyson asked if we minded if they joined us, and I indicated for them to sit. As he sat down, Dyson asked "So where've you been Tiger, I've been trying to get in touch with you," my mouth was full with steak, so I held up my finger for him to wait for an answer, but Darlene blurted out, "he's been in Columbia and Panama," as soon as she saw the look I shot her, she shut up, realising she'd spoken out of turn, I swallowed down the mouthful I'd been chewing, and said "Yeah I've been out of the country on business, what have you wanted to see me about, because a man in my line of work, can't wait around waiting for casual invites."

He looked at me taken back a bit, and replied "Columbia huh, did you bring home any coke or H? Nah, forget that, just kidding, so what line are you really in Tiger? He was looking at me shrewdly, so I matched his stare, and replied "If I'd have brought anything back, I sure as hell wouldn't be telling anyone, now would I? And to answer your question I deal in the import and export of various pieces of merchandise, but usually by the container load." My gaze hadn't left his face and eyes, and he inclined his head to the left, as he replied "I'm having a bit of a party at my place on Sunday, why don't you and Darlene come, and while she's having some fun, you and I maybe can talk over some business." I nodded my head, and said "Sounds good, what time, and what's the address?" As he answered his eyes were still boring into mine, until he got up "Midday, Darlene knows where, see you then." And as he started to move away from the table, I looked at Darlene and said "When it comes to business sweetheart, please do me a favour and keep your mouth closed, and let me handle that part."

She looked at me with a pout, and said "I'm in this as well!" I let go with an exasperated sigh, and replied "Yes dear, however if you'd have been with me during my last deal, we'd both be dead now, what I'm trying to say is, that if you're not sure of anything, keep your mouth shut, and don't say or do anything that could jeopardize things." Then she became a bit more animated and enthusiastic, as she thought over what had been said between Dyson and me, she leaned forward and whisperingly asked, "Did you bring back any drugs?" I looked her sternly, and in a harsh voice replied "No! However, the last deal was for, nine million dollars, and because the guy might be good for repeat business, I cut my profit, and made half a million in US Dollars clear profit in cash."

The rest of the night went well, but she seemed to be on tenterhooks, and as we walked home I quizzed her as to what was making her so jittery, so she replied, "Well you know how you said you made that profit in cash, do you have it with you?" I answered "Yes" knowing that there were more questions coming, and she asked "In the flat and in cash?" I nodded my head and replied "Yes, why?" She went quiet for a while, and then replied "Well because I've never been able to do this before, how about I make love to you with all the money spread all over the bed, which should be a humongous turn on, don't you think?" I laughed for a while, and replied "Ok, if that's what you want to do, I'm game."

That was easier said than done, and the bills kept sticking to us while we romped thankfully none of them tore, next morning after cleaning up and putting the money away again, while Darlene made breakfast, I showered and got ready to drive into the office, and while we ate, she told me that she would be back by one at the latest, would start to get her stuff sorted out, and then she kissed me goodbye and headed out, while I finished my breakfast. Not that I didn't trust Darlene, but I transferred the cash into a smaller bag, and also added the hundred and sixty-eight thousand I'd won at the casino, and when I went down to the car I took the bag, with the intention of later depositing it into my account at the bank.

As I strolled into my office past Janice, she flashed me a smile and started to rise, I kept going into the office and found that Callaway wasn't in yet, and as Janice brought in the cuppa's for our together time, I asked if she had been able to confirm the early afternoon meeting with all involved, and she assured me that she had. Then we got down to the daily business, and as we got to any correspondence in, she excused herself, went into her office and brought back a piece of paper which she handed to me, saying "This came in earlier for you," I took the paper and it was a message from Alex and Mose in the states, saying *Tiger, everything went down ok, we used your suggestions, and apart from destroying everything including plant and equipment, we now have an extra ninety six million in operating capital along with a ton of gold bars. Morales' wife was taken into custody by the Columbian Federales on attempted murder charges after she tried to shoot them as they stormed the property, so looks like she'll be joining Jose in jail, but both in separate countries, I somehow think however that Jose will have the better time of it, thanks for everything, and hope I can repay the favour one day, Alex.* I smiled as I mentally filed the fact that the DEA and Alex Stein now owed me a favour.

Janice smiled, and said "It seems that the entire operation was an extremely profitable success, as well as getting rid of one whole crime cartel, I'd like to express my congratulations to you, sir." I smiled, and said "Thank you Janice, but you of all people know that it wasn't only me, it involved a whole lot of agents, both here and more importantly in the States, Columbia and Panama, I'm just glad that we were able to help, and how many times do I have to tell you, it's Tiger, not sir!" And we both laughed.

At the meeting in the operations room that afternoon was John Callaway, Harry, John, and me, also waiting outside was Ross and Bob, why they were waiting would probably come from Callaway, so we would have to wait to find out why they were waiting. After we discussed the ongoing operations, and had dealt with them, it came time to discuss operation deep silence, so I filled everyone in on the latest developments, and about the upcoming meeting on Sunday, and as I looked at Harry told them that I'd record the meeting if it was possible, and that we'd have to visit it again during the week, because things were developing faster as I got in deeper, so it was decided to keep at it and if it required extra meetings, then so be it.

After taking care of that, we moved onto new business, it was then that John Callaway said "I've got some new business, and it involves the two I have waiting outside, but before we bring them in, I'd like to run what I'm about to do past you. Before Tom came on board with us, we used to have arguments about how this branch required its own aircraft, and I always told you that we didn't have the aircraft available, well now we do, last week the agency seized another plane through the proceeds of crime act, and I must say we really had to beat ASIO to the punch, anyway we got it, and now mainly because Tiger may need it as part of his cover, I've decided to leave the jet he used on his last very successful mission be based here in Queensland, and I'm prepared to transfer Ross here as senior pilot, but not Bob, I need him down south. So gentlemen you will need to have another agent to take Bob's place as Deputy Senior pilot, do you have a pilot that can be promoted up and trained for 737s?" John answered "Yes I've got just the man."

Callaway nodded and said "Good, but remember both Ross and this other pilot are first and foremost operating field agents, so they can be used in this role, if need be, but only sparingly. I'm also going to propose that the safe house near the airport will become the Higgins residence, and we'll look for another safe house nearby, so if we're all agreed, let's get them in here, and let Ross know."

Ross was happy enough with the news, and even more so when he was told that he would be flying back to Sydney with Bob, and with Callaway. Callaway also told him that after a week of sorting things out for the move to Queensland that the agency would arrange, he would fly back up here with his wife Jenny and the family. Then I told him that when he got back he'd be teamed up with another pilot to train up to get him 737 qualified, and that it was up to him as senior pilot to organise a permanent hangar for the jet. Ross was smiling as he nodded in the affirmative.

After our meeting broke up, I left Callaway to make his arrangements with Ross and Bob as to regard the flight that they would all be taking back to Sydney, but I had asked Callaway to have Ross see me before he left the office. I took my stuff back to my office, and the told Janice that I'd be out for fifteen or twenty minutes, and then return, but I needed to get something down, downtown. As I left the building, I went to my car and retrieved the bag of money, and strolled a couple of blocks down to one of the main branches of the bank, and when I was inside I took the extra hundred and sixty grand out of my wallet, changed my mind and put the sixty-eight thousand back into my wallet, and then went to the foreign money counter changed the US Dollars into Australian. After receiving eight hundred and twenty-two thousand Australian dollars, due to the exchange rate on the six hundred grand I gave them, I deposited eight hundred and twenty into my account, keeping two thousand cash in my wallet, thinking *no doubt if Lisa makes more appointments I'm going to need to pay her so I may as well have it available. After doing my banking, I retraced my steps back to the office.* As I was about to walk into my office, Janice told me that Callaway had Ross in there and were waiting for me to return.

I walked into my office wearing a smile, and said "Ross glad to see you finally get to make the move to Queensland as you've been wanting for some time, and I'm glad to have you aboard, after you've flown back up Janice will assign you an office, and that's where you and your new 2IC will spend your time, unless of course I need you both in the field, but that'll only be if I'm shorthanded, but as I said earlier it will be up to you to organise, and equip the permanent hangar for the jet, so you both will be spending time out there getting things setup, I don't know if John has told you but the house you are in now will be your home, so I hope you and Jenny enjoy it, if nothing else it's damn close to the airport, and the schools nearby aren't all that bad, I know I used to go to one of them many moons ago.

The next day, because I woke early I decide to get Darlene up, and while she woke herself up I made breakfast, and as we ate, I suggested that if she got into getting all her stuff together, I'd pack it in the car, and then we'd probably have most of it moved by the end of the day, any washing could be done at my place. By three o'clock that afternoon everything was at my place, even my stuff that had made its way to the apartment was home again, so that night after having a nice bistro style dinner at the local league's club, she organised her side of the wardrobe, as I started the first load of washing.

After she got used to being back at my place, and the amenities there, she told me that she'd forgotten how life could be so luxurious there, the only problem that she complained about was the fact, that she'd have to use her car more often, later that night we were both quite drunk, and then she wanted to have sex in the spa, so what else could I do, but accommodate her before we went upstairs to bed. Now it wasn't easy and eventually after a lot of experimentation we found that the only way it really worked well, was if she sat astride me with her back toward me, which wasn't bad, because I was also able to play with her breasts and manipulate her nipples to bring her really intense orgasms. Next morning was a late one, before we got ready to go to Dyson's place for the party, and she gave a disapproving shake of the head, as I put my holster on underneath my shirt, but after I explained to her that I was going to a meeting that could be profitable to both of us, but also could be quite dangerous, it paid to be armed. Besides, I told her I never went anywhere unarmed these days, because I didn't know when I would need my gun, and it would be a bit silly if I reached for it and it wasn't there.

CHAPTER 9

Dyson had a house in the area that more or less straddled two suburbs Kelvin Grove and Herston, but I guess as far as the post office was concerned it was in Herston. As I pulled up in the street, I noticed the van that Harry had arranged to be there, wasn't too far away. The house was two story, and a bit like mine with a garage and I assumed a games room downstairs, with the living area upstairs, and it had a large deck that extended from the lounge and kitchen which had a large spa pool in one corner. Most of the people at the party were part of Darlene's crowd with some others that I recognised, one being a judge, and a couple others that were instantly recognisable as cops, along with some I didn't know, and I thanked Christ for Harry's foresight to have arranged a small video camera that would fit a jacket lapel, hopefully the van would be receiving the images.

After a bit of socialising Dyson had disappeared, but I had been drawn into a conversation with one of Darlene's friends, so I wasn't able to go looking around for him, however I was able to move over to where Darlene was talking about economics with a couple of her mates, and I whispered into her ear that if she saw Dyson anywhere, to try to let me know, and without missing a word she was saying just nodded her head, as I moved off again, and found myself talking insurance with one of the cops, until we were interrupted by Lyle Thomas, and he said "Sorry to interrupt, but Trevor wants to pick Tiger's brain about an insurance issue he's having," as he escorted me into the house and down to what I thought was a games room, Dyson had made it into a lavish office with couches and recliner chairs, and with shelves lined with books. Behind the desk and built into the shelves behind it was a large safe, and I wondered what treasures it would contain, as I took a seat opposite Dyson at his desk.

Dyson asked what I thought he'd done with the house, and I laughed, as I replied "I don't think you invited me here to get my praise over what you've done with the house, so let's do us both a favour and stop beating about the bush, and put our cards on the table, so come on Trevor put your cards on the table, and I'll answer you in kind, what do you want?"

He smiled as he looked at me, as he said "Touché Tiger, I guess I should have expected that, no matter how you try to hide it you're smarter than a lot of people think, and I think we can work together, because you have international contacts, and I've got them here in Australia, do you mind if I ask a question?"

I looked at him, he was probably thinking that I was thinking over what he had to say, and I smiled as I knew he was so wrong, I'd already thought of how things would go during this conversation, having mentally gone over this scenario many times prior. So I said "Look if we're going to discuss business, let's do it in a gentlemanly manner, over a drink in comfortable seats." With that I got up and moved to one of the reclining chairs, as he did the same, Lyle had moved behind the bar, and started pouring a drink for Dyson, as he said with a smile "From what I hear, you have a preference for Jonny Walker Blue label with only one ice cube." I nodded my head, and replied "You've done your homework I see, thank you Lyle." As I took a sip of my drink, and gave a sigh of satisfaction as I sat back in my chair.

Looking at him with my tumbler in hand, I smiled and said "Now to your previous question, please go ahead with anything you wish to ask." And I took the time to light a cigarette, as I did Lyle came forward and placed an ashtray on the table beside my chair, as Trevor asked his question, "You know from your wife that I know you've recently been in Columbia, so I'd like to ask you why you were there, and just saying you were doing some business, is not really an answer is it." I smiled, before answering with "Fair enough, I was there after a call from a friend, who had another friend who is looking to buy a good deal of weapons." Dyson nodded his head, as he digested this information, as he asked "Are you able to supply what is needed?" I laughed replying "Not yet, but I've put it about that I'm looking for supply, now I'm not sure what your line of business is, but if you can put your hands on a shitload of weapons, then you and I need to talk, so that's all I have to say at the moment, is there anything else you wish to discuss?"

He smiled, and replied "Well it just so happens that because of the line of business I'm in, which seeing you asked so subtlety, is mainly drugs supply and procurement, but every now and then I come across other merchandise, and there's a good chance that I may be able to supply what you need." I smiled and scoffed my reply, saying "Hah, Yeah, well, I've already been down this road with one of your, in crowd, and not only did Kevin not have the quantity of items I wanted, but I was arrested into the bargain, plus he's responsible for my now being known to the cops, so unless you can talk in hundreds, don't waste my time or yours, and unless there's anything else you wish to say, I'll be going." He stared at me without saying anything, so as I rose to go, he said "How about a container load of weapons?" I sat back down, and stared.

He knew I was waiting for him to go on, and so he drew it out, and laughed as he smilingly said "Kevin is a dickhead, and deserves what he gets, he told me he could get me a buyer, so I let him try, and I'm sorry you got arrested, just because he couldn't keep his damn mouth shut. Yes, I did hear that you'd been mixed up it; however, let me assure you that Kevin's days of speaking out of turn will be over soon, if not already."

I was scowling as I lifted my gaze to look at him and scoffed, "What are you saying that you've arranged to have him killed?" he smiled as he nodded his head, and said "Well it's not unknown for people to have fatal accidents in jail is it." I smiled, but didn't say anything, as he continued "So shall we discuss what we can do for each other?"

Before answering, another drink was placed by my side, and I took the opportunity to light a smoke while Lyle placed another drink on the table beside Trevor, and then I said "Ok let's, but there is something bothering me, and that is that Kevin said he couldn't get me all the items I was after, so if you were supplying him, that means that you may not have what I'm after anyway." Dyson smiled in the chair opposite me, and calmly said "I gave Kevin a few weapons, and told him he could only have so many, at that time I wasn't aware that you had come on the scene, if I had of known we would have been having this conversation before you even went to visit Kevin." I nodded my head, and replied "Makes sense, so how many and what type of weapons do you have available?"

He laughed for a while, and said with a smile "Well there you have me Tiger, to tell you the truth, I really don't know how many are in the container, and I can't tell you exactly what they are, but what I can do is, I'll get the container moved to one of my sheds, and have everything in it unloaded, and then when that's done, I'll contact you, and you can have a look at everything while it's all out unpacked, and then you can make me a fair offer, and if you need more, I may be able to arrange it."

I nodded with a smile, saying "Sounds good to me, so you'll be in touch in a day or two?" His smile dropped, and a worried expression took its place, as he replied "Uh no, because I didn't have a ready market up here, I had it moved down south where some of my business associates are, but they don't deal in bulk, so I will have it brought back up here, but it could take a couple of weeks." I nodded and told him that was ok; I wasn't under any time restraints.

He smiled and a look of relief passed over his face, as he said "Well then that's good, that's our business all fixed, I have your number, and I'll be in touch, now I suppose we'd better get back to the party." So we both downed what was left in our glasses, and stood up as we did, we shook hands, and moved upstairs to the party, as we joined in Darlene, with a worried expression on her face came to my side, and whispered "I couldn't find you, and you've been gone nearly an hour, I was starting to get worried." I looked at her and smiled, saying "You can put your smile back on now, everything's cool, we were just talking business."

As a waiter passed by with a tray of nibbles, I took a sausage roll and spring roll, and moved toward the deck railing that was empty of guests, and said into my pen microphone, "I'm only hoping that Harry gave you the other recorder and that you have got all of that conversation on tape as well, just in case it was too far away from my car, but I think it'll be ok." After taking a couple more sausage rolls off another passing waiter, I moved back into the main group, and had a couple sandwiches, while I was waiting for the waiter to come back with a drink.

Next morning, I drove into the office early, and was joined in the lift by Janice, so as we went down I asked to arrange a meeting with John and Harry for eight thirty, if not earlier, so she pushed the button for John's floor and got out, telling me that she'd stop a Harry's floor as well on the way down and would then come and make coffee, and then we could get the afterhours correspondence sorted before the meeting. As I sat at my desk, a note had been left for me along with a thick folder, and the note read *"Sir we have enclosed transcripts and tapes of Sunday's meeting, have also made still photos from the video tape, and have enclosed also, a copy has been left on the deck of each Department head."* The note was signed by Michael from the surveillance team, I smiled and thought, *Damned fine work Michael, thank you,* and I opened the folder and pulled out the still photos and looked at them as I moved toward the operation board, and pinned each photo up on the opposite side under the to Be Identified section, then stood back to admire my handiwork.

After all of us had seen the video played in the tactical room, it was decided that John would liaise with the AFP about the threat to Kevin's life, and we'd send a complete copy of everything to do with that meeting down to Callaway in Sydney, also Harry would run the photos through the library to see how many could be identified that way, and I told them that I would be absent from the office most days that week, but would still come in early 'til ten each morning.

Once we finished the meeting, I finished up the outstanding stuff that needed doing, and then it was time to head over to Stafford, and do some of my cover work. Lisa was glad to see me, and she gave me a kiss and cuddle before saying "About time you came back to doing some real work, but first I'll put the kettle on and we can bring each other up to date," I laughed and then went back outside to grab the small bag that would soon be emptied from the car, and I took the bills out of the bag, and onto my desk, before I unlocked the built in safe, as I was doing that Lisa came in with the coffee, and gasped as she put the drinks down and spied the money, and exclaimed "Good lord where did that all come from?"

I smiled, and said "It's just some of the money I won gambling in Columbia, but I don't want it around at my place, because Darlene knows how to get into the safe over there." She nodded and after I had placed the money in the safe, I joined her sitting across my desk, as she proceeded to tell me that her life was going well, and she thought that Reg was getting ready to pop the question, and I asked her how she felt about that, and she said "I really don't know, I like him a lot and we get on well together, but sometimes I find myself comparing him to my dead husband, and at other times. I think that I'm lucky to have the possible dream of having two such wonderful men in my life, three if I include you, but I know that you're really not ready to settle into a mundane job without any thrills, and of course I will always love you as a true friend, but Tiger, truthfully my dear you're not the marrying kind yet, maybe in the future, but not yet."

While she took a couple of sips of her coffee, I told her that she really hadn't answered the question, and she laughed, saying "I know, aren't I terrible, but honestly, I think that if he does propose, I will accept." I smiled, and replied "Good, nothing would please me more than to see you happy, ok, enough of this mushy stuff, time to get down to business, what have you got for me?"

She smiled and told me that I had three appointments, the first was another company that had been referred by the first one, and the owner there was my second appointment, and the third one of the employees from the first. The first two were during the day and the third was scheduled for five that evening. At the first one, not only did I sell thirty endowment policies, but the owner and his wife took out a further four policies, and also wanted me to refer them to the superannuation team. The second appointment was with the owner of the first company, he and his wife took out a further five policies, and told me that the superannuation team had done the right thing, and now had his super scheme.

I was on a roll, and that evening wrote a further three policies, which really made me happy, in one day I'd written nearly six months' worth of normal business, poor Shirley would have a fit when I went in tomorrow with forty-two policy proposals. Next morning was quiet in the office, so I left the city at nine and headed out to Newmarket, and as I had predicted, after going through the pleasantries of seeing me back, Shirley shrieked as I gave her the bundle of paperwork, and then while Shirley was in the store room getting a stock of sixty blank proposal forms for the types of proposals I'd been selling, I phoned the Superannuation team, and spoke to Miles the team leader, and when he knew it was me, he informed me that they owed me a far bit of money as my part of the commission on the super sale I'd setup, so I gave him my agency number and my commission account number, and that way it could go straight into my commission account and I'd get the cheque at the end of the month, and then I gave him the new referral, and filled him in with the background information, and he told me if I kept going like I'd been doing he could very well ask me to come onto his team. I laughed and told him it was not likely, and then we hung up from each other.

Before I left the office I checked my wallet, and saw that I had enough cash to cover what I owed Lisa, and then drove over there, to find out I had three more appointments that day, and so told her not to make any more appointments for the rest of the week, and gave her the two grand that I owed her and she told me that she'd take a whip to me to keep me working if that sort of money kept coming in to her, and we both laughed. After telling her I'd see her the next day, I left and went home before I went out again later in the day, when I got home that night I'd made another eight sales, which made fifty in two days, and I figured that was more than enough, so after I left the city and Newmarket offices, where I informed Shirley, that she'd get a break because I wasn't going to work anymore that week, but would be there for the sales meeting, and then I dropped into Stafford to give Lisa a further six hundred, after dropping into the house to change, and collect my clubs, I went out to Samford that afternoon and played a game of golf.

Friday came, and after spending a productive morning in the office, because now everyone that had been at the party at Dyson's had been identified, with names and addresses and other details written below their photo on the second situation board, and as I stared at the boards I thought, *I hope we wind this op up soon, otherwise I might have to get a bigger office for the situation boards.*

Then I had a light bulb moment, *bingo, I know what'll do, I'll get the boards shifted into the ops room, because that's where we gather for our Monday meetings, and where we also come to when we're discussing the operation, I'll get Janice to arrange it, and that way they'll be there Monday for our meeting, top idea Tom!* I called out to Janice, and when she came in, mentioned what I had in mind, she nodded her head, and told me she'd get it sorted. I smiled at her, and then told her that I was heading off, and also invited her to have an early day if she wished.

That afternoon at the sales meeting, I was the centre of attention, and lauded for the amount of business I'd written that week, and I was asked how I was able to do it, and in answer told everyone that I had a very good secretary who's strike rate on canvassing was at present one to one, and that instead of concentrating on only one policy to sell I spread out the options that my clients had, and invariably I would make at least two or three sales in the one household, not only the one. Then I mentioned that I didn't knock myself out trying to make sales, and by that I meant that I'd made a rule not to have any appointments made from Thursday to Monday, therefore effectively only working three days a week, and if I didn't make a sale I wasn't bothered by that at all.

On Monday we were having our usual meeting, and as yet I'd had no word from Dyson, so there wasn't much to be added to operation deep silence, just as we were about to move onto any new business, when the phone beeped, and Janice came on the line saying that Callaway was on the line with something urgent. So I got her to patch him through, and switched him to speaker and said "Ok John we're listening, go ahead." He told us that the NSW police had caught a prisoner in Byron Bay that had been picked on an unrelated charge, and after running her through the criminal database, where she was red flagged by the AFP as being wanted by British authorities, they contacted the AFP and she is now in their custody in Brisbane which was the closest to Byron.

Then Harry interrupted him by saying, "Good for them, but what has that got to do with us?" We heard Callaway laugh, as he told us that they'd contacted him because the prisoner is wanted by MI5 which is ASIO'S opposite agency in Britain, and so they wanted ASIS to take custody of the prisoner and transport her to England, and because she was already in Brisbane, it would be up to me to get her there. I looked at John and Harry, and then I asked "So how am I supposed to get her there?" He answered that I'd have to go by commercial airline because as I knew the jet wasn't equipped for transporting prisoners.

What I would have to do was arrange a flight, and contact Jack McCord and let him know which one and he would have the prisoner taken from the airport cells, to meet me in the immigration departure offices and then I would board the plane before any other passengers. As he carried on he told me that I wasn't expected to come straight back, but to rest up for a couple of days after I'd handed over my prisoner to the MI5 agents that would meet me at the other end, and I'd have to contact them to say what flight I'd be arriving on. He went on to tell me that when he knew this had come up, he had requested for the latest whereabouts on Dumper, and that he was at home having a holiday, and made the suggestion that I could visit him while I was there, and that he'd fax me up all details, and then rang off. I looked at Harry and John, John was smiling and said "Well looks like you get a few days in the sunny UK."

As I went to walk through Janice's office, she told me that a two-page fax had arrived from Callaway, and it was on my desk, so asking her to follow me in and sit, we both made for my desk. I read the fax and then told Janice what was going on, all she did was raise her eyebrows a bit, and then I started listing things for her to do. To book me a one-way flight for one, and a return for me in business class on Singapore airlines to London. I wanted three days in London before the return flight, next she was to book me a suite at the Marriot at Marble Arch, for my time in London, and to make sure I had use of a vehicle from the hotel while I was there, and to use the rank Colonel with my name for the booking. After she had the outgoing flight confirmed she was to ring Jack McCord upstairs and let him know the flight I'd be taking.

While she was still listing what had to be done, I unlocked the safe and counted out fifteen thousand dollars, and after telling her that was for expenses asked her to check the count, as I told her I'd go downtown while she was sorting all that out and change the US dollars into British pounds, so after I relocked the safe we both left my office. At the banks the exchange rate was just over two to one, so after changing the money, I was carrying just over thirty thousand pounds.

When I got back into the office, Janice was on the phone so I carried on into my office, and then rang Lisa to tell her not to book anything until further notice, and that I'd be away for a week or two, as I hung up Janice came in to tell me where she was up to, and said "Your suite is booked, and yes you will have a car available to you, the flight number is SP 351, and departs at fourteen hundred tomorrow afternoon, and arrives at Heathrow at zero eight hundred Thursday, your return departs Heathrow at zero nine hundred on Monday."

I interrupted her, by asking "And the tickets?" She smiled, as she replied "I will pick them up this afternoon, and I'll have them for you in the morning, also I was able to get your return upgraded to first class, and I was just about to call the AFP." I smiled, and said "You're a darling for doing that Janice, don't worry about McCord, I'll go up and see him, but I need you to call MI5 before they shut, Tom McFadden is the operations chief if I remember rightly, tell him what's going on and who I'm bringing in, I'll go see McCord now, and be back soon."

Jack smiled as I sat down opposite him, and as he passed across the file on the prisoner, remarked "So you drew the short straw huh," and I nodded my head and asked if I could take the file, and he nodded. Then I told him what flight we'd be going out on and departure time, and what time I'd get to the airport, as we made arrangements to have his officers meet me in the outgoing flight crew customs and immigration lounge. After we'd made all the arrangements, we shook hands and I left with the file.

Back in my office, Janice informed me that everything was taken care of with MI5 and they would have agents there to meet me when the plane arrived, after thanking her, I continued into my office and sat down to read the file, which contained a head and shoulders mug shot from the Byron Bay police station. A redhead with green eyes the file listed her as five foot four, weight fifty kilos, and in the photo she was wearing a tank top, and according to the file she was an active member of the IRA and was personally responsible for six shootings and two bomb attacks against civilians in Belfast, and the file was stamped in red Shoot to Kill, as I saw this my mind wandered back to the time my team and I had spent in Northern Ireland with Eric Wetherby and his troop of the British SAS, and also to the day of the bombings, and I felt that in this case my impartiality might go out the window.

That night at home, I told Darlene while we had dinner together, that I was off on another business trip, and would be back within ten days, and should she hear anything from Dyson to tell him I was out of the country and when I was expected back. As I was packing my go bag that night, she wandered into the room and asked where I was going, and after telling her she asked if she could come, I frowned and luckily I recalled that she was into exam times, and so I said to her "Are you really sure you want to go this time, you told me these exams were important, besides most of my time will be taken up with business, so I won't be doing any sightseeing, or have the time for any."

She looked at me, and replied "Oh ok, but how about next time?" I lifted my head and smiled, before replying "We shall have to see what next time brings, won't we?"

As she left the room, I put in my handcuffs, and AFP ID that I had slipped under the bag as she had come in. After I satisfied her desires that night, and we woke she had an early exam that would go most of the day, so she kissed me goodbye as I got up for a shower. I arrived at the office with my go bag, and after transferring my cuffs and ID to my person, I was ready to go at a moment's notice. Janice came in with the coffee and we went over our usual routine, and as she was about to leave handed me the tickets for all my flights. Before she left the office, I asked her what sort of car she drove, and after she told me a little Toyota corolla, I asked if she like to drive a mustang while I was away, and her face light up and she beamed, as she replied "Would I ever."

So I said to her, "Alright, now if you drive me to the airport today, and promise to take the rest of the day off, you can use my car until I get back, how's that sound?" The indecision and smile on her was something to see, as she replied "I'll be ready to go when you are boss!"

CHAPTER 10

Well I found out that Janice was a competent and reasonable driver on the trip to the airport, and we arrived there at twelve forty-five, and after wishing her a good afternoon off, I grabbed my go bag from the back seat as I climbed from my car and she drove off. Outside the international terminal, before going in I lit a final smoke until I arrived at Heathrow. While I smoked I transferred my AFP ID to my jacket pocket, and my handcuffs, I folded over the belt of my strides at my back, where they were readily accessible.

After finishing my smoke, I went to the Singapore Airlines check in counter, and after having a brief discussion with the senior clerk, she allocated the seats so they were beside each other, she asked to see where my gun was, and after an approving nod that it couldn't be seen, she then escorted me to the outward bound crew's customs and immigration lounge entrance. After giving the officer my passport, and showing my gun and ID, I was able to walk into the lounge after the passport had been stamped with the exit stamp.

It was easy to pick out the AFP officers, as they stuck out like sore thumbs, each officer had a wrist handcuffed to the prisoner that was standing in between them, Mary McAfee looked very much like her photo, the only difference was that her hair had been combed, and she was wearing a pink shirt, jeans and a pair of sneakers with small socks. Walking over to the two AFP officers, I introduced myself, and they checked my ID, and after that I asked the officer on her right to uncuff her wrist, because I knew from her file that she was right handed, while I pulled my cuffs out from behind me, I replaced his cuffs with one of mine on her wrist, and the other cuff, I secured to my left wrist, and then the other AFP officer unbound his cuffs from her left side, leaving her left arm free, and then they shook hands with me and moved off and out of the lounge.

She looked up at me as I told her we'd move over to the seats and sit down while we waited to board, and when we were seated, I looked at her sideways and lay down the law to her as to how she was to behave during the flight, and then asked if she had any questions, and she asked in a heavy Irish accent about going to the toilet, and having a shower, I glanced at her ankles, and told her that if she behaved, and didn't break any of the rules I'd laid down, I'd transfer the cuffs one at a time to her ankles, but if she broke the rules or acted up in anyway, she would have to go to the toilet and so on with the door open and me standing there watching her do whatever needed doing.

She looked at me with wide eyes, and said "Fair enough, because I won't give you the joy of watching and looking at me."

I nodded my head, and smilingly replied "Good I hope we understand each other." Then I reached into my bag and drew out another pair of handcuffs, and slipped them into my jacket pocket with a smile, knowing that I'd been smart thinking that the extra set of cuffs out of my desk drawer would come in handy.

Half an hour later, I was allowed to board the aircraft with the crew, and once we found our seats, I was able to place my go bag into the overhead locker one handed, and then indicated Mary to move into her window seat. As I sat down the hostess that would be looking after us came to me, and told me that there weren't too many people booked in business, only six, and they had all been assigned starboard side seating in front of our position which was at the back of business class on the port side of the plane, and that it would be half an hour before take-off, and should I require any drinks before that I only had to let her know, so I asked Mary if she wanted a coffee, and she told me tea would be better, and so our hostess made a black tea for her and a black coffee for me, and put a couple of biscuits on my saucer as well.

As we sat there waiting for everyone to board, while we drank our cuppas, Mary turned to me, and said "You seem to be kinder that the other agents, but I think that you still don't like me,"

I looked back at her with a grim smile on my face, and replied "It's not that I don't like you, I just don't like what you stand for."

She immediately retorted with, "How would you know what I stand for, you've probably never seen what happens in Belfast, we're fighting the struggle for independence from British rule."

I was starting to get a little annoyed, so I looked at her, saying quietly "By blowing up, or shooting your countrymen, women and children, that are all innocent, they're not British, and for your information I have been to Belfast with the British SAS that are there to try and stop you lot of fanatics from killing the innocent people that you pick on, I've had to pick up bodies of women and kids that IRA bombs have killed and maimed, so don't tell me they were your enemy, and if you don't want to end up with your ankles handcuffed to the foot rail, I would suggest you keep your mouth shut unless you want something, and don't forget what happens if you break the rules.

Also it won't pay you to anger me either." I must have looked and sounded pretty fearsome, because the colour drained from her face.

As she sat back facing forward murmuring a quiet "I'm sorry." Behind us I heard the crew closing the entrance door that was behind the business class galley. The hostesses went through the emergency procedures, and soon after the plane started to taxi out to the main runway for take-off. I experienced the G force as the plane's engine thrust hurtled us down the runway with joy before the wheels left the ground and the mighty jet clawed with full thrust into the blue sky, once we reached cruising altitude, the seat belt signs went off, and the smoking light came on, as the captain came back onto the intercom, to advise us of the route we were taking, and telling us that we would be overnighting in Singapore, after the nine hour flight, and that we would be transported to our accommodation by bus from the terminal, and back again early the following morning.

After the announcement, the hostess came past, and I signalled her, and I asked her if the Singapore police were aware that I was travelling with a prisoner, and she smiled and told me that two female officers would be waiting as I departed the plane, to take her to the overnight cells, and that they would present her the following morning in the crew departure lounge as in Australia, and then asked if I would like a drink, and I ordered two scotches. As they came I gave one to Mary with a small bottle of ginger ale, mine I would drink neat, and also lit a smoke.

The first inflight movie before we were served lunch, or dinner was Octopussy, the latest James Bond movie with Rodger Moore, and I settled back to watch it. Then came the dinner service, and that was followed by another inflight movie, which was Return of the Jedi, the latest Star Wars movie, which I considered quite good. After having another drink and smoke, we started to descend into Singapore, and when I left the plane after all the other passengers I handed over my charge to the airport police, and went to the hotel in the transit bus. I learned at the hotel that an earlier transit bus went to the terminal an hour earlier than the scheduled one to take my flight, and so arranged to have an early breakfast so I could grab a ride on that one, so I could retrieve my prisoner.

The following days flight went the same way, except with the differences of the flight being fourteen hours, we had two meal services and three inflight movies, which were, in order Trading places, Lone Wolf McQuade, and Christine.

We did arrive at Heathrow on time, and when we landed, after the skywalk was linked to the plane, Mary and I were first off, and as we left the plane, after thanking the staff, and checking the two MI5 agent's credentials, we went down the stairs from the skywalk and into the terminal that way, once we went through customs and immigration, Mary was handed over to the airport police, and as I retrieved my handcuffs, the MI5 agents escorted me to their car.

I was escorted into Thames House, which is the headquarters for MI5, and I was taken to meet Tom McFadden, and after realizing we'd met before while I was in the army and with Petula at the Prince's Christmas party. After that we got on like a house on fire, and after our small talk, I asked what was going to happen with the prisoner I'd brought over, and he told me that she was actually going to go on trial in Belfast, and if she was found guilty, which seemed a foregone conclusion, she'd be hanged for the deaths of six kids and two women.

Readers Note: Sorry, but my proof reader has pointed out that I haven't mentioned how my prisoner was able to go to the toilet without my watching from the doorway as I'd threatened, if she broke my rules. Ok the answer for those that wish to know it is simple, remember the extra pair of cuffs I had? Well after I escorted her to the toilet, I fastened the spare pair of cuffs around her ankles, and removed the cuff on her right wrist, so to get where she was going, she had to shuffle quite slowly, and I would wait until she was finished before reversing the procedure.

McFadden asked me if I had booked in anywhere and I told him that I was booked into the Park Plaza, and he was impressed, but I explained that I was using extra funds that we'd seized during an operation, so I was making good use of the funds to my benefit, and he laughed as he told me he'd get me dropped off there after we'd finished talking, and then we brought each other up to date on what advances had been made in electronics, and how we used them, we parted two hours later the best of friends, or as close to you can afford to make in our game, and then the same two agents drove me to the Park Plaza.

After checking in I went up to my suite, and before having a shower, I rang the phone number I had for Dumper, it was answered with a gruff hungover voice, saying only one word "Marsh." I smiled, and asked "Dumper is that you?" Dumper answered with the statement, "No one calls me that anymore," and I replied back "Yeah, well I still do, now wake up!" I heard some noise and fumbling around, and he answered, with "Boss, is that you? Where are you?"

I smiled thinking that's better, as I replied "Yep it's me Dumper and I'm in London for a couple of days, I had my agency find you, and I thought I'd come and visit you before I go back home, how about I drive down to see you early tomorrow, say around ten."

He stammered as he answered, saying "Yeah sure boss, ten is good, my place is the third driveway on the left going up to a house on the hill, after you leave Sevenoaks, that's me, gee it's good to hear you, boss and I can't wait until I see you." After restating the time, we hung up.

Then after I had a shower and freshened up, I went down to the restaurant for a lazy lunch where I took my time, and then I went back to my room, and slept until twenty hundred hours. I felt really refreshed after the snooze, and now my body was in tune with the time zone, and I went down to have a lovely dinner of beef wellington, which I accompanied with usual drink of malt scotch. After dinner I had a couple more drinks in the cocktail bar, and then went back to my room, and rang for a wake-up call at seven just in case I slept in.

I finished breakfast, and strolled to the reception desk at eight thirty next day, and had the car brought around, and asked the best way to get to the M25 going south to Kent, the receptionist told me there was a roadmap in the car if I got lost, but also told me the easiest way, and because I knew London fairly well I was able to follow her verbal instructions, after all it was only three roads that I needed to get to the M25, it took a while to get out of the city proper, because of a hold up to traffic at Waterloo Station, but once I was on the A34 I was able to move faster, and after getting onto the M25 the rest was easy. I knew which exit I needed and soon after crossing the Kent County border, I exited and drove through Sevenoaks slowly, and outside the town limits I started looking for the turnoff into Dumper's place.

As I pulled up to the house, which was an L shaped double story house with a thatched roof, Dumper came out the front door dressed in cam trousers and a grey T shirt, and walked toward me, as did I toward him when I got out of the car, we shook hands and embraced each other as two old friends, and then he showed me into the house, and gave me a tour of the downstairs, and explained the upstairs, it was a six bedroom house with two communal bathrooms and the two master bedrooms both had full sized bathrooms, the large lounge had a big fireplace at one end, and a large TV at the other, with couches and easy chairs in the middle of the room.

It faced out toward the back of the house onto a large timber decked patio. Dumper offered me a cuppa which I accepted and when he made them he brought them back into the lounge, where I was seated in one of the easy chairs, he sat in the other one with a coffee table between us, I guessed that I had sat in the one he usually sat in because near the right hand arm was a packed box of H.E. grenades, and when I commented on them, he told me that he kept them there to fiddle with while watching TV, and that he used them to measure how drunk he was by pulling out a pin and trying to reinsert it, and if he was too drunk he tossed it out into the back yard, I laughed and casually told him he was nuts, he was laughing also and agreed with me.

Then while I sipped my coffee, which I told him was really excellent coffee, he smiled and told me that he'd brought back twenty kilos of ground coffee from Kenya after his last trip to Africa, and he laughed as he said it was one of the perks of the game pun intended. I laughed along with him, and then our talk turned to the old days, and I asked "So what happened to you that you didn't come to Tag's and Buzz's funeral, I know that Mark Ryan had left messages for you everywhere?"

His face took on a saddened look, as he replied "Yeah I got the messages but by then it was too late, I got one of them a month after the funeral date, I'd been doing a three-month stint in the Congo, communication is shit in there, so I missed it, and I didn't even know how they died."

So I told him about the crash, and as I was telling him, he shook his head, and with the saddened look still on his face, remarked "Just goes to show you, they go through all our shit without a scratch, just to be done in by a bloody accident the poor bastards." I also told him that Wires, JJ, and Lizard were still ok, and still working in the machine, and he asked whether I was still in, and I told that I left about a year and a half after going across to Transport, and then I asked him what he was up to, and he replied "Well you know that I went into being a mercenary, I've done ok I'm a captain now with the same unit of old Mad Mick's company, or what's left of it, that stint I told you about, it paid for all this and the land, and I still had a heap left over, but it's not the money Tiger, I'm a millionaire twice over it's the game it keeps my alive and on my toes, I really don't know how to explain it."

I smiled and said "I do Dumper, when you're operating every sense you have is alive, ready to spring, I thought I was getting past it when I transferred.

But I missed the action Dumper, I guess it's the adrenaline surge. We went from full on operational action to nothing, so I do know how you felt, so in a way I went back to it, how do you think I knew where to find you and whether you'd be here, this isn't my first trip to England you know?"

He looked at me with a smile, and replied "I was wondering about that Boss, but wasn't sure how to bring it up, but you've saved me the trouble, what are you doing these days?"

I smiled as I replied, saying "Well hold onto your hat, I'm a spook these days, I'm a senior agent with ASIS, and I work in an undercover role as well, and so as far as money is concerned I'm raking it in, in fact one of my main concerns is what I'm going to do at tax time, because the undercover part of my cover is as an insurance agent, and I've become a natural at it, Christ just last month I sold over a hundred policies, which is almost a normal years work."

He looked at me laughing, and said "So you're back in the job more or less doing what we used to do without the kill factor, and making a shitload of money, hah, we both like the job we do, and don't really give a shit about the money we make, we are definitely cracked Boss, but hey that deserves a proper drink." He got up and went out of view, came back shortly with two tumblers half full with one cube of ice in each, and passed me one as he sat down, and said "To the old days." I repeated the toast and took a sip, I smiled, and he'd gone and poured us Jonny Walker Blue Label malt.

After we nattered for an hour or so, Dumper said "Tiger I don't really feel like getting lunch made up, how about we head off into town and grab a counter lunch, there's a pub I go to that has great meals." I was getting a bit peckish, so I replied "Yeah sure Dumper let's, we can take my car seeing it's in the drive." We headed out to the car after he grabbed his keys, and when we were in the car he asked, "Hmm Merc, nice, is this you're new one then?"

I looked at him, smiled and answered, saying "No it belongs to the hotel that I'm staying at in London, actually I haven't seen my BMW since I left it with my aunt before we left for Australia, any trip I've done here since have sort of been fly in, fly out leaving no time to catch up with family, or others."

He nodded his head, saying "Yeah know what you mean boss, so where are you staying, and for how long?"

I told him where I was staying and that I was flying out the next morning, but in actual fact it was the day after I told him, mainly because I didn't want to get stuck in a drinking session with him that night, because I knew it wouldn't end until one of us had passed out. He whistled when I told where I was staying, and commented "Christ that'll cost you at least a thousand a night, but I must say boss we were able to stay at some really classy joints because of you making sure we were ok, I'll never forget those times boss."

I laughed, and replied "Well I don't give a shit about how much

122

it costs, and like you the money means nothing to me, and besides, yep we have stayed in classy places, but we've also had to make do with sleeping in the mud or dirt ground in jungles, sometimes still covered in bloody uniforms, so now give me comfort."

We both had a good laugh, and as we reached the village, he started to give me directions to a pub called A Soldiers Arms, and he told me it was run by an ex para that had been with the Coldstream Guards. Dumper introduced me to him as Colonel Davis, as we ordered our lunches, and I told Dumper it was my shout, so as he grabbed a table I ordered a bottle of Blue Label two glasses and a bucket of ice, the landlord smiled and told me he'd keep the top of the bottle.

I nodded knowing what he was doing for us was strictly illegal, but he was turning a blind eye to servicemen, so after paying for everything I included a twenty-pound tip, he came to attention behind the bar and saluted grinning saying thank you Colonel, I saluted back with a grin, and headed to the table.

We left the pub two hours later, and as I handed back the half empty bottle of Blue Label to the landlord, I said "You may have the rest of the bottle with my compliments best wishes sergeant,"

He answered "Thank you very much sir, and please come again." Luckily the road was quiet and the coppers weren't out, because we both would have been over the limit to drive, but we made it back to Dumper's without any mishap, once there he made coffee, and for the next three hours, not only did we sober up, but we talked all that time about things we'd both experienced, and about things that other people wouldn't or couldn't understand, however we could because not only were we soldiers in the same army and had both seen and experienced the same thing, we were more than that, we had served together as comrades in arms.

Just after six, well and truly sobered up by this time, I told Dumper that I had to go, so we headed out to the car, we embraced each other and said our goodbyes, and I told him not to get himself killed and to take care, and he wished me the same, and I told him I'd contact him the next time I was in the country, and he told me that he'd look forward to the visit, and then I started the car, and headed down the driveway turning left towards town, even though it was late evening I had no trouble with the sunlight, it was summer there so the sun wouldn't set until midnight, I drove into the hotel driveway just over an hour later, and after giving the keys to the concierge, I went into the restaurant for a dinner that I took my time over, and then went up to bed.

After having a nice lazy breakfast, I left the hotel taking a cab to Harrods, and did a bit of browsing, and then I walked around to oxford street, finally found what I'd been looking for, a tobacconist that made up packets of cigarettes to order, and I had him make up two hundred of a mix of Turkish and Balkan tobacco in packs of twenty. Fifteen minutes later I left the shop with my smokes, and I would try to only have one as a special occasion when I got home. After that I did a bit of window shopping I decided to give it away and hailed a cab, and had him return me to the hotel. As I walked in, I went to the concierge and asked if he'd be able to get me a ticket to The Phantom of the Opera that was playing in Piccadilly Square for that night, and he told me he had a few A class seats, so I asked him for it to be charged to my room.

He nodded and he told me that he could make sure that the hotel limo took me there and would be there after the show to pick me up. After he gave me all the details, I smiled and then arranged an early morning wake up and the limo to take me to Heathrow the next morning at seven. He made all the arrangements while I was there, so I thanked him and slipped him a twenty pound note for his help. Then I went up to my room, and after changing went to the hotels heated pool and gym, and had a long swim and workout, before going back to my room for a shower and changing, before going down to eat prior to going to the show.

The show was good, and I enjoyed it immensely, back at the hotel I was in bed almost as soon as I was undressed. When the wake-up call came I was already up and showered, and after packing the last minute items, I went down to breakfast, taking my bag with me I left it with the concierge, while I had breakfast, and then checked out. As I made my way to the concierge desk he was just putting my bag into the limo, and as I walked out to the driveway, he opened the door for me.

As I thanked him I slipped another twenty pounds into his hand, he smiled and wished me a good flight, and he hoped to see me back again soon.

The limo driver got me to Heathrow by eight, and this time I couldn't shortcut the wait, and had to go through normal passenger service line up for customs and immigration, as I showed my ID, gun, and passport I did however get ushered through quicker without any hindrances. While I was seated at the boarding gate waiting, I was paged over the PA system to present myself to the air crew at the boarding gate counter, and when I did, I was escorted onto the plane and shown up to my cabin and the first class lounge where a hostess was waiting to make me a drink. While I was sipping a hot coffee, I enquired if there were any more passengers coming into first class, and she informed me that I was the only one from London, but another two couples would be boarding in Singapore, and then she passed me a list of movies available besides the main inflight movies that would be shown through the flight.

After perusing the list, I elected to watch the Terminator, first, to be followed with War Games, she asked whether I preferred to watch here in the lounge where it could be played through the VCR, and I could pause or stop it if required, or in the privacy of my cabin, and I elected to watch here in the lounge in comfortable chairs, and she smiled and said she'd get it ready for after we were in the air, and then the captain came on the intercom, and after his announcement, my hostess went through the usual emergency information.

Then the plane started to taxi, and the safety belt light came on and the smoking light out, so I moved to one of the chairs and buckled up, soon after came that lovely familiar surge as we started to gather speed for wheels up. The trip to Singapore was a mix of watching movies, eating, sleeping, and then doing it all again, but when we landed in Singapore, this time there was no overnight stop, but we had to exit the plane and wait in the transit lounge for four hours, while the plane was refuelled, and reprovisioned for the next leg into Australia.

We finally landed in Brisbane at Seven the next morning, and only about a hundred people got off the flight, all of the rest were going onto Sydney, I smiled as I went into the customs and immigration hall, because I had all my luggage in the go bag, the rest had to wait for their bags before following me into the hall. As one of the customs officers went to call me over to a bench for an inspection, I cheated and flashed my ID, and he waved me through, and after getting my entry stamped it was off to the duty free.

Where I bought another two hundred cigarettes and two large bottles of Blue Label, after putting them in my bag I turned my Sat phone on, and found a message from Janice that she would pick me up, and to meet at the money exchange kiosk. So after getting through the exit doors into the terminal proper, I headed towards the kiosk, Janice and I saw each other at the same time, and as she moved toward the front entrance, I joined her at a tangent.

Outside I smiled as I saw my car, and it had a security guard beside it, and as we neared it, I flashed my ID and thanked the guard, I got into the passenger seat after putting my bag in the back, and Janice popped it into drive, and we took off.

CHAPTER 11

As we were pulling away, I laughed and looked at Janice saying, have you been throwing your weight around Janice, I'll bet that poor security guard will never trust a woman again. She laughed and told me, well he started getting stroppy about me parking there, so I flashed my ID and told him that this was a security matter, and if he knew what was good for him he'd stay there and make sure that no one went near it. I was really laughing by then and I said, "So how do you feel after scaring the shit out of him?" She told me, "Oh really exhilarated boss it was fun; it's the first time I've ever done something like that."

Getting to the office took nearly an hour because we had to contend with peak hour traffic, and as we drove, I had Janice fill me in on what had been happened while I'd been away, and how she liked having my car to use. Ross had arrived from Sydney, and had moved into the house near the airport, John introduced his new co-pilot to him, and they had spent a lot of time out at the airport, and Ross had been able to get a hangar for the plane that had access by the road, and a gated entrance to the tarmac, and Ross considered it as ideal for the purposes.

Nothing new had happened with Deep Silence, due to me not being in the field, the usual Monday meeting had been put on hold 'til I would be in the office that morning, and as far as my car was concerned, she told me that if I ever wanted to get rid of it, that she wanted the first option. I smiled as I slowly shook my head, as we pulled into the carpark, I noticed that she gave me the keys back with a slight reluctance, and I smiled again. As I continued into my office Janice started to make our morning cuppa, then we got back into our usual routine of going through everything to bring me up to speed with what was happening on all fronts of operations ongoing and pending within the office, and then she left me to carry on with my work, and went off to do what I'd instructed.

I sat back in my chair and reflected, *no matter what I, or anybody did, to some people life would go on the same as normal, unaware of what happened in the world behind closed doors, a few weeks ago I'd been instrumental in bringing down one of the largest drug cartels in Columbia at the time, and I'd just delivered a fanatical bomber and murderer into the hands of justice, and apart from a very select group no one was any the wiser! Even in our own office! One thing taken care of, now back to business as usual, get back to taking down more bad guys!* I sighed and inwardly laughed as I placed a wry smile on my face, got up and headed to the tactical room for the usual meeting.

This meeting, and every other, of course was to make everything right in the world, after all we were the guardians that stopped anything bad from taking place in the country, so everyone could feel safe and not worry about what went on behind closed doors. I smiled as I received handshakes from John and Harry, as I entered the TAC room, and fielded the questions as to how things went. Then we got down to business, two more operations were about to wind up, one in the north, that involved liaison with customs being ready to make arrests, this dealt with a supply of drugs that were coming in from the Solomon's via PNG, Customs and AFP officers were going to hit two targets that were yachts, one in Cairns and the other in Bundaberg, both raids were due to take place the minute the vessels tied up at their respective berths.

The second one in the city was to raid a drug house out in the Kenmore hills, after we'd verified that it was being used, it was now up to the Queensland police and the AFP that had originally made the enquiry with us, this now freed up eight agents in total between both operations, and considering the scope that Deep Silence was progressing and expanding they could be well utilised with the investigation of the reaching arms it involved, two of the agents could be used particularly because they were recognised bike club members, and after discussion with the others over the snippet about using bike gangs as interstate couriers, they would be well placed to investigate that side of things, and report.

Then we moved onto Operation Deep Silence, which was mine, there wasn't anything to report as to what had been happening with it, due to my being out of the country, and as yet hadn't been home to see if there had been any messages from Dyson. I informed both of them that now that I was back, I had every intention of turning up the heat and get things moving, but that I would need another agent as backup, who I would pass off as my 2IC come bodyguard, John told me he'd start scouring the local agent files as soon as we were done, and bring me the files that he would shortlist as suitable candidates. I nodded and thanked him, and as there was nothing more to discuss the meeting broke up and we all headed to our respective offices.

As I sat down behind my desk, I reached for the phone and dialled Lisa to let her know I was back in the country, and that she could make appointments for me, but to only work from the red hot list, or if any were businesses to only book one of those a week. My next call was to home, but Darlene didn't answer, so I left a message to let her know I was in town, and that if we didn't come across each other before, I'd see her at home that night.

I informed Janice that because I was feeling a little weary, I was going to have a shower and get changed before heading to the canteen for lunch, as I was about to go into the living quarters of my office, the Sat phone rang and it was Lisa, she told me that the first call she'd made turned out to be another company presentation, and they wanted to see me on Thursday afternoon at two, and she wanted to know what I wanted to do about it, so I told her to go ahead and confirm the appointment, and tell them I'd be there half an hour before to have a quite word with the company owners prior to the meeting, and to make sure they'd be there, and then told her not to make any more appointments until the following week.

After having had a long warm shower and changing my clothes, I felt a little bit more human as I headed to get some lunch. While

I was there John came and joined me, and he was carrying three personnel folders which he passed across to me saying, "Any of these three should fit the bill, and the best part is that all of them live within five or ten minutes' drive from your place, I'll make sure all three are here in the office tomorrow, and when you've made your pick send the other two back to me." I nodded with a smile and thanked him, and while I finished my lunch he had a cuppa, and we made some small talk before I told him that I was going to push Dyson on his other operations to see what I could learn, especially about his distribution setup, which would give us some insight as how big his network was.

John nodded smiling, and said "Well we already know quite a bit thanks to you, just don't go too hard on the pushing in case he starts to smell a rat, the last thing we need right now is him or any of his mates coming after you, because when we finally take them down, we want to make sure we have them all." I looked him in the eye, as I replied "Don't I know it." With lunch over he headed for the lift, while I went back to my office carrying the three files, as I sat at my desk, I lifted the first file, and started reading. I read all three files, and every now and again I would go back to a previous one to check some detail that occurred to me, and in the end, I had made my top choice and written his name down on my desk pad as number one and the other two in descending order, but I would wait until I'd interviewed all three before confirming my decision. Then I reached for his file a third time to be sure and read.

Name David John Sutton and his address, security classification which was a six, he was six foot one with black hair and brown eyes, he'd been born in Moree, New South Wales in nineteen fifty-five making him twenty-eight.

He had been recruited to ASIS from the army intelligence sector where he'd held an officers commission as a lieutenant, prior to that he had been with the commandos, before accepting officer training where he gained a reputation for unarmed combat roles, but he also held marksman status with

130

weapons, since joining ASIS he'd been involved with two undercover operations that had been successfully concluded, and with the help of customs officers and boats arrested a group of pirates that had been preying upon lone sailors between Indonesia and PNG.

After making sure of my choice, I smiled as I stretched in my chair, and decided that I'd done enough for the day, so I gathered up my go bag, and told Janice that I was calling it a day, and then headed up to my car and home. Darlene's car was outside the garage as I used the remote control to lift the door and drive into it, and after closing up, I went upstairs to the lounge where she was sitting and waiting as she saw me, she got up and rushed to give me a kiss and cuddle, and told me she'd missed me, and as she walked with me into the bedroom to unpack, she asked "Did you miss me honey?" She got quite annoyed when I told her that I didn't because my mind had been focussed on business, but she soon got over that when I suggested that we go out to dinner instead of cooking, and she told me about a new Thai place that had opened in Arana Hills down by the shopping centre, and suggested we give it a try, and I agreed with her as I took my gun off.

During dinner at the restaurant, which was licenced much to my enjoyment, while we were waiting for the dessert, I asked "So have you heard anything from Trevor while I've been gone?" She nodded her head and told me that he'd left a message to ring him when I was able to, and that he would be home most nights, with a smile and a nod, I told her I'd give him a ring after we got home. She was also able to tell me that she'd passed her exams, and that they were now on a fortnights break between semesters, and intimated that we could spend longer in bed in the morning because of that, I smiled and said "Well without trying to put a dampener on that, I've still got to work, so I'll be going into the office each morning, but you know you can have your wicked way with my body any night you wish." We both laughed as she made the comment that because I'd been away for some time, she'd be taking full advantage of having me in bed with her that night, and not to count on getting too much sleep.

When we got home, I rang Dyson, and he told me that everything was ready for my inspection, and we made arrangements to meet at his place the next evening.

The next day at the office, was busy, starting from when Janice and I had our morning catch-up after which I got her to get John and Harry down to the TAC room for a meeting, once that was sorted I told her that I'd probably buzz her during our meeting, and that if I did I wanted her to get Callaway on the Tac room com line, and then I warned her about having the three agents coming in for an interview, and to make apologies to them, but they were to wait for my return.

In the Tac room, I filled John and Harry in on the latest developments with deep silence and brought up the fact that now we had to make a choice, whether to take them down now that the guns were all in a recoverable spot, or for me to remain on the inside to see how much more could be learned and during our discussion I buzzed Janice, and shortly the call from Callaway came through, after being appraised of the latest developments we asked for his thoughts, and he answered "Well this operation is ballooning right out, I think it would be great if Tiger could stay on the inside, and try to get involved with everything, but I don't want to let those guns get away either." After I told him that it was possible to achieve both objectives, he said "Alright, I'll go along with you, and whatever decision you make I'll back it, and let's hope for all our sakes there's no screw-ups, otherwise we'll all be in the shit, all I can say is Tiger trust your instincts, if you feel it's time to come out, you come out, good morning gents."

With that he rang off, and John asked "How do you think that we can possibly make arrests over the gun shipment, and keep yourself in play at the same time?" I smiled because I was just thinking if there were any flaws to what I had in mind, as I looked at them both and said "I don't think that they'll let me know where the guns are kept, so Harry, I'm going to need two things from you, one a small tracking beacon, silent if possible, and two a couple of bugs that I can plant in Dyson's home, John, I'll need you to have a surveillance team near Dyson's to monitor and record all the goings on from now and until we close them down." They both nodded and said that these things were easily done.

I nodded my head and told them good, and then I told them I'd come to them each individually later in the day, but after our meeting I had some agents to interview, one of which was going to become my wingman on the operation from now on, and soon after I closed our meeting, and then I made my way back to my office, and as I went into Janice's anteroom I saw the three agents waiting there in chairs taking everything in but not appearing to, and I smiled and walked in and apologised for keeping them waiting.

I continued through to my office, and after taking my seat picked up the first folder, had another quick read to refresh my memory, I buzzed Janice to send in the first one. I had prepared Janice earlier as to what order I wanted to see them in, and the first was my last choice, and after talking with him and checking some details I closed down the interview, and told him to report back to John's office, and to ask Janice to send in the next agent. After going through the same routine he came very close, but something was telling me no, so again he was sent on his way. Sutton was a different kettle of fish as to the other two, he confidently walked up to my desk and sat without being invited, and waited, eventually during our talk we branched off into the army and I gave him a gruelling about the commandos being a mob of pussies, and I could see that I was getting a rise from him, even though he was hard pressed holding it in.

Bristling he said, "Alright sir, I've taken your jibes about the commandos, and I'll have you know that there is only one unit in the rest of the army that is any tougher than the commandos, and that would be the SAS, and I'll admit that I failed their training, and that's why I ended up in the commandos which are second best only to them, and if you think that reflects on whatever job I'm here for then send me on my way!"

I smiled, and then told him of my background, and as I did I watched him visibly relax, and then I asked him to tell me more about himself, and some of the things he'd done since joining ASIS, and I got a clearer picture of him. I treated him to a briefing on the present operation and what his role would be, and then said "Now it's up to you, I've told you what you needed to know to make up your mind, are you work prepared to work with me as your partner?"

He thought for a while, and then answered "Yes sir," my head came up sharply as I retorted quickly "I'm either boss or Tiger, nothing else, and you, do you prefer David, Dave, or what?" He smiled and replied "Well boss, DJ works better for me, and I get called that more often, even by my wife." I smiled and said "DJ it is then, now what sort of handgun do you use?" He told me that he was partial to using his nine millimetre Barretta, and I warned him that due to our cover story, he'd have to be wearing his gun most of the time during the duration of the operation, and I hoped that he had a comfortable shoulder holster, and as he shook his head I asked why, and he told me that he used a belt holster at his back for his gun, but also wore a sheathed knife sewn into the inside back of his shirt as a backup weapon. I laughed, and said "Good for you."

Still laughing, I said "Right well we've got work to do, so first off we'll make some visits, and then we'll come back here, where I'll give you the complete file on the operation you're now involved in, besides we'll be at a meeting with the main players tonight, but you'll get that from the case report later, right ready to go?" He smiled and nodded, and I said "Right let's go."

As we left the office I introduced Janice and DJ to each other, and asked her to call up to Harry and let him know I was on the way to see him. I introduced Harry to DJ as my new partner, and then asked what he was able to come up with. He passed me a microchip that had an adhesive pad on it, and what looked like a miniature antenna, and as I passed it to DJ, Harry told us that was the bug and it had an effective range of a kilometre, so therefore the listening van didn't have to be close to the house, which would avoid arousing suspicion. He told me he'd give me three to plant in the house, and I nodded, and then he passed me a matchbox, and when I opened it there was a small location transmitter stuck to the side and bottom of the matchbox and there was, also some live matches in the box, Harry explained that when the box opened, it activated the beacon so once activated it could be thrown down anywhere, and it would give off a location signal for only four hours, and had a range of twenty kilometres.

He smiled, and said "Therefore it would be prudent to have agents prowling the streets with receivers waiting for the signal to turn on, and then locate the premises as quickly as possible, we only need to know where, and we can send surveillance into action." I told Harry that I doubted whether we'd be taken to the location in my car, which would mean the recorders wouldn't be much use, but I needed another microphone pen and recorder for DJ, and Harry told me that it wasn't a problem because once the initial two worked well he'd ordered and received about a dozen of them, and then he setup one set for DJ and showed him how to use it, after getting the radio frequencies for the bugs and the location transmitter written down, we thanked him and then went up to John's floor.

The first thing I needed from John was a surveillance van and team to start that night keeping tabs on the bugs I'd be placing in Dyson's house that night, and I told him that they didn't need to be too close because the bugs ha a range of a kilometre, and I gave him the radio frequency they'd be on. John smiled and with a sigh told me that not having to be too close went a long way to avoiding suspicion, and I smiled and agreed with him, and he asked if there was anything else that he could help us with, and I nodded as I told him yes.

John smiled again, saying "I knew there would be more, oh before I forget, DJ you will now be posted to Tiger as his official partner, so you'll be working from the office from now on, ok Tiger what else do you need?" I looked at DJ, and let him explain about the location transmitter its range and also its limited operating time, and then I gave him the frequency. John sat back in his chair thinking, and then leaned forward, saying "I can give you four cars with two men each and a direction finder, but what I'll do is put a car at each end of Dyson's street, we know his cars now, so if any of them move around seven, we'll follow at a distance, don't want to get too close, and then when you activate the beacon we'll move in and get the location of the premises, it should go like clockwork."

I laughed and told him that clockwork doesn't always work the way it should, but I thought that we'd covered most contingencies, and hopefully by the end of the night we'd have the location of the guns, one way or another. He sighed and told me, that he agreed, and that everything would be in place by the time DJ and I arrived at Dyson's. Then we left the communication floor and went back down to my office, and when we got there Janice told us that she'd arranged the empty office across the hallway to be DJ's and that everything pertaining to Operation Deep Silence had been put there on his desk, I smiled, and said "Thank you Janice, you've done all of what I expected you to, so once you've squared away DJ, can you come into my office and bring a cuppa with you please."

After I sat down, I realised that I still had to go out to Stafford that afternoon to make another presentation, and figured out that I'd have an early lunch then leave to do that, and then have DJ pick me up at my place at six thirty that night. When Janice joined me, I took my first sip of coffee before inclining my head upward, and saying "Well what do you think?" Janice knew by my head movement that I was referring to DJ, and smiled as she said "He's got a bit to learn, right now I don't think he knows which way is up, and you must admit you've thrown him in at the deep end, but yeah he'll work out ok, he catches on fast." "Good" I replied, and then went on to tell her what I'd be doing for the rest of the day, and asked her to give DJ my address because he was going to have to pick me up that night. She nodded and we made small talk over the rest of our cuppa, and after that we both went back to our respective work. One of the things I did was ring Lisa to tell her I'd be there just after one, and then left my office headed for the canteen, but first invited DJ to join me.

He did join me and also brought along the case file, so as we had our lunch DJ was asking me questions in regard to deep silence which I answered for him, and then as I was finishing my lunch, I told him that I was going to be spending some time on my undercover job that afternoon, and that he would be picking me up tonight, and that Janice would give him the address, I made clear to him to be on time, and as far as my wife was concerned that he was my bodyguard.

I drove into the driveway at the Stafford house /office, and Lisa came and cuddled up to me showed me her left hand that had a new engagement ring on her ring finger, and she told me that she had finally decided, Reg and her were going to be married in about a year, but she'd let me know as time got closer. I laughed and told her I was pleased for her, and playfully said, but I pity poor Reg, and I received a playful punch in the arm from her as we walked into the office.

I arrived right on time at a large factory, it was a family business, and as I talked to the owners I arrived at a few possible suggestions for them and by the time I was escorted down to the lunch room for my presentation to the factory hands. I'd already sold six policies, but they already had a super scheme in place, however they wanted me to send out the super team to look at their options, which I was pleased to do. When I left the factory at four o'clock I had sold another forty-two policies. As I left I considered my options, I wasn't that far from the Newmarket office, so I drove over there and lodged all the proposals, by now Shirley was getting used to me turning up with a bundle of paperwork, and the only thing she muttered, was "Forty-six, is that all, you're getting slack Tiger." We both had a good laugh at that, and as she started processing them. I rang Miles in the super team, he informed me that I had a lot more money to come from them, thanks to my last referral. I laughed as I gave him the gen on the next one, and he asked which super scheme they had, and he told me that our figures made theirs look sick, so I'd probably end up with another sale share. I laughed and told him that it suited me fine, and we ended the call with him telling me he'd be in contact.

As I left with another load of proposal form blanks, Shirley informed me that Rick Walsh had moved the sales meeting forward to eleven instead of twelve the following day, and I told her I'd be there, besides I wanted my commission cheque, there should be at least three hundred thousand coming my way. I had just enough time to get to the bank and withdraw twenty-three hundred dollars, which I gave to Lisa as her pay from the transactions, and then headed home.

When I arrived home, I had only enough time to eat, and then have a shower and get changed before I was due to be picked up, while I was in the shower Darlene stood outside it complaining to me that I never took her anywhere, luckily she couldn't see my eyes raising, or read my thoughts. I tried to tell her that if she wanted to go out all the time, we'd never be able to make enough money to retire early, and live the good life, which she countered with the fact that if I was able to buy Trevor's load of guns, I'd be making a two hundred percent mark-up on the sale, which was true, but I told her out of that have to come setup monies for the job and transportation and shipping, plus the cost of actually being on site at the sale and hoping that we weren't ripped off.

She argued that, if I bought the consignment for nine million, I'd probably offload them for anything from twice to four times the value, which would mean thirty-six million, if I paid out say six million in transport and shipping, that would leave twenty-one million clear profit, which was more than enough for us to live the high life, anywhere in Asia, and she was right. I could live like a king in Thailand or Cambodia, but my argument was, that what she said was true, but she'd most likely end up with a pissed husband, because I'd have nothing to do.

The doorbell rang at six thirty on the dot, and I was saved any further argument, my last comment to her was, but first everything hinges on tonight whether your so called mate is up for a deal, now I have to go and I'm not sure what time I'll be home. Then DJ and I got into his car, he drove out onto the road, and we made our way to the rendezvous with Trevor Dyson.

CHAPTER 12

We Arrived at Dyson's at ten to seven, and when I rang the doorbell, it was answered by Lyle Thomas, and I introduced him to DJ as one of my men, so considering this was the first time DJ had been on the scene. He wanted to search him, which I allowed and DJ told him about his gun, Lyle seemed to be satisfied and he led us down into the office to wait for Dyson. I took the opportunity to plant the first bug underneath the desk, I had just finished securing the bug under the desk, when DJ warned me of footsteps on the stairs, as I turned and was casually leaning against the desk, as Lyle said "I'm sorry Tiger, but the boss meant for you to wait upstairs in the lounge, my fault I'm afraid." I smiled and replied, "No probs Lyle, come on DJ back upstairs," and we followed Lyle back up the stairs, when we reached the lounge, Lyle took my drink order and poured me a scotch, however he must have known DJ's role, because he didn't even ask if he wanted a drink.

I moved toward the end of the lounge that contained the chairs and lounge, and pretended to admire the painting that was close to the business end of the lounge, and as I went closer to the painting, I gripped the edge of it, as I bent closer to see the Artists signature, but in actual fact my fingers had curled around the frame and secured the second bug, and I thought, *two down, now where shall I put the last one? As I figured that sometimes I talked business while I was relaxing in the spa, so I casually strolled out onto the balcony, and moved toward the spa,* and I became interested in the way the light shone into it, by bouncing off the overhang of the roof, but one section was in complete darkness, and so number three ended up being secured. I was still looking into the spa pool while Dyson made his way into the lounge, met and shook hands with DJ, and then drink in hand joined me near the spa, and I told him that the refraction of water at night tended to mesmerise me with its beauty.

He laughed and then upended his drink, and said "What do you say we head off and have a look at the inventory, and then we can come back here and discuss business," I smiled, and replied "Damned good idea, please lead on." We made our way to the garage and as Lyle opened the door for us, Trevor and I got into the back seat while DJ had made his way to the passenger seat up front, when we were all seated, Dyson said "I'm sorry Tiger but you can most probably appreciate that security needs to be maintained, so I'm afraid I'll have to ask you both to wear blindfolds." I looked at him and smiled, as I replied "Trevor please have no worries on that issue; please go ahead, security is everything."

As I saw Lyle start to place a covering over DJ's head, I felt the cover come down over my head, and started to concentrate on feel, just in case all else failed. After half an hour of driving, the car pulled up, and I thought that from where Dyson's house was to where we pulled up, the way we'd been driven and my own mental map of Brisbane I figured that we were near the river at a spot close to Newstead or Teneriffe, and my mind went through a list of buildings that I knew were in that area, and I speculated that we were near the old wool store buildings. Soon after what sounded like a roller door being raised and the deeper sound and echoing of the car I surmised that we'd driven into a building.

I heard Trevor say, "We're here, I'm just going to lift your blindfold, there's a lot of light in here so you may be better off closing your eyes, and let them adjust to the light afterwards," I nodded, and then felt the hood being raised, and I slowly opened my eyes into slits at first, before opening them fully after the few seconds of adjustment, and then I had the car door opened by DJ, and I got out. As I looked around, I saw work tables with stuff on them all over the place, an empty container with its doors open, and stacks of rifle boxes, that were stacked neatly beside tables that had rifles sitting on them, and about twenty men sitting around.

I reached into my jacket and pulled out my cigarette packet, and then into the other pocket for my matches, the first match I blew out sideways, and reached into the box for a second, while I murmured, bloody last one, which blew out too, and I growled "DJ" as I went over to him, while at the same time I threw the open matchbox into a pile of rubbish, he lit my smoke and I looked at Dyson, and said "Well let's go see what you got."

The first table we approached had four RPG launchers sitting on it, and after finding out that there were three hundred rounds for them, I noted that in a notebook, looked at Trevor and asked "What do you want for them?" He looked at me with a smile, and replied "Why don't you work out your best price for the lot and then we can deal afterward." I laughed and said "Good idea. Ok DJ, take your book out as well, so we can cross check everything." He replied "Yes boss." Then I went from table to table, every now and then asking a question as to how many, conferring with DJ, and only then again breaking down a rifle or rocket launcher, or checking grenade pins, and I asked "How much ammo for what?" Dyson looked at one of the men, and he stepped forward, and started giving me the inventory of all the ammunition, and then DJ and I went through our notes making sure we had everything on both lists.

DJ and I looked at each other, nodded, and then I looked at Dyson with a smile on my face, and said "Ok, now do you want to discuss business here, or would you rather head back to your pad where we can be comfortable while DJ and I work out a price for you?" Trevor smiled, and replied "Back to my place we'll go then, but security you know." I laughed, and answered "But of course Trevor, just pass me the blindfold when we're in the car and we'll quite happily put them back on."

On the way back to Dyson's, I put my senses to the test again, and by the time we arrived back there I was convinced we'd been near the wool stores. After our blindfolds were removed we went back up to the lounge and as Lyle served drinks, this time DJ was asked what he wanted, DJ and I sat on the lounge, and compared notes, while Dyson sat in one of the easy chairs. DJ and I made a show of come up with figures beside each item, and after an hour I pulled a calculator out of my jacket, and sat back with my notebook and started entering figures. Lyle took my glass as I held it out toward him, and as I reached a final figure, I sat back and took an appreciative sip.

Then I looked Dyson in the eye, and said, "Ok Trevor, considering the fact that the weapons are a bit old hat but still serviceable, I won't ask where you got them, but I would hazard a guess as to them coming from an army depot somewhere, however that's beyond the point, I'm prepared to offer you six and a quarter million for the lot, but you throw in the container."

He smiled, and returned my look, saying "Well yes they were part of an army shipment that got lost, however I'm thinking that eight mill would be closer to the going price." I was shaking my head and smiling, and replied "Well there you have the crux of the matter, they're old these days but because you're a mate, I'll make it seven and a half, but that's the best that I can do." This is where the haggling got interesting, if he didn't come down in price, I'd most likely have to pay that, but if he came down, I'd have won the bargaining, but the trick was not to make it look like that.

Still smiling, he said "Well I know you have expenses, but so do I, also people to pay, but I'm treating you as a friend, so the most I could come down could maybe be a couple hundred grand to seven mill eight." Ok now I had him, so after making it look as if I was really thinking hard, I casually took a sip of my drink, and replied with a smile "I'll give you seven and three quarters, but in the way of a sweetener, I'll give you a two mill deposit in cash."

He sat back still smiling, and then leaned forward, saying "I'd need the deposit within a day or so." I also leaned forward and replied "I can have it for you on Saturday, but you still supply the container." He leaned forward even further and held out his hand, as he said "Deal," so we both shook hands on the transaction, and then we both sat back with our drinks, and after a few minutes, I asked "Trevor, you got anything urgent to do this weekend?" After he told me that he had nothing special on, I explained that Darlene had been on my case about me not taking her anywhere lately, so I decided that DJ and myself and our partners were going to fly down to Melbourne to see the new Andrew Lloyd Webber show of Cats, and if he and Lyle and their partners wanted to join us, more the merrier, he laughed and smiled, as he said "Tiger we'd love to, how about we make it a business trip as well, and we'll meet up with all my associates down there, you never know we may have more business to throw your way."

I sat back in my seat with a smile of triumph, and told them the address of the hangar at the airport, and suggested we all meet there at ten on Saturday, and told them I'd arrange it all, and that it was my treat. After we left half an hour later, I immediately reverted to character, and told DJ to get on the radio and find out if they had found the right address, he was able to raise the comm's room and they confirmed my assumption that the shipment was in the lower part of Newfarm two buildings away from the wool store, I also had DJ ask the comm's room if the surveillance van had begun receiving input from the bugs, and as they confirmed it we told them we were going radio dark, I smiled as a looked at DJ, who was also sporting a smile.

During the trip home, I asked DJ "Is your wife aware of what you do and who you work for?" He told me that she did and used to be an agent herself, so she had no problems mixing in undercover roles. I nodded and told him to pull over, and then I told him the whole story of Darlene and me, and as I finished, he said "Shit, no wonder you didn't want her to know that all of this is a sham. Christ boss! You've got balls I'll give you that, I don't think I could allow myself to get married without love of some kind, but to do all that just to infiltrate this setup, well believe me that takes real balls. Yeah I'll fill Marley in on the operation, and the situation with you and your missus, and I must admit flying the company jet down to Melbourne to see a show, I've got to hand it you, boss, you're one in a million, but she'll love this, she wanted to see Cats, and you've just made it possible."

After he had said what he wanted we continued on home.

The next day was an early one for me, because I had to have a meeting with John and Harry after the previous night's events, and a briefing combined, which required the presence of Ross and his co-pilot, so as soon as Janice came in I had her contact Ross with the intention of having him and his co-pilot at the meeting / briefing that morning. Then after that was done, I had her find an attaché case and after I unlocked the safe, had her count out two million into the case, as she started the procedure she commented that it was all still in US Dollars. Shit! Ok after some quick thinking, I had her get the current exchange rate, and after doing our sums decided that that amount of cash would go into the case. Then because the exchange rate played into our favour, I Phoned John and asked him to send down four very big and armed agents to accompany Janice to the bank, she was to change one hundred grand into Australian dollars for me to use for expenses, and the rest of the money in the safe and case, she and her guards would take it all to the bank and change it into our currency. *That was some time ago, and I won't bore you with the details, except to say that when Janice returned, I had ninety-six thousand dollars for expenses and apart from what we had taken out, the safe contained eight million six hundred thousand Australian dollars roughly.*

Now while she was away with her escorts, the meeting / briefing took place, and I was finally introduced to the new co-pilot, his name was Jerry Hellmann, and after we talked briefly, I knew he could be counted on, and that I liked him. There really wasn't much to say in regard the meeting side, everyone in the TAC room had listened to the previous night's reports and recordings, DJ and I were applauded as we entered and sat, and then we gave a verbal report of the night's events. Once we were finished, John asked "So what's this idea of a jaunt to Melbourne, and how are we going to come up with two million in cash?"

I leaned back with a smile, and said "I'll answer your second question first, don't worry where the money is coming from, suffice to say you should all recall I was in Columbia recently, and right now Janice is at the bank and with the help of your agents John, she'll be bringing back more than enough." Then I explained that the reason for the so called jaunt to Melbourne was to provide an alibi for all concerned when John and the feds raided the warehouse and seized the weapons shipment, and hopefully made quite a few arrests. This started everyone laughing and cheering, and then I said "Now here's the inventory DJ and I took of what's there, hopefully it tallies with what was stolen.

I passed my notebook across to John and so did DJ, after taking a sip of water, I continued "Now the reason for the jaunt as you know is to give us an alibi, so therefore the raid is not to be conducted before eleven tomorrow morning, but it must be wrapped up before Sunday night, so John I would suggest you get together with McCord later today and get it worked out, Ross, you and Jerry, would you both like to take your wives to Cats, and have a suite at the Hilton for the weekend?" They both were smiling and nodding their heads, so I continued again, "Good, now your wives know what you do so fill them in, as to what we're up to, but on no account is anyone to assume that my wife knows, so she's to be treated like a target, Jerry I'll need to know your wife's name, because remember we all know each other and are all friends, got it?" He nodded his head and told me that his wife's name was Rhonda.

I nodded my head, and then looked around the table, saying "Ok Ross, Jerry, wheels up at ten in the morning, anyone got any questions, okay let's adjourn, and I'll see everyone for a de-briefing when we get back, John, stick it to them, but be careful, right thanks all, let's go." We all got up and filed out of the room, DJ followed me to my office, where Janice had the case out and was counting bundles of bills into it. I assumed she had it all in there as she closed the case, and then started putting the rest of the cash into the safe, except for a pile of bills she had left out, these she passed to me, saying "Ninety-six grand boss, and we have two mill in the case and eight mill six hundred in the safe." I laughed as DJ whistled, and nodded my head with a smile, and then told her what else she needed to do, which was make the hotel accommodation for six suites, book twelve first class theatre seats, and arrange for limos from the hotel to pick us up at Avalon airport, which was easier to use than Tullamarine, and as she turned to get started DJ followed her out heading for his office.

Then I had time to make a couple of calls, the first being to Darlene, who I knew was at home, and I told her to pack for a weekend away, and to include a formal dress, she was full of questions, but I put her off by telling her it was a surprise, and that she'd enjoy what we were doing. The second was to Lisa, to make sure she would be home so I could drop some money off to her after the sales meeting, and she told me than she'd already been out and she'd be home the rest of the afternoon. Then she asked if I wanted her to make any appointments for the following week, and I told her to hold off until she heard from me, and then we both rang off after I said I'd see her later. It was close to ten thirty when Janice announced that everything was taken care of.

I smiled as I heard her shout, and I got ready to leave, as I walked through her office she told me that the tickets would be waiting at the hotel reception, and everything had been booked in my name. I smiled and nodded as I wished her a good weekend, and that I'd see her the following week, as I passed DJ's office, I poked my head in and asked him to pick me up at nine in the morning, and he confirmed by saying, "Roger boss."

I arrived at Newmarket at five to eleven, and as I entered the office, everyone cheered, and parted so that I could see Rick standing at the sales tally board, and then he said, "Now here's someone that's only been with us for a short time, but in that period he's written more business, than in the whole metropolitan area, and has been awarded two trophy's from head office, the first one goes without saying, Most Improved Salesman, and the second more importantly Salesman of the Financial Year." As he presented me with the trophy's, he also passed across cheques from the society that went with each award, the first was for a thousand, and the second for ten thousand, and then he also gave me my commission cheque, and when I saw what it was made out for, I really had to think how my calculations of the amount due to me were so far out, because it was for six hundred and ninety-seven thousand dollars, Shit! I was gobsmacked, and thought, *There's got to be some mistake, let's have a good look at that payment summary.*

So while the rest of the meeting went on, I was sat near the back looking at the payment summary, and then realised that with my share of the commission on the two super schemes that Miles had been able to sell was almost equal to the commission I'd made on all the other policies I'd sold, *shit maybe I might move into the superannuation side after all, Christ what a shitload!* I smiled at the thoughts that were going through my brain, and then looked at the sum now in my retention fund. *Now the retention fund was where ten percent of every policy sold was held back from being paid for a period of three years to cover the eventuality of the policy holder cancelling his policy, and if that happened the society took the money already paid in commission from that fund. If at the end of the three-year period everything was fine, that money was released from the fund as an extra commission to the salesman.*

After all the presentations and in house prizes on performance were given out, I was approached by one of the long term salesman, and he told me that if I ever considered selling my agency, he was interested, not really sure what he meant I nodded, and then dismissed it, I would ask Rick about that at a later stage.

The next morning the doorbell sounded at five to nine, and as I answered it, I was faced with a five foot eight or nine redhead that had green eyes, and was smiling, as she said "Hi boss, how you doing?" Darlene joined me, and the girl continued "Hey this must be your wife, why haven't you shown her off before, and are you going to introduce us?" I laughed, and replied "Hi Marley, long time no see, this is Darlene, Darlene Marley DJ's wife." Marley laughed, and said "Ah yeah speaking of him, he's in the car waiting boss, so you ready to go." I nodded as I moved our suitcase out onto the landing, Darlene joined Marley in walking down the stairs, as I locked up, and brought the suitcase down, DJ popped the boot and the suitcase went in with his, Marley was holding the door for me, and gave a slight wink as I got into the car.

The gate to the tarmac was open as we drove through to see our plane already out with the boarding steps in place, and as we drove into the hangar and parked, I took Darlene over and introduced her to everyone, and as DJ and Marley joined us the other wives said "Hi Marley, DJ, been a while huh?" Jerry had been placing the luggage in the cargo hold, and as he finished he told us another car was arriving, and he directed the driver to park beside our cars. I went and shook hands with Trevor, and as his party joined him I made introductions to my staff, and the wives, and he did the same with his and Lyles girlfriends, Darlene knew them, so she took the girls by the arms and joined the other ladies, as the last of the luggage was loaded, and then I looked at Ross, and he nodded, so we made our way onto the jet after the women, as Ross and Jerry locked the cabin door, he looked at me, and said "We'll be in the air in a few minutes boss, as soon as we start to taxi is a good time to buckle in."

While we were still climbing, Ross turned off the seatbelt sign, but kept the no smoking one lit, and came on the PA, saying "Well good morning ladies and gentlemen very soon we'll be levelling off at thirty six thousand feet which is our cruising altitude, and our ETA at Avalon is eleven thirty, the weather in Melbourne is forecast as sunny and mild with a temperature of twenty four degrees, please feel free to move about if you wish," this last was said as the plane levelled off and the no smoking light went out.

I was seated opposite Dyson, and as Jenny got up she asked if we'd like anything, Dyson ordered a coffee and so did I, I also asked her for the attaché case I had place aboard earlier, and she nodded, and brought the case to me before going back to make our drinks, Rhonda also started asking if anyone wanted anything, and then joined Jenny in the galley.

After Jenny had gone I picked up the case and passed it to

Dyson, saying "Your deposit Trevor would you like to count it or will you trust my bank, because they're the ones that packed the cash for me." He smiled and lifted the lid and his eyes lit up, he rifled through a couple of stacks of notes and smiled as he closed the case, and asked "How about we put this somewhere safe 'til we're on the way back, that way I'll be less tempted to use it," and he laughed, and I joined him in the laughter, as I said "Sure I'll put the case in the safe in my office, if you'd care to join me." So we both moved into my office and I unlocked the safe, luckily it was fairly large in height and width, but was only twelve inches deep, and Dyson watched as I put the case on top of the Ingram sub machine gun sitting in there.

While I'd been doing that Dyson had sat in one of the chairs facing the desk, and after closing the safe, I sat opposite him, and he said "This is a pretty good setup, is it yours, the plane I mean?" I nodded my head, and replied "Yep, you probably won't believe this, but I actually won the jet in a poker game, and since then it's been invaluable, but I must admit keeping up with registration numbers can be a pain, but Ross only uses the registrations that he knows for a fact have been scrapped, so every now and then we paint on another set, but it keeps me ahead of the law." He laughed and nodded his head, and replied "Tiger you really are a real smooth character, I can't wait to introduce you to some of my associates, you my friend have style and you're a cool operator, but what do you do if someone screws with you?" Now it was my time to laugh, and then my mood went deadly, as I replied with menace "I kill them, and sometimes I cut off their heads as well, and send them to their business partners as a warning."

His face had gone white, and he swallowed hard as I stared at him coldly, and then I reverted to myself, saying with laughter "But I haven't had to do that for a while now, I think the last one belonged to one of the Mexican cartels, but I'd have to check with DJ, he'll know." I shrugged my shoulders, and smiled as I said "But what the hell," and he stared at me for a short time before swallowing hard again, saying with a sigh "Yeah well remind me never to get on your bad side." I moved from the desk to the minibar, and took out two tumblers and a bottle of blue label, and held it out for him to see, and he nodded, so I took the tumblers back to the desk and poured two good sized shots into each, and passed him one, and then we sat back and savoured the drinks, and then he said "I've also found out something more about you Tiger."

I raised my eyebrows in a query, and he continued "You've got excellent taste in scotch, my lord that's good." So I poured us both another round. After making small talk for a while, we finished our drinks, and I suggested that we head back to our respective women before we both got castrated, he laughed, but got up all the same, and we went back into the main cabin.

Soon after we started the descent into Avalon, and after taxiing to a hangar, we disembarked, and the waiting limo drivers gave Ross and Jerry a hand in cross loading the luggage, and then after Ross had arranged the refuelling we all climbed into the limos, and they started the drive into the Hilton. When we got there our luggage was sorted out and we registered, each couple were given the keys to their suite, and we all arranged to meet in the restaurant for dinner at six and leave for the show at seven that evening in the limos.

At five thirty that evening, as I was getting ready for dinner the only thing I needed to put on was my suit jacket, the Sat phone buzzed in my trousers pocket, and I reached for it, there was a message for me that read, "Raid a complete success, all weapons seized with twenty six arrested," I called to Darlene that I was going to see DJ, and went to his room and knocked, Marley answered and invited me in, and I showed DJ the message, we were both smiling, but I warned "Now we can't give this away under any circumstances, business as usual, now I'd better head back, see you at dinner."

CHAPTER 13

When Dyson and his party joined us at dinner, he wasn't in a good mood, and tended to be a bit snappy, I assumed that he'd had some rather bad news, but ignored it, until he went just a little too far, with his snappiness. So I got up and asked him to join me as I moved out onto the restaurant balcony, once we out there I rounded on him, and said "Listen Trevor I don't know what's happened, or how bad a mood you're in, you don't shout at the staff, now if it's something you want to talk about, fine I'm here, if not just get your shit together, and try to have a pleasant evening."

He looked at me, and replied "Yeah sorry Tiger, but yes I've had some bad news, and it involves you as well, but let's talk about it later, now I think I ought to go in and apologise to that waiter, and the rest of you." Then we re-entered, and I saw Dyson having a word with the waiter he'd told off, and slip him a twenty, before returning to the table and apologise to us for his rude behaviour with the waiter." As we were finishing our meal, Darlene leaned over and whispered in my ear, "Where are we going next? None of the girls told me." I looked at her and smiled, and then leaned over and told her we were going to see Cats, now I'm not too sure which, but she didn't show any reaction, maybe she didn't believe me, or didn't think I'd think of something like that, but she did lean over into my ear again, and scoffed "Yeah right, as if you could get tickets to that on a whim," so I just shrugged my shoulders, and said "ok."

As we were waiting in the foyer for the limos, I leaned across to her again, telling her to reach into the inside right pocket of my jacket, which she did and pulled out the tickets, and as she looked at them stunned, I slipped them out of her hand, and told her that there was nothing that money couldn't buy. Then she seemed to come out of her stupor, and was smiling and telling me she loved me, and saying that it was a wonderful surprise, and I really didn't care what she thought either way, because by now she come to the end of her usefulness, and if I stayed with her now it would only be for convenience sake.

Readers Note: I suppose that with my last comments I could be called a male chauvinist pig, (which is what it was called in those days), and probably by now alienated my female readers because I tend to tell the truth, and yes, I could be called that for stating the obvious, as she would only be a plaything and used to satisfy my sexual urges from time to time, but you have to remember ours wasn't a marriage based on true values, I knew her before she was a criminal.

She would have been arrested as an accessory, if I hadn't of intervened, my marriage to Darlene was merely a means to an end, there was no love involved in it for me, I was merely using her as a convenience, and I admit that without reservation, some would say she was being treated terribly, but don't forget, she was with me for what she could get out of it, so by logic, one must admit that we were using each other. Anyway, after that casual interlude and losing half of my reading audience, let's get back to the story.

The evening was perfect and the seats we had for the show were perfect, the first row in the middle section of the balcony, from the aisle inward, the show itself was stupendous, the only time I've seen it done better was back in London Piccadilly Circus, but we'll get to that later. During the intermission Dyson, DJ, Lyle, and myself got together and Dyson told us what had occurred prior to dinner that night, both DJ and I both pulled off the acting award for the job we did, as I said "Great now I don't have my guns, what the hell is going to happen now, I've promised delivery, and your guys have fucked that up, and screw the deposit it stays in my safe, now what the hell am I going to do, I've killed people for less than this, but bugger that what are you going to do to make this right?"

Dyson was sweating, but told me that everything could be worked out, but he would need to make calls later that night, and that DJ and I should be available to travel with him the next day at whatever time, because he was going to call a meeting of all his associates, and that he would like us to attend. I seemed as if I was thinking it over and after a reasonable time delay, I nodded my affirmation, and said "Ok, we'll have breakfast at eight, and be ready after that," and he nodded, and then we started discussing the show so far, as we casually strolled back to the ladies and the pilots.

The second part of the show was just as good as the first, and at the end of the evening we all decided to have some drinks in the bar before going up to our rooms, but Dyson excused himself, so he could make his calls to arrange the next day, and Lyle and his partner went up as well, after a couple of drinks, Darlene started yawning, so I told to go on up to the room, and I'd be along soon after. Once she was gone, there was only those associated with ASIS at the table, so keeping my voice low I proposed a toast to, a successful raid, and also to our trip being a success with the way things were falling into place, and lastly to a very good show, then after a couple more drinks, and looking at DJ, I made my goodnights, and told him I'd see him at eight for breakfast.

As I stepped into the bedroom of our suite, Darlene said "Don't you worry about getting undressed I'll do that for you, and then I'm going to throw you on the bed and ravish you," I chuckled, and replied "Now with an invitation like that how can I refuse, go right ahead and be my guest, just as soon as I've had a leak." She laughed, and replied "Such a romantic, go on hurry up, before I change my mind, not." When I got back into the bedroom she was naked, and proceeded to make good in stripping me, all the time rubbing her breasts and nipples all over my back and front, groaning all the while, before taking my strides and jocks down, and as she went down to undo my shoes, she blew her warm breath on my now hardening penis and ball sack, after my shoes and socks were off, then came my strides and jocks, and as she moved back up, she started kissing my lightly all the way up until she reached my penis, which she sucked into her mouth, while she was sucking on me her groans were becoming more intense, until she stopped, got off her knees, grabbed my penis in her and guided me to the bed, and then pushed me backward, as she straddled over me and remarked, "God I'm likely to come as soon as you're inside me." Then she raised herself up and guided my penis into her wet vagina, and slowly lowered herself onto me, as I entered her she gave a sigh and moan, then raised herself a little and then drove herself downward, I went into her as far as she could take me, which resulted in convulsions, a small scream of pleasure, and then satisfied moaning as she came. After her initial orgasm, it was easy to keep her in the zone, so to speak, and I brought to five more orgasms, before I poured my warm fluid deep inside her, which drove her over the edge one more time.

As she collapsed onto the bed beside me, she was murmuring things like, "God you're good, how do you do that, Christ I'm glad I'm on the pill, that one would have impregnated me for sure, you're so wonderful." Soon after we drifted into sleep. After waking at six I got out of the bed without disturbing Darlene, and shut the bedroom door as I moved around the suite, I made a coffee for myself before I got in for a long hot shower. Darlene already knew that I was going to be on the move early, and so she stayed in bed asleep, at least I hoped as I silently sorted out what I was going to wear, my shoes and gun, and then carrying everything into the main lounge again I closed the bedroom door once more. After I was dressed, I made my way down to breakfast, and sat relaxing over another cuppa as I waited for DJ to join me. When he arrived, we took our time and had a relaxed breakfast, as we talked over business. We both hoped that we would be able to pick up a lot of useful information as the day wore on, and I made a joke about probably ending up with the Carlton crew.

As we were both sitting back relaxing over a final coffee, we were joined by Lyle, who asked us if we would join Trevor and himself at a café in St. Kilda. When we got to the foyer, Dyson came forward with all smiles and handshakes, and said "I've just arranged a limo for the day, because we'll have a few stops to make, but there's a good chance we'll be out most of the day," I nodded, and replied "Well that's ok the women will have to care of themselves, so you're the travel guide Trevor, lead on by all means."

The first stop we made was at a café in St. Kilda, and Trevor told us that we would be meeting a few people known to him. When we walked in, my senses were immediately on full alert due to the atmosphere, and I noted a table in the centre of the café that had a few spare places, and ringed around at other tables were bodyguards, and I presumed they were all armed. I noticed that Lyle had barred DJ's way and indicated a table that they moved to, as Trevor and myself walked forward to the table, and as we did the head of the table watched us and then stood to come forward and greet us, and bid us to join them, introductions were made all round, and I found myself seated down with to breakfast with, Domenic (Mick) Gatto, Alphonse Gangitano, Graham Kinniburgh, and Lewis Moran, the cream and ranking members of the Carlton crew, shit so much for jokes anymore.

Gatto told everyone of Dyson's troubles, and while there were commiserations, nothing else was forthcoming in the immediate future, after I'd finished a coffee, most of them were making preparations to leave, and we all shook hands and embraced, as people exited. Finally, we were left there with Mick Gatto, and he started telling us that, even though the Carlton crew didn't want to have much to do with the Calabrese family, that they may be able to help, or even the Serbian mafia. He gave us a piece of paper with contact names and where they were known to hangout, and as he passed it to Trevor he pointedly suggested with a cold warning look that we could use his contacts, or use Dyson's own, because he knew that Trevor had had dealings with both in the past. Then everything was back to all smiles and so on as we made our farewells.

Next stop saw us backtracking to Footscray, where I was to meet the head of the notorious Honoured Society Frank Benvenuto, and an underling Tony Romeo. The Honoured Society is part of the Calabrese Family, both Calabrian Italian Ndrangeta groups, more commonly known as Mafioso, or just plain mafia, that day I met the heads of both, the second being Francesco Barbaro.

At both we had no luck, and so we headed towards the Clayton Mulgrave area to meet with the Serbian mafia and met with Zorz Stankovic, who suggested that we'd be better off dealing with the Nomads motorcycle club, who were doing a lot of stockpiling and stealing of weapons lately. Once we were back in the car I told Dyson that it was getting late, and I had no wish to talk with a bunch of drugged up bikies, and he agreed with me, so we instructed the driver to take us back to the hotel.

Apparently while we'd been gone, most of the wives had gone out shopping and touring, while Jenny had taken herself off to the museum, Ross was telling us this in the foyer. While he'd been waiting with Jenny who'd arrived back, when we arrived the rest were still out, and he'd been waiting to account for everyone. As he was informing us of what had taken place a limo arrived in the driveway, and all the wives piled out. Most were a little drunk and raucous, and grabbing at their shopping once the boot was opened by a staff member. They were unaware that we were watching them, and I noticed that Dyson's face had tightened while he watched his girlfriend, and I sympathised with him because I wasn't too pleased over Darlene's actions either.

As they entered the hotel finally making enough noise to wake the dead, I saw Darlene spot our group, and she yelled out "Hey honey," and headed our way, and draped herself over my shoulder when their little group got to us, I was furious, and I turned to Ross, saying tightly "Well looking at this bunch, I don't think we'll be going anywhere today, so we'll fly home in the morning Ross, and we can all have dinner in the restaurant tonight at seven, those of us that can, that is." While I'd been talking I'd looked at everyone and received their nods of ascent, and glanced over the other wives and girlfriends, Ross gave his acknowledgement by saying, "Sure thing boss", and then the party broke up and we all headed up to our rooms.

That night as we all gathered for dinner there were a few empty spots, I was first down, and I made apologies for Darlene, who was sleeping it off. Jerry made his excuses for Rhonda, and Dyson told us that the other two girls were a little the worse for wear, and had decided to forgo dinner. I gathered from his demeanour that he was none too pleased, but we all had a good diner and took our time over it, and then after drinks and coffee, we drifted back to our rooms. Next morning after breakfast, as our luggage was being loaded into the limos I paid for our stay and checked us out, and then we were driven back to Avalon, and the limos pulled up next to the jet, which was already to go.

We arrived in Brisbane at midday, and made our farewells, and Dyson and I arranged that we would get together the following evening, and then he, Lyle and the girlfriends drove out of the hangar, Rhonda volunteered to drop off Darlene, and Marley on her way home, and I think some of the offer was due to her being contrite over the way she had acted the previous day, god knows what sort of telling off she was going to get from Jerry, if he hadn't already done so, but that left all of us free to drive into the office for a debriefing.

I used the hangar office phone to ring Janice at the office, and asked her to have everyone involved with deep silence in the Tac room, when we arrived, which would be in roughly twenty minutes. She told us she'd take care of it and that she'd also arrange that lunch for the four of us would be waiting in there also, I thanked her and rang off, and then the four of us started the drive into town, DJ and I in DJ's car, and Ross and Jerry in their car.

When we arrived at the office, we all headed straight to the Tac room, as we passed my office, Janice fell into step beside me and started filling me in about who was in the room beside John and Harry, McCord from the AFP was also there, and the head of the surveillance unit that were monitoring Dyson's house, and that she'd been waiting for us to arrive before having a sandwich and pastries lunch served, so I asked her to organise that and drinks, and to stay after the lunch was brought in. She veered off toward the canteen, as we continued along the hall to the TAC room, and entered.

Inside I saw the six occupied seats, and as I moved to mine, the other three fanned out and took seats on both sides of the conference table, and before sitting, I addressed them all, saying "Gentlemen thank you all for attending, while we are meeting lunch will be served very shortly, only sandwich's and so on I'm afraid, but you should all know what it's like at short notice, now for those that don't know each other in the room, in a minute we'll go around the table, and I'll get you all to introduce yourselves, and tell us how you are involved with Deep Silence, I'll start and we'll go around to the right, ok I'm …", and I told them who I was and that I was the lead investigator in the field for the operation. While all the introductions were being made Janice entered, and behind her were canteen staff that she directed, and then closed and locked the door behind them, while the food and drinks were being setup and placed by them, the introductions had stopped, and then resumed after they left, as Janice took her seat beside me on the left, and I motioned her forward, and told her what was happening, so she knew when it came to her turn.

As each person finished his introduction, they would reach for something to eat as the progression round the table continued. After it was all finished, I put down the sandwich I'd been eating, and after clearing my throat, said "Thank you all for that, now because this meeting has elements of a debriefing, and a briefing of latest developments, I'd like to return to after I ordered the raid and have my team that were with me be briefed thoroughly on what happened, so I'll pass to John and whoever he needs to call on, to bring us all up to date, John."

John told us all, that after I'd given him the task to make the raid, he'd gone up to see McCord together they worked out the different tasks to be undertaken and how many men would be required, all of this was made easier because we were able to supply floorplans from our surveillance team, and that they would be the eyes of the raid until it was carried out. Then we worked out the time of the raid and decided that it wouldn't be after dark because any traffic noise would be heard and couldn't be disguised as normal for a weekend, but we needed it to be at a tiring part of the day. So we decided on four thirty on the Saturday, because we already knew that there was a TV at the warehouse, and there was a good possibility that most of the occupants would be watching either the VFL or the League game being televised, which would provide a distraction and make our entry easier, and I'll now pass over to Jack.

McCord took up the story, after we'd made all those arrangements, we decided on the briefing time for the assault team was to be fifteen hundred Saturday afternoon, and I asked John to step up the surveillance to fully operational standing that morning, but I later learned he had stepped it up from the Friday night, so I'll pass to Tim. Tim was the senior surveillance agent in charge of that operation, he told us, he had been in the communication van which was a block away from the target site when one of his men that were ringed around the building keeping the exits monitored, left his partner in the car while he went to relieve himself. Whilst doing this spotted a way onto the roof of the building, so he took it on himself to check it out, and found that the roof was unguarded, and that the skylight was in such a position if a camera was mounted through it the whole of the interior was visible, as soon as he got back to the car with his partner, he called me over the radio, and told me what he'd discovered. I went to check his report, taking a transmitting camera with me in case we could mount it. The agent led me to the roof, and we found a place to secure the camera, and I also thought it would be an ideal entry point.

With that thought in mind, we tested the panel, it was unsecured, and moved noiselessly, quite frankly I couldn't believe our luck, after climbing down I thanked the agent, and went back to the van to see if the camera was working, and sure enough it was, and

I couldn't wait to morning, when I reported all this to our boss. John then took up the story again.

As soon as Tim informed me, I got onto Jack and let him know, and he told me he'd be in the office an hour later, so during the time I waited, I got onto Harry, and we decided that it was about time that he knew where we were located, and so I collected him at his office and brought him down here. McCord interrupted saying, "I got the biggest surprise of my life, you've been right under my bloody nose this entire time, no wonder you could get to my office so quickly!" John took up the story where he left off, I brought him into the Tac room and I contacted Tim, and He told what he'd found, and also patched the camera feed to the Tac room monitors, and then Jack asked Tim for more detail on the skylight as a means of entry while we watched what was taking place in the warehouse. Between us we made the decision to leave our ASIS agents to cover all the exits during the raid, and that the assault team comprised of AFP officers would enter via the skylight. It was also agreed that the surveillance team would listen to the briefing via radio, and that I'd arrange that with Tim, and then I escorted Jack back to his office where I would meet him and his team just prior to the briefing, now I'll pass over to Tim again.

Tim told us after hearing from John, about his team being the exit guards, and therefore they would be included in the briefing, he decided to have one man from each car come to the van, for a briefing, and then they would pass on what was told to them to their partners, and also that all his teams had radios that would be listening to the briefing at three o'clock.

Jack now continued, and told us about the briefing he gave his and our people, John had made it possible for his officers to see the camera feed in their briefing room, and had our agents all tied in via radio, the raid was timed for sixteen thirty, and entry would be via a roof skylight. All other entries and exits were manned by armed ASIS agents, thirty officers would make entry, in three waves of ten. First ten to enter would be vulnerable and were to be covered at all times by the third wave officers. Once everything was secured the main entry would be opened to allow access to all our field agents and vehicles, and the prisoners removed to the federal police watch house for processing, each member of the assault team had to be in full combat gear with flak jackets.

As Jack continued, he now told us of the actual onsite decisions and how the raid was brought to a successful outcome. After arriving onsite with John at the surveillance van which was going to be used as a mobile command post. Tim showed the assault team commander the best place to have his men positioned to gain access to the roof on a street map, and then they went in on foot to have a good look. At sixteen hundred the main assault force arrived and the commander went with them to the staging area, and then each man made his way to the roof silently, while four officers removed the skylight panel slowly and quietly, and took it out of the way, anchors were set for the ten abseiling ropes, and then the first wave of ten buckled themselves to the lines that would payout as they lowered themselves down into the warehouse. John and myself were able to see what was happening because while Tim and the assault commander had been on the roof they had sighted another camera that gave view to what was happening on the roof, and once the commander radioed in that everything was ready to go, I waited for the allotted time before I gave the go order.

We watched as the first wave went down, and there was no opposition, the same for the second wave, and eventually all thirty officers were inside without the opposition knowing of their presence, we nabbed all but two of them in watching the football, the other were in the toilet, and grabbed as they came out, all in all the prefect arrest scenario, and without one shot being fired! Once the prisoners were taken away, we cordoned off the entrances and had all our people move into the warehouse. Then an inventory of the weapons was taken, and Tiger it looks as if they hadn't put anything away since you visited them, we compared them to the list you gave us and the stolen guns from the army, and apart from a dozen handguns and two rifles, we've recovered the lot. So I would like to thank all the ASIS personnel that have been involved with this investigation and recovery, thank you all.

After Jack had been applauded for his accounting of events, I looked at John and asked "Anything further to mention about the raid?" John smiled, and replied "Yes, just to say that after our people left the site and we got back here I sent a message to your satellite phone giving you the advice." I looked around the table, and at the same time, said "Yes I got the message, thank you John, and also I'd like to thank Jack McCord for the cooperation that we've received from the AFP, and congratulations on a job well done to everyone. Now it's our turn to bring you up to date with events of our weekend."

Before I continued, I took a sip of coffee that Janice had poured for me, "Now once you've heard what we have to say, every one of us here will have to make a decision, and because Ross and Jerry weren't involved in what DJ and I were doing over the weekend we won't hear from them, unless they have anything to say," and looking at each of them they shook their heads, and then I spent the next hour going over what we did from start to finish. Then I called on DJ for his input, and apart from saying that everything I'd said was backed up by his report he went over a matter that I'd omitted, and told them that he'd been able to tape most of the conversations that we'd had with the underworld elements while in Melbourne. So I told them that there would be transcripts available of the conversations at a later time, for those that were interested, and naturally Jack McCord's hand went up.

After they'd had time to process what they'd been told, I said "Now it's that time when we have to make a decision, we've successfully recovered the stolen weapon shipment, and uncovered quite an extensive crime ring that's been operating right under our noses. We've also gained access into information we never would otherwise have had, but I think as the field agent running this operation, now we've gained as much as we're likely to, apart from interrogation after arrest, so I'm making a recommendation that we proceed no further except to arrest the main players, and close down Operation Deep Silence. I'll take a vote around the table, yes for close them down, which will make a significant difference to the organised crime along the whole eastern seaboard, or no, which will mean we continue to suck as much intelligence out of it as we can, if we haven't already done so, my vote is to close them down now!"

CHAPTER 14

Well as the vote went around the table each agent and department head voted I guess on my summation, and the effective cost of what more could be gained, and as the vote reached McCord, he said "I'll abstain from the vote, due to the fact that it is more to do with your own in house observations, you've all gone far above the brief that I asked for, but I'll be ready to offer whatever assistance you require." So as the vote moved on, the result was a direct result of the time that had already been spent on the operation since its start which was coming up to almost a year, and trust they all had in my leadership, it was unanimous in closing down the operation.

So we discussed how to take down the two ringleaders, and considering the fact that I'd made an appointment with them for the following night, this seemed the perfect opportunity to take them down, so I looked at McCord and asked "Jack how would you like some more fish to fry in your cells, and can you have a raiding party available to back my agent's tomorrow night?" He smiled, as he replied "You have no idea of how much pleasure that would give me, you let me know the details, and I invite you to brief your team and mine in our briefing room upstairs if you would like." I smiled and answered, by saying "Done deal Jack, I'll give you all the details tomorrow, now then considering we've taken up most of the day, I'm going to adjourn this meeting for my staff until tomorrow morning, Ross, you and Jerry are exempted, but for the rest we'll resume at zero nine hundred, Jack I'll talk to you later tomorrow once everything is sorted, thank you all, go and get some rest."

As everyone shuffled out of the Tac room, John volunteered to escort McCord from our headquarters, Janice and DJ remained until I was ready to move, but before I did, I told Janice that I'd be in at the normal time, and DJ was told that there was no need for him to pick me up in the morning, as I would drive in my own car, then we left the Tac room, and DJ and I headed home.

During dinner that night with Darlene, an argument ensued of her own making, after the fact that I'd let her be driven home as if she'd been dismissed, and I'd spent the whole day at work, instead of coming home with her, and then she said "You spend more time working than you do with me, it's like when we first met, with you being in the army, and working as a spy as well." Then she came to a halt mid-sentence, and then continued "That's it, isn't it you're still playing at being a spy, but against who, I have no idea."

Then her mind really started to wake up! She continued "Unless it's against Trevor, which makes me one of your targets as well, is that, it? You've never loved me at all! I'm just a convenience, a show thing, just like those pieces of jewellery you've given me over the time we've been married for my birthday and Christmas, shit you're an arsehole."

I had to put her off track, but I was fuming, so as I replied I got up and stood over her at the table, as I shouted back at her "As for me being back in the spying game, forget it, I have enough shit to deal with, without that sort of crap, and as for me not loving you, well I have to agree with that one, how could someone love somebody who doesn't even know how to behave properly in the public eye, you can't even be trusted to be able to behave at closed affairs like parties and BBQ's where people know you, let alone those that don't, and as far as being a convenience is concerned, that goes both ways, you may be able to hold up your end in bed, and sometimes cook a reasonable meal, but you use me as your own private bank, I need this, I need that, and you're always pushing me to retire to a comfortable life, that wouldn't last, because of the way you go through money! Christ's sake, I've had enough of this shit, I'm going to sleep at the office!"

She burst out crying, which I ignored, as I went into the bedroom, grabbed my go bag and packed some clothes into it, and reached for my keys, as I passed the kitchen where she was still crying, and continued downstairs into the garage, and hopped into the work sedan, and triggered the door remote before starting it up, and reversing out. I had just made the office carpark in town, when my Sat phone rang, and as I looked at the number that was calling, which was my home phone, I ignored it and let it ring out. After putting my go bag into the bedroom, I took my jacket off and hung it up, and then settled at my desk with a drink, and relaxed as I went over the reports sitting on my desk, and after a few more drinks I had a shower and went to bed.

I was awoken by sounds of movement in my office, and I quickly put on a pair of shorts that were handy, because of course I sleep naked, I grabbed my gun and cautiously made my way into my office. I relaxed as soon as I saw Janice filling the water jug, and leaned against the door jamb, however as Janice turned and caught sight of someone, she nearly jumped out of her skin, as she jumped and screamed, so I put my gun into the back of my shorts, and went to help her up from where she'd collapsed in a heap, as three agents burst into my office with guns drawn, I quickly raised my arms up, and identified myself to them.

They helped me get Janice on her feet, and we sat her on my lounge couch, and then I dismissed them before I gave her some water to drink, she asked what had happened, and I told her that it was my fault, but she'd fainted as she caught sight of me in the bedroom doorway, and then I apologised for forgetting to leave her a note saying that I was there, and told her to stay and recover as long as she liked, I was going to have a shower and get dressed, before we both went to the canteen for breakfast.

After a shower, shave and dressed in clean clothes, I re-entered my office, Janice wasn't in there, so I made my way to her office and found her at her desk, and after apologising once more, I enquired how she was, and she told me she'd recovered alright, and that it was her turn to apologise for being that silly, and I told her that it was nonsense, she'd got an unexpected fright, so I was buying breakfast and she was to join me without any buts. In the canteen, I had a well-cooked breakfast, while she settled for just coffee and raisin toast.

Back in my office we went through our usual ritual of going over everything during the day over a cup of coffee, and once all the routine business had been caught up, she left me to contemplate and plan the arrests that would take place that night. During my mental planning, I decided I required a whiteboard to draw the floor plan of inside Dyson's house, as I passed her desk on the way to the TAC room, I asked her to get DJ to join me when he arrived, and told her where I'd be.

When he arrived, I was working on the office level floorplan, and asked him to have a look to see if I'd missed anything. He told me that it all pretty much as it was, and then we discussed how we'd make entry, I told him I was thinking that it would be a soft approach, because we were already expected anyway, and we'd be taking them by surprise, but it would pay to be on the safe side, and have a couple agents with us out of sight of the door until we take care of Lyle, and have four quietly force entry through the garage, once we were in. Just he told me that it sounded good, the door opened, and everyone else trooped in.

As we all took our seats, I looked toward Tim, and asked "How's things with your surveillance team on the house?" He told us that everything was normal, and that there hadn't been too much business chatter, but everything was being recorded anyway. I nodded and replied "Ok, but don't forget to let that team know that we'll take them down tonight, so they go onto step up status at fifteen hundred." He smiled and nodded replying "All in hand boss." And I smiled.

Then I got up from my seat and moved to the whiteboard that I'd positioned near the end of the table, and said "This gentlemen, is the floorplan of Dyson's house, and this is the plan I've come up with...", and I told them what I had in mind, and that the key target was getting to his computer, we needed to get hold of it intact, so that would be one of the priorities of the team going in the garage. Then we worked out the required manpower, and that John would

168

join Tim and would be second in command onsite, and the assault team command would be mine. We also would have a full briefing for all personnel involved at fifteen hundred, Harry brought up the point of what we would do with the prisoners, and I told them that I'd arrange with McCord to have a couple officers available to take them to the AFP cells, and then the meeting broke up to resume as a briefing later that day.

Back in my office, I rang McCord, and asked to see him, and I was told that he was free at the moment and to go on up, so hung up the phone and went up to his office. I was shown into his office as soon as I arrived, and Jack and I sat down to talk. I told him that I was planning on taking down Dyson that night, and that I'd be happy if he could provide some officers to take the prisoners to the AFP cells, he smiled and rubbed his hands in glee, saying "No problem, they'll be available to your onsite commander, do you mind if I sit in on the briefing?" I smiled and told him he was more than welcome, and told him to be at the lift at quarter to three, and I'd send someone to escort him down.

On my way back, as I walked through the carpark, I spotted John at the entrance having a smoke, so taking out my pack I joined him saying, "Mind if I join you?" He gave a sigh of relief, as I lit up, and said "I'm glad that you're here I was waiting for you, something urgent has come up, it's come in from the surveillance unit, and I really think you better listen to it, we've got a bit of a spanner in the works, and some re-thinking maybe required." So I threw down my smoke, and ground it out with my shoe, and then we both headed for the lift, and as we went down we stopped on his floor, and we went to his office, where a tape player was sitting on the desk with a set of headphones, and he told me go ahead and listen, passing the headphones, I think you better listen to this yourself, and besides I've already heard it, it came in about half an hour ago.

The recording was of Dyson and Darlene having a conversation in the lounge of his place, and he obviously was giving her a drink to calm down to calm her down, as he came into voice range, I heard him saying, "Come into the lounge and sit down, here that should calm you down." I heard ice tinkling in a glass.

I hit the pause button and asked John, "Who else has heard this?" He replied "Only the surveillance team of two, me and now you," I nodded, and then hit the play button. I heard Dyson ask "Now what's your problem Darlene, what's wrong?" Her reply was, "That frigging husband of mine, I should have known better." I heard him say, "Oh come on, what has he done, it can't be that bad." She said, "Well I had a go at him the other night, about giving me a dressing down in Melbourne because we got drunk while shopping." Dyson laughed and replied "Well good on him I did the same with Jane; you were all pretty pissed when you got back, and a tad embarrassing."

Darlene said, "Well, ok maybe, but he really lost it after I had a go at him about being away all the time, and told him it just like he was in the army and being a spy again." Dyson replied "Wait a minute, did you say he was a spy?" *I groaned and thought, that's stuffed it,* as I waited for the tape to give me the reply, she said "Yeah well he used to be in the army, and this sort of super unit, where he'd be overseas, and then back in Australia, and then he'd have to go back overseas again and do some spying, or exercises, and of course it didn't help he always went back to Western Australia where he was based, instead of coming here, until he transferred into a company in Brisbane, but then he quit, and he hasn't said why, but said something about being discharged for something he'd done, he never really talks to me about it, but he used to."

I closed my eyes and put myself in Dyson's place, and figured that if alarm bells weren't ringing in his head, he was a fool, but I continued listening to the tape without saying anything, and then came Dyson's voice saying, "Well we both know that he used to be in the army, and that's where he got his start in what he's doing now, sorry it's only toasted sandwiches, but let me get you another drink, and you can tell me what's troubling you." She replied with a mouthful of food, "Umm, their nice, well after we had this barney the other night, he stormed off saying that he was going to sleep at the office, and I haven't seen him since, and he won't answer his Sat phone either, if I knew where his office was I'd go and see him to say that I was sorry, but I don't even know where it is." And she started to cry again, but at the same time took a slurp of a drink, from then on Dyson tried to get more information out of her, but thankfully she didn't know the answers, and eventually he gave up, and told her eat her lunch, and then he'd pour her another drink, and as he put another drink on the table, I heard him ask, "So how come you think Tiger is a spy?" She laughed and answered, "He told me once."

Dyson wasn't about to let that one go by and pushed her a little more, and by this time her voice was slightly slurring, so I imagined that he really been doubling the alcohol base in the drinks he'd been giving her, as he asked "What do you mean by that?" She replied, with a giggle, saying "Well it was when I found his gun for the first time, and I told him that I knew army people but they weren't allowed to carry pistols, and he told me that in his super unit everyone carried a gun, and I asked him if he was some kind of James Bond, and he told yes something like that but, better and more real, anyway you've listened to my whinging like the kind person you are, I better get home now before I'm too pissed to drive, I might get lucky, he maybe there when I get home, see ya."

There were sounds of her leaving, and then after the sound of the front door closing, I heard Dyson yell "Lyle get in here!" I heard footsteps and then Dyson's voice again, "Looks like we've got a problem, seems our friend Tiger has been playing us, he's a government spy! He and his mate are coming at seven; get hold of some of the boys, half a dozen should do and make sure they are armed, tonight we'll grab them, and see how much they know."

I was furious, and I exclaimed "Shit!" out loud without realising I'd done so, so I took off the headphones while John was looking at me, and said "My feelings exactly, now what are we going to do?" I looked at him, and replied "I'm not sure yet, I need time to think, but it's going to make the job a bit harder, our element of surprise is up the creek, Christ lucky we had the bugs in there, do you have a copy of that?" He nodded, and I said "Good, I'll take a copy with me, and thanks for the heads up John." He gave me the tape, and back on my floor, I called into DJ's office, tossed him the tape, and instructed him to listen to it, and then come into my office, then I continued to my office, and made a cuppa before sitting back at my desk just to relieve the tension I felt, hoping it would relax me a bit, at least enough for me to come up with a counterplan.

As I slowly sipped my drink, my thoughts were slowly starting to focus on the job at hand, as I ran jumbled scenarios through my brain, by the time my coffee was finished, my thoughts were starting to cooperate, as I started piecing a plan together. *What if I take two from the garage team to reinforce DJ and me? No that won't work, I need four to handle that effectively. Could just the four of us take twice as many considering the first thing to happen would be DJ and I would be disarmed, unless we have backup weapons. What if they search us after we're disarmed? No, we definitely need two more agents for the front door; now how do I keep the door lock from operating properly, think I need to talk to Harry.*

I was about to ring Harry as DJ walked in, and sat opposite me, he raised his eyebrows as he looked at me, and said "Well that's put the cat among the pigeons, I know you won't scrub the mission tonight, so I'm guessing that you've got something up your sleeve." I nodded and told him I was working on something, but to give me a minute while I talked to Harry. After speaking with Harry he said he had just the thing, and he'd bring it down to the briefing, and also the tool for opening the garage quickly and quietly. Then I turned to DJ, saying "Now we've got a decision to make, whether we just go with four at the door, or do we make it six, because don't forget we'll now be expected to hand over our guns, if we knew they weren't going to search us, that would be fine, all we'd have to do was have backups elsewhere, but that's

172

something we're not going to be certain about, any ideas?"

He smiled, and suggested that I start packing a knife, as well as my gun, so I opened my desk drawer and pulled out my bush-master, his eyes bugged out, and he whistled as he saw it, and said "Well that's definitely a knife, but a bit too big for what I had in mind, here try mine." He pulled his from the back of his shirt, it was about eight inches long, and flat with no blade guard, and the blade itself was double sided with razor sharp edges and tapered to a point, it was light and made for throwing, I flipped it a couple of times and then threw it at the corkboard on the wall, that had Dyson's picture on it, and I'd aimed at the nose, and that's where the knife struck, I was impressed and I let DJ know it. Then he suggested "Boss you and I are about the same shirt size, and I've got a couple spares in my office, and each one has a knife in the sewn in sheath, what do you think?"

I smiled and told him that could solve the problem, because the last time Lyle searched you he didn't find it, so we'd go with it and keep the assault force the way we planned it in the beginning, DJ went to his office to get me a spare shirt, and when he came back he hung it of the coat rack, and I told him I had a call to make but would see him in the canteen for a belated lunch before the briefing.

The call I made was to Darlene at home, and she sounded quite pissed, and I asked her if she was going to be home that night, and she slurred that she would be, and I told her that I was seeing Dyson earlier in the night and that our business may take some time, but I'd be home after that, even if it was late. Then I went and joined DJ, for a late lunch, and then after that we both headed for the Tac room, but I made a side trip to Janice and told her where we'd be, and that she was to attend the briefing at the same time as everyone else.

At fifteen hundred, everyone filed into the TAC room, and I started the briefing, by saying, "Ok gentlemen and lady, we're all here to end Operation Deep Silence, and this is the culmina-tion of nearly a year's work, some of you already took part in part one of the operation that recovered the weapons stolen from the army, that was a great job, and I'd like to add my personal thanks to John and his whole team, and because he did such a good job you have to put up with him again as my 2IC tonight. Who will be running things from the surveillance van, I won't be on air and neither will my partner DJ, for reasons that will become obvious during this briefing, now there are to be two assault teams, team one will consist of me and DJ, and two assault agents, team two will be four assault agents. Team one, our job is to go in the front, now DJ and I are expected at the address, but we also expect that our primary weapons will be taken from us, due to the fact they now know were intelligence agents."

I let the murmurs, muttering, and comments run around the room before I started to continue, "So as you're all aware DJ and I are going to be in a very precarious position, now the two assault agents in team one, you need to have silenced weapons, and any action will be conducted in close, so no theatrics with having rifles or assault weapons please, pistols and subs will suffice. As DJ and I go into the premises, we will attach something to the front door that will stop it from closing, and a minute after we're inside you make your entry, now because of the situation DJ and I will be in you need to get into the lounge area ASAP, so no screwing around shoot to kill anyone in your way with getting to us. Team two, you will insert two minutes before team one heads to the front door, you will be provided with the implement to allow you to force the garage door quietly, again anything you do is to be quiet, now you have two objectives, one is to recover the computer in the downstairs office intact! That takes priority over your second objective, which is to make your way up the interior staircase, and be ready to backup team one, and if I can make it blunt, save our sorry arses." This allowed some of the tension in the room to dissipate as laughter accompanied my last comment, and I let it continue for a little bit before speaking again and rapped the whiteboard with a pointer, which was my old swagger stick from the army, the noise ceased abruptly, as I rapped it, before I said "Come on people we've got a lot to get through.

Team one; this is the interior layout of the floor we'll be on. Team two, this is the downstairs floorplan, now I don't care if you're a man down when you are ready to backup team one, as long as that computer gets to our Technical division head in one piece, and speaking of Harry, he'll now take over and give us instruction in the tools he's come up with to aid teams one and two on their entry into the premises, but before I give him the floor, are there any questions?" There were none, and Harry made his way to the end of the table, and he was carrying an odd looking device, which he placed on the table, and then pulled something out of his pocket that he put down beside the weird looking item.

After he explained the workings to us, it really was quite simple, and the ones DJ and I were to use were just simply a case of slipping them over the door striker, they were magnetic and would stay in place, but would for all intents and purposes the door would feel and act as if it was secure. The weird item going to team two was also a simple device that slipped in against the locking catch at each side of the door, and would release the catch, but the only problem was that he only had one, and that would have to be passed from one side to the other while maintaining pressure on the garage door, but not enough to send it flying up when the other side was released. John as 2IC was next, and he gave everyone the radio frequencies for the man to man comm's and also all the others that were going to be used, and told whoever in team two, was bringing out the computer that it had to go to the van, and he made sure everyone was aware of where it was stationed, also because DJ and I weren't wearing any comm's, and would for all intentions would not know what was happening with the strike teams, we would be wearing our transmitting pen mic's but that would only be heard in the van, so sign language was a must between the other members of the strike detail and DJ and I.

Then I introduced McCord, and he told us that he would have a couple of unmarked cars in the vicinity, ready to take any prisoners, and that he would be in the van with John should anybody need him. After he was finished I resumed the floor, and then gave the threat assessment. When I told them the numbers we were facing, the assault force commander raised his hand with a query, "Sir, how do you know that we will be facing those numbers?" I smiled, and replied "Because we've had the place bugged for months, and it's also how we found out that the targets now know that DJ and I are involved with law enforcement, and that number of opposition was the latest, as of two thirty."

Jack McCord then made the comment, "I better get you some more cars and officers then." This was treated with mirth as laughter and smiles went around the room. Continuing, I said "Alright now the assault teams, except for DJ and me, all in your black combat gear, and flak jackets, I want everyone to go home tonight without a scratch, so take extreme care out there tonight, that's all thank you, oh and the debriefing will be tomorrow with your own department heads, and again take care out there."

After I finished there was a lot of talking in minor groups, as the leaders moved to the device that was team two's and the floorplans on the whiteboard. Jack came up to me, and told me he could only give me two more cars and four more AFP officers, I smiled and told him that if we ran out of room, some of them could sit on each other's laps, and he burst laughing, and said "Yeah, I'd expect that from you, you're a mean man Tiger, but I certainly like you and your thinking, I'll be off and I'll see you tonight." As he walked off towards the door, I motioned Janice to go with him to see him out; she nodded her understanding and joined McCord near the door.

Alright, now came the worst part, after the final briefing and the getting onsite was that time that had to be killed in between, and this is where a lot of people tended to get nervous and let fear seep into their thoughts, but because I'd been in this position numerous times, I just went ahead doing my normal thing, and as the time passed I'd done paperwork, had a shower and got dressed for the evening's entertainment, and taken my time having a nice and filling dinner.

CHAPTER 15

At eighteen thirty everyone was in position, our first call was to the van, and Tim had taken charge, and told us that even though the team stepped up their activity, there was no way to know how many were in the house, except from what chatter had been picked up from the bugs, however Dyson and Thomas had been spending a lot of time in the office, and we were able to gather that while Dyson and Thomas were going over some names, that apart from them, there were six more in the house, two near the front, two on the deck, and two in the lounge, just then Dyson's voice came over a speaker saying, "That was an excellent dinner Lyle, but I suppose we'd better go up to the lounge, and get ready for our guests, there that's shut down you can turn the lights out on the way up, I think all our entertainment will be in the lounge tonight."

I looked at Tim, and asked "How long before team two moves?" and he told me five minutes, and then I told everyone that DJ and I would do a blockie, and arrive just after they went in. once team two were in, they were to wait five minutes before doing anything, to allow DJ and I time to be taken inside. As we reached the house and parked out front, I scanned the area and located the other two agents in my team, and as DJ and I walked past them to the front door, I gave a thumbs up, and then DJ pressed the doorbell.

Lyle answered the door smiling, and as entered, brushed my hand against the doorjamb and slipped the magnet into place, there were two men in the middle of the hall holding weapons pointed at us, from behind us Lyle's voice said, "Tonight we have a change in plan boys, please hand over your guns, and that way there'll be no unpleasantness, not yet anyway." Lyle stepped forward to take our guns, and then as we followed him the other two brought up the rear, as we went into the lounge room, near the lounge and chairs, Lyle said "That will do, stay put and if either of you move, these men have instructions to shoot," and as he finished saying that, Dyson came inside from the balcony, and muttered "Well, well if it isn't my two favourite federal agents, separate them please."

As he moved into the room and took a seat in one of the armchairs, DJ was moved to the end of the couch where Lyle was sitting with a smile, he gave a signal and we were both forced to our knees, as Dyson spoke again "Well Tiger, I'll bet you're wondering how I know that you and your mate are cops, well I had a very interesting chat with your wife today, or should I say widow?"

Playing for time, I looked at him, laughed and said "Trevor, are you out of your mind? What the hell are you talking about? Come on you really think we're cops, Jesus, what shit did that stupid Darlene tell you?

He got up and picked up my gun from the coffee table, where Lyle had placed both of our weapons, and as he picked it up, he smiled and replied "Well to tell you the truth I was a bit dubious, but one thing she said sort of convinced me of what she was saying, that you admitted to her that you were a spy, and don't tell me I'm out of my mind!" During his last comment, his voice got louder and he swung his arm at my head, my gun which he was holding cracked into the side of my head, and I fell on my right side, seeing stars for a while, and then I shook my head, looked around, and levered myself up again, and my voice took on its usual menacing tone, as I warned "You're going to regret that you did that asshole!"

During the time I looked around, I had noticed that the two thugs at the hallway, were white faced, and slowly stepping back into the hallway proper, which meant that the other two agents in my team were in, and were taking those two out of play, so now I needed everyone distracted, and looking in my direction, so I continued threatening Dyson, saying "When we get out of this, I'm going to make your life unbearable, you piece of shit!" Again

Dyson swung and my head was cracked again with my own gun, on the opposite side this time, and with the stars still flashing in my eyes, I got myself upright again, stared at him, saying "Do that again, and I'll rip your frigging arm off!"

Finally, I'd seen what I'd been waiting for, team two were on the internal stairs and ready to assist, and I knew the other two agents of my team were ready, so with my head now clear, I asked "Do you really think DJ and myself are going to take this lying down Dyson?" This was the signal to let DJ know to get ready for action. Angrily Dyson swung at me again, but this time I avoided the pistol whipping by leaning backward slightly, but I grabbed his hand and pulled him toward me as my right hand pulled the knife from its sheath, and sliced his arm, which resulted in him dropping my gun on the floor in front of me, and as he screamed, I flipped the knife and threw it into the chest of one of the thugs standing guard. During this time DJ had gone into action, and smashed Lyle in the face, as he reached for the other pistol, the last guard went to point his gun at me but was shot by the leader of team two, and Dyson tried to make a run for it, but I sprang toward him after picking up my gun, and as I reached him I hit him in the head with my gun, that gave off a resounding whack.

I smiled with satisfaction, he was completely knocked out, as I looked around all the guards had been taken care of, and DJ subdued Lyle with a cracker of a punch to the nose, who sat sullenly with blood dripping from his nose, and his hands secured with a zip tie, I asked if everyone was alright, and they were, all except for the opposition, four of the guards were bound, two were wounded, one of which was the one I'd thrown the knife into and the other was nursing a shoulder wound, both would require hospitalisation. Then I moved and spoke directly into the bug, "Ok we got them all, but we'll need ambulances, for two wounded thugs, and the Feds can move in please."

As I looked around again, Dyson was starting to come to, so I went and bent over him as I secured his wrists behind his back with a zip tie, and said "I told you, you'd regret hitting me, hope you've got a nice headache, you, sad piece of shit." As I rolled him over and dragged him to the couch by his collar, and then I went and retrieved DJ's knife from the one I'd thrown it into, and after wiping the blood off it, I replaced it into the sheath in my shirt, as I heard distant sirens approaching, and John and McCord came into the lounge, and looked around at the scene. I went over and knelt in front of Dyson, and asked him for the safe combination, he glared at me and remained silent, until I grabbed him, and applied pressure just below his right ear, and I kept applying more and more pressure until he screamed, and blurted out what I wanted to know, telling DJ that he wasn't to leave 'til I came back, I went down to the office and opened the safe, inside it was roughly a hundred grand in cash, and paperwork, that hopefully would be incriminating, so I went to the bottom of the steps and asked for two bags, they were thrown down to me, I put the money in one and the documents in the other which would be looked over by the feds for any useful data.

When I got back upstairs the scene had undergone a change, the wounded had been removed, and the feds were taking all the rest of the prisoners outside, so I motioned DJ to bring Dyson over, and we escorted him to one of the vehicles, and waited for one of the feds to put him inside, as he was being placed inside, I smiled, saying "I'll be seeing you in a couple of days Trevor," as he sat sullenly glaring at me. Then I put the bag of money into the car, before going back inside. One of the team medics cleaned up the dried blood and cuts on my head, as McCord told us he'd have a forensics team at the house in the morning going over everything, and if anything turned up he'd let us know, I nodded and DJ passed over the documents to him as I told him I'd left the safe open for them.

I told McCord that I'd probably want to talk to Dyson in a day or two, and he nodded, and said "Yeah I can arrange that, but I'll need some charge to hold him on, that doesn't entitle him to a lawyer, can you think of one?" I smiled, saying "I'm not sure if this is right, but with anyone charged with treason in some manner, you can hold for thirty days without the right to a solicitor." He burst out laughing, and replied "Yep you're right." So I smiled, and said "In that case charge him and Lyle Thomas with Conspiracy to Commit Treason and Conspiracy to Murder, namely me and DJ." McCord smiled and said "Done."

After that I had a quick word with John, and told him the location of the bugs, telling him that I didn't want them left for the feds to find, and that he needed to collect them before leaving, and to clear the place of any of our personnel, and that no debriefing would be required and to pass along my thanks to the men. Then DJ and I headed for home, I told him along the way that he was to drive in by himself in the morning, because I was going to drive my car, I also told him to bring the cash into my office when he got in next day. When he dropped me off, I went up the front stairs and let myself in, and as I went into the lounge Darlene stood up, and was shocked at my appearance, and asked "Good lord what happened to you?"

The headache I had was really starting to take hold now, from the cracks to my skull, so I wasn't in a really good mood, and her comment was just enough to spark my rage. I grabbed her loosely by the throat and backed her up to the wall, and at the same time I took my gun out, and stuck it under her nose, as I answered her question, "You is what happened to me, I was almost killed tonight because of you and your big mouth, you told Dyson that I was a spy, you bloody stupid bitch, whatever possessed you to tell him that, unluckily for you I survived, and he's been arrested for attempted murder, and you should thank your lucky stars that you won't be joining him on a conspiracy charge."

Then I let her go, her face had gone white, and she stood there frozen, not knowing what to say, so I continued "Now this is what is going to happen, you and I as a couple are through, I will be moving my stuff out of here bit by bit, and you can keep the house, I will start divorce proceedings after twelve months of not living together, and you had better sign the papers when you get them, now I'm giving you the house, so you have no further claim on me, try it, or if you don't sign the divorce papers, you will have me hunting you down, and I will kill you, understand? Good, tonight you can sleep in one of the other rooms, now get out of my sight!"

She rushed off out of the lounge room with tears streaming down her face, and I went into the kitchen, grabbed four Panadol out of the packet, and went downstairs to the bar, and poured out a good measure of scotch to help me swallow the pills, and then sipped on a second glass, letting the liquor sooth away the stress, I thought about having a spa, but decided against it, and had a long hot shower in my ensuite instead, before going to bed.

Next morning, after driving into office, while Janice and I were going through our morning ritual, DJ arrived and excused himself, as he placed the bag of cash on my desk and left, Janice's eyebrows raised in question, and I told her it was all the cash from Dyson's safe and she asked if I wanted it counted into the safe and I shook my head saying that I'd take care of it later. I also told her to make note of the date, and to inform me three months prior to, and on this date the following year, in case I couldn't get my divorce approved before then. While I was telling her this I recalled something I'd have to do, and so after we were finished with the routine business, I made a call to Lisa.

Before I had a chance to tell her anything other than it was me, she told me she'd been waiting for me to contact her, but because her news was so important she needed to see me as soon as I could arrange it, so I told her I'd get out there that day probably in the early afternoon, so I decided not to say anything until I saw her later, and I wondered how she'd take the news that I'd be moving into the house. So I made a mental note to go out after lunch if there wasn't anything else that required urgent attention.

After Lisa greeted me outside we went into the office and I sat down at her desk as she made us a cuppa. Then she came and sat down, and was jumpy, really hesitant about what she wanted to say. So I told her to just blurt it out and not bother beating around the bush. She smiled and told me that I was a darling, and that she didn't want to leave me in the lurch, but she had decided to move in with Reg. So everything could be sorted out before the wedding, but she would still come over and work if I needed her, but it would mean no one would be actually living there, and that thought worried her. I laughed and then told her what had happened between Darlene and I, and I was going to be moving into the house anyway, and that's why I'd rang her earlier to tell that, and then I asked if she would still be doing the cleaning, and after she informed me she would, she told me that she only had to put some things into her car, because most of her stuff, she and Reg had moved bit by bit. We arranged that she turn up three days a week, and if she wasn't cleaning, there would be office work.

Things started to settle down a bit after the end of Operation Deep Silence, Dyson did end up letting the feds know everything about the organization he'd built up in return for a more lenient punishment which ended up being thirty years with a non-parole period of twenty. I moved my stuff from one house to the other, and I sold my mustang to Janice, so it was still in the family so to speak, and I used the company sedan. Every now and then I would make the time to sell a policy, but the truth was I was bored with it; there was no challenge, one Friday during a sales meeting I asked Rick Welsh about this selling my agency thing that had been mentioned. As it turned out I could sell off my society number and agency, which meant that whoever bought it took over the retention fund, and the client list and any referrals that had been made, and he advised me that if I was thinking of doing that, my agency because of the amount of business that I'd written would be worth well over a quarter of a million. That both shocked me, and gave me food for thought. For some time, I'd been toying with the idea of giving it up and doing something that really interested me.

The next morning, instead of going into the office, I went to a dive store in Alderley that I used to pass on the way to work, and I talked with the owner and his wife, Mark and Mary Penny, and it was decided that I would pay for dive courses all the way to

Assistant Instructor, and I would work in the shop with them, and learn the dive business, and Mark would prepare me as much as he could to become an Instructor, and because I wasn't being paid for my services, I could have as much time off during the week that I might need, unless I was assisting Mark with a course.

Once everything was settled I left, and I drove to the Newmarket Insurance office, and the agent that had asked me about my agency was in, so I went to see him to ask what he was prepared to pay for my agency, and after we worked what he wanted, which included all my referrals and contacts, my client roll, and my goodwill, he was willing to pay me six hundred thousand, in six increments of one hundred thousand each month, and if one of the payments was missed, the sale was considered null and void, and any payments made were non-refundable. I agreed to the deal, and the paperwork was drawn up, as Shirley signed as a witness, and he handed me a cheque for one hundred thousand, and I was to give him everything included in the deal, as soon as the cheque cleared into my account, with special clearance I would be taking him everything on the Friday when the monthly commissions were distributed.

That following Friday, I took in everything, and because I hadn't written any business for the last two weeks of the month previous, I received my last commission cheque from the society for sixty two thousand, so all in all I had plenty of money at my disposal, and if it really was required could live off my weekly government pay, and if I didn't have that, I could survive for at least four years before I'd need to get a paying job, so I was sitting fairly pretty financially, and that didn't take into account that a further five hundred thousand was yet to make its way into my bank account.

During August of nineteen eighty-five, I took a month off from work, so that I could attend my dive instructor evaluation course on the sunshine coast, and if we the candidates passed the evaluation there could be another dozen diving instructors working in the industry. Mark had booked my place on the course, and hadn't told me who the course director would be, or anything else like who would be the examiner, so when I arrived at the hotel that everyone on the course was booked into, the day earlier, I was surprised to run into my old mate from Jordan, Colin Cloud, he was with his girlfriend Sharon and someone else who he introduced as Robert Ballzinger.

When we all having dinner together that evening, Colin asked what I was doing there, and so I told him what was happening, and asked him if he knew anything about the course director, Rob sat with a smile on his face as I was told that Colin knew the course director really well and half way through Colin's description that the course director was tough but fair at times, Rob burst out laughing, and told me not to be taken in by Colin's bullshit, because Colin was the course director. "You shit," I said, and then everyone was laughing, and Rob told me he was doing the same course, and asked how I knew Colin, and so we did some reminiscing about our time in Israel and Jordon, Sharon told me that she'd heard from Monique shortly after I left Cairo, saying how much she missed me. I laughed and told Sharon that if Monique ever came to visit, she was quite welcome to look me up. Once dinner was over Colin and Sharon was going to head home after a couple of drinks, and when they departed Robert and I decided to call it a night, and as we went to our rooms, we found out they were beside each other. The next morning over breakfast Rob and I made a pact to help each other as much as possible during the course, and that was the start of a friendship that has lasted for years, and still endures to this day. During that day most of the others on the course filtered into the hotel, some I knew, and some Robert knew, but we never let on we knew the course director.

After the two week course learning how to become Instructors, that was followed by a three-day Instructor Examiner course, and was presided over by an instructor examiner from the dive association, and in our case the examiner was the only female examiner in Australia. I had been warned not to try any charm on her by most of the guys under examination, but Sharon had quietly told me Narelle was getting over a divorce, so even though I didn't try to win with her by using charm. We had a few discussions together that did end up being a little on the personal side, and she discovered how smart and capable I really was. She remarked to Colin that I would be a very good instructor, and asked if he knew anything about me, and as part of her staff he was obligated to tell her what he knew of me, and after hearing what he told her, she'd remarked that I was a person she'd like to get to know, all of this was passed onto me and Robert at dinner one night, when Colin sat with us, but it was to be kept under wraps that he'd told us.

Robert and I passed the course along with all the others except one who failed, and I finished as top of the course with the highest marks, and that night at dinner Narelle and I ended up talking well into the night after all the others had left, but we didn't go to bed together. Next morning, she left to go to the airport to catch her flight south, so Colin drove her, after we'd said our goodbye's to her Colin and Sharon, and then Robert and I said our goodbyes, with the intention of getting together at a later date.

The following day I was back in the office feeling rather pleased with myself, as Janice and I went through our usual routine, during the department head meeting there was nothing new on the agenda, and only one more operation that was in full swing, but Tim's surveillance people were on top of that, so the meeting only lasted an hour, and afterwards I returned to my office, and just as I sat down the phone rang, and it was John Callaway in Sydney, and he sounded a little hesitant, as he said "I really hate to tell you this Tom, but we've just received word from Campbell Barracks at Swanbourne, it seems that corporals Jensen and Lawrence, and Sergeant Ellis, have all been killed in two separate training incidents, I've already been in contact with the Air Force, and Ross can fly into Pearce, you can take as much time as you like just leave somebody competent in charge 'til you get back." I thanked him for what he'd done, and then hung up, and I immediately phoned the Swanbourne barracks and spoke to the Headquarters CO and found out when the funerals were to be, and informed him that I would be attending, and he said he'd arrange my accommodation.

I asked Janice to get hold of Ross for me, as I went through into DJ's office, and told him that I was heading to Western Australia in the jet for the funerals, and he would be in charge of our department while I was away, and that I would be gone probably about a week. While I was in his office the phone rang, and he passed it to me, Janice told me she had Ross on the line, and I asked her to patch him through, as he came on the line he asked "Are we going somewhere Tiger," and I told him we would leave for WA at eighteen hundred, and we were cleared to land at Pearce and to pack for a week away and that I'd see him and Jerry at the hangar that evening.

DJ took me home after that, and told me he'd pick me up at five to run me to the hangar. Inside I took my time packing my go bag, and placed in it a couple of sets of cams, my dress shoes, a beret, and my cap, my dress uniform I placed in a suit bag that could be hung up, and I took out another set of cams, and my combat pistol holster which I would strap in place on my thigh after I got dressed, and I left these ready to put on later. Then I went into the lounge and poured myself a drink, added some ice, and then sat down to do some internal commiserating. As I thought, *I recalled all the names and the faces of, Pep Salter, who'd been one of my real friends he was lucky, he went down in action, Snagger Brown, Sparks Riley both disabled in combat, Gecko Martin and his entire family, Tag Wilson, Buzz Tyrell, all killed in useless car accidents, and now, Wires Ellis, Lizard Lawrence, and JJ Jensen killed in training accidents, and the woman that would have been my wife, killed in a hail of gunfire by an Arab terrorist instead of me.*

I smiled as I recalled we'd all played with fire, and I wondered was this to be my curse, my fate, my divine retribution, to watch everyone I care about die around me, to be the last man standing? Then I remembered I wasn't the last one, Dumper was still around. So I recalled all their faces again into a group, and raised my glass in a salute and toast to all my now absent friends, and I wondered if I was the catalyst that enacted change into their lives, would they still have died if I hadn't come into their lives? What would have happened to me without having had them in my life? I smiled wryly as I considered the variables that life throws at each and every one of us, and then wondered that age old question, what is the meaning of life? Then I laughed out loud as my mind instantly gave me the answer forty-seven, as I had recently finished reading The Hitch Hiker's Guide to the Galaxy, for those of you that haven't read it, a super computer worked for a billion years to arrive at that answer.

An hour passed before I shook myself out of my maudlin state, I got up and put the bottle away, had a shower, and got myself dressed and ready to go. After having breakfast at the airbase, a car and driver was assigned to me, and I was driven to Swanbourne, I dismissed the driver outside the headquarters building, and stood staring at the rock, which was the monument to every soldier that had died whilst with the regiment, and I noticed that the three new names had been added already, before going into the building.

The funerals were conducted at the same time, the only other person that I recognised at the funerals was Mark Ryan who had flown in that morning, and was due to fly out again that night, so after the services we got together in the mess and reminisced, I told him that Dumper was away in a war zone when I tried to contact him, but that I'd hear from him sooner or later when he got back to England. Mark nodded and then asked what I was up to, and after I told him he laughed about it, saying "So they got you to be a spook after all?" I laughed with him as I agreed.

CHAPTER 16

Well for the next few days after the funerals, I really wasn't too much of a happy camper, so I stayed away from the dive shop, and concentrated on work, and slowly I returned to my normal self. I was in my office one morning looking over the completion report of another drug operation that had been shut down in the wide bay area, when the phone rang and Janice told me that John Callaway was on the line, and as he came on the line he asked me to switch the phone through the scrambler, these had been installed two weeks earlier into every state office, I did as was instructed, and then Callaway came on the line again, asking "Tiger how are you?"

I knew with that greeting, that something was going on, and replied "Fine, now how about getting to the point." He laughed and said, "You know that problem we had on your first assignment, about a possibility of a mole, well there was, and it has been dealt with, but the person in question not only had ties with the CIA but with someone else as well, now the person she had other loyalty ties with will be told to you by the boss when he gets up there, because he wants you to take care of this one, so I won't say anymore, or than to expect him soon."

Well, well, well, so we're going to get a visit from the head honcho, better make sure this place is ship shape, I thought. As I reached for the phone intercom button, and asked Janice to come in, and when she was seated I informed her about the visit we were going to get from Colin Gorman. I told her that I needed her to get the word out to everyone, that he was coming, and to make sure that the place was tidy, and would withstand an inspection, she told me that she knew what had to be done, and she'd get onto it and so I left it in her hands. After she left my office I phoned John and Harry respectively and told them about the visit, they were grateful, and said they'd put things into place should there be an inspection of the whole building.

Two days later, the boss Colin Gorman the Director of Special Services Department of the Foreign Office the head of ASIS, walked into my office behind Janice at ten, I immediately stood up and we shook hands, and sat opposite me, while Janice asked if she should bring coffee, he smiled and told her yes, and to shut the door on the way out. I'd only met Gorman once before and that was when I first joined ASIS, he took my oath of service, as I looked at him, he did the same, and he smiled.

He stated "Well Tiger, it seems you've been making quite a name for yourself since I first saw you, and I hate to tell you, but you don't look as young as you did anymore. However, I can tell you you're not the only one, it seems as if it's in a Head of Department's job description, must have something to do with what we do I guess."

We both laughed, and then Janice knocked on the door, and brought in a mobile tray that had a small urn of percolated coffee, milk, sugar, and a tray of biscuits and Danishes, and with a quick glance at me left the office. Catching the glance, I gave a quick nod of approval, as the Director poured the coffee asking how I had it, and having told him, he stated "Ah a man that likes the taste of his coffee, good for you, but I haven't been weaned yet, and I'm definitely not sweet enough." I laughed and filed the information of how he took his coffee in my mental useless information file.

After our morning tea break, not one to mince words, he said "Tom I've got a job for you, and I think you're one of a very few that could possibly pull this off!" I stared at him, and said "Sounds interesting, go ahead and continue boss." He looked at me, and said "This may interest you for two reasons, one it involves the mole that was recently detected for passing along some of our information to her countries intelligence organizations, oh didn't you know she was originally born in the US, and that's how they got to her, but before that she had formed an alliance with my predecessor, who I've been informed sent you on a hairy assed

191

mission that I'm sure will come back and bite us in the future, and at the time that happened, I've also been reliably informed that you weren't particularly too taken with him even then."

He took a break, and poured another cup of coffee, before continuing "Since then he was transferred and demoted, and I assume, he wasn't too happy with that, anyway he was farmed off to our UK office, and put into a non-superior role there, now obviously he wasn't too happy with that, and started to send out feelers as to who may be interested in the intelligence that our country had been gathering, and some of it goes back to days when you were still with SAS, so needless to say he'd accumulated a massive amount of data. Once our US cousins became aware of this they have decided to step into the current auction of this information, because a lot of it concerned them, but as luck would have it, the frontrunners at present are the soviets, and as I'm sure I don't need to tell you, that would be a disaster of nearly biblical proportions, therefore he needs to be stopped, and I think you're the right man to do it."

I was already aware from the way he'd been talking as to the identity of the operative, but needed it confirmed, so I pressed the issue, saying "If I'm supposed to know who this is, can you tell me who it is, considering I'm already supposed to know him or her, sir?"

He looked at me sharply, and replied "Terry Dumthy, and he has to be stopped in giving this information over to anyone, your job will be to find all that he has, and even if that can be done, you are sanctioned to stop him by any means possible and that includes killing him, from verbally passing on that information to his so called saviours, and it has to be done quickly, do you understand?"

I instantly replied, "Yes sir, if I take the company jet we can be wheels up in an hour, so where are we heading?" He looked pointedly at me, and answered "As of when I left Sydney, he was still working in his office in London, and ASIS agents have been briefed to keep him under surveillance without alerting him to that fact, but should anything change you will be informed through our regular communication with your pilots, but at present you can assume he will still be in London at our embassy there, how long before you can leave?"

Smiling, I answered "I can be out of here within twenty minutes, sir." He nodded and smiled also, saying "Good, start the ball rolling." So I nodded and flipped the intercom switch, saying "Janice get in here please." As my office door opened, I was opening the safe, and told her over my shoulder to get onto Ross and Jerry, and tell them we were headed to England in a hurry, and to pack for a week or so, wheels up as soon as I got there, before she scurried off, Gorman told her that he was in town for the week and would be at the Crest International should he be needed. I took roughly one hundred thousand out of the safe and put into my wallet and go bag, that was in my personal quarters, and then I unlocked the guns cabinet, and pulled out my Uzi for long work, and my Ingram for close quarters, my go bag was already packed with clothes for several days, so I only had to add my toiletries and shaving gear to go in plus ammo, the suit I was wearing already had my passport in the jacket pocket from the desk drawer, and so ten minutes after being given the go order, I was walking out of the office, and as I passed DJ's office called, "You're in charge 'til I get back!"

Twenty minutes later, I pulled into the hangar at the airport, to find the jet already humming, and the boarding ladder in place, so I parked my car, grabbed my go bag and weapons, and made my way up into the jet, as soon as I was inside the stairs moved away and Jerry was closing the door.

As he cross locked it, I said, "I'll talk to you both when we're in the air," he nodded and headed for the cockpit leaving the intervening door open. After the rush of getting airborne and climbing to our cruising altitude, I made my way forward to the cockpit, and sat in the unoccupied engineer's seat, and talked to both Ross and Jerry.

I told them that the mission was to catch up with an agent,

and dispose of him prior to him getting to his handlers in Russia, and so if things didn't go well in England, we may end up flying all over Europe in pursuit, so the jet had to be ready to move at any minute, so apart from normal radio traffic, they needed to keep monitoring the company frequency for any updates as to the target's whereabouts, then I enquired about the route we were taking, and was told that first stop would be Singapore, and then a possible refuel in Bahrain, or straight into Gatwick, dependent on headwinds, I nodded and then made my way back to my office, and stretched out on the couch for a snooze.

The intercom came on about an hour out of Singapore, with Ross saying that there was a radio message from the agency coming in in code. So I made my way into the cockpit and Ross glanced at me and nodded towards Jerry who was intensely focused listening, and busily writing on a pad on his knee, when he was finished he reread the message back to whoever was on the radio, and then, he nodded and acknowledged, turned around to me and handed me the coded message.

After I'd decoded the message sitting at the engineer's station, I sat and read it before making any decision, it read "Target has made a run for it by flying to Oslo, luckily had agent following, target and shadow are booked on ship destination Riga, eta Riga port three days, agent will meet you at Port customs hall." *"Bugger, he couldn't wait till we got there could he*, I thought, and then after consulting a map, and doing some mental calculating, asked "Ross if we only refuelled at Singapore, could we make it to St Petersburg in Russia, and would you guys be able to do that without a break?"

He told me that as far as him and Jerry and the flying, that was ok, because if need be one of them could sleep, without needing the other in the cockpit, unless something drastic happened, and they both looked at me with smiles, and I told them that it was just my luck to be landed with a pair of comedians, and we all laughed, before Ross told me that if we did a quick refuel at Ataturk airport in Istanbul, Turkey, we'd have no problems.

We'd land at Pulkovo airport St. Petersburg without any problem. I considered this before making a decision, but the majority factor that could help was the fact that we had a High Commission in St. Petersburg, and therefore I could get assistance from them as to regard a car and so on. So I instructed Ross to make the necessary changes to our flight plan when we landed at Singapore Changi airport, and then drafted a reply to the message, and asked for assistance from the Commission in St. Petersburg, and then after coding it passed it to Jerry for transmission.

The reply came after we were in the air again, after refuelling and making our flight changes with air traffic control at Changi that would be passed onward, Jerry passed me the reply as we levelled out at our new cruising height, and I decoded it, the message read "Roger all previous, require to know what flight number you are using, for ground agents at St. Petersburg." So I asked Ross for the flight number we were using and an ETA into Polkovo. I wrote all of this information into my reply, coded it and then passed it back to Jerry, who started transmitting it.

Then went back into the galley and made something to eat, and while that was cooking I chose a video to play, and watched it while I ate, I had thought that the first Rambo movie was reasonable, but this second one, well let's just say, I knew it to be bullshit, and I got quite a few laughs as it played. Then I replaced it with 'Back to the Future' which wasn't all that bad, if you prescribed to that sort of science fiction. Soon after that I settled down to sleep once more, and was only woken by our descent into Ataturk. Whilst we were on the ground, as well as the refuelling I arranged for more provisioning, so that we had plenty to eat and drink on board, and after three hours on the ground, we were in the air on the last leg of our journey into Russia.

After all the immigration business had been taken care of, with our commission representative present, and arrangements made for a hangar and refuelling for the jet, our escort from the High Commission office helped smuggle my weapons into the car that was at my disposal from the plane, and then after he informed me it was only an hour's drive to Riga, I decided to follow his car that had Ross and Jerry as passengers to the hotel where we were all booked in, I had tonight and then next day before the ship carrying my target docked in Riga, so I took full advantage of the rest prior to going to work the next day by driving to Riga. I must say I was surprised by the hotel; Russia wasn't as bad as I thought, and the hotel would easily hold a four-star rating anywhere else.

The next morning, I took my time getting up, before going down to the restaurant for breakfast, and again took my time and had a relaxed breakfast, before going back to my room, and getting ready for my drive to Riga that day.

I hadn't spotted Ross or Jerry before I left, and decided not to disturb them, that'd probably be worn out by the air time we'd racked up without a real break for either of them, so I left them to relax, while I went about what I had to do. The High Commission staff had provided a map with the best route marked on it, and notations as to where border crossings were, and other blow ups of streets and places in both cities, and it was easy for me to navigate to whichever road I needed, because the road signs were in English, as well as Russian, but it gave me the opportunity to update and practise my Russian, by speaking out the directions.

I drove towards Pskov, and crossed the border into Latvia soon after, and then into Riga, the trip had only taken me an hour, even with the stop at the border, I found a fairly decent hotel, and booked in, and went to my room. Then I went out again to reconnoitre the port customs building, and ascertain the ship's arrival time, which was at eleven the next morning, and then with nothing better to do I returned to the hotel, and went into the bar area for some drinks.

After breakfast the next morning I checked out, and made my way to the port, and I went into the hire car agency beside the customs building, and made enquiries to see if Dumthy had any car booked, by flirting with the blonde receptionist, and it turned out that he did, and it was the one nearest the gate a light blue Zill.

After arranging to meet the woman later that night at the bar she'd told me about, which of course wasn't going to happen, I left the rental agency, and after going to the gear in my car, retrieved a silent tracking beacon, turned it on, and as I passed near the car Dumthy would be using, I had to retie my shoelace, and while I was doing that I secured the tracker to the vehicle.

Inside the customs building, I lounged about like the other people waiting, and then I spotted Dumthy walk through the foyer, so I turned side on, just in case he spotted me, and remembered what I looked like, and then I spotted his tail, our agent, so I approached him, and whispered in his ear, as we both moved to the front window of the foyer, and as he filled me in on what had taken place on board, I watched Dumthy go into the rental agency. Then I told our agent that he should go get some rest that I would take over now, we shook hands and he made his way out of the building.

Where he was going to go I had no idea, his part of the job was over, and as I watched him walk toward the city centre, I waited for Dumthy to come out of the rental office, which he did five minutes later heading toward the car I was told was his. Now that his vehicle was confirmed, I breathed a sigh of relieve, and made my way out of the building and to my car. I followed Dumthy's Zill out of the city, and let him gain some distance from me, I had a tracker on the car, and I didn't want him to know he was being followed. At the border station he was pulling away as I reached it, with a car in between us. Again I had no problems at the border, and pulled away slowly, the tracking signal had stopped near the centre of Pskov, and as I passed Dumthy's car I spotted him in a store buying groceries, I pulled over a block further on where I could watch his car in the wing mirror.

Soon after I saw him climb into the car again, and drive in my direction, so I hunched down in the seat as he passed, and then slowly started the car, and followed about a kilometre back. Then according to the receiver he had slowed down so I did the same, as I drove past a side road, the signal started to fade, so I

197

surmised he'd turned off down the side road, so did a U turn and took the side road, a little further on I passed another smaller road that had a sign post, and again the signal started to fade, and so after another U turn I approached the road slowly, it looked like a driveway track to a cabin so I looked at the sign, and it said Perskovic, I looked at the map, and there was no town of that name, but I knew the name from somewhere.

The tracker had stopped, so I had time to search my memory, and then I had it, Dmitri Perskovic, he was a high echelon domestic KGB officer in Moscow! *Shit, I'd better have a quick look around, and hope like hell they're not meeting yet,* I thought. So I looked for a place to stash the car with some sort of cover, and I was able to drive under some foliage near the side of the road that almost obscured the car completely. I quickly changed into a pair of cams, and strapped both pistol holsters to my thighs, grabbed my Uzi, and made my way alongside the track in the bushes, sure enough about four hundred yards down the track, it ended at a double storey cottage, and I saw Dumthy's Zill parked outside, but no other vehicle. Needing to know the layout and whether there was anybody else there, I moved slowly and silently around the cottage, looking in the windows and doors. The bottom area didn't have any bedrooms, so I assumed the internal stairs in the front room led to possibly two bedrooms upstairs, given the size of the cottage.

I returned to the car, and changed into the set of black cams, strapped on my guns again, and lay along the back seat, and settled down to snooze until it got dark. I was thankful that we nearing the end of the year, because that meant winter in Russia, and therefore it got dark quite early, I moved silently from the car at seven pm and by then it was really dark, and I slowly made my way to the cottage, I saw Dumthy in one of the armchairs in the lounge room, and he was drinking vodka, and judging by the level of the bottle, quite a bit.

Moving toward the rear of the cottage, I was able to force the back door without any noise, and I silently moved into the cottage shutting the door behind me. The only light that was on was the one in the lounge, and from my earlier turn around the house, I'd noticed that he'd at least got a fire going in the fireplace, so the only light was from those two sources. As I crept down the hall toward the lounge, I saw the switch for the lounge light on the opposite side of the hall from where I was, so I took as step to the other side and inched my left hand toward the switch, but as I flipped the switch to off the light went out, but at almost the same time if felt a sharp sting on my wrist, and the PHUT of a silenced weapon.

Ignoring the pain in my left wrist I immediately sprung catlike into the lounge, and fired my silenced pistol, my shot took him in the right arm, which resulted in him dropping his gun, so I swiftly moved forward and swung my gun against his head, and he went down unconscious. By the time he woke he was arms were tied to the arms of the chair, and his feet tied together, the light was back on, but I'd drawn the curtains, and I was looking in disgust at his gun, and my left wrist, luckily he'd used only a twenty-two calibre, otherwise my watch would not have stopped the bullet going through my wrist, however my altimeter watch that I'd been given years before for topping my HALO course was completely destroyed, I was not a happy camper!

As Dumthy opened his eyes, I said "You owe me a new watch, that was special, and I've had it a long time." He stared at me and enquired "Who are you?" So I smiled realising I still had my balaclava on, so I took it off, and asked if that was any better, to which he replied "You look familiar, but I can't place you." I said to him, "No I guess not, I was younger when you sent me on a mission to a certain country in Africa," With that his face went white as he looked around the room, and his voice held a tremor in it, as he said "Davis, surely you're not alone, I suppose the rest of your murderous team are outside, I suppose you've been sent to take me back to face a charge of treason."

I stared at him for a while before I replied, to his query "No as a matter of fact most of them are dead, and yes I am alone, but as for taking you back, no I don't think so, I'm only after the information and files you copied, so be a good boy and tell where they are."

He started laughing, and said "Well what are you going to do with me? You can't arrest me, and if you kill me you won't get what they want. I sat down opposite him, and looked into his eyes, as I replied "Hmm, if I was still with SAS, you're right I couldn't arrest you, but you see I now work for ASIS, and you know what that means. Now let me give you some advice, next time use a bigger gun, you see if I was to shoot you in the knee with this, it wouldn't do much damage, however if I shoot you with this one, it would destroy every bone in your knee, you'd never walk properly again." I'd lifted up first his gun, and then mine, and as I spoke his face had gone completely white, and he'd started sweating.

Then he must have summoned some bravado because he looked at me, saying "You wouldn't do that, you're one of those decent types that require a reason to do things, you can't do anything cold bloodedly." He started laughing, but his laughter turned into shrieks of pain as my silenced weapon went off, and tore through his right knee, as I said "Oops, sorry." After his screams died down, I told him in the deadliest tone I could muster that I would shoot him in every joint in his body until he told me where the stuff I wanted was, and to add emphasis to my statement I put pressure onto his knee, which resulted in further screaming, but also where the stuff was, he'd been clever and transferred everything to microdot, so after retrieving the dots, I went back into the lounge.

Sitting opposite him again, he answered the question I'd asked by telling me that no one was coming for him, he was supposed to drive to the Kremlin the following day and present himself. I nodded and got up again, as he asked "Are you going to kill me?" I shook my head, and replied "I was going to but the KGB doesn't have much time for people that can't deliver what they promise, so I'm going to leave you to them."

I turned away from him, but kept my pistol in my hand, and moved toward the door as I heard muffled thump, and the scape of his gun being picked up from the table where I'd left it. I swung around and fired as I saw the gun pointed in my direction. My shot went into the centre of his forehead, and he was thrown back against the chair with the force of the bullet striking.

I continued to and out the door, and this time I walked all the way up the driveway to my car, took the time to change again, and then headed the rest of the way into St. Petersburg and pulled up at the hotel. I'd hidden the Uzi and Ingram again and the Colt was in my go bag that I grabbed from the back before the car was taken away and parked, while I went up to my room, and after showering I went to bed, and drifted off to sleep almost straight away.

Next morning, I joined Ross and Jerry for breakfast, and told them that the mission had been completed, and we could leave whenever they wished. Ross thought this over and he and Jerry had a discussion on the best way home, and it was decided the way we'd come was the best way back, so they would leave for the airport at two, and get the plane ready, and I could meet them at three for take-off. They would take the car with the weapons and transfer them to the jet, and I told them I'd make my own way to the airport.

After we parted I went out to do some sightseeing while I was there, and had a lovely time just wandering around, I had lunch out, but was back at the hotel by two, had a shower and got ready to go, and then rang the High Commission, they would send a car and a spare driver to collect me and transport me to the airport, and pick up the other car. At fifteen zero five local time we said goodbye to Pulkovo airport and St. Petersburg.

CHAPTER 17

When we got to cruising height, I moved into the cockpit, and as Jerry flipped on the auto pilot, they both looked around at me, as I told them not to worry about calling the agency and reporting the mission over, unless they contacted us. Then I filled them in on what I had in mind for the trip back, saying "How about we stay in Istanbul for a couple of nights, and do some sightseeing, and then fly to Singa's during the day we leave, and we'll overnight there as well." They were both smiling and were nodding in the affirmative, so I continued saying "Good, ok it'll be your job Jerry to get us three suites booked at the Hyatt, while we're in the air and to have them send a limo to pick us up at Ataturk, book them under my name, and I'll be picking up the tab guys, but now I'm going back to watch a movie." With that I left the cockpit and made my way back to the main lounge, and picked up the latest James Bond video, A View to a Kill and placed it in the player.

Jerry came through from the cockpit half an hour later to say that the hotel and transport was arranged; I smiled and gave him the thumbs up, and continued watching the movie. We landed at Ataturk airport at eighteen hundred, and after having made all the arrangements for refuelling and a hangar, and the customs procedures, we got into the limo a half hour later, and were driven to the hotel, and after checking in, our luggage was taken to our rooms as we went into have dinner. Over the relaxed meal it was agreed that we'd head for Singapore the day after next at nine in the morning, and I told them that I'd arrange the hotel in Singa's and transport from Changi airport. After dinner we had a few drinks, and then headed up to our suites.

After breakfast the next day, I took off to do some sightseeing of the city buildings, markets and bazaars, and I also took a trip along the Bosporus river that split the city, I was tempted to take a fast boat up to the black sea, but decided that it would take too long, as it was I didn't get back to the hotel until after dark, and ended up going straight into the restaurant for dinner.

Both pilots were already at a table, so I joined them and over pre-dinner drinks we swapped stories of where we'd gone for the day, they both seemed pleased at the bargains they'd gotten in the grand bazaar, and were taking home Turkish jewellery and silks, and Ross told me he'd also bought a carpet, Jerry piped in saying "You should have seen us trying to get it back here, one in front and one behind, Christ talk about comedy routines."

After taking a drink he continued, "And that smartass concierge took it off us when we got here and told us he would make sure it was tied properly and ready to transport when we were ready to take it, now why hadn't we thought of that in the first place?" I was laughing as the story unfolded, and Ross grumbled as he told me I wouldn't have been laughing, if I'd been in the bazaar, he wasn't sure how many people they knocked over carrying the stupid thing. After dinner we arranged for an early breakfast, and headed to our rooms after arranging to meet at breakfast at seven.

Before I went to bed I had a long soothing hot bath, and woke really refreshed the next morning. I had a quick shower and chose the clothes I was going to wear from my go bag, and then took it, and left the room. I dropped my bag with the concierge, and went into breakfast. Then I checked us out as the boys loaded the limo; however, I wasn't too happy with sharing the seat with a six-foot wide carpet, even if it was rolled up and tied. On the jet the carpet was placed in the aisle near the entrance to my office and secured there, and after going through the customs and immigration criteria, we were in the air at eight fifty-five.

The stopover in Singapore went well and instead of flying on the following day, we ended up going out to Sentosa and having some fun in the water park, and we flew that evening just prior to midnight, which had us arrive back into Australia at zero eight hundred, and after going through the customs and immigration clearing, I had Ross drive me into town. On the way in I said to him, "You know you're damned lucky that the customs guys ignored that carpet of yours, I hope Jenny appreciates it, and the trouble you went through to get it." He started laughing, and said "She'd bloody better or she won't get lucky tonight, or get the bloody jewellery and silk dresses I got her." "You're such a smoothie Ross," I answered and started laughing as well.

In the office, I had Janice place a call through to Gorman, and when he came on the line we transferred to the scrambler, and he enquired "Well how did it go?" I replied "You pointed me at a target, with carte blanche in the way of control, suffice to say I have the information in my possession and will send it to you via internal mail, the target has been eliminated, and no trace can be traced back to us, I will send you a copy of the full written report with the information, and I would appreciate it if this office has an operation going that requires funding, that request is not overlooked." He replied "I understand what you're asking, and it will be acted on, and thank you Tiger."

After the call I started writing up the mission report, and when it was finished I gave it to Janice to type up and file, with a copy to me, that I would send to Gorman through our internal mail system, and then I went to lunch.

Janice and I had our usual catch up session after we'd both had lunch, while I was waiting for her to finish her lunch I went ahead and read the report she'd typed, then signed it and put it into one of the internal mail envelopes dabbed some hot wax across the seal and marked it 'eyes only' only on Gorman's office address. After the catch up session, because everything was progressing well with all ongoing operations, I announce to her that I was having a couple of weeks off, but would be available on the Sat phone, and as I told her she was in charge, which really wasn't the case, but she knew what I meant, it was at her discretion whether I was contacted or not should something go wrong. Then leaving her to it I drove home.

The next day I went into the dive shop see what was happening, and then went into the back area to catch up on any of the servicing requirements that needed doing ASAP. During this time, I was earning a reputation as being one of the best repairers and service technicians of Scuba Equipment in Brisbane. The dive shop I was working for as an instructor had its own boat, so most of the time when teaching the open water sessions, I would also skipper the boat, (having obtained my boating qualifications years earlier).

Upon reflection the mid to late 1980's was a very volatile time for dive shop operators and this proved to be the case with the shop I was working for, luckily I was starting to see the writing on the wall, due to under capitalizing over expansion, and decided to look around for another job elsewhere *in other words get out before everything went under (pun intended)*.

I had started hearing rumours of this small outfit down the road that were going to be doing some radical things within the dive industry, this went along with my way of thinking, so I decided to go see them first.

I walked into what was an old car yard, you know the sort of set up: plenty of open space at the front on the main road with a little office at the back. I remember thinking *that there's no way this could be a dive operation, or if it was it would have to be a dodgy one,* and I almost walked off, but just as I was going to walk away, someone came out of the office and asked if they could help me. Well in for a penny in for a pound, I asked if the boss was around, the reply was that he would back in a tick and I could come in and wait if I wished, so I did.

The first room was full of dive posters and had a set of dive gear assembled on an air tank, in a corner, while I was looking at this, the door slid open and heard a voice say: "Just can't keep the riff raff out of here can you guys!" I looked up to see my mate Robert Ballzinger standing there laughing, and as it turned out it was him that I'd been waiting for, after initial introductions all around, Rob and I went outside to talk. I filled him in on what I was doing, and he told me all about the operation, and how the company was still looking for investors, and as I filed this information for later, he asked me "How much notice do you have to give before you come and work with me? Two weeks later we started working together for the first of many times.

Once I started work, Rob showed me the outline marks of the training pool that was going to be built, and I asked what was holding things up, and he told me that money coming from the biggest investor hadn't come through yet, so I asked "Ok, how much is it going to take to get the work started?" After we went over the ideas and plans I reckoned that if I put in half a million in cash, the work could start, and I would become a shareholder in the company, the way I thought of it was, I was securing my job, and it was agreed that I would become the service manager.

As the end of the year fast approached, *have you ever noticed that? As the months go by in a year, the last three months seem to fly by, it's as if the year picks up speed as it goes downhill,* we were only conducting three operations, and they were in the far north, one each in Townsville and Cairns which had us investigating a link between people doing contract work in PNG and flying into Australia on leave, it was believed by Customs that somehow some of them were smuggling in gold from the PNG mines.

The other one was on Thursday Island, and concerned the trafficking of weapons to agitators on Bougainville, from Australia; this operation had some drawbacks when we were first asked to investigate. Mainly because Thursday Island inhabitants are either aboriginal or Torres Strait islanders, the number of whites on the island would have been six at most, which were medical and police staff, so sending a couple of Caucasian agents there would have been as tantamount to hanging a sign around their necks saying "I'm a Federal Agent, tell me what you know," as if that was going to happen.

Initially the request had been made to headquarters, and they had passed it to us because we were the closest state office, luckily someone with some brains had figured out that we didn't have any aboriginal agents to do the job, and had sent us one agent from

Western Australia, and the other from Sydney that would team up, and handle the investigation, but that operation was just in its initial stage, and so I was expecting anything for at least the first three months.

At this particular time period ASIS like most government agencies was predominately staffed with white personnel, and to come across an agent of other ethnic backgrounds was rare and far between. However, over the years this issue has been addressed and now like other government agencies we have multicultural staffing. Anyway getting back to what I was saying before I transgressed, we were moving into the period of the year that we referred to as the dead zone, which was the period between the start of December through to the end of January, and we called it the dead zone because nothing of any importance took place during this period, theoretically we could have all gone a two-month holiday.

During this time, I was grateful for being in the dead zone, because work at the new dive complex was pushing ahead, plus the dive courses and trips we were running were filling up in numbers from repeat clients as well as new people and referrals from other clients. All of the instructional staff were all scheduled for back to back trips away due to our policy of conducting the open water dives, up where the diving was great the great barrier reef, and we had charter boats in Gladstone that we used, and the second trip I was rostered for was with a newer boat that was based in Bundaberg. So it was also my job to assess the new operator, and introduce him to our usual dive sights in the Capricorn bunker group of the reef, and because this trip was a ten day one it meant that I'd also need to do a lot of entertaining, because we would be away over the Christmas new year period, not that I was averse to that, because I wouldn't have been spending Christmas with anyone anyway.

Prior to that trip however, I took part in a combined course that involved all of the instructional staff and dive masters we had available where we were going to be based on Masthead Island for two weeks with a school camp from one of the gold coast colleges, so that the students could complete their open water dives. Everyone was bused to Gladstone and we went aboard the boat the school had chartered for the trip, once at the island, all the equipment was taken ashore along with all the food and drinks required for the stay. All of the company personnel were housed in one of the three huts available, the second one was for the school support staff that had organised the trip, and the third hut was the kitchen, the students were all to sleep in tents for the duration of the stay. I must confess even though we had enough staff, all of us were in the water most of the days, and it did get a bit exhausting after ten days of solid dive teaching and examining, but in the end all the students passed and we spent the last day on the island issuing the dive certificates to everyone. When we arrived back in Brisbane, I only had a days' break in which to prepare for the following trip, so I made sure I had enough smokes and booze for after hour activities. That evening my dive master and I loaded up the company coach with our gear, and all the paperwork, I had in my briefcase that was beside the driver's seat.

I had six open water students, two advanced diver students on the trip, but two of the open water students were going to be doing the advance course after they'd finished the basic open water, and I had four others that were already certified but doing the trip for the diving. Only two of the students on the open water and the two advanced were mine, the other students had done their pool sessions and theory with one of our other Instructors. As Evan my dive master and I waited for people to arrive to catch the bus we chatted and smoked while we discussed the fact that we were away for Christmas and New Year's Eve, and we decided to include a night dive for New Year's Eve prior to midnight, and after the dive we'd party.

The first person to arrive really took my eye, as I watched her get out of her car, a little yellow Mazda 323, she lifted the boot, and then came over to us, and said "Hi, I'm Dawn Young, I thought I'd be late so I came here after leaving work, and I wondered if there was somewhere I could get changed, I don't particularly want to travel in my work uniform." I laughed and replied "Well hello Dawn, I'm Tom and I'll be running the trip, this is Evan the dive master, sure come with me and I'll open the office and you can change in there." I passed the clipboard with all the passenger names to Evan, and showed her the way to the office and she grabbed one of her bags from the car as she passed it, I unlocked the office door and waited until she was finished changing. When she came out again, I decided that she definitely look better in civilian attire than her nursing uniform, not that she didn't look good in that either, and as I moved to the coach after her, I looked a little closer at her, she was the same height as me, or maybe an inch shorter, had brown eyes and hair, she had a nice figure, and every time I looked in her direction, I would find her looking my way.

Eventually everyone else arrived, and the gear loaded, and as I started the coach, I turned on the intercom, and then drove out of the yard on our trip north, as I drove I introduced myself and Evan, and told them that I was the instructor for the courses, and that if they needed anything while we were on board the boat to see me or Evan, and where we would be boarding, and to settle back and enjoy the trip.

There was going to only one stop on the way north, and that was going to be at the twenty-four hour service station at south Maryborough, while we were stopped there, Dawn hadn't stirred from her sleep, so I decided not to disturb her until we got to where we were going, and then went and had a coffee and toasted sandwich. When we got to Bundaberg, I followed the mud map Robert had given me, and we pulled up in a lighted yard, just under the bridge on the northern side of the river, I parked the coach as close to the jetty as I could, and then after everyone else had gotten off, I went and woke Dawn, who said, "I'm sorry, I must have dozed off ten night shifts followed by a day one kills you."

I laughed, and said "Well you'll be able to go back to sleep once we get you on board." As I gave her a hand up and escorted her to her luggage, Evan had already taken my stuff on board, so I grabbed her gear for her and walked her down onto the jetty, and aboard the boat, her dive bag I left on deck, and I carried her other bag below to her cabin for her, her cabin I noted was across the hall from mine, and as I put her bag on the bed for her, she gave me a kiss on the cheek, and said "Thank you, you're so sweet." Back up on deck I checked where my dive gear was and then shook hands with the skipper, Joe, his wife Valéry who was the cook, and the deckhand Paul, I introduced Evan and myself, and after a discussion of where Joe was to head for with the boat which was named SeeWah, I went back to the coach and locked it up. Then I stayed with Joe in the wheelhouse as he glided up the Burnett to the open ocean, and he invited me to take over skippering the boat anytime I wished, and I told him that during the trip there was no doubt that I would take him up on his offer, but at present I was going to get some much needed sleep, so when we got to the open ocean, I said my goodnights, and went down to my cabin.

Next morning, I woke with the feel of the boat slowing, and so getting into a pair of swimmers, and taking a sleeveless shirt with me, went up to the wheelhouse, as I walked in I noticed Paul down near the bow, and Joe was concentrating on the sounder, I looked around saw where I wanted to be, and asked to take over, and then increased speed and moved the boat to where I wanted it, and looked at the sounder, leaned out the door, and yelled "Now" to Paul, who let the anchor drop. I pointed to our position coordinates, and said "We're right above the coral gardens here Joe, max depth is ten metres, and this is one place we use for the first two dives of an open water course." "Righto," he replied and started writing in a notebook as he looked at the coordinates.

After positioning the boat I left the wheelhouse, and went down to the back deck where Evan was getting our gear ready, after a quick check, I was happy, and told him that I was going to have some breakfast, and moved into the saloon, where Valery was ready to serve breakfast I had a plate of bacon, eggs scrambled, sausages, mushroom and a hash brown, with toast and juice, while I was eating some of the others came up, Joe came down from the wheelhouse, and apart from the generator the boat was quiet in the warm sunlight with hardly a ripple on the sea. When everyone was seated having their breakfast I announced the first dive of the day would be between nine thirty and ten, and that a briefing would be held here in the saloon at nine o'clock for all divers, even those already certified.

I was back in the saloon before nine the large table had been folded down, and Joe and Valery were in the galley doing the dishes, and I asked how they were situated for fresh fish and lobster.

I was told they had plenty of food on board, but if anyone was to catch anything, it could easily be cooked up. With a smile and a nod, I left them to it as the divers started to troop into the saloon, once they were all in the room, I stood up and started the briefing. Saying, "Well first off the first part of the briefing is for all the certified divers," and I told them where we were, and the maximum depth, and then pointed out that Evan and I would be near the anchor line with students on their first open water dive, and asked for them to be considerate. Then I pointed out areas that were great dive spots, and finished with that fact that should anybody happen to entice a coral trout or crayfish into their catch bags then Valery would be only too please to cook them up for them, and this brought some laughter from the group. As I continued telling them that we'd be spending the day here, and a second dive would be done after lunch, should anyone wish to do any snorkelling or swimming, to make sure that Evan or Paul were made aware that you're not on the boat, and to log in when back on board.

That ended the briefing for the certified divers and I told them they were free to go whenever they wished, and as they trooped out Evan came in with my teaching slate, and I proceeded to inform the students what I expected of them, and the exercises they would be performing on the bottom and said "Now what we are doing here, you've done before in the pool, and from what I've seen you all blitzed the pool sessions, after that we'll all go for a swim around in your buddy pairs with me and my buddy leading, and Evan and his buddy bringing up the tail end, any questions?" I was asked about the buddy pairing, and so with my slate I wrote the buddy assignments up as I announced them, using a reverse alphabetical format for pairings, and so my buddy for the dive was Dawn, and I told them that how we entered the water and everything we did mirrored what happens on an actual dive trip, and to take notice of all that took place, and then I said, "Ok first pair in the water at zero nine thirty, so be ready!"

Dawn approached me after the briefing, and asked "Am I ok in my bikini, or should I wear a one-piece?" I laughed and gave her a lecherous smile, saying "Oh I don't know you look bloody great as far as I'm concerned sweetheart, no seriously if you can get into your wetsuit without losing anything you'll be fine, your choice. Now I'm ready to go out and start gearing up, what about you?" She smiled and nodded her head, and joined me on the rear deck beside my dive gear, after bringing hers over beside mine.

As I assembled my dive gear, she took a keen interest, and was surprised as I only got into a one millimetre lyrca suit to ward off the chill, and after she asked about it, I explained that I was used to the water temperature, and didn't need the extra thickness of the three mill suit the students wore, and then I had her help me into my tank and BCD (Bouyancy Compensating Device).

Then it was my turn to put her gear on, once that was done we went through a buddy check to make sure everything was ok, and then gave each other the same ok signal, before moving to the entry from the boat into the water, I was the first to enter the water, and gave Evan exaggerated signals to say everything was ok. Then it was her turn, and her entry into the water was spot on perfect, as she surfaced and gave the ok signal, once everybody was in the water, we moved up to the anchor rope to slowly descend into what for the students was a whole new world.

Once on the sandy bottom, I arranged the students into a semi-circle facing me, and Evan stay at the back keep watch over them, while I signalled to each student what exercise I wanted them to perform for me, and as each student did each exercise properly, I gave them the ok signal and smiling gave them the thumbs up. Because the first exercise was to get neutrally buoyant, after they'd done all the exercises perfectly, I signalled to them that we'd have a bit of a swim around, and going over to Dawn I grabbed her left hand in my right, and we led the way, and as we made our way through the coral gardens, I would point out things of interest to everyone, and after checking my watch, from time to time, I led them all back to the anchor rope, I signalled for Evan to ascend first, and then each one of the students, one at a time after him, and as I kept watch, Dawn was the last to go, and I followed her.

After we were all back on board, I spoke over everyone, saying "Ok that was excellent guys, now break down your gear, and have the tanks ready for filling, there will be a debriefing in one hour in the saloon, make sure you have your tables and log books with you please, Evan grab the cray hook let's go for a swim." With that Evan and I went back underwater, and we started to hunt some crayfish, and after twenty minutes we went back to the boat with four decent sized crayfish, as an appetiser for lunch.

During the debriefing I asked for each student thoughts of the dive and all up the consensus was that they were overcalled, and wanted to do more, then we addressed the issue of how long we were underwater, and at what depth, and had them all work out according to the dive tables what grouping they were in, and more importantly, how long before all the excess nitrogen had left their bodies, and they were considered ok to dive again, as I went around the room to look at the written answer, they were all correct, and I told them so, and then told them how impressed I was with their skills, and got them to write up their first dive log in their books, and told them that Evan or I would sign each logbook, as the verifier.

While the debriefing had been going on Valery had cooked the crays that Evan and I had caught, and when we were finished brought the cooked meat out on a platter with thousand island sauce, and with a cheer to Valery. I told them that this was the freshest seafood they'd ever taste.

While they were all having a feed of the crayfish, I disappeared up to the bow of the boat and lit a cigarette, and relaxed in my own company, then after fifteen minutes or so, I was joined by Dawn who brought me a cup of coffee. She said "I hope you don't mind me joining you, I thought you'd like a coffee, I was told you take it black with no sugar, but I'm not sure if I heard right." I laughed and answered "You heard right Dawn my dear, black no sugar is how I take it, that way you get the flavour of the coffee without it being adulterated with all the other crap." She burst out laughing as I told her that, and then I lit another smoke.

As she saw me light up, she said "Sorry, but the nurse in me is about to come out when I say you really shouldn't be smoking you know." I laughed and said smilingly, "Well my dear it's something I've been doing for over twenty years now, and because I enjoy a smoke, that means I won't be stopping it anytime soon." She smiled and nodded, and then she asked what time we'd be diving next, and I asked her to tell me when they'd be ready, and I smiled as her answer was right, and then I told her that we wouldn't be going back into the water before two, so she could have a rest if she needed one. Again she kissed me on the cheek and thanked me, and then took my empty cup with her as she headed into the boat interior.

CHAPTER 18

Well lunch was good and then at one thirty I gave the students the briefing for the next dive, when I'd finished I then had them switch buddy pairs telling them that unless they had a permanent partner to dive with sometimes they would be assigned a dive buddy and they had to get used to that idea, so we would be swapping dive buddies each dive, all the tanks had been refilled by Joe and Paul so everything was ready for the next dive, again we geared up and made our way to and down the anchor line, and apart from them completing different exercises the second dive went pretty much the same as the first one.

After the debriefing, I told them they were able to go snorkelling or swimming or lounge around and rest, for the rest of the time the boat was stationary that day. Then I went to the wheelhouse and had a talk with Joe about where I wanted to do the next days' diving. I had decided to go to one of our sites at Bolt Reef, and that way we'd be close enough to steam overnight to Flinders Reef for a special Christmas day dive I had planned for everyone. After giving Joe the coordinates for the site at Bolt, I asked what the forecast was for the following week. He told me that it was fine weather all over the Christmas period, and asked why, so we discussed my plans to dive different parts of Flinders for the three days after our next days' diving at Bolt, and he agreed with the special dive I was planning for Christmas day, and we arranged to get together each afternoon to talk about the following days' diving.

Just before dark Joe fired up the main engines, and after the anchor was winched in, I felt the boat start to move slowly, Joe and I had calculated that we'd arrive at Bolt close to midnight, and that we'd anchor away from the reef until daylight, when we'd have better vision of the reef and bottom. So that night we had a lovely roast pork dinner as we cruised along, which was followed by a great dessert of cheesecake, custard, cream, and ice cream. During dinner I announced to everyone that I had a special surprise dive planned for Christmas day, and it was a place that not too many people knew of, and it would be my Christmas present to them.

Once dinner was finished and clean away, the bar opened and Evan bought me a drink, and I strolled out onto the back deck to light up, and soon Dawn had joined me at the rail, and asked "This dive on Christmas day will we all be able to do it, because it sounds exciting?" I smiled, and replied "Don't worry you'll be certified after tomorrow, and if you want you can be my buddy."

I took a sip of my drink, and decided to do a little flirting, and said "And if you're real lucky, I'll even hold your hand." She smiled and moved closer so that we were touching each other as we stood against the railing, and she said "I'd like that, very much," and as we looked at each other she leaned forward and gave me a light kiss on the lips, and continued saying "You really do have a wonderful lifestyle, you've got all this, and I suppose women just throw themselves at your feet and probably into your bed, no wonder your single, who'd want to give up all this."

While she'd been explain how I had such a wonderful life, I was roaring with laughter in my mind, and thought *sweetheart you have no idea of the lifestyle I lead, and you probably wouldn't want to know, Christ you'd run a mile if you really knew,* but I smiled, and answered "Well yes I suppose so, but as for being single, no I'm in the middle of a divorce at present, she couldn't hack my lifestyle, probably because I was away most of the time, and as for having females falling all over me, well I have my own set of rules for that and I don't break them."

She looked at me rather thoughtfully I assumed, and asked if I'd like another drink, and what I was drinking, as she headed inside to the bar, I lit up another smoke. When she returned, she handed me my drink, and enquired "Before I left you were going to tell me about the rules you set for yourself, and how you never break them." I smiled, laughed, and then started telling her my rules, the first being that apart from polite conversation I never got involved with a student under my care. I never took any female to bed that wasn't unattached, they had to be single or without any boyfriend even if one wasn't on a trip, and that I never took sides in any couple's arguments, and should someone tend to throw themselves at my feet, it was up to me if I took up the offer, because I might not be interested in that person, but if I did take up the offer, the other rules still applied. When I'd finished explaining that to her she laughed and looked at me quizzically and told me she thought I was a very complicated sort of person, so I laughed and agreed with her, and said, "Dawn you have no idea how complicated I am," and at my suggestion we went back inside to join the others, that were watching and making comments on the movie Blazing Saddles which was a Mel Brooks comedy about the wild west.

After a couple more drinks, sitting beside Dawn, she was starting to fall asleep with her head on my shoulder, so I woke her, and suggested that I take her down to bed, and she just nodded with a smile.

After saying my goodnights, I escorted her into her cabin, and had her lay on her bunk, and I flipped a blanket over her, turned out the light as I left her to sleep, and went into my own cabin. While I lay in my bed doing my usual nightly mental debriefing of the day, as my thoughts came around to Dawn, I smiled thinking, *Tiger that woman has designs on you, I could do far worse, she was intelligent, attractive, and only a year younger than me, and seemed to have her head screwed on properly, wonder what she's like in the sack? I guess I'm going to have to find out I think, but not until she's finished her course!*

Next morning, I woke early, and after grabbing a coffee from the galley I went and joined Joe and Val on the bridge. Joe told me that he was going to leave firing up the engines until six, which was still twenty minutes away. I glanced up at the course plotter and he'd already keyed in the coordinates for the dive site, so I nodded. Just as Joe fired up, Evan joined us as well, and Val told us that now the engines were going she'd put on an early breakfast for those of us that were up. Paul at the bow gave a thumbs up as the anchor snugged into its housing, and we started to move slowly toward the reef.

Joe positioned perfectly, and as the anchor went down, I clasped him on the shoulder as he shut down the main engines, and then all of the crew, Evan and myself, had an early breakfast. While we ate I discussed the possibility of a late lunch, explaining that if that was done I could get the last two dives for the open water students completed before lunch, just have morning tea between dives, and after lunch we could move the boat to the site at Flinders during the afternoon, and that way we'd be on station already for the morning. They all thought it was a great idea, and so it was decided we'd do that, after breakfast I told Evan to start waking the open water students, we'd have the first dive at eight.

Shortly after I was leaning on the back deck rail, as I felt Dawn sidle up to me and say, "Thank you for helping me to bed last night, and for behaving yourself, oh yeah, I know your rules, but thank you all the same." I nodded and smiled, as I replied, "Yeah it was difficult but I managed," as she looked at me with a sly smile, and said "Well I better have some breakfast if we're diving at eight." I watched her as she moved inside, sighed, and then reached for my smokes.

While everyone was having breakfast Evan and I got our gear together, and got into our lyrca suits, and I grabbed my teaching slates, and moved inside to give them the briefing while they were finishing breakfast.

I told the other divers that we would be moving on earlier today to get to tomorrows sight, so to stay in their buddy pairs and that they were free to explore the reef, and I pointed out where there was, the remains of a wreck. If they were interested in seeing that. The students finished their breaky and moved off to get changed into swimmers ready to assemble their gear on the rear deck.

The first dive went well, and all the students excelled with the exercises, and then during the swim around, I showed them a couple of moray eels, and they saw a big Maori wrasse and I showed them how to play with clown fish, and then took my gloves off and clicked my fingers and start wiggling them to entice a coral trout to nibble on the palm of my hand. It would have been so easy to hook my fingers into his gills and take him to the surface for lunch, but I fought the temptation, a little further on in our swim, I spotted a wobbegong shark lying on the bottom. So I got them to stay and watch as I went to play with it, by grabbing his tail and shaking, he swung up and around as I wrapped him in my arms we both went for a circular swim before I released him, and after doing a circle around me it went down to lie on the bottom again. Looking at my watch, I decided that that would be enough for that dive, and headed back to the anchor rope. I stayed away from the rope as they ascended one by one, and I swam to the back of the boat watching the students swimming on the surface as I started a free ascent to surface at the rear of the boat, and waited till they were all out of the water.

Two hours later I led them on their last dive as students, and after they did all of the exercises I shook their hands underwater, took my breathing regulator out of my mouth and smiled at them, giving them all a thumbs up, before we went off to explore the reef. Evan had found a turtle and was riding it around while we all watched, then I had some fun by pulling out some bread, and crumbling it above them, within seconds the students were mobbed by all species of fish swimming around and through them, but as the bread disappeared so did the fish, and with that we all swam towards the back of the boat, and all did a free ascent to finish their last qualifying dive.

During the debriefing session, I congratulated each one of them, and signed their logbooks, and then filled out all of their paperwork and gave them an interim dive card while they waited for their official card which would be posted to them, then I told them that once all the dive gear was put away, and their tanks made ready for filling the rest of the day was free time.

For those that hadn't heard, I told them also that we'd be moving the boat after lunch, so if they wanted to do any swimming or snorkelling to let any of the crew know they weren't on board, and where they'd be, and the most important of all that the first round of drinks were on me that night. Then I went out onto the back deck and lit a smoke, Dawn came to join me as I stood there relaxing, and said, "You know you really shouldn't smoke, but I've decided not to say anything more about it, but I would like to thank you for looking after me, all of us, you're really a very good teacher Tom, but now that I'm not a student anymore can I be allowed to throw myself at your feet?" She was looking at me quite intently, waiting for my answer I supposed, so I smiled at her, and said "Yeah well it'll be difficult to take, but I think I'd be able to handle it, come here." As I held my arms opened, she smiled rushed into me, and kissed me at the same time.

Later after lunch Joe started to make the trip from Bolt to Flinders, and everyone was either seating along the starboard side of the boat, watching the football on the TV, or lazing in their cabins, I was out on the back deck helping Evan and Paul with the tank filling as we motored along, and as soon as the first two tanks were filled I strapped one to my BCD, and then Evans, because when we got there I wanted to dive the entrance to the underwater to the lagoon, and mark the entry, so that we could find it the next day. Dawn came and started talking to me and we got into a conversation, about our hopes and dreams, and she was telling me about her parents, as I was sitting back enjoying a smoke. Then there was a lot of commotion on the bow and side of the boat, so I looked over and saw a pod of dolphins swimming alongside, and I assumed riding the bow wave.

I smiled and told Dawn to get her camera ready, I raced inside, and Evan was on the lounge so asked him to get ready to toss me my mask, and then continued up to the bridge and wheelhouse and asked Joe to slow down, stop and drift, explaining I'm going to try something, and with that I went through the side rail it was fairly high but I'd dived from higher in my time, and dived into the water as the boat started slowing. Underwater I somersaulted and kicked to the surface, and as my head came out of the water a dolphin dived into the air over me, and came down with a splash. Evan was standing by the side rail with my mask, and as I raised my hand he tossed it toward me, it landed short, but I swam to it and was putting it on as a couple of dolphins came in close to me and I rubbed their bellies for them, as more came over to play.

Then one was nudging my feet with his nose, so I stiffened my legs, and next minute I was launched into the air far enough to do a somersault before slicing into the water, but as I did, I noticed that the dolphin that had launched me had also come out of the water and was somersaulted itself beside me. Well I had hoped that they'd stop and play, so I was on cloud nine when they did. Joe had kept the boat close to keep me in view, and also I think so that everyone could go snap happy, because when I was between two of them holding their dorsal fin, I glanced at the boat and he even had a camera with a long lens out, and with a zoom lens like that he'd be getting some great shots, and then after twenty minutes or so of playing and frolicking with me, the dolphins carried on, and feeling elated, and a bit sad I swam towards the boat, and as I reached it everyone was crowding around me as I climbed up to the rear deck. Dawn came through the crowd with a towel, as I was passing my mask to Evan, and she wrapped the towel around, and gave me a kiss in front of everybody.

As I was drying myself, Paul asked if I'd go and see Joe, when I got up there, he was smiling, and asked "I hope you let me use the photos, and how did you know they wouldn't just swim off? I told him most definitely use the pictures as long as he sent me a copy, and I was mentioned if they were going into the newspaper, and then I told him I really hadn't expected them to stop but keep going, but I'd decided to give it a go. Val spoke up, saying "It looked like you were having fun out there, Tiger." I smiled, and replied "Val, I was stoked, and yeah I had a ball." Then Joe nodded to the window and told us he could just make out Flinders on the horizon, as I did some calculating and told him that we should reach the coordinates with an hour to spare before dark. So Evan and I will go down and mark the entrance of the swim through, explaining that you'd swim right by it if you didn't have any idea where it went. I told Joe I'd come back to the bridge as we skirted along Flinders so we could position the boat just right.

After leaving the bridge, I went down to my cabin to get into some dry shorts, and I noticed Dawn was in her cabin, as she saw me she smiled and told me she thought I'd come to change soon, and had brought my sleeveless shirt with her. I smiled and told her she was an angel, she moved toward me and circled her arms around my neck, and then we shared a long passionate kiss, and she asked in a whisper, "Do I get to sleep with you tonight?" I smiled, and replied "We could go there right now if you like, I wouldn't say no, if you feel that." She grasped my penis through my shorts.

She smiled and murmured "Oh god you are ready, and big, but let's wait till later, I really want to enjoy this, as she fondled me again, and told me she'd see me back up on the deck soon, and walked off. I closed her cabin door with my shirt in my hand, and went into my cabin and changed shorts taking the wet ones back up with me to dry. *Now some of the guys out there may know what I faced changing and trying to hide the fact that I had a raging hard on as I left with dry gear on.* I made my way to the back deck and hung up my shorts to dry overnight, and moved to the rail and lit a smoke, as the stern of the boat started to glide past Flinders.

I was approached in drips and drabs by the passengers wanting to know what swimming with the dolphins had been like, and I answered their questions as good as I could, and each promised to send copies of the photos taken, and one even told me he'd got it all on video, so once it was edited and copied he'd send me a copy to keep. Then I saw Evan and Dawn at the same time and they both joined me. I told Evan that we'd probably only enough time for a short dive to mark the entrance, and to bring along a couple of catch bags and torches, as I looked at where we were. I figured we had half an hour until we reached the spot so changing into dry gear was probably a mistake, and I took down my swimmers and dropped my shorts while Evan and Dawn surveyed the area and got into my swimmers, dawn took my shorts for me, and took them down below while I got into my lyrca suit.

Back on the bridge I helped Joe position the See Wah into the place it would stay that night and next day, and then while Joe gave Valery a hand with dinner Evan and I made the dive, we had a few onlookers as we dropped below the surface once I located the entrance, we marked each side of it with a yellow balloon that we tied to a piece of sturdy coral, and then we went hunting, after forty minutes underwater in the thirty foot depth, we had just about expanded our dive limits and so we surfaced with appetisers for dinner as our catch bags contained three big crayfish and a large lobster, which Paul triumphantly took to the kitchen, as we started getting out of our dive gear, and both smiled as he said "Time for a durry," as I nodded and joined him, as he lit both smokes.

Because it was Christmas Eve Joe had decided that dinner was to be a formal occasion, and that meant long sleeves and ties, however long trousers were optional, for those that didn't have ties (which was all of us), Paul was able to supply them from one of the property lockers, and some of the outfits we went to dinner in was a comedy fest in its own right.

We all vied for the most outrageous dress, and I ended up wearing a dry pair of swimmers, a three quarter sleeve red T shirt, with a wide black tie that had daffy duck on it, Dawn who sat beside me was wearing, a bikini under a little blue wrap, belted at the waist, and was sporting a wide purple tie with white horses on it, that she had gotten me to tie for her. Joe opened the bar so we could have drinks with dinner, and I gave him first prise for ridiculous with what he'd decided to wear, a pair of white shorts, two white long sleeves that were held in place by a length of blue strapping sewed to each sleeve, and a wide red tie with a hula girl motif that flashed and wiggled by battery power. As the drinks were being dispensed Valery brought out the cray and lobster meat on a tray leaving the top half of the shells on each side of the tray, and announced that entrée had been provided by Evan and myself, and as we received three cheers she then brought out another tray with toasted garlic bread and some thousand island sauce.

Dinner was a long and happy affair, and I think everyone enjoyed themselves, and half way through the night, I announced "My thanks to the crew of the SeeWah for such an excellent meal, and I expected everyone to sleep in the next day, so no diving would be done before ten o'clock, when I expected everyone to dive, even the crew because what I was going to show them was quite magical, and so until tomorrow Merry Christmas all!" After my speech, it seemed everyone had something they wanted to say, and as each person tried to outdo the previous, Dawn and I snuck out to the back deck with our drinks so I could get some nicotine into my system, plus we also indulged in a fair bit of foreplay which had her moaning a fair bit, as I explored various erogenous areas of her body.

When we went back inside, I asked everyone to help with the dishes and washing up, so that we didn't leave a massive mess for the crew to clear by themselves, as one of them had to stay awake and keep watch, once all the cleaning up was done I told everyone to have a good night, but I was going to get some sleep, and Dawn and I took a bottle of scotch with us, as I led the way to my cabin.

Inside my cabin we embrace for a long passionate kiss, and while we were doing that, I undid her belt, and slipped her wrap off her shoulders and body, and unclipped her bra, as she pushed her pelvis into me with a moan, and her moaning increased as I played with her back and sides, and then she shivered in ecstasy as I ran my fingers lightly up her sides to her armpits.

She broke our embrace, saying huskily "No fair, you've still got your clothes on!" I smiled and said "Well I took yours off," she smiled and then proceeded to strip me slowly kissing me all over as she took off my garments, until we were both only left with my swimmers on, and she had the tie and her bikini bottoms, so as I kissed her I travelled down her body from her neck to her breasts, and as I moved lower I slipped my fingers into each side of her bikini pants and lowered them slowly as I kissed her stomach, moving slowly to her sides, and then I moved to her legs as I lifted each one in turn to take off her pants from around her ankles, and then kissed her on the clitoris as I made my way back slowly up her body to her breasts and neck. She was a little unsteady on her feet, and moaning quietly in ecstasy, as we shared a deep tongue kiss.

After our kiss, she recovered a little, and then she started doing the same to me, and she murmured "Oh god" as she saw my swollen and enlarged penis, and took it into her mouth, and after sucking on me quite vigorously she stood up again, and whispered "I can't take anymore I'm so wet, please take me, I want you inside me," and slid back the covers and sheets on the bed, and lay there with her legs opened wide for me to come down on top of her, there was no need for any guidance as I slipped into her vagina, and pushed myself all the way into her, and as I did she shuddered and convulsed in spasms as she orgasmed straight away. After her shudders slowed I started to move and I took her to another orgasm within minutes, this time as she came she bit her teeth into my shoulder as she moaned quietly. After bringing her to the pinnacle half a dozen times, I couldn't stand holding back any longer, and when she started to come again, I poured myself into her which produced another series of convulsions and shudders that I held her through, and she whispered "Oh wow, I wasn't sure if I could take anymore." My swollen penis was no more after some minutes of lying inside her, and I slipped out of her and moved my position so that we were side by side with my arms around her, and we drifted off to sleep, with her snuggled into my chest.

We both awoke together the next morning, and as she was waking up, she kissed me on the chest, and then on my cheek and murmured "Morning," and I replied "Merry Christmas sweetheart," she stretched and quietly said "Umm, certainly is, I feel like the cat that swallowed all of the cream." I chuckled, and then replied with a smile, "Well it's definitely in there somewhere." She laughed and replied. "Oh yeah, and talking about that, we should clean up a bit, what time is it?" as she rolled over on top of me.

She kissed me again, but didn't wait for an answer as she kept going into the bathroom, I heard the toilet flush, and as I got up, I picked up the clothes that were laying around the floor, and draped them over a chair back, as I heard the shower start. So I waited a little for her to warm the water, and then I went in and joined her in the snug little shower. It really wasn't big enough for the two of us so I got out and scrubbed her back for her from the shower door.

After we were showered and sort of dressed, she had me open her cabin door and she scooted into from mine, and came back into my cabin dressed in a one piece bathing suit with a terry towelling wrap around, I put on my swimmers from the night before, and my sleeveless shirt, and put my smoke packet and lighter into the pockets, and before we left the cabin we had a long kiss wrapped in each other's arms, and she remarked "Umm, I could get used to this," and I smiled as I replied "Well I do have a vacancy for a bed mate," and then she looked at me intently, and smiled, as she said "Be careful, I might just take you up on that offer."

CHAPTER 19

When we went into the saloon, we were greeted with "Merry Christmas" from all the early risers there, and the only member of the crew not around, was Paul who was sleeping after taking the dog watch. *The dog watch is so called due to its timing being from three am onwards to dawn it can be very gruelling in that you want to keep drifting into sleep, and not being able to make too much noise as others sleep, so you have keep moving around and was generally referred to as a dog of a watch, and over time is referred to as the dog watch. Evan was also up and a couple of the others, and I took my coffee* outside to light up while Dawn chatted inside, while I was out there I tested the shorts that had been left to dry, and they were. So I made a mental note to take them with me the next time I went down to my cabin.

While we had breakfast I suggested that during the dive, we all stick together within the group, until the return where Evan would take over the lead and guide the group out and back to the boat, while I stayed behind with Paul and Joe who would carry some catch bags and cray hooks. We would do some foraging for seafood, before returning to the boat, it was agreed on, but I noticed Valery looking a little glum, and so asked her if she was ok, she looked at me, and said "It's all fine for you lot Tiger, but I get stuck behind cleaning the breakfast things and getting stuff ready for our lunch. I would have liked to have seen what you'll be showing the others, I'm a qualified diver and there are times I'd like to go for a dive as well."

I was thoughtful for a minute, looked at Joe, saying "Val's right Joe, if you would look after the breakfast clearing up and cooking, if Val was to go and get into her swimming gear, I'm prepared to take her for a private tour of her own, before anyone else, and Evan will give her a hand with her dive gear." Before Joe could say anything, she came around to where I was sitting, grabbed each side of my face with her palms, and kissed me on the forehead, and said "Oh thank you Tiger, I'll go and get changed now," and walked off upstairs to hers and Joe's cabin, as I looked at Joe, and said "Sorry buddy looks like you don't get a say in it!" We all burst out laughing, and I leaned across to Evan and told him quietly to make sure she was carrying a torch, and that everyone is in here at five to eleven for the main briefing.

I took my dry pants down to my cabin, and then returned to the rear deck for a smoke as I got my diving suit on; I was joined by Dawn, Evan, and Val.

Valery now had a swimsuit on and was wearing her wetsuit unzipped, and she zipped it up just before she put her weight belt on, and then Evan gave her a hand to put her BCD and regulator onto a dive tank, I shrugged into my gear, and we did a quick buddy check while on the duckboard, and then we both entered the water. As I looked down into the water with my mask on, I saw that the stern of the boat was right over the entrance markers, and as we bobbed in the water I gave Val a quick briefing, and then we lowered ourselves beneath the water.

When we were near the entrance to the swim through, I grabbed her free hand and guided her, the light dulled perceptively as we entered and I switched on my torch, and she did the same, and as we swam through, I showed her the sleeping night fish, Harry and Sally two moray eels that shared the same hole, she also saw crayfish some prawns skittering upside down along some fan coral, sea fans of different colours, a couple of turtles, and all around us as we swam there were fish of every species, and some sea slugs on the floor of the swim through. The swim through was four hundred yards long but near the middle it is shaped like an S, so that the internal exit is not straight across from the entry, but about one hundred yards further to the west, and when we came out into the lagoon, going through the swim through had taken half an hour.

As we got into the lagoon Val was rather insistent about

surfacing, and as soon as we did she spat her Reg out and exclaimed "My god that was unbelievable, I had no idea, no wonder you don't tell many people about that, I didn't think there was a way in to this lagoon, but I do now, oh thanks Tom, now where's the boat." I swam her around so she could see the boat, and someone had seen us, and were giving the ok signal, in other words asking if we were ok, so I returned the signal with a large ok using both of my arms over my head, and then asked Valery "Are you ready to back through again?" She replied "Oh yes please, let's." So we slipped below the surface and went back the way we came.

We surfaced right at the duckboard, and just slid onto it to take of our fins, Evan came down as Val undid her BCD, and he lifted it up to the main deck, and then climbed the steps up to the deck, as all the people that were crowding around made way for him, Val followed him up wearing a grin like a Cheshire cat, and I brought up the rear, I shrugged out of my gear and looking at the pressure gauge, I told Evan that I wouldn't need another tank for the next dive, there was more than enough air left in my tank, so I left my gear in one piece, and got out of my lyrca suit, but stayed in my swimmers, and reached for my smokes.

When I went into the saloon for a cuppa, every chance all the others could get they'd quiz Valery on the dive, and she would just walk around with a smile on her face, until eventually she couldn't hold off saying anything, and so she said "Joe and I have had some spectacular dives in this group over the years, but Tigers Christmas gift is one of the most awesome dives I've ever done, you have no idea of how much of a treat you're in for." I was quiet chuffed at her compliment, as I sat in the lounge with Dawn resting her head against my shoulder.

Eventually everyone started to gather for the dive briefing , and I told them what we be doing, and what would happen at the other end, and then warned them of the dangers, particularly with Harry and Sally, and I told them that Harry was docile, but Sally would snap if anyone's hand got near, I told them to be careful and try not to touch anything, and also told them that I would be going slow and so not to bunch up too much, and encouraged those with underwater cameras to them with them, they may get some shots of the night fish sleeping in some of the crevices, also after the dive no more would be done that day, so they could break down their gear for tank refills and so on, but as usual swimming and snorkelling would be available throughout the rest of the day with the usual provisos.

Half an hour later everyone was in the water, except Valery, who would be doing some special cooking while we were away, and as I asked if everybody was ok, with a resounding yes, I said "Ok let's do it!" And we disappeared from the surface in a group, on the bottom I once more assured myself everybody was ok, and then Dawn and I led the way into the swim through. This time it took forty minutes, because I was moving slowly so they could all see what I was pointing out, and there were numerous flashes throughout the dive as cameras were activated for photos, near the S bend I settled to the bottom to let a couple of cuttlefish swish past us going in the opposite direction, and they were closely followed by a red octopus, then we continued, at the exit I had them all surface, and then told them that Evan would lead them back and to be at the entry/exit point in two minutes. I also told Joe and Paul to stay on the surface with me.

We watched as the others all descended, and they both told me what they had thought of the swim through, which they said was an awesome dive, and then I suggested we forage around the inside of the reef, and give the others at least a ten-minute head start, so we descended again, and then we went on the hunt.

Near the bottom of the lagoon, we came across a large coral trout, and as I looked at Joe, he nodded his head, so I started to entice the trout into my hands and palms, and as it nibbled at one palm I slowly moved my other hand near its gills, and then caught it by grabbing it through the gills, it fought to get free, but by now it was already inside the catch bag as I released it. As I looked at Joe and Paul with a smile they were both shaking their heads in disbelief.

On the way back through the swim through, we gathered a further haul of food for the table, four blue swimmer crabs, six large crayfish, and eight good sized lobsters, and I was able to entice another big coral trout, and he went into the bag as well. As we surfaced at the boat, I had nearly used up all the air, I was down to the last fifty bar, not really the done thing for an instructor, but I had done both dives on the one tank, and there were no students around to see what I'd done, and I said nothing. After we got out of our gear, we headed into the saloon, and inside everyone was gathered and waiting for us to enter, and yelled "Surprise!" as Val came forward, and looked toward someone at the back of the room, it was one of the non-students, and he said "Tiger on behalf of everybody on board, we would like to thank you for your gift to us, and so we came up with one of our own for you. We have all voted you king of the sea, and if you'll please kneel to receive your crown we can get on with the festivities." With a smile I did as requested, and a smiling Valery placed a yellow plastic crown on my head, and then pulled me up, as someone called "Three cheers for King Tiger!"

I was laughing and smiling as Dawn passed me a large glass of scotch, and as the cheers died, there was a call of speech, so laughingly I said, "Well thank you my most, humble subjects, I have come to bring bounty so everyone can feast," and I waved my hands in the direction of Joe and Paul who entered with smiles and holding up the catch bags, as applause rang around the room. Valery put her arms around Joe's neck and kissed him as they headed to the galley with all the fresh seafood, and then everybody drifted off to other parts of the boat, as Dawn and I slipped out onto the back deck for me to light up.

During lunch the main topics of conversation were the dive, and how Joe and Paul had watched me catch the fish, after the main lunch the table stayed up with food on it available to any who wanted to pick something to nibble on, and so it seemed that dinner was an extension of lunch, but before that during the afternoon some would go swimming, or just laze around the boat, after a second nibble and three scotches, Dawn and I drifted back to my cabin for a snooze.

Well that was Christmas day, Christmas night while we were in bed, Dawn had asked me if she wanted to do the advanced course, would I teach her, because she would fall into two categories, one as a student that I'd declared I wouldn't touch, and two, my girlfriend. So with a laugh and smile I told her that if she paid the money for the course, I'd teach her, and so it was agreed that she would pay for the course during the week we got back after the trip, and therefore she became a student once again, and so that night I taught her all the theory and asked her the exam questions verbally, which she passed without any help on my part. I wasn't the sort of person to give her a pass mark if she didn't earn it. So we went to sleep quite late. Then for the following day we anchored at a different part of Flinders reef, as I commenced the first of five dives for the advanced course students.

The first dive was designed to master perfect buoyancy, so once I assigned the buddy teams, because I now had an odd number of students, I buddied Dawn up with Evan after the briefing we all took to the water, and at fifty feet about ten feet from the bottom, I had them start to show me their mastery of buoyancy, but first I showed them what could be achieved. I hung motionless upside down, but perfectly straight with my feet towards the surface and my head facing the bottom, and for a bit of a change I continued to stay that way for the remainder of the dive.

During the afternoon I conducted the second dive which involved underwater navigation, and I added a little element of search and recovery for fun, but first they had to show me that their navigation skills were appropriate for advanced level divers. I was quite pleased with the progress and skills the students were making, because I didn't have to retest anyone so far, and navigation is usually one of the dives that need retesting, so I was well pleased. Once I was dry after the dive, I went up to the bridge, where my briefcase was, and had a word to Joe, about where I wanted to conduct the next dive, and after consulting the chart he worked out that it would take seven hours steaming to get to the coordinates, and so it was decided that we'd move the boat after dinner, and then he asked me why I wanted to go there, and he was shocked at my answer, that the coordinates were of a shipwreck in sixty feet of water, that had been a steel hulled pleasure cruiser nearly one hundred foot long, that had sunk in a storm in nineteen sixty. Because he'd never knew it was there, and was consoled after I told him not all that many people knew of it, and I knew about it because a Marine Park Officer told me about it being a good dive.

During the debriefing session, I told the students to think of a list of hazards that could occur during a wreck dive. I would be asking them for them at the next day's briefing, and after being asked what sort of dive it would be. I told them that it was a surprise that probably no one would work out, until I briefed them the next day, after the debriefing, I updated the student files to include the previous two dives. As I was finishing, Evan brought me a drink, and asked about the next dive, so I told him, but to keep it under wraps, he whistled with a smile, and said, "That should be great, how do you know of it?"

Dawn tried to get me to tell her what the dive was going to be, but I remained tight lipped, and only told her she'd require to having her torch and compass with her, and her response to that was they always had them on a dive, so I wasn't really helping too much. Then at breakfast the next day I announced that I would give all divers a briefing at nine, as to where we were and what the best sort of diving to be done in this area.

The room was full as I gave the briefing, and there were some gasps at the fact that a wreck was the main area for a dive, and I said, "Now as far as I know there is only one of you present that know this wreck as you were with Rob after I gave him the position, the rest of you were like everyone else and didn't know that a wreck dive existed on the barrier Reef, except for way up north, and I would ask that before the certified divers do dive please wait until after I've completed my dive with the students, then you can explore to your heart's content, thank you all, and advanced students please stay for your briefing."

At the student briefing I had them reiterate the hazards of wreck diving, and then had them work out how much time they had for the dive considering the wreck was lying in sixty feet of water, and as I went around the room they had all written the right answer. *Now I won't bore you with the details and work that has to be done during a wreck dive, suffice to say that all the students did remarkably well and passed with flying colours, as I observed while floating just above the wreck, as I was able to follow their progress by the air bubble trail. Also I won't bother with details of the night dive, which would be done the following night, just to say this one has a tendency to create fear in divers, a night dive is just the same as a day dive, but fear of not being able to see anything around you because it's dark does affect some divers, because of the fear of the unseeable.* After the students all surfaced, the other divers had been waiting, and as soon as we were out of the way, after logging off the boat.

Paul was the one in charge of the logging out and in process as the boat dive master, so after that they entered the water, and I smiled as I noticed Joe and Valery taking the opportunity to have a dive themselves.

Taking pity on Paul, knowing he would have loved to dive the wreck, I had Evan take over his duties, and I buddied with him for the dive, leaving the debriefing until after my second dive, but before diving I made an exaggerated show of consulting the tables to see how long I could be under in full view of the students, so they knew it was definitely a case of do as I do, not as I say.

During the rest of the day repeated dives were made on the wreck, and I even allowed the students time off for a dive of their own, but I was seen not to be diving again that day. Even Dawn went for a second dive with Evan as her buddy, and I think that all of them enjoyed their second wreck dive, mainly because there was no pressure to pass exercises for me as an examiner.

That night the boat was moved again, and by morning we were anchored over the top of entrance bommie, just off the Lady Musgrave Lagoon. The dive was to be a deep dive, the bottom of entrance bommie is one hundred and twenty feet below the surface, and is the maximum depth for recreational diving.

I changed things around that morning and after the all diver briefing the students stayed behind while I let the experienced divers go first. There were three of them so Paul volunteered to dive as the buddy for one of them, so Joe took over his duties as boat dive master. While they were diving I had a long briefing with my students, the first thing I got them to do was a three-digit maths take away problem, and they were timed, then I warned them of the effects of nitrogen narcosis. How it fogged the brain, and made people act as if they were drunk. Then I showed them a tennis ball that I was taking down to show them the effects of pressure at the depth they were going to, and why it was impera-tive that they ascend no faster than the prescribed rate of ascent, and to make it easier for them, I made it simpler, telling them they came up no faster than their own air bubbles, and that we would be stopping ten feet from the surface for a ten minute decompres-sion stop, to avoid getting bent, or more commonly called the bends, due to the effects of the excess nitrogen getting trapped in joint areas, if surfacing too fast. Then I took all of their slates, and wrote another math problem on each one, it was hard to get seven sets of sums to have all the same answer, but I did it, and told them I would give them their slates back after they'd worked out the sum and I'd seen the answer.

As we started gearing up, the first experienced buddy team surfaced, and was followed five minutes later, by the two other teams, once they were aboard we logged out, and entered the water, once we were all in the water and okayed the boat, I swam them to the anchor line, and we descended. On the bottom as they settled in a semi-circle around me, both Evan and I were keeping a close watch on them for signs of being narked, one of the guys had a smile on his face, so I quickly got them to focus by pulling out the tennis ball, and I showed them the pressure effects.

It looked as if it had been sucked in from the inside, or imploded and crumpled into a new weird looking shape, and they all nodded, I approached each one of them in turn, and passing their slate to them, I timed each of them doing the maths problem, and wrote the time on the slate and circled it, and handed them the slate, and then it was time for a swim around, and as we swam near the sea fans, I turned on my torch and instantly the colour of the fans exploded into view as far as my torch beam went, and the I swam them through a small swim through at the very base of the bommie, and then looking at my watch, I signalled that it was time to surface, so we swam to the anchor line, I went first then the students in their buddy pairs and then last up was Evan. I ascended at a slower rate than normal to get them used to slow ascents, and at the ten-foot mark I stopped so no one could come by me, and watched my watch, after the ten minutes had gone by, I signalled the ascent to resume.

Back on board, I told them to get their logbooks, slates, and tables after they'd put their dive gear away, and to join me at the bow area in the warm sun. I grabbed my shirt, and leaving Evan to look after my gear I went to the front of the boat and lit up. When they all assembled, I asked Evan if he had anything to say about the dive, and he mentioned that Jack had looked like he was a little narked, so I asked jack if he thought he had been narked, and he told us that he didn't think so. I looked at his dive buddy asking if he noticed anything, and the reply I got was he did think that he was acting a little weirder than normal, and this made everyone laugh.

As I nodded my head, I said "Ok remember this, because nitrogen narcosis can affect people in different ways, but it's easily fixed by going up a little so that five feet or so can make a difference, but if someone starts to go to the extreme, if they take their Reg out and want to chase fish for a kiss, then it's time to end the dive and surface." That comment had them all laughing, so I continued "Ok you can laugh now, but be warned getting narked is dangerous and can kill."

Then I collected all the slates, and as I did, I asked "Did everyone see what happened to the tennis ball because of the pressure down there?" They all said they did and also some other comments how to really scrunch up, I pulled it out of my pocket and showed them again, saying that it was the same ball, and they knew it by the mark I'd put on it underwater, it was back in its original shape and still bounced as I showed them, and told them the only reason we didn't go the same way as the tennis ball was because our bodies were seventy percent liquid, and I let that fact sink in before continuing.

I held up the slates, saying "Now remember I had you do that math problem, well let's look at the results, now remember it only took less than a minute to do this on the surface. Ok Jack you're first seeing you said you weren't narked, let's see. It took you three goes to get the right answer, and four times as long with a time of four minutes sixteen seconds, and yes you were narked." Giving out the slates after everyone bagged Jack, I continued "Now it won't do for you to bag Jack because each of you showed signs of being narked, look at how long you each took, the times circled, and only two of you had the right answer straight away, you all took at least double the amount of time it took on the surface."

Letting that sink in for a few minutes, I continued "Now of course none of you failed and there will be no retesting, but please be aware of the dangers of going too deep! Now who can tell me, how long is it before you're safe enough to dive again?" Dawn stuck her hand up, and I told her to go ahead, and she said "We were at one hundred and twenty feet for thirty minutes; therefore, we've got to wait at least six hours before we're clear of nitrogen, and fit to dive again."

I smiled and nodded, and said "Correct, so you won't be diving anymore today, however you're next and final dive will be tonight at eight pm, the briefing will be at seven thirty, until then rest, thank you and well done all of you." After they had made their way back from the debriefing, Dawn stayed with me as I lit another smoke, and I told her she'd done well and I was proud of her, and that after I was finished having a break I'd be going up to the bridge to see what time Joe was going to shift the boat, so she said she'd go and have a sleep in her cabin, but I was welcome to join her later if I felt like ravaging her. We both laughed, and she made her way into the boat while I headed for the bridge. When I got there, Joe told me that he'd decided to shift into the lagoon now, seeing everyone was still on board the boat, Paul had made his way to the bow, and I went to the rear deck, to make sure everything was secure.

As I felt the main engines start, I grabbed two coffees from Val, and returned to the wheelhouse, and passed Joe his drink, and the we both sipped while waiting for the anchor to come up, when Paul raised his hand to say the anchor was all in, Joe told me that I knew where I was going, so to take us in through the channel, I put the controls into gear, and did a lazy wide turn to line up with the channel mouth, and then slowly took the boat in, because I knew from past experience that the entry channel was only navigable for one boat at a time due to the closeness of the coral, once in however I chose a great spot with ten metres of water under us to anchor, and as I kept the boat in position, I signalled Paul to drop the anchor, I made sure we had plenty of swing room, and then placed the main engines in neutral to cool down before shutting them off.

With small coral bommie's underneath us and only ten metres in depth, I considered this perfect, considering we would be here for the next few days, and then Joe, Paul, Evan, and I got together to unload the two tenders. After attaching the outboard motors to them, as we would use these for any diving while we remained here at anchor in the lagoon, also the tinnies would also be used to ferry anyone that wished to explore Lady Musgrave Island by foot.

CHAPTER 20

Well the mood at dinner was sombre, and glancing around, I smiled knowing that the apprehension of the dive was getting to those who were to night dive for the first time, my gaze settled on Joe, and trying to lighten the mood, I asked him if he was going to dive that night and he told me, you bet both Val and I love night diving, and sometimes think it's better than diving during the day, because in the right places like here you get to see all the day fish sleeping while the night fish and crustaceans come out to play.

After dinner, Dawn and I were out on the back deck while I went through my usual after dinner routine, and I could sense her tenseness, and said with a smile, "Sweetheart, there is nothing to fear, except fear itself, nothing is going to come and grab you, and drag you away, except maybe me. It's just the same as a day dive, and trust me after you've done your first night dive you'll want to do more."

As they assembled for the briefing, I looked around at the apprehensive faces, glanced at Evan who was wearing a wide grin, and I turned away from the students so they wouldn't see my grin also, and then looked around and started the briefing. After we would head to the anchor rope to descend, the other divers would descend free fall from the duckboard, I told the students how I would sequence the dive, and then assigned buddy teams, Dawn would be my buddy, and Evan would trail along, and keep an eye on everyone, and then it was time to gear up.

Needless to say the dive went without hitch, and we were underwater for fifty minutes as we toured slowly around the closest bommie's and then stopped to watch a troop of crayfish move from one bommie to another in the style of a train, this was the first time any of them had seen this and so they were enthralled, and as the crayfish progressed, it was hard to get the students moving again. The progress of the dive was purposely slow so they could see as much as they could, but eventually I came to the deeper shadow of the boat and looked up, looked at my watch, and then waited for everyone to bunch up and signalled a free ascent.

It was a far different mood as we surfaced, and made our way back on the boat, log in with Paul, and then I had to shout to make myself heard, as I told them to strip down and place their gear away, and place the used tanks near the filling station, and that the debriefing would be in thirty minutes.

This gave everyone time to get into dry and warm clothing, I as usual was quite happy in shorts and a sleeveless shirt, and after getting a couple of drinks from Paul who opened the bar, while Evan had taken over the logging in duties. I took his drink out him, and we both lit up while we were laughing and smiling as we discussed the change of attitude from the students after the dive.

When they were all gathered for the debriefing, I had completed all the signing and comments of the necessary paperwork, and had put it all away back into my briefcase, but kept all the temporary certification cards in one of my pockets, everyone had passed the course without any problems, so I was quite happy. While they sat with their tables and logbooks at the ready I asked, "So who of you would like to do more night diving?" Everyone's hand went up and chatter erupted, and I smiled, as I asked "I thought you were all scared of the night dive, at least it looked that way earlier, didn't it Evan?" He smiled and told them all, well it certainly looked that way Tiger, but I guess we might be wrong, and a chorus saying that we were rose from the students. So I laughed, and said "Well I'm pleased to hear that, now that was the last qualifying dive of the course that you have all passed, and on behalf of Evan and myself I would like to congratulate each and every one of you, so as I come around to signoff your logbooks, I'll pass you your temporary cards, and then first drinks are on me.

The night became quite festive, and Evan and I were the recipients of a lot of drinks, eventually I got the time to ask Dawn what she thought of the dive, and she told me that I was right, and she was addicted, she'd loved every minute of it especially that crayfish migration, and thank you for helping me through it, I suppose that's one of the reasons why I love you. As she realised what she'd said, she reddened in embarrassment, and looked at the deck without saying anymore.

As I told her, well looks like it's certainly out of the bag now, and I'm pleased because you've got to me as well, so don't feel about telling me the truth, but there is something you'll have to understand, if you feel like taking it to a higher level, I can't until my divorce is through, so you either have to wait for that, or we don't act on our feelings after the trip ends, and it won't do any good if you feel like complaining to me about how long it's taking. So I'll leave you to think that over, while I get another drink. I returned with two drinks, one for her, which I handed to her, and then had a smoke, while she told me, well yes I'm falling in love with you, and I would like us to stay together. So I'm willing to wait as long as you want me to, then we could eventually marry at a later date.

I looked at her with some surprise, and told her we could talk about that at another time when we're back in town, and as we worked out other things out as well, because we had a lot talk about if we were thinking of making a life together, and besides I wasn't sure if I wanted to get married again. She nodded and agreed with me, and then asked were we went from there, so I laughed and told her to bed of course sweetheart, let's go, she laughed and started to head through the saloon and the stairs to our cabins below, as we passed through the saloon I noticed that the party was starting to break up, and looked at my watch to confirm it was close to midnight.

Over breakfast the next morning, I asked if anyone had experienced drift diving, and no one had so I proposed that during the day, I would take four divers at a time outside the lagoon with one of the tinnies to the fringing reef. After a drop line had been place, each diver would enter the water and find a spot on the drop line, and I would then motor slowly along the fringes to give each an idea of drifting, and told them that most times this would be done in a current with a boat following to pick up divers, but because there was very little current this was the best way to simulate it. Joe asked if I wanted to use both tinnies, and I enquired if he wanted to keep one to ferry anyone to the island, that may wish to go, but looking around the table no one was interested in that, so it was decided to take both tinnies, and that way we could double the number of divers. After asking for a show of hands as who was interested, everyone put their hands up, so it was decided that all names would go into a bucket, and the first eight would be drawn out, but because Evan had done this sort of thing before, I wanted him to drive the other tinnie, so both he and I were relegated to the last group.

The first group was drawn out, and included Joe, Val, and Paul, and because Dawn wasn't in the first group I asked Evan to take her through the logging out and in routine, so she could stand in for Paul. Then I warned them of the only danger of this kind of drift diving, which was not to let go, if they did they would have to swim very fast to catch up with the guideline again, or to surface, now because another boat would be following. So they would have to wait until it had passed over before coming to the surface, and wait for the returning boats. I was going to make the down and back trip last fifteen minutes each and that way the second group should be ready to leave forty minutes after the first group, and the first group could get their dive gear ready after breakfast. Now because everybody enjoyed the first time, we did another that afternoon.

That night we also did another night dive, and the following day both tinnies went outside again, but this time went to entrance bommie for another deep dive, but I asked all the divers not to go below one hundred feet, and told them there was plenty to see without having to go right to the bottom. To facilitate making it easier for the divers, each tinnie would put a towline out the back and once we left the bommie, we would tow the divers back in at a slow pace to the boat. During the afternoon as long as they logged out and in, they were free to do dive anywhere in the lagoon, because being New Year's Eve there would be no night dive that night, due to it being party time.

To say that we had a party and a half that night would be an understatement, everybody was quite drunk, and most didn't go to bed before three am. The following morning the alarm woke me at seven, somehow I must have turned it on when we came to bed, which is just as well the first dive was scheduled for nine. I had a magnitude seven hangover, and I not feeling really well, but I put my swimmers on, and headed to the back deck, no one was around except Paul and I told him I was going to clear my head, and so I wrapped my weight belt around me put my regulator on a tank and opened it, grabbed my mask, and stepped off into the water with the tank wrapped under my arm, because I hadn't bother about my BCD or Lyrca suit and I sat on the bottom doing nothing but snooze for half an hour or so, breathing pure air, and this did the trick. Then when I surfaced there was no hangover and I was feeling great, so I made my own breakfast in the galley and put on a pot of coffee, and then went to the bridge, as yet no one had relieved Paul, so I did and he went off to get some sleep.

There was some sorry looking sights that morning, and so the day ended up becoming a recuperation day, and no diving was done, but they all took part in the night dive, with buddy teams going in all directions. I swam with Dawn over toward the entrance channel, and we dived along both walls, and she even went for a cruise with a turtle that let her. As the time to head home came closer we did a lot more talking about the future, and then I invited her to my place the night the trip ended, and she accepted on the proviso that I went to her place the following night. After a couple more days it was time for the trip to end, and Joe headed the boat toward Bundaberg after breakfast of the last day.

During the cruise back to Bundaberg, everyone started packing away their dive gear into the dive bags, and then went below to pack their personal gear. I took my gear and Dawn's up to the rear deck and put them with our dive bags. After the boat docked I went ahead, and unlocked the coach, and all the baggage lockers and started it up, and then went back to the boat, all the bags were unloaded and, the dive gear was taken to the bus first and stored, and then all the personal bags, I made my gear along with Evans and Dawns were kept separate to all the other baggage, so we wouldn't have to scramble to pick out gear at the other end.

Then it was time to say goodbye to Joe, Valery, and Paul and I told Joe that the company would definitely be using him as one of our preferred charter boats in the year ahead, and he told me that he was glad it had been me, for the first time trip, as he had learned a lot about the way we worked and liked it, and looked forward to working with me again, so with a final handshake from Joe and Paul and a kiss on the cheek from Val, I headed back up the jetty and into the driver's seat of the bus.

As we neared the outskirts of Brisbane I received a radio call from the shop, it was David one of the instructors, and he asked what my ETA was because he was due to leave for Gladstone at seven that night with another class of students, and I told him I'd probably be pulling into the yard before five thirty, and he asked about how much fuel was in the tank, and I let him know that there was just on three quarters of a tank, so he had plenty of fuel to get up and back. He told me that seeing I was that close he'd wait at the office till I got in, so I rogered his call and told him I'd see him soon.

When I drove into the yard I turned the bus around ready to go out again before opening the door and shutting down, David was standing at the office door as I got out and he enquired as to how the trip went, and I told him it was great, and everyone had a ball. He told me he was taking ten students up and one of the dive masters for five days using the voyager, which was a boat we used for small numbers and no more than a five-day turn-around. I laughed and told him to give my regards to Barry the skipper, and he said he would, by then everyone had collected their luggage. So I took my personal gear and all of Dawn's to the cars, and left them there as I went and unloaded my dive gear which I was leaving at the shop. Then I asked Dawn whether she was going to follow me to my place or did she want to leave her car, and we could pick it up the next day, but she elected to follow me home because she lived at Stafford, and I smiled.

We left the shop and on the way home I did some thinking about what people had been saying to me all of last year about getting into the stock market.

I decided to check it out with the bank sometime soon, and left worrying about my finances as I concentrated on watching Dawn behind me. When we pulled into my driveway, she exclaimed "You shit, no wonder you were familiar!" As I asked her what she was talking about, and she said, "I go past this place every time I'm on shift, and I used to see that insurance sign you had on the fence with your picture on it, see that block of units, well that's where I live!" As she pointed to the first unit block three houses up the street, and I said "I thought you lived at Chermside?" she laughed and replied "No, that's where my parents live."

Looking at her I laughed, and then said with a smile "Well let's not worry about this palaver now, let's go inside," and she nodded and followed me to the door, once we were inside I gave her a quick tour, starting with downstairs, and her eyes lit up as she saw the spa, then we went upstairs, and I told her to have a snoop wherever she wanted, while I collected the bags. When I got back upstairs carrying both bags into the bedroom, she told me the place was marvellous and well set out, and kissed me on the cheek. Instead of cooking we ordered a couple of pizzas delivered, and while we waited she suggested that a soak in the spa after dinner would be nice. So I went down and turned it on to heat up the water, and then poured a couple of drinks. Then dinner arrived and after we'd eaten, I combined both uneaten bits into one box, and placed it into the fridge, she had started a conversation about my history and as we finished dinner I was telling her about my stint in the army, and it was continued while we were soaking in the spa naked.

After telling her about the end of my first marriage, she didn't agree with my thinking, and told me I should have asked why she'd done it, but then switched and asked why I got married again. So staring at her while I thought, I said, "What the hell, you're going to find out anyway, when you get vetted." She laughed and asked what I was talking about, so I told her that if she was going to become my girlfriend or partner that she would be investigated and vetted by the agency I worked for, and then I preceded to tell her everything. After I had finished she stared at me in silence, and I could almost see the cogs in her brain working, deciding whether she believed what I had told her, and she asked me if I could prove any of what I'd told her, and I told yes, I'd show her just as soon as we were upstairs, but I stressed that she couldn't tell anyone what I'd told her, as far as everybody else was concerned I was a dive instructor, but she would find that out for herself during the vetting process.

After that she stayed silent, until we were up in the bedroom, where I showed her my ASIS and AFP ID's, and after looking at them, said, "So am I supposed to think that you're some kind of spy, surely for that you'd have to carry a gun in case you got caught out wouldn't you?" I smirked and opened my bedside drawer taking out my holstered gun, and then took it out of the holster, ejected the magazine, and locked back the slide ejecting the round in the firing chamber at the same time, and threw the colt onto the bed towards her. She stood there stunned for a moment staring at the gun, and then said, "Holy shit you're telling me the truth aren't you? How do you close it?" Then she looked at me, and I nodded and told her, unless I'm working I do tell the truth, sometimes to my own disadvantage.

Going around the bed to her, I held her waist as I reached for the gun, and put it in her hands, and showed her how to unlock the slide, which she did, and flinched almost dropping it, as she remarked how heavy it was, but I seemed to handle it effortlessly. I told her I'd had it for a long time, and then I leaned over and picked up the magazine and loose round and I put the mag in, cocked it to feed another round into the chamber, and then ejected the mag again and put the loose round into the magazine and replaced it into the colt, and then put the safety on. Took it around the bed and placed it back in my holster, and into the drawer after that I looked at her, and she met my gaze as she asked "What happens now?"

I smiled a wry smile, and said "Well that really depends on you, if you still wish to continue to be my lady, then I have to report that I'm seeing someone on a permanent basis, and then the vetting process begins, where your every bit of your background goes under the microscope, and then you're called into an office for an interview with the vetting officers, and you get given verbal instructions on what you can and can't do, and during all the time this is happening you're followed, your phone is bugged and everything you do is reported and recorded. Now it's up to you, now you know all that, do you still wish to be involved with me? Before you answer consider this fact, I may get a call anytime, and I'll have to disappear but I won't be able to tell you where I'm going, or what I'd be doing, that's the worst case scenario, but could you honestly be able to put up with that?"

She stared at me as I told her all of that with a serious business look on my face, and then told me quietly, "Yes, I can do that, as long as you help me, I'm in love with you and want you in my life, so when you report in, start the ball rolling."

Then she said "Can we get into bed now? All of a sudden I've got a chill, and I need you to keep me warm." After she'd cuddled into me, she started to let go her apprehension and started to arouse my body, which was followed by an intense session of lovemaking. When we were done, she fell asleep in my arms, as I considered what I'd done, and I debated with myself whether I should have divulged that information so early, as I thought to myself, *well it's been a long while since I had someone in my life that I did care about, maybe this was my chance to be happy and settle down, Christ it's nineteen eighty-six, and I ain't getting any younger. It just so happens that that year proved to be one of the most volatile years of my life, in every shape, with my work, my business front, my finances, and my personal life, but I didn't know that until it ended.*

Next morning, we lazed in bed talking about when she had to go back to work, the fact that she still has another two months before her lease was up on the unit, and when she would like to move into the house permanently, and then what would we do with her furniture, would we keep both cars and so on, all the sort of incidental things that occur after deciding to live with one and other.

Dawn wasn't due to go back to work for another two weeks, I on the other hand had three days off from the dive shop after each long trip, but I had expected to go into the office during that time. Not that much would be happening, because we were still in the dead zone period, but Dawn did want to go into the shop to pay for the advanced course she did, so we decided to go into the shop later in the day, and then I said jokingly to her, that I suppose I'd better take her home to her place sometime considering she was cooking me dinner that night and I had such a long drive to get there. She jumped on giggling and stated that I didn't have that far to go, besides I was going to be helping her cook dinner, and I retaliated with, since when did that happen, and she told me it was either that or I had to get up and cook breakfast, so I opted to make breakfast.

We arrived at the shop at one pm, and Rob came out the office door as we were getting out of the car, I was going to ring you earlier, but I figured you'd still be in bed. Dawn giggled as I told him I was till an hour ago, and as he nodded with a smile I introduced him to Dawn, who had been one of Tony's open water students. They shook hands, and she told him that while she was on the trip I'd convinced her to do the advanced course, so she came into pay for it, Rob smiled and told her, well in that case you'd better come in and we'll take your money from you, I take it your Tiger's new girlfriend. I looked at him sharply and he told me Evan's already been in, and told us about the trip.

While Dawn was fixing up the course fee, I asked Rob if much else was going on for the next two weeks or so, and he told me, no so if you want some time off, now's the time, the builders aren't back for another three weeks, and I've got a trip to do on the Kanimbla when David gets back, so take as much time as you want, if I need you I'll ring. I nodded and told him thanks, and asked about his marriage, because I knew it was on real shaky ground, and he told me it was much the same, she was still wanting the house renovations done, and more money, which was strange considering she ran her own business and it was running at a massive profit according to the accountant, and that she was pissed off that he was spending too much time with diving, and he smiled as he told me that he only came into the shop to get away for a while, but what the hell, and we both laughed.

When Dawn came out, Rob told her with a smile to look after me, or she'd have to deal with him, because I was his best mate, and we all laughed as Dawn and I got into the car and headed back home, that night we spent at her place, and she was curious when I put down the Sat phone, and asked me about it, so after I told her about it, she laughed and said, "Rubbish, there's no such thing!" I smiled and told her ok, that's the number ring it, you'll see. She laughed again and took the card with the number on it, and dialled it on her phone, and then the Sat phone rang, so I answered it, saying "Are you satisfied now? I told you I don't lie," and then hung up as she nodded and amazed said, "Well I'll be, I didn't think that was possible, could I get one?" I nodded and relied "Sure if you're ready to fly overseas and buy one if you have a spare five thousand dollars, and can pay the call charges which are a dollar a second." Her eyes went wide and said "I don't think I really need one, but how come you've got one?" I just looked at her, without saying anything with my lips pursed, and head cocked at an angle, after watching me she said, "Oh, yeah right."

Over the following two weeks we started moving some of her stuff into the house, and we spent most nights at my place. We'd also called in at her parent's place so they could meet me, and I got on well with them, and we were even invited over for dinner on a Saturday night. When I met the rest of her family, another older sister married to a fireman, and a younger sister that was also a nurse in Mt Isa, and was home on holiday, everyone got on well, and they were pleased that she'd found someone who cared for her like I did. That was the last weekend of her holiday, and she had phoned the hospital to find out her shifts for the week, and was on days from seven to four for the first four days.

After that she had three nights of midnight to eight, and then three days off before switching to the afternoon shift of four to midnight, for ten days straight. We had already discussed the fact that she'd have various shifts to do, and that sometimes we wouldn't see each due to our different work schedules, but we'd work our way through it.

The dead zone was almost over, the day I walked into work, and slowly the place was getting back to full strength with staff returning from holiday, but still wasn't at full strength that Monday that I went into work, while Dawn had gone to work an hour before I left, deciding to have breakfast in the canteen.

There were no urgent things to take care of, so I pottered about with all the non-urgent stuff that had to be caught up on anyway, and after I'd taken care of that I went downtown to the bank, and asked about the share market, and was given a list of brokers that would be able to help me with investing, and while I was there I got the balances of all my different accounts. Back in my office I contemplated that considering I'd lost two huge amounts, the first being nearly seven hundred thousand that was paid to a law firm, that had ended up losing the case I was funding anyway, and the second being the half a million I'd invested in the dive shop complex, I was treating this as a loss, until I saw some return on the investment. After accounting for those, I still had just under a mill and a half, so if I kept the million to live on, I could afford to invest the five hundred grand.

CHAPTER 21

Well over the next few weeks I contacted brokerage firms, and finally focused on one, and after accepting their advice ninety percent of my share portfolio was made up of stock that could end up making me a lot of money and also some on the short term money market, the rest was put into blue chip stuff, that didn't earn a lot of interest but was a safe haven, and real estate. During one of our usual Monday meetings at the office we were interrupted with a call coming straight from the boss Colin Gorman from Foreign Affairs, Janice had patched it through, and stayed on the line in case she was needed.

Gorman, told us that he'd called me straight away to do with a situation that had developed overseas, and he required my planning and strategy for the operation that was going to happen because of the situation, but told us that, the only part I would play in the mission would be to plan and oversee the operation from start to finish, regardless of the end result. I would be given full command of the operation and it would be run from my operations room, and asked what I would require. So I looked at Harry, and he rattled of a list of things, which included the ability to task satellites to our bidding including the use of not only communication but real time photo and infra-red capability plus night vision, all this Gorman agreed to without question, so that meant this was a really serious operation.

As Harry finished his list, I interrupted and told Gorman, all this is just on speck we may need more when we know the full parameters of the operation and what has happened precisely, so we required a full briefing, and he agreed and told us he would arrive in Brisbane as soon as he could get to the airport, so I told him I'd have a car waiting to bring him straight to the office, and we would all await his arrival.

I flicked the switch that terminated the call, and then told Janice to alert Ross to Gorman's arrival and to bring him straight in when he arrived. She rogered my instructions, and then Harry, John and I discussed the upcoming briefing, and the fact that it must be damned important considering the speed at which things were taking shape, and we surmised that a SAS TAG team had already been put on alert considering it was an overseas operation, because there was only one or two ground agents in each particular country, so if this was a big operation, which it sounded like, then we'd be using a SAS TAG team for the job, mind you this was only our speculation at this point.

So It was agreed that I make use of my former association with SAS, to see if one of the TAG teams was on alert, and that we could find out while Gorman was in the air and unaware of what we were up to. So we adjourned the meeting until Gorman arrived, and in the meantime I would call Western Australia.

Back in my office, composed myself and what I was going to say, before getting Janice to make the call to Campbell Barracks, and after being connected, I spoke to Major Carl Nabors, who was the headquarters CO, and that meant he was the CO of the TAG teams as well. He knew me by sight and reputation, and after we exchanged pleasantries, got down to business, by telling him of my current position and that I wished to speak to the TAG team commander that had been placed on alert, Carl laughed and told me the commanders name was lieutenant Terry Witherspoon, and that he'd patch me through.

I spoke to Witherspoon, and found out that TAG teams now numbered ten men, and he gave me a list of the current communication devices they were now using, and the only thing new was personal locator transmitters, and he explained to me that they'd only been place on alert only two hours before, so I told him that when I had all the details I'd be letting him know, as to what I came up with in the way of planning, and that I would be running the operation from my headquarters Tac room, he knew of my reputation with the regiment, and therefore was prepared to wait until he heard from me, and I advised him to get in as much practise at the killing house as they could in the meantime.

Two hours later, Janice told me that Ross had called in, and was on his way to the office, so I told her to alert John and Harry to meet me in the TAC room, and that she was to bring Gorman there when he arrived, and then I went into DJ's office and told him he was to join me in the Tac room. I had plans to make DJ my protégé and 2IC in the planning and strategy area so it time he started to learn, and what better time to start.

In the meantime, Janice had taken it on herself to have the canteen make up luncheon food for everyone in the TAC room, and even though there was only six that would be present she catered for ten, so at least we wouldn't go hungry during the briefing that was about to come. We didn't have long to wait Gorman came into the TAC room with Janice five minutes after the food had been brought in, so we were all having a sandwich as he entered, he sat down and grabbed a plate and put some food onto it as he addressed us, saying "Ok I don't know all of you yet, but the reason we're all here is because of an attack."

He looked around at all of us, and continued "By that I meant that last night an attack was made on a compound of aid workers in the small village of Milange, in Zambezia, which is a part of Mozambique. The attack was made by Malawi rebels from across the border, and two school teachers were kidnapped, one Australian, and one a US citizen. Now our cousins are going to let us run the recovery operation, but will give us access to everything they have available, and that includes intelligence from their assets in country, which is how we and the CIA have learned about this already, and I would assume that the press will find out about it very soon."

I interrupted, asking "Ok we know where they were taken from, but do you know where they are now, and how they were transported away?" He looked at me and smiled, and then said "At this present time, no, but they left in three utilities, and one of the US assets (native agents) was following them at a distance, and we should have some solid intelligence soon, I hope. Now I've already put a TAG team on alert, but I would like to get them into the area as soon as possible, but do we send them into Malawi or not."

"No," I stated, "Get them into the air soon, yes, but can they be sent to a military base near Pretoria, or somewhere near the northern border, but first I want to have time to talk to TAG commander, and fill them in as we go along, so I'm going to need constant communication with them."

Gorman looked at me, saying "Yes I can get them into South Africa, but I don't want them to be briefed just yet until we know the full picture." I scoffed, and harshly replied "Callaway can confirm this, but I swore to your predecessor that I'd kill him if he didn't give me the full picture, when I was with SAS, and he sent my team on a mission, so I know what it's like to be left guessing, and I refuse to do that to people who are working with me, so if I'm to run this recovery, we're doing it my way, or I don't do it at all!" He stared at me, and then finally sighed and nodded his head and agreed. Then I looked at Harry, and had him bring up a map of the area on the monitors, and I told Janice to make the call to SAS and get me Terry Witherspoon. Gorman started laughing, and asked "I suppose this is a silly question, but how did you know TAG Bravo was the team on alert?" I smiled, and replied "I have my way of knowing things."

Witherspoon came on the line, and I told him he's on speaker and that after I filled him in, different people were going to be asking for different things for him to supply, and then I gave him all the information we had to date.

Then after I was finished, I told him that as I got information in, I'd be passing it along, and then I passed him onto Gorman, who told him that the RAAF would supply them a Hercules and be at his disposal, but that they were to head for South Africa and the aircrew would be told where to make for on route with instructions to be pass everything onto him. I interrupted to tell

Witherspoon to make their way to Pearce by eighteen hundred and they were to be in the air by nineteen hundred, then Harry took over and asked for all the technical data and radio frequencies, after that I told Witherspoon to note the phone number I was going to give him, and then go to Major Nabors and have him ring me back.

Five minutes later the phone rang and Janice answered, looked at me and nodded, so I flicked the speaker switch, and told Carl that Mr Colin Gorman of the department of foreign affairs was about to come on the line and give the go order, and then Gorman told Carl everything necessary, and then ended the call. I looked around the room, and told them all, that now the operation was official and happening that the TAC room was now operational, so John said "I'll get the staffing sorted, and everything will be available in thirty minutes." I nodded and we adjourned for an hour.

When we filed out of the Tac room, Gorman told us he would go up to the Foreign Affairs office in the building above us, to try and get the latest, and I suggested that after that, they contact him through our Tac room, and he nodded. DJ, Janice and I headed for my office, and when we were alone there, I asked "Janice are you able to stay, this could take a few days?" She nodded, and replied "I've got enough clothes; all I'd have to do is make a call to arrange some things to be looked after." I looked at DJ, and asked the same thing, and again he had enough clothing, but like Janice would need to make a couple of calls, which I had to do myself, so I looked at them, and said "Ok go make your calls, and Janice arrange for some camp beds for you and DJ in your offices, also confirm that the canteen know that they'll need full staffing requirements, ok away you go, I've got a call to make as well, I'll see you back in the Tac room."

After they had left, I quickly made the call home, I knew that Dawn was on nights this week, but I wanted to let her know that I probably not be home anyway for the next few days. She answered and I let her know a situation had arisen at work for a few days, and she told that it was ok, because she was going to be on nights until Friday, and I told her that if she had a couple of days off after that, we might go somewhere for the weekend.

She seemed happy with my suggestion, and told me she'd leave it in my hands, and also told me to be careful, then she had to get showered before work, and we hung up. After the call I went into my wardrobe and selected a comfortable pair of trousers and a warm sweatshirt and a pair of Ugg boots to wear for the first sojourn in the TAC room after I'd had a shower.

After my shower, and change into casual gear, I made my way to the canteen, and decided to increase my sugar level by choosing a large piece of cheesecake to go my coffee, and as I turned from the counter I saw Gorman was back and sitting alone at a table, so I joined him, asking "Anything new Colin?" He looked at me and smiled, and replied "Yeah we've got a location, and the Herc will land at Pietersburg military base in the northern province of South Africa." I nodded, and asked "Good, tell me is this the first time you've gone through one of these situations?" Gorman replied with a smile, "No, but it's the first time I've been privy to what actually goes on in a tactical room." I laughed and smiled, and jokingly said "Well in that case, I'd better not screw up hey! Look all you have to remember is that there's only one person in charge in the TAC room, and that is me as mission commander, my decisions are final and there are no arguments, if I screw up then I'm accountable later, but in there, my word as commander is law, no ifs or buts!"

He laughed and smiled, and said "Ok I'll go along with that, but in that get up, I'm not sure." I laughed and answered "Well get used to it, we're only into the first stage of the operation, which is a sort of a settling in period, this is just the lead up, while the operation on the ground is taking place everyone will be on top of their game., and if they're due for a break, that break won't be taken, because they won't want to relinquish their posts while the operation is in a flux situation, and the ground operation isn't finished. They'll wait until the rescuers are back in friendly skies."

Gorman stared at me and questioned "So what'll happen then?" I replied with a smile, and said "Well those that have been on shift without a break will be ordered to have at least six hour's kip, before reporting back, and then once the mission is finished everyone will be given three days off to recuperate, which includes you, me and all our staff." He looked at me incredulously, and asked "What the hell does that mean?" I smiled with my reply, "Think of it this way, at times you'll be in that room for upwards of forty-eight hours straight, and no one functions without sleep and food, why do you think I'm giving my body such a high dose of sugar at the moment, if food is available you take it."

Gorman responded, by asking "But won't that just put on fat to the body?" I laughed, and answered "No, your body will need the energy that the food gives you, because trust me almost everyone in that room will be running on pure adrenalin, and that's all, no matter how much you eat, you'll probably find that you've lost weight. Now let's get ready to go in, and where are the hostages being held, and are there any demands as yet?"

Gorman answered with a wry smile, saying "No, on any demands, but they are being held at a rebel base just outside Limbe which is about half an hour's drive from Blantyre in Malawi." As we headed towards the TAC room, I surmised "Hmm, I wonder how many rebels are there; I'll get Harry onto it as soon as we get into the TAC room."

A lot had taken place during the hour I'd been away, as both of us entered, I noticed the monitor screens each had a different picture, DJ and Janice, along with Harry and John, and the rest of the staff were all dressed in casual gear, expecting a long haul operation, and they were right in their assumptions. After giver Harry instructions to bring up the town of Limbe, I told Colin to give him the coordinates of the rebel base, and the screen wavered for a minute, and then focused on the particular group of housing. After watching for a couple of minutes, I asked John if he could go to infra-red to determine a count of personnel, and then what we saw was that there were only two in a constant area, while around the rest of the buildings there were at least thirty targets moving freely around the complex, so I assumed that the two constant heat signatures were the hostages being held in a cell or room.

After determining that Terry's team would be facing odds of three to one, I asked for hard copies to be faxed to the base where the Herc would land, and then asked for direct radio communication with the TAG team. Witherspoon came on line, and I told him what we'd found out, and that hard copy faxes would be waiting for him when he landed, and also that I would be looking at things with a fine tooth comb to see what I could plan, and that by the time they landed I'd have something concrete for him.

His reply showed me how much my reputation was still alive within the regiment, when Witherspoon replied that he trusted my judgement, and looked forward to hearing my plan of action, and as he signed off, he told me he'd contact us via radio as soon as they were on the ground. By this time, I'd been in the TAC room for over three hours.

After asking DJ to get me some topographical maps of the target area, I told Janice to go and get some rest, and asked her to rouse me when we had confirmation the TAG team had landed, and then headed to my office quarters for some sleep, and I smiled as I saw Colin Gorman with his head on his arms at the table fast asleep, as I turned to leave the room.

As I lay down I worked out that Witherspoon still had at least six hours flying time before landing, and set my internal clock so that I woke after five hours. While I slept the beginnings of a plan had started to formulate in my mind, and so when I woke, I contacted the Tac room, and asked for John to have a screen up with the satellite view around the target village, and for Gorman to find out if it was possible for us to land a military plane in Mozambique.

An hour later, after having some breakfast, I walked back into the Tac room, and the maps I'd requested from DJ were on the table in front of my chair, and I looked them over comparing, the map with the satellite view that John had up, and the more I looked the more my plan formed, and then I looked toward Gorman, who was on the phone handset, and a smile came to his face as I watched, he looked up, and while still holding the handset, gave me a thumbs up signal, and I couldn't help but grin, it was all coming together nicely. Then I asked for the satellite view of the border crossing on the Blantyre Mocuba road, and decided that it was undermanned, which would make the escape easier.

Soon after finalising the plan in my mind, Witherspoon came through on the radio speakers, alerting me to the fact that his team was on the ground. So I asked him if he had access to a large computer screen, and the base commander was with him, conveyed the fact that they had a fully operational tactical room much like the one we were using, and after Harry obtained the computer address from the base commander. I told Witherspoon to let his team rest and be ready for a video briefing in ten hours' time, and to have the RAAF pilots at the briefing, because we would be giving them position coordinates. For tasks that would require completion prior to the mission completion. Then after signing off with Witherspoon, I stood down all but a skeleton staff to rest and sleep, telling them to report back in eight hours.

In my office Gorman and I were drinking coffee on opposite sides of the desk, and I told him needed I needed to speak with his CIA contact as to regard the use of the assets they had in the area.

After ten minutes it was arranged that I could use two of their assets for the rescue, and I was told how to contact them with instructions and the code phrase to use as authentication.

Later that night after a couple hours' sleep, and something to eat, I went into the Tac room, and over to Johns seat at the table, and asked him to bring up the area around the target location, and we looked particularly at the golf course as I worked out the course layout, and found that the clear area I wanted to use for insertion was the second fairway. Then I had him transmit a message to the two CIA assets with the authentication code, telling them to be on the second fairway of the country club at twenty one hundred with torches, and to flash them straight up for a minute at the sky, then they were each to spread out to different parts of the fairway, well away from any trees and wait until they heard the plane, and then turn on their torches and shine them straight up until they were joined by our soldiers, and then they would lead them to the rebel compound. John looked at me with a smile, and said "Oh you figured the insertion point out very well, cunning and it's only a hundred metres from the target; tell me will we have to pay green fees?" We both burst out in laughter.

When Harry walked into the room I went over to him, and told him I wanted blown up hard copy photos of the golf course, the compound, the main road border crossing into Mozambique, and the military air base outside of Mocuba. He smiled and told me he'd have them ready for me in an hour, and I asked to get a video camera set up at the end of the room so I could brief Witherspoon's team live, he nodded and went over to John, and they talked for a while before Harry left the room again, as Gorman entered. I went over to his seat and told him what I needed, which was permission to land at the Mocuba military air base, for our Herc, and access onto the base for the TAG team that would arrive in a maximum of three vehicles, he nodded and smiled as he told he get onto it, and he reached for the phone handset.

Everything in the TAC room was ready and set up for the briefing by six thirty that morning. The photo blow ups and all the relevant maps and coordinates had been faxed to the Pietersburg Tac room for Witherspoon and his men, our monitors were displaying up to the minute satellite images, and one display was blank, but it was hooked up to the incoming computer signal for the camera in the Pietersburg Tac room so we'd see the TAG team.

At five to four in the afternoon South African (Bravo) time, the monitor from there became live as the wide angle camera swept the room, and a deep voiced Afrikaner asked if we were getting the video feed and voices, by now I had a microphone attached, and so I reported that we were seeing and hearing everything, and I enquired if they were receiving our feed, which they were, so we were all set to go. I had a monitor facing me that showed what they were seeing, and so I could adjust accordingly, Harry was going to operate the camera at our end, and we'd rehearsed what I would be showing them, so there was less camera swing.

I watched their monitor, and saw them all taking seats, and at eight am our time I started the briefing. "Good afternoon gentlemen, I'm the agent in charge of this operation, and for those who don't know me my name is Tiger Davis, I'm ex SAS, and was the leader of the first ever Special Response Team, so believe me when I say I know what you're going through and into. The mission is to rescue two school teachers that were kidnapped from Milange and transported to Limbe in Malawi by a rebel group a couple of days ago. The mission is to be wheels up by twenty hundred hours your time, now to the RAAF crew, you'll be inserting the TAG team at this first group of coordinates that you should have received and I've estimated that they're two and a half hours flying time from your present location." I heard a voice interrupt and say "Just checking that now, and that's spot on estimation sir." I smiled and continued.

"From there you'll fly to the next set of coordinates, which is for the military base at Mocuba in Zambezia, you will have permission to land there and refuel and also take on fresh food, after you give them your flight number and inform them that you're the expected Australian flight. Once there you'll wait, to be re-joined by the TAG team. Now Captain will you have enough fuel to fly straight back to Pearce from there?"

A voice replied, "Just checking, it'll be a long haul, but yes we'll have enough and with some left over." I smiled into the camera, and remarked "Good, trust the RAAF thank you captain, that's you guys taken care of," and laughed.

"Now then Lieutenant Witherspoon, your team will insert by parachute, your landing zone will be marked by two local assets holding torches, and they'll lead you to the target location, which will be one hundred metres away. Now you'll by landing on the second fairway of the local country club, so please don't dig it up to bury your chutes, bag them and give them to the local assets."

As I waited for the mirth to finish, I added another joke to relieve some of the built up tension in our TAC room and theirs, "And please place your green fees in a bucket as you leave the course." While I'd been saying that Harry had placed the camera on the golf course blow up, and the target compound, so I said "You've probably seen the copies of these photos that we faxed earlier."

"Now I'm going to have the camera show you our monitor of the target location, and it's in infra-red to show us the heat signatures, now these two have been here for hours, and don't move from this location. So you could probably assume that is the hostages, whereas everyone else moves about in the complex, you'll also need to steal at maximum three transport vehicles, destroy the rest, because your escape will be by road into Zambezia and making for Mocuba, now the only bug bare, maybe at the border. Now here's the photo of the border control, if you have to, shoot your way out, the Zambezia authorities won't stop you, because they have already been informed of your mission, any questions gentlemen? There were none so I continued "Ok, we'll be able to monitor your SR Ten headsets, and we'll be able to communicate that way, good luck Terry, gentlemen, and thank you, dismissed!"

CHAPTER 22

Well after the briefing which had taken half an hour, I stood down the Tac room staff until midday, and a skeleton staff took over, and most of us went to eat and rest in the canteen, but before I went to my office for a rest, I left the building for a couple of smokes, and found out I wasn't the only one needing a nicotine dose. When I went back down, I asked Janice to wake me at fifteen thirty hours, which was approximately thirty minutes before the attack took place. I was trying to get as much sleep as I could, because after that I wouldn't sleep until the mission had reached a successful outcome.

Just before I was ready to get into bed the phone rang and I picked it up in my bedroom, Janice told me that John Callaway was calling, and I told her to put it through. Once he was on the line, he told me that he knew I was busy with the operation, but he'd had some news from the legal department, and that my divorce had been granted, and I would receive the paperwork in a couple of days, I smiled and thanked him, and after he wished me luck with the operation we hung up, *great* I thought *someone's going to like that news, but right now I can't be bothered with it*, and then I shut my eyes and swiftly dropped into sleep. I was woken by Janice prodding me with a broom and telling me it was time to wake up, and I grumbled the question, "What the hell are you doing?" She replied rather seriously, "Boss, I'll do almost anything for you, but to get anywhere within striking distance of you, when you're woken from a dead sleep is not one of them!" Thinking, nothing wrong with her logic, I replied as I inwardly laughed and asked "Time to get up I take it?" She responded, with "Yes Tiger, and before you ask, the ground assets confirmed being on sight where you wanted them." "Good" I replied "I'll be along in a tic," and she left me to get dressed, and soon after I was at my place in the TAC room, along with everyone else, a mug of hot coffee within reach.

The first thing I did was look closely at the target site on the monitor, and asked Harry to change the colour of the hostage's heat signature to blue, and instructed him to change the TAG team colour to green when they came into viewing. Then I asked John to get Terry Witherspoon on comm's, after a few minutes he told me that he couldn't get the team on their headset's, and he was assuming that they hadn't turned their sets on yet, so he was trying to get the aircraft, and have him put on the radio. After a couple of minutes Terry's voice came over the speakers, saying "TAG Bravo, go ahead." I replied and requested, "Terry this is Tiger, your LZ is confirmed and will be lit."

Then I turned to the request, which was "Please turn on your personal sets, how far from are you from drop coordinates?" After some muffled conversation he came back online, saying "two minutes from drop will do as requested, but must go, out." I smiled as I knew that right now he'd be racing from the cockpit into the Herc cargo bay as the plane depressurized and the loading ramp was being lowered in readiness for the jump.

I could almost visualize him running through the cargo bay yelling to his team, "Gear up, turn on comm's, and go, go, go!" Soon after we heard the crackling of the headsets as each team member passed on information to each other, the lead team member came through, saying "Have spotted two landing lights about four hundred yards apart, will head for the forward landing light." Then we heard "One down boss," and each consecutive call after that was consistent with a team member landing, and I knew when Witherspoon landed and announced "last man down all ok, switching to night vision equipment." I breathed out and sighed in relief, knowing everyone was down and ok.

Looking at the monitor, I could see the bunch of green dots that signified the TAG team and with them were two red, which were the local assets. Then as we watched, we heard Terry announce "Team Bravo to base, moving in on target." Watching the monitor, I said "Base to team Bravo, target fifty yards in front of you, three signatures moving, one to your starboard, and two near the gate in front of you," "Copy that," I heard as I watched the team split up, and then the heat signature near the rear of the complex faded out, and we heard "One down," as five of the team neared the gate to the complex, but the other five were moving across the compound, and then the two heat signatures went out, as we heard "two, three down, opening up boss." I smiled and brought my bent arm down in a proud yes gesture.

Then the team split up again, four headed toward the hostage area, three towards where we'd seen vehicles parked earlier, and three toward the remaining heat signatures that I assumed were sleeping rebels. Now as far as I'm concerned, if these guys woke up, then they would stop at nothing to shoot our troops, so I gave the kill order, by saying "Base to Tag Bravo, waste that lot before they wake up, you're outnumbered." The response was instantaneous, "Copy that base," and the signatures started to fade out, meanwhile the group with the hostages started to move toward the group near the vehicles, as I heard Terry's voice say, "Multiple enemy down, reform at the vehicles men, Bob you got the prisoners?" Another voice announced, "Roger that boss."

Then we watched the monitor and saw three different groups of friendlies moving away from the compound, as we heard Terry say, "TAG Bravo to base, civilians recovered, twenty-nine opposition forces down, and we are moving towards rendezvous, ETA eight hours" I smiled, and replied "Base to TAG Bravo, copy that, will alert reception, good job Terry and all your men, call into base before you tackle the border crossing, we will be sitting on the side, call if you need, Tiger out." As I finished speaking, applause and cheers erupted from the personnel in the Tac room, as I looked at the wall clocks, Bravo local time was zero one thirty, our time was seventeen fifty. So from the last time I'd spoken to Terry on board the Herc, the takeover, recovery of the hostages, and escape from the compound had taken two hours, I thought that was pretty good.

Now we had to wait until the border crossing which I estimated would take place within the next three to four hours, so I decided that this was the best time to go and eat, Janice and DJ volunteered to stay in the Tac room, so Gorman, Harry and John joined me in the canteen, and after they had finished heaping kudos on me for the way the operation had gone. We had a nice roast dinner, while we talked business, and about what was to come. Satisfied with the meal, I smiled as I leaned back in my chair with my hands linked behind my head, and announced, "Well I don't see there being any problem, they'll get to Mocuba ok, then board the Herc, take off and sleep on the way home to Western Australia, it's just a pity we can't be there to welcome them home."

Gorman started laughing, and as we looked at him, he explained "Well you could welcome them home, you've got a jet here, wait until the border has been crossed, alert the RAAF crew to be on standby, and then fly to Pearce your TAC room can stay online and reach you in an emergency, that way you'll be there to greet them when they arrive. I'll authorise it, and in the meantime I'll pick up my opposite number from the US embassy in Canberra, and meet you all at Pearce." I smiled and looked with a query in my eyes at Harry and John in turn and they both nodded smiling, so I said "Ok let's do that then! We can all go to the airport in my car, just take a small bag of clothes each." So before going back to the TAC room, we each went our separate ways to go to our offices, and pack go bags, except Gorman whose bag was on his plane.

When we got back to the TAC room, I talked quietly in Janice's ear, telling her to have a couple of days off when the job was finished, and also to get hold of Ross, and tell him to prepare the jet for take-off to Pearce air base in WA.

Ross was also to alert Gorman's air crew that they would be taking off at the same time, headed for Canberra. Then I informed Colin that the planes would be ready for flight as soon as we got to the airport, and then told DJ what Harry, John, and I would be doing, and that he would be in charge of the TAC room. Once the Hercules crew announced that they had the airfield in sight, he could wind down the operation, and give himself and the TAC room staff two days off before returning to work.

Just before eight pm, the room speakers announced "TAG Bravo to Base, we're a couple of minutes from the border, and I'm looking at it now while two members are reconnoitring, will report back soon." I looked at DJ and nodded and then while he answered, saying "Base to TAG Bravo copy that." I looked at the clocks, they were making better time than I thought, it had only taken them two and a half hours to get to the border, so they'd make the crossing under the cover of darkness, and hopefully sneak across while the border guards were asleep.

Five minutes later Terry called again, saying "TAG Bravo to base, scouts have come back and report everyone is asleep at border gate, and it's only a timber pole on a swivel, do we engage? Over." I thought quickly, and asked "Base to Tag Bravo, Terry do you think you could crash the barrier? Over." Witherspoon was silent for a minute, and then replied "Terry to Tiger, I've been told that's affirmative, it'll snap like a matchstick, over." Thinking quickly, I came up with the way to deal with the crossing, and said "Base to TAG Bravo, put your strongest vehicle in the lead, with your others behind it, crash through the barrier and don't stop for anything until out of rifle range, only engage if any of the guard's fire on you, when you're over call in, base out." I smiled and watched the monitor, as Terry replied "TAG Bravo to base copy that, moving in one, out."

Everyone's eyes were glued to the monitor that gave the satellite view of the escape vehicles, and would follow the progress of the team until after they made it to the military base and were airborne, after that it would be re-tasked, but at this time we watched as they approached the crossing, I got Harry to zoom in, and we all saw the lead vehicle smash through the barrier and keep going, and then each vehicle followed close on the rear of the previous vehicle, and were way down the road as the first person rushed out of the hut. I was chuckling as the speakers came alive, with vehicle noise and "TAG Bravo to base, crossing made without resistance, continuing to rendezvous, out."

I was still chuckling, as I listened, and replied "Base to TAG Bravo, copy that, well done Terry, see you and the team in Western Australia, base out." By nine pm our time, I had handed over command to DJ, and Harry, John, Colin and I were in my car headed for the airport hangar.

When we arrived, I drove into the hangar, and as we got out, Colin shook hands with us, and then headed to his jet that had its engines already turning over, while I gave Ross who was seated in the cockpit looking at me, the signal to start turning the engines over, and we made our way to the boarding stairs.

Ross landed the plane at Pearce airbase, and we taxied towards the main hangars where a refuelling truck waited, along with a rover that was being leaned against by Wing Commander Luke Roberts the base commander whom I'd met several times, so when we stopped and the boarding steps were in place. I preceded the others and went down and shook his hand, and introduced him to Harry and John. Luke told us that we were three hours in front of the returning Hercules, and an hour in front of a ministerial flight coming in from Canberra, and I smiled as I informed him who would be on that flight, and he thanked me for the heads up, and suggested we make ourselves comfortable in the aircrew's mess.

Which is exactly what we did, and after we'd finished breakfast, and were relaxing with our coffees, the ministerial jet landed, and I saw Colin Gorman greet Luke, and then introduce the rest of the passengers. After the introductions Luke escorted them towards the mess where we were sitting with our drinks, and as they entered Colin Gorman introduced me to the American ambassador and his boss and ultimately my boss Mr Bill Hayden the foreign affairs minister. During the time we waited for the arrival of the Hercules, we all chatted about different subjects, until the US ambassador put me on the spot, by saying "Tom, from what I hear from Colin here, it was you that put this whole rescue mission together, and planned it down to the last detail, now I have to tell you there's certain people in the CIA that would give their eye teeth to have you on staff, because you seem to know how to get things done, so if you ever think of living anywhere else, I'm sure we could find a place for you."

The Minister Mr Hayden had drifted over toward us as he been stating his offer, and smiled as he also waited for my answer, as I replied with a smile "Well sir the only reason I can get things done, is because I'm good at what I do, and I don't publicly embarrass anyone, or get caught, but elsewhere I'm not sure."

The ambassador started laughing, and then noticed the minister, and said "Bill old buddy, I've just been trying to head hunt your strategist, and I think he just put me in my place, but I'm not sure if he did or not, you're an Aussie, you tell me." Hayden laughed and replied, with a wink at me "Well I hate to tell you Jake, but not only did he put you in place, he stomped all over you." They both were laughing out loud, the ambassador turned to me and stated, "Son you ever find yourself out of a job, you come see me, ya hear." I smiled, and said "Yes Sir." As they started to move away, the minister murmured in my ear, "Well done Tiger, the pompous shit needed that, hopefully we get time to talk later."

Shortly after the Hercules carrying the TAG team and hostages landed, and everyone was ushered outside as the plane came to a standstill, and powered down, and then the loading ramp opened, the hostages were first off, and were greeted by the ambassador and minister, and then as the team filed past they were introduced to both dignitaries, and then Witherspoon spotted me as they were heading into the mess, and led his men to me, saying "You've got to be Tiger Davis, no one else has the easy look of command that you exude, it's an honour sir." As he held his hand out, and then I introduced Harry and John, and we in turn were introduced to Team Bravo. After all the dignitaries had gone inside, I suggested that we better go in and make an appearance, and that way we'd get the bullshit out of the way before some heavy drinking, the whole team laughed, and Witherspoon smiled as he remarked, "Sounds like you haven't changed much since your days in the regiment, Tiger." We both laughed as I replied, "I should hope not."

We overnighted there in VIP quarters and flew back to Brisbane the following morning, and landed at fifteen hundred, after the drive into the city, I went to my office to clear any backlog, and then decided to have an early day, and drove home, and it turned out that Dawn was on her first of three days off, so that night we went out to one of our favourite restaurants at the grange for dinner. While we having dinner, she told me about the hospital administrators being on her case, about taking some of her accrued leave time, and asked if I had any solutions. So I asked her to give me a week or so, to see if I could come up with anything, knowing already I had an idea playing around in the back of my head.

Next morning, I called into the dive shop on my way through to the office, and found out that nothing much was happening due to it being winter, and I told Robert that I would use the time, and have an overseas holiday.

He laughed and jealously said go right ahead Tom, but don't you dare be going to the pacific for any diving, and he laughed as I told him I'd probably end up going to England. In at the office that day, I asked Janice to get hold of John Callaway for me, and when she did, I asked him for some leave time and he asked how long I needed. So I informed him I wanted five weeks, and also that I'd need an update on Dumper's whereabouts. Then he asked when I was thinking of going, and I had to tell him I'd let him know as soon as he got me the update on Dumper, and he told me to leave it with him.

My next call was to Dawn at home, and I asked her if she could apply to take five weeks leave straight away, and she told me that she'd have to check, but she thought that it wouldn't be a problem, and so I asked her to find out ASAP, and leave a message on my Sat phone, and she told me that she'd get onto it straight away, and it was only then that I enquired whether she had a passport, and thankfully she did. Half an hour later my Sat phone vibrated in my pocket, it was a message form Dawn which read, "On holiday for six weeks after my days off, where are we going, ring me please."

As I was about to pick up the phone handset, it rang, and Janice told me that Callaway was on the line, so I got her to put him through, and as he came on he said "Jeez you're a lucky arsehole, the boss has told me to tell you that you can use the company plane to go to wherever you wish, and the agency will pick up the tab for the pilot's accommodation and fuel, so they're at your disposal, for five weeks only, however this is a onetime offer for doing such a bang up job on that recovery. Now your mate flew into England two days ago, so I presume that he's at his home for the rainy season, good luck, and let me know when you get back." As I replaced the handset I thought, *brilliant everything is falling into place when I need it, wow damned lucky on being able to use the jet though, ok, now what have I got to do, oh yeah somewhere to stay.* I flicked the intercom switch, and asked Janice to come in.

When she'd come in and sat down, I told her I'd have a few things for her to do. The first was to book me a suite in London for five weeks, and make sure they had a car available to me to use, and that a limo would pick me up at Heathrow. Then get hold of Ross for me, after I finish with the call that I was about to make, and then I opened the safe and took out one hundred thousand, and gave it to her and asked her to go to the bank, and get that changed into UK money. So she told me she'd get it done first, and then worry about making the hotel booking, I nodded and told not to worry about Ross because I'd do it.

When she left my office I decided to take another hundred grand with me as a backup, and called Dawn after I closed the safe. She answered the phone with a "Hi sweetheart, would you like to let me know what you're up to?" I laughed and said "Well I have to go see someone in England, and I thought we could have a holiday there if you wanted to go with me. We can do all of the touristy things, and I can show you around the country, and maybe even visit some of my relatives, but we'll base ourselves in

London, and we'll be flying there by private jet, so how does that sound to you honey?"

She was ecstatic, and replied "Oh darling that sounds wonderful, please come home soon so we can talk about this, and I'll even take you out to dinner tonight, because I love you so much." I smiled and then said, "Ok honey I'll see you when I get home." I looked at the clock and did some quick mental sums, and then reached for the phone again. Dumpers number rang three times and went to the answering machine, and I left him a message saying that I would be coming to into the country soon and would ring him from London. My next call was to Ross, and I asked him if he and Jerry would like to take their wives on a trip to England for a holiday, and after he told me that would please them both, told him to start getting the plane ready then, and we'd take it in easy stages first into Singapore, then Bahrain, and finally into Heathrow. Then I told him that the agency was covering the costs, so to arrange their accommodation as well, and that we'd be over there for at least a month. He asked me when we'd be going, and I told him that it would be in the next couple of days, and I'd ring him.

After that I went into DJ's office and sat down, and then I told him my plans, and we discussed what he'd need to do while I was gone, which was just that he'd be charge of our department while I was away, he'd done it before, so there wouldn't be any difference to then. While I was in his office Janice returned, and after she gave me the British money, she said she'd get onto my booking, so I nodded and told her that while she was trying to organise that, I'd go and grab some lunch in the canteen.

Back in my office, Janice was sitting across from me as she told me that she was able to get me a suite at the Hilton Metropole which was on Edgeware road down near Marble Arch, I nodded because I knew it and told her it was close to Harrods as well, and she told me that they'd have a limo available to pick me up, and I just had to give them an hour's notice of arrival, also there would be a car at my disposal during my stay, after that I left for the day.

When I got home Dawn greeted me with a kiss, and then offered to pour me a drink as I got changed, not one to refuse a drink I took her up on the offer, and we sat in the downstairs barroom as we discussed the trip, and she asked how I'd managed it on such quick notice, we'd only been discussing it the night before. So I told her that, I'd asked for and been given holidays from the office job, and as a reward for such a good job on the last operation, the boss had given me free use of my agency plane. She stopped me there, with the question, "Wait a minute, are you telling me you have your own plane?" Now that she'd been vetted and approved to know some of the internal workings of the agency, I told her that as the officer in charge of the state office, I did have a jet at my disposal to get me from place to place as required. She looked at me with a smile, and said "Oh this I can't wait to see, when can we go? Oh wait a minute what about the dive shop?"

I laughed and got up to make us each another drink, and replied by saying "I stopped in this morning and there's not much going on over winter, so I can take as much time as I like, and as for when we can go, well that's up to you we can leave tomorrow if you wish, but you'll need time to decide what to pack, so how about day after tomorrow?" She nodded and said "You're the boss."

Next day I slept in a bit, and went into the office for only a couple of hours to tidy things up, collect my go bag, and take care of any last minute details. After that I drove out to the airport, and saw Ross and Jerry at the hangar, and they told me that their wives about the trip, and couldn't wait to go. I laughed and told them both that when they got home to tell the girls to start cooking, because we're go to fly out tomorrow, and that's why I'm here to work out the best time to take off. Then I suggested that at times I could take over in the cockpit, and Ross asked what aircraft qualifications I was signed off on, when Jerry heard about the Harriers, he was excited and asked all about them, and then Ross told me that if I could fly a Vulcan I'd have no trouble picking things up on the 737, and so we went up into the cockpit, and he had me take the captains controls, and ran me through a few questions about what did what, and he was well satisfied, and told me that I could take the controls anytime I wished.

Finally, we decided that wheels up would be nine am and that way we'd have time to refuel and take off again from Changi while it was still daylight, and then we'd land in Bahrain in the early morning, refuel again and get into Heathrow around two in the afternoon. Then I gave the hotel number to Jerry and told him that he'd have get London airport to ring the hotel with my ETA.

He told me not worry, that he'd make sure the limo was there to pick me up, and then I warned them that my current girlfriend would be coming on the flight, but she already been vetted by the agency, and as they heard that both of them visibly relaxed, and after telling them I'd be there by nine, and saying I'd see them all in the morning, I drove home.

The following morning, Dawn and I arrived at the hangar at quarter to nine, and I drove the car into the hangar, and as we got out I was greeted by Jenny, so I introduced them to each other, as I was taking out the bags, Rhonda came rushing over kissed me on the cheek, and said "Hey boss how are you, haven't seen you for a while." Then Jenny introduced Dawn to Rhonda, just as Jerry and Ross came down the stairs, so after further introduction, Jerry went to lock the gate, and Ross started to close the hangar door as we made our way onto the plane. As she looked into the cabin of the plane, Dawn remarked "Wow." Then back to face me and asked incredulously "This is yours?" I smiled and then nodded my head, and told her I'd give her the grand tour once we were in the air.

As Jerry and Ross closed the door, while Jerry cross locked it, Ross said "Boss we have to wait for some incoming planes before we can taxi, so it'll be ten minutes before we start rolling, I'll come on the intercom just before we move." I nodded my head, and then held my hand toward Dawn and told her I'd give her a quick tour before we moved.

CHAPTER 23

As we were sitting in our seats and buckled up to take off Dawn was remarking about the plushness of the seating, and the fact that the seats converted into full length beds, and the size of the toilets and showers and when she found out the lounge in my office was a little larger than a double bed. She stated that we'd be sleeping on it that night. I think that she was overawed by the jet, and amazed at the same time. My comment about her reaction of anybody would think you haven't been on a private jet before, earned me a punch in the arm, and when I told her that sometimes I would be taking over the controls to fly the plane myself, that led to questions about my flying skills.

When she asked Jenny about joining us while she served us coffee and cake, and she was a little taken back by Jenny's answer, "No Dawn, this is the boss's flight, and even though I met Tiger, as a soldier back before he was Ross's boss, now he is the boss, and he is one of the best bosses I've ever come across. Why it was at his insistence that we were able to make this trip with you, even though we'll be doing our own thing while we're there, but miss as far as Rhonda and I are concerned even though we don't work for him, we're just married to Ross and Jerry who do work for him, he's the best boss ever, and there's nothing we wouldn't do for him, now if there's anything you need just press the call button and Rhonda or I'll be able to help, boss we were going to serve a hot lunch at thirteen hundred is that ok?" I replied "That'll be fine Jen thanks," quite frankly I was feeling a little embarrassed because of her open praise.

When we were two hours out of Singapore, because Dawn as asleep I went into the flight deck and took over from Ross while he had a break. He came back into the cockpit as we were on the approach to Changi, but I told him it was ok. I'd land the plane, so he sat in the engineers seat behind Jerry in the co-pilots seat, and watched, and as we were given permission to land, I lined up the plane with the path of the runway, and had Jerry bring the wheels down, once he told me they were down and locked, Ross's voice said in my headset, "Everything's looking good, just remember to be aware that a hundred foot off the deck be prepared for a cross wind gust, it's usually not strong, but it can take you by surprise if it's your first time landing here." He was right it almost took me by surprise, but because I had warning of it I didn't make the mistake of over correcting, and soon after I felt the wing wheels contact the tarmac, and slowly lowered the nose until it made contact. Then both Jerry and I brought the engine levers into full reverse thrust, as I softly applied the brakes to slow us down.

I felt Ross slap me on the shoulder, as he said "Hah perfect landing boss considering that it's your first time at the controls of this sort of plane, you can fly this thing anytime you wish." Jerry took over the taxiing, as I took off the headset and got out of the pilot's seat, and Ross told me we'd be on the ground for an hour while we refuelled, if I wished to take my missus for a tour of the terminal, I nodded and opened the cockpit door as I made my way back to where Dawn was now wide awake.

After the immigration and customs formalities we killed the time on the ground by touring the terminal, and while we were having a drink she told me that she wouldn't mind coming back here, so I told her we could stop over a couple of days on the way back if she wished, and she nodded. When we boarded for the next leg, Jerry got some sleep while I took over as co-pilot, and Dawn came into the cockpit and sat at the engineer's station while we took off, and once we were at cruising height, she went back into the cabin and was going to watch a movie. When Jerry returned to the flight deck, he took over as pilot and Ross changed into the co-pilot seat while I went back to my office, and found Dawn already in bed there, so I joined her, and slept until we were an hour out of Bahrain.

When we landed because our stopover was going to be longer

than the refuelling time at Singapore, we all ended up having a nice breakfast together, at one of the terminal cafes, and after three hours on the ground; we took off again on the last leg into Heathrow. We arrived a couple of minutes in front of the projected time we'd worked out a few days ago of two pm in the afternoon, I had to wait for Dawn to go through the customs and immigration formalities, I'd been able to go straight through because I held a British passport, and I went to where a driver was holding a sign with my name, and after I told him we had to wait a couple of minutes for my girl to join us, and then we could be away.

An hour later we were checking in, and went up to our suite and Dawn was amazed at the luxury of our suite and looked at me and asked "Is this the way you live when you're away on business?" I laughed and nodded my head and told her there were sometimes when I'd have to rough it, but I did like to live well when I was on an assignment. Then we got down to discussing whether I'd get my stuff out of the way, by seeing the people I had to first, or if we'd play tourists for a couple of days, before I went to do that. It was decided I'd get my stuff done first, after all it was the main reason we were here, but first we'd enjoy the rest of the day, and the night relaxing together, before we settled down to the business at hand, and then she headed into the bathroom.

I asked what she was up to, and she told me that she was running a nice hot bath for the both of us, and I smiled as I went into the lounge area and made us each a drink to have while we soaked in the spa bath. That night we had a lovely three course meal in the restaurant and a few quiet drinks in the bar, before going to bed.

Instead of going down to the restaurant the next morning, I Took Dawn to the executive lounge, which we were entitled to use due to having a suite, in those days you could have a full cooked breakfast there, but apparently that doesn't happen anymore, but at that time our breakfast was a marvellous buffet style, and had a choice of some exquisite delicacies along with the normal fare of bacon, eggs and sausages and toast along with brewed coffee. Dawn told me with a laugh that if she kept having decedent food like we'd been having, she would definitely put on weight. Laughing I told her that there was a gym and pool in the hotel, and we both laughed. While we were there I phoned Dumper's number and when he picked up I told him I was in London, and would see him just before lunch time, and he told me he'd be waiting for me.

Back in our room I warned Dawn that I would be away most of the day back by night I could be away the whole night, she told me she wanted to look around by herself anyway, and asked me where she could go within walking distance, so I took her to the balcony and showed her Marble Arch, and mentioned that Harrods was down a little further, and I also showed her where oxford street was, and told her she'd get her fill of window shopping along that road. She told me she'd have a quick look at Harrods's first while I was away, and I said "Honey if you're going to have a look in Harrods's you could be there for days on end." And we both laughed, after throwing some clothes into my go bag, just in case, I left the suite and went down to the concierge's desk to get the car that was on loan to me.

The car they gave me was a fives series BMW, up until then I had been toying with the idea of taking it to Peterborough and my Aunt's place, and swapping into my BMW, but seeing they'd given me one, there wasn't any need to do that, and as I left the hotel the traffic was pretty busy. It took me about an hour to get to the Sevenoaks turnoff and then only took a couple of minutes to get to Dumper's Farm. As he came out to greet me, I noticed that he wasn't at all well, he'd lost weight, his neck seemed swollen, and I noticed that he had a coppery coloured rash on both arms, he quickly backed off when I went to embrace him, and didn't move to shake my hand, and he told me he'd explain inside.

Inside the house I immediately noticed a change, the house was tidy and clean, and there were covers on all the lounge seats except one, the one that Dumper used all the time, it was easy to tell he used it all the time, because it hadn't shifted position like the others from my previous visit, and also the table beside it had a half empty bottle of scotch sitting on it, and as usual at the other side of the seat was his grenade box. He asked if I'd like a hot drink or something hard, but I elected for a coffee, and as he made it, I noticed he was meticulously cleaning everything after use.

When it was made, he turned and said "If you'd like to grab your mug, we can go out on the deck." I nodded and we both took our mugs with us outside, and after he'd lit his smoke, he said "Boss I'm sorry for before but I've got a bit of a medical thing at the moment, and don't want to risk it being contagious." I laughed and told him that was all right as long as it didn't stop us going down to the pub for dinner later, and he laughed as he told me that it wouldn't. A little later I made us both some lunch, simple fare, just a couple of sandwich's each with chicken, ham and cheese, and we ate these as we discussed what he'd been up to, and then I got around to telling him about the death and funerals of Wires, JJ, and Lizard.

Then most of the afternoon we spent reminiscing and laughing over some of the things we'd gotten up to, and also some of the things he'd seen and experienced in the Congo, and he asked me about how I was getting on as a spook, and I told him about the Mozambique incident, and he told me he heard about the kidnap while he was in Kenya on the way home, and had decided to make further enquiries. Eventually heard about the rescue, and the more he picked up the more he thought it sounded like I had a hand in it, we laughed about that and the fact that my handiwork had a certain signature to those who knew me.

We walked into the pub, and it hadn't changed, and as we breasted the bar the ex para sergeant now publican greeted us, saying "Marshy, Colonel, what'll be?" I ordered a pint of Guinness while Dumper had a pint of Falls Lager, and as I paid, said "Thank you, sergeant and I hope you have a bottle of Blue Label back there for later on?" He smiled, and replied "Ah that I have Colonel, just let me know when sir." I smiled and nodded and then asked him what was good on the dinner menu, he laughed and told me all of it, and we all laughed. After a few more pints, Dumper and I went into the dining room for dinner instead of drinking out in the bar, and the meal lived up to its reputation by being perfectly wonderful, and after a nice sticky date pudding, we returned to the bar.

As the publican approached, I said "When sergeant," and he about turned to a shelf and reached out to grab a bottle two tumblers and a bucket that he put some ice in. He placed the tumblers in front of each of us, put a cube of ice in each, and screwed off the bottle top and left us to pour our own. I paid the going rate for the bottle, plus added a fifty as a tip. The publican winked and walked off after telling us to enjoy ourselves.

Unfortunately for the sergeant this time we emptied the bottle before making our way back to Dumper's farm, I can't say we were exactly sober, but what the hell. When we got inside Dumper tossed me a bottle from behind the bar, and then collapsed into his chair. We didn't bother with glasses, and drank out of the bottle beside us. Then I'd had enough of the bullshit, and said "Ok Dumper, you've been down in the dumps, and no pun intended, since we started talking about the rest of the team, so it's about time you spit out the truth, what's going on?"

He smiled wryly, and replied "We never could put anything past you, boss, ok, I wasn't telling you everything earlier, it happened about four months ago, I was on leave in Kinshasa, and ended up screwing a highly priced whore, she told me she was clean, obviously she wasn't but by the time I got around to seeing any medico, I was already in stage three, and I got the full results yesterday, I'm actually dying boss, of believe it or not frigging Syphilis! All I've got to look forward to is major heart problems, maybe dementia, and blindness, so one way or another Tiger, I'm screwed, so it looks like out of our whole group, you're going to be the last man standing, you and I are the last of a great idea boss, but it looks like I'm stuffed so you have to stay alive, tell our story boss, even if you only tell our story to only one person, then maybe we won't be forgotten, I'm sorry I have to heap this shit on you, boss, but I'll be lucky if I live longer than three months, so I kind of hoped I'd get the chance to talk to you before I joined the rest of SRT one, hey just think, it's going to be a brilliant reunion."

I had to take a long pull on my bottle, before I could actually look at him, and then it was through misty eyes, it wasn't full tears, because I'd cried myself out years earlier, but John 'Dumper' Marsh had been handed a death sentence, and he was leaving me all alone, I would be the last of one of the most effective fighting forces since World War Two, and I said to him "Dumper, I don't know what to say, shit man, why don't you come home? What about your family, they need to know, Christ brother don't give up yet!" He smiled a wry smile, and replied "Well you know us boss, we all knew we could die any day, even you."

He took a pull out of his bottle before continuing, "At least unlike some of the other guys, I get to make the choice of how and when I go out, so I guess we're the lucky ones boss, we have that choice, but I'm glad that I had the time to talk to you before I go out Tiger, because if you grab that envelope on the mantelpiece, that gives you power to be executor of what goes where to my family and friends in Australia, and also my solicitor here, he's been instructed to pass on what isn't distributed over here to you, and those are the things I want done, and you're the only one I trust to do as I wish."

I nodded and told him I'd see to it when the time came, but that wouldn't be for some time yet, and then I asked him "Do you want me to talk to your solicitor before I go back, because he'll have to arrange your body going home?"

Dumper laughed and took a pull of his bottle, and replied "Well boss I thought that I may as well stay here, I like it here and back in Aus. I've no real close family and you're my only real mate alive, the rest are in that pitiful cemetery in WA, besides I'll be with them before my body ever gets near there." I nodded and took a pull of my bottle. Then I made him promise to call me on the Sat phone if he thought the time was getting close, because It would only take me a couple of days to fly in, and be with him.

He smiled and nodded that he would, and then had another drink.

After a while he started to really give the bottle a nudge, and then started to play with a grenade he pulled out of the box beside him, and I said "Look Dumper, if you're going to start playing with those things I might head back to London, its only nine, so I should get there in an hour, but I'll call down to see you before I go, if you need anything I always carry the Sat phone so you get me fairly quickly."

He nodded and we shook hands, as I left the second bottle beside him, and walked out of the house closing the door behind me, I started the car before closing the door, and then reversed toward the house to line up with the entry drive, and started down the drive. I was about three quarters of the way down the drive when I heard a muffled boom, and felt a concussive wave of wind, as I slammed on the brakes and the gear stick into park; I exclaimed "What the fuck was that!" As I got out of the car looking toward the house, as I did I saw the end of a massive fireball mushrooming into the twilight sky from the back of the house were the lounge was. I jumped back into the car, slammed it into reverse, and floored it all the way back up the drive.

As I slammed on the brakes near the front of the house the screaming of reverse gear faded away, as I put the car in park, threw open the door and raced toward the back of the house from the outside. The back of the house where the lounge had been, was completely obliterated, the wall and doors had been blown out, the second story had collapsed down into the room area, and timber was spread at angles in all direction, and made it difficult to make my way into what was left, and try to locate Dumper. So in disbelief, I made my way back to the front of the house and opened the front door, and walked in as far as I was able, and again found there was no way I could go any further.

I walked back outside, and reached into my pocket for the Sat phone, and dialled the emergency services number, and after telling them the county, I was passed through to the Kent Police, and reported the explosion, and gave them directions to the farm.

While I waited for the police and fire brigade, I smoked and had time for a lot of thinking and not all of it was complimentary. *Shit Dumper that wasn't thrown out the door, what did you do, drop it or something? Wait a minute, did you set this up? You were certainly keen for me to take that letter, and you knew that I'd walk away if you played with the grenades, plus you were talking about choosing your own time, or is it just my suspicious thinking? Am I doing you an injustice my old friend, well amigo you certainly made an exit! I hope that you are with the rest of the boys, and if you are, the last man standing considers it an honour, to have served and known every one of you, I salute you all each and every one of you, my comrades!*

At that last thought, I brought my self to attention, and snapped a minute's salute to each direction, east, north, west, and south. As I finished paying my honours, the first of the police cars, and a fire brigade unit rolled into the forecourt of the house. The policemen were young constables and they walked across and asked what happened, and after I told them briefly what had happened, one of them asked "What so someone is still in there?" He yelled to the firemen to follow, as I lead them to the back of the house, and they saw the full extent of the damage some of them swore, and the fireman in charge told his men to get hoses around here, and then some of them headed to the debris that was the back of the house. I moved to go help them, but the coppers held me back, and told me I had a lot of explaining to do, as I heard the jangling of more police cars. As the second wave of cops arrived the first pair called "We've detained a Colonel Tom Davis as being a person of interest in being involved with a murder and arson."

Then one voice cried, "That can't be, my uncle is a Colonel, and his name is Tom or Tiger Davis, but he's Australian army officer!" I was only partially listening to the proceedings, in a confused state of a cross between bewilderment and shock, until I heard that last statement and I snapped out of my brain fugue, and snapped an order "Come forward that man!" As a young constable came forward with a plain clothes detective, I looked at him and questioned "William, is that you?" He snapped to attention, and replied "Yes Sir!" My god! It was my Aunt Dorothy's youngest boy, and he was a rozzer (cop)!

The detective stepped forward and introduced himself as detective inspector Allun Hunt, and asked me to accompany him to Sevenoaks police station, and said "You too constable." I looked at Hunt, and replied "That's not a problem inspector, as long as I can drive my own car, it's a rental you see, he smiled, and replied "I think you can do that, the young constable Davis can go with you, sir." I smiled and nodded as we headed towards the forecourt, and then got into the car with my cousin William in the passenger seat. He started asking questions as soon as I started the car, but I fobbed them off, until we arrived at the police station, and I was shown into an interview room.

When Hunt came in with his sergeant, who he introduced as Mike Townley, they let William stay as long as he remained quiet, and then Hunt asked me if I could verify my ID. With a smile, I played my ace, and handed them my security ID, and said "Tom McFadden at MI5 can confirm my ID, and will vouch for me inspector." As Hunt asked "So what about what young Davis claims, that you're a Colonel in the Australian Army?" Townley left the room I looked at him with a smile, and replied "Well inspector not all of my family is current with what I do, yes I was in the Australian army as a Warrant Officer, but I also held the honorary ranks of Colonel in the US and Israeli army, and also that of Major in the British army, due to the specialised work my team did, however I eventually put in my papers and moved into the security services.

Just as I finished, Townley came back in, and was saying something into Hunts ear. Hunt nodded and said "Hmm yes I see, now what can you tell me about tonight's incident?"

So I gave them a whole account of the day, which started with me arriving at Dumper's farm and up to calling the emergency services to attend the farm, and when I was finished accounting for the day, Hunt seemed satisfied.

Then told me that the one thing that puzzled him was why I insisted in calling Mr Marsh Dumper. So I told them the whole story of why we used nicknames, and how Dumper came by his nickname. After I finished explaining that Sgt Townley was laughing out loud, and Hunt was smiling, and young William was laughing quietly. Then a uniform Sgt interrupted, and asked to see Hunt outside, so he left the room, as Townley asked if I'd ever been in the army here, and smilingly told him of the time I was training the British SAS, and the time I spent in Belfast with them, it turned out that Townley was ex-military, having served with the Queens Horse Guards.

Hunt returned with a sombre face, and asked if I'd like a cuppa while my statement was being typed and I accepted, and so William was sent to make the tea and coffee, and Townley went to type my statement. While they were out of the room, Hunt said "I'm afraid they found the body, your friend was pretty torn up, so let me give you my condolences Mr Davis." I nodded and with a grim face replied "Yeah well a case of H.E. will do that, perhaps you can tell me what happens next, with the body I mean because I'd like to see him buried decently. He took my details and told me that he'd pass them on to the morgue, and they would contact me or the funeral directors I chose.

He was telling me of a decent funeral home, as William brought in the cuppas, and as I was half way through my coffee, sitting back having a smoke with Hunt, Townley came back in with a sheath of papers, which was my statement, and had me initial each page and sign at the end. Townley looked at me saying, "there won't be any charges against you Mr Davis, but in due course there will be an inquest into your friend's death, but I don't think you'll have to attend, it's pretty much death by misadventure, and I'd like to thank you for your time and patience." I thanked them both and we shook hands, and then they had William show me out.

Outside the police station I looked at my watch and it was a bit after seven in the morning, I should have been feeling tired or hungover, but I wasn't, I turned to William and asked where I could get some breakfast, and freshen up a bit, he told me that he'd show me a good place, seeing he'd been off duty for the last hour, he'd come with me. On the way to the diner, I saw the funeral home Hunt had mentioned, and I intended to return there later. Over breakfast I explained that I was only a cousin, not an uncle to William, and also if he wanted to tell his mother he'd seen me, it was alright, but tell her I'd be visiting while I was in the country, and would probably stay overnight.

After a relaxed breakfast, I used the diner's facilities to freshen up a bit, ordered a take away coffee, and William and I said hooray to each other and shook hands, and he walked off towards his flat just up the road, while I lit up a smoke to have with my coffee.

Eventually I went back to the funeral home, and waited a further fifteen minutes for them to open, and then arranged everything with them to bury Dumper, then chose a coffin and went through all the necessary rigmarole, and then told them that his body would be at the morgue, and they'd have to liaise with them as to when the body would be freed, also they would advertise Dumper's death and funeral notices, and I gave them clear instructions on how to contact me, and that I needed two notice prior to the burial, so I could attend. The whole thing from go to whoa cost me ten thousand pounds, but at least Dumper would have a good send off.

Then I headed back to London, and Dawn was out shopping when I got back, so I went down to the pool and gym, and to give myself a vicious workout in an effort to rid myself of my frustrations and anger, after a three-hour workout, I returned to the suite, and Dawn was there, so she kissed me, and asked if I had fun with my friend. So I sat her down and told her what had happened, and what I'd been doing until getting back, and warned her we would be going to the funeral.

CHAPTER 24

For the next few days I was moody and out of sorts with the rest of the world, after I told Dawn the news she knew that Dumper had been a great mate, and tried without much luck to cheer me up, but even though I didn't say anything, she really over compensated, and tried to do everything for me, and it got to the stage where I really felt like snapping at her, and jumped down her throat, but I let my anger dissipate without saying anything, because I knew she was only trying to help me over the loss.

The next morning, I phoned Dumper's solicitor for an appointment, and was able to see him that afternoon, at two o'clock. His offices were in a firm that was based in Que square just around from the Old Bailey law courts, which was in walking distance. So after lunch Dawn and I set out for the walk, she had been determined that she was going to accompany me, and so to save any argument I let her come with me, besides there wasn't anything I was going to keep secret from her anyway.

We reached his offices, but along the way I gave Dawn a running commentary of where we were, and that particular spot's claim to history, because by now we were off the beaten track of where tourists usually went, we had been past the houses of parliament and Big Ben at Westminster, and passed into Downing Street, where a flash of my ID was enough for us to pass through, and then into the law precincts of the Old Bailey, the home of the British legal system and crown courts. The original Old Bailey building had been preserved, and it was a one room stone affair, where lawyers used to wait outside for the client to appear before a judge, and a crier would announce the upcoming case, and if the lawyer didn't make it inside in time, to argue for his client, well that was it for the client, all over red rover. It was also the place, where two hundred years before the first convict was sentenced to transportation to the colonies of New South Wales, for the term of his natural life, and his family was condemned as well, the crime, the poor bastard stole a loaf of bread to feed his family, his name Daniel Lawson, and his youngest son who was only five at the time was named Charles.

Dawn was still correlating all the history that I was firing at her as we reached Dumper's lawyer's office, and we went inside to reception to announce our presence. Deciding to throw my weight around, I flashed my security services ID and it wasn't long before we were shown to the solicitor's office.

We were shown into an office that was rather well lit considering there were case files all over the desk, and a small figure seated behind the desk, as we approached with the secretary, he stood and introduced himself as Jonathon Hyde-Spiers, and shook our hands as I introduced ourselves, and then he said "Ah yes you're here in the matter of Mr John Marsh, late of the Australian army, and now domiciled here in the UK." As he reached for a file and placed it in front of himself, and asked "Now what can I do for you Colonel?"

My temper started to rise, but Dawn squeezed my hand, and I dropped back into my seat, as I said "Well I'm here to find out what provisions Dumper made in his will, and what I have to do to finalise them." He looked at me in a sort of astonished look, looked at the open file in front of him, and replied "Sir have you looked at what has to be done?" I shook my head, and answered "No, I only got as far as your address and phone number, and that's why I'm here, to clear everything up." He looked at us pensively, and shaking his head, said "Well I'm afraid that until Mr Marsh is dead, I can't divulge what is in his will, so if you would like to return in the company of Mr Marsh, then we'll see where we can go."

That was it, my temper boiled over, as I yelled at him, "You stupid jumped up want to be, listen you, fuckwit, I wouldn't be here unless I needed to know, Dumper is dead! He died two days ago, now I happen to be here, and was with him prior to his death,

I've spent all of one night with the police, I've travelled back to London, and now I'm with you wanting answers, now I've gone ahead and paid for his funeral, so what else needs to be paid out and after that what happens? I'm only here for a limited time, and I had plans to be doing other things while I was in the country, so what can be looked after while we're in the country and then where do we go from here?"

Taken back and visibly upset by my anger and outburst, seeing his face whiten in shock I toned down a bit, and he recovered quickly, as he said "I see, well I think it would be best if you were to open the letter he gave you please." So I reached into my jacket pocket and brought it out, and opened it fully, there was only one sentence, and I passed it to Dawn, and her intake of breath was enough to know she was as dumbfounded and as sentimental as I was, because it had read "Boss, you're the only mate, I've had, and consider you and SRT one all of my family, so everything I have goes to you, to distribute amongst the surviving members of our team in equal shares, I love you all, your mate John 'Dumper' Marsh."

With a mist before my eyes, I looked at Hyde-Spiers asked with a controlled voice without waver, "Alright, I've read it, now what?" He looked at me and nodded, and then turned the page on the file, had a quick read, and said that we may as well have morning tea while we went through all the legalities.

After paging his secretary, she came in and took our drink preferences, as he started saying, "Well it seems Mr Marsh has a fair sized estate, apart from his property in Kent, which is worth one and a half million pounds, he also has cash assets of two point three million pounds gathering interest in the Westminster bank. So as soon as I get a copy of the death certificate, I'll close his accounts and have his bank transfer the sum into our holding account. I'll also need a copy of the receipt you paid the funeral people so I can reimburse you the sum you've paid for the funeral, we have the title deed to the farm here, so all we'll have to do is set enough aside to pay the transfer stamp duties for the change of ownership, and I should think that we could have the whole matter resolved within a fortnight, if you can get me those copies."

I nodded at him and fished around in my jacket pockets, some pieces of paper I gathered into one hand, I balled up to go into the rubbish while I kept others, and then I found the receipt from the funeral home, and passed it across, and then asked "So Jonathon, where do I get hold of the death certificate?"

He looked at us, and said with a smile "Well usually they're issued by the coroner's office, so I would assume that you'll be able to have one issued by the relevant morgue authorities, it would also help if you could get a copy of the police report as well." While I'd been fishing through my pockets I had found Allun Hunts police card, and so I nodded, and then asked "Jonathan could I use your phone please and would a faxed copy be alright for both documents?"

He smiled, and replied "Yes a fax copy of both will be fine; we only need to show proof of death to the bank management so a fax copy is fine, and here's the fax number, that's outside with my secretary, would you like me to give you some privacy for your call?"

I told him no as he passed me his phone, and he told us that he'd organise another cuppa while I was making my call, and he left the office while I dialled the number on the card. Hunt answered on the second ring, and I told him what I needed and he took the fax number assuring me that he'd send what was needed after he hung up, but before he did, he gave me the number and name of the person to speak to at the morgue in regard to the death certificate.

He also told me to tell them that he had authorised it being faxed, so after thanking him I hung up, and was dialling the number he gave me as Jonathon came back carrying a tray with the drinks and a plate of biscuits. As he set them down, the phone was answered by the person I needed to speak with, and I told what I needed and how I was involved, and lastly told him what Hunt had told me to tell them. They were very helpful and told me that they'd send it as soon as I gave them the fax number, which I did and as we were talking he said that he was sending it as we spoke, and I thanked him very much, he also told me that the body had been released to the funeral home, so I thanked him for that also, and hung up after saying my goodbyes.

After my calls I passed the phone back, and while we were having drinks and a biscuit, the secretary came in carrying what I hoped were the two faxes, Jonathon looked at me respectfully and told me that I must have some pull, because he'd never gotten that sort of cooperation before, and I just flashed a knowing smile thinking, It's not what you know, but who you know buddy! Then he asked how Dumper had died, so I told him, and about the aftermath. Soon after that we left his office with him telling us that he'd contact us at the hotel as soon as everything was ready to be finalised.

As we headed back to the hotel, we discussed what we were going to do with it all, and I told Dawn that we had more than enough money and that I'd rather give it all too some charity that could make use of it. That opened up an ongoing conversation about which charity to give it to, and whether it would be really used to benefit people instead of disappearing in administrative funds.

Then bugger me we both noticed a sign in a building window ahead of us that read "Your donation saves lives." It was a Red Cross sign, and we were standing outside of the Red Cross building, we both looked at each other, and I was able to read what was going through her mind because they mirrored my own, that they were a worthwhile charity that did do a tremendous lot of good for all sorts of people, we both smiled, and I looked enquiringly at her, and she nodded with a smile, so we both walked in hand in hand.

Readers Note: In one way or another, I'm a believer in what goes around comes around, or Karma whatever you like to call it. Now the reason I'm saying this is because what happened next was one of those such occasions, and in a way I was glad that it did happen, not only did it make me think of a past that was a bit hurtful, it also gave me a chance to payback that help to a family member.

We were escorted to the office of the donations director, and as he looked, and stood up for introductions to be made, I had to do a noticeable double take, as I thought this impossible. In front of me stood the spitting image of Michael 'Pep' Salter, and as Dawn and I were introduced and shook hands with Gabriel Salter, he said with a smile "Please sit, you look as if you've seen a ghost Mr Davis."

Dawn was also looking concerned, so as I sat down I asked "maybe I have, do you have any brothers Mr Salter?" Looking at me quizzically he replied "Aye, I have three brothers and a sister, but one of my brothers immigrated to Australia, and we've since learned that he died, that was just before my parents died." I nodded and then stated, more than asked "I'll bet your brother's name that went was Michael." Salter smiled, and replied "Aye that it was, and how come you would be able to tell me my brother's name Mr Davis."

I looked at him and a feeling of sadness went through me, as I said "Mr Salter I'll answer your question in just a moment, but can you tell me if your brother was married when he, and did he serve with the British army prior to going to Australia?" Salter looked at me suspiciously, and replied "Aye he was in the commandos, and he was married, you know him or knew him didn't you Mr Davis?"

I looked at him sadly, and said "Yes I did Mr Salter, Pep, that's was his nickname as in pepper and salt, was one of my best friends, and he taught me all I knew while we were both in the Australian SAS, I was also with him when he died in action sir." And for the next hour between cups of coffee and cake, I shared with him some of my background that involved Pep, along with some of the things we used to get up to, and the forming of SRT, and the other members of the team.

This brought me back to why we were here, and so I told him

that during my stay in the country, the last of my team died, and had left everything he had, money and property, to me as the last surviving team member, and I told him that if any of the others had been alive we would have all shared, but it wasn't to be, so I already had enough money and property, so I was considering donating everything to a charity, and that was what had brought us to his office, because it ranked in the millions, we wanted to make sure it would be put to good use. He nodded his head and told me that he would try to alleviate any fears we had, and then asked how much we were actually talking about.

I smiled, and told him what the farm acreage was, and told him that at present it only had half a house on it due to an explosion, and that it was valued at one and a half million pounds and the monetary value in the bank was in the vicinity of two point three million pounds. He whistled and told me I had very good reason for being concerned, and asked where the farm was, and as I told him, he nodded and smiled, and then said "We've been looking around that area for some land to establish a retirement home that we would manage, and this sounds like just the ticket, we could call it the SRT Team Retirement Home, and list all of you as our benefactors, because not only would you be supplying the land, but the rest of the donation would more than pay for the construction, we could probably get a couple more soup vans as well. How does that sound to you?"

Dawn and I looked at each other, she gave a small nod, but I asked the question "Sounds good, but how do I know that will actually happen?" He stared at me and replied, "Aye I can see your point, but let me assure you that as my own brother will be listed as one of our benefactors, I will be pushing all the way to see this happen, I give you my word as the brother of your best friend." I stared at him for a short while, and then told him I accepted his word, and that as soon as I heard from the solicitors I would be in contact with him to accompany us to the solicitor's office, so everything could be transferred legally. As we stood he passed me his business card, and shook hands with both of us, and escorted us to the building entry.

After we left the building we asked each other about our thoughts on giving the money to the Red Cross, and we were both happy with the decision, and then we strolled back to the hotel, and when we arrived in the suite I told Dawn that considering we'd spent most of the day out, I was all coffeed out, but I was hungry, and asked if she wanted anything to eat from room service, in the end we ended up ordering a pizza to share, and while we waited for it to arrive we had drinks.

For the following three days, Dawn and I played tourist, and we went to such places as Parliament house, where by a stroke of luck we ran into my cousin Robin, who was making his way to the house of lords, we chatted to him for ten minutes before he really had to start making tracks to the house, and so Dawn learned the full story of the title, and how I'd passed it on. Then we went to the tower of London, and apart from everything else there, we viewed the Crown Jewels, that still have a four-man guard team from the horse guards.

They were still wearing traditional Beefeater garb that hadn't changed since the nineteenth century. There were a few people looking as I started to tell Dawn the story of the Cullinan diamond which was named after the man who unearthed it in the Transvaal, South Africa in nineteen zero five, and to this day was still the largest colourless diamond ever discovered, it was also named the Star of Africa and weighed in at over one thousand carats. It has since been cut down into two large segments and a lot of smaller segments that make up some of the Queens everyday jewellery, but the two largest pieces have been renamed the largest is set into the sovereign's sceptre, but removable, and can be worn as the centrepiece in one of the pendants, it's still called The Star of Africa, and weighs five hundred and thirty carats, while the smaller piece, is the front centrepiece of the crown there, it's called the Star of Africa Two, and weighs three hundred and seventeen carats, and I finished telling her, considering the engagement ring on your finger is only half a carat, and you know roughly how much that cost me, so try to imagine what those two diamonds are worth.

As I finished everyone applauded, because they'd also been listening intently mesmerised at what I'd been telling her, so I decided to be a show off, smiled, and spread my arms out to my side, took half a step forward and took half a bow, and spotting a small bucket near one of the sentries, I retrieved it, and put it on the floor, saying "Ladies and gentlemen, I hope you enjoyed my story of the Cullinan diamond, any donations you decide to give, go to the very expensive upkeep of the traditional uniforms worn by those four that would shoot you if you tried to make off with anything not bolted down, I thank you one and all."

Thunderous applause came again in that smallish room, and shouts of here, here, I even noticed one of the soldiers smiling, and gave him a wink. As everyone left, they passed by the bucket, and put notes into it, no change, but actual notes, and I mused, that I must have done a fairly good job. Dawn and I were the last to leave the room, and as I passed the soldier with sergeant stripes on his uniform, I inclined my head to the bucket, and said "Share that amongst your lot Sarge, and all of you have a drink on me tonight, see ya." He smiled, and muttered out the corner of his mouth "Thank you, sir, we will." After the Tower I showed her St. Paul's Cathedral, and then we headed towards Oxford Street, where I found my tobacconist and order two thousand, of my special mix to be made up, and after that we strolled up to Trafalgar square, and across into the mall, and headed up to Buckingham palace.

As we went up the mall, I pointed out the minor palaces, one being Kensington, which was the home of my old mate Prince Charles, who'd years before, made me a Major. Dawn asked me about that, so I told her the story as we strolled towards Buck House. After that first day, there was a message waiting for me at the hotel, which informed us of the day and time of Dumper's funeral, which was in two days' time. So in the meantime I took Dawn to the Tate gallery, and that's where we spent the two days, and probably could have spent a few more.

The morning of the funeral, we had an early breakfast,

and then I had the car brought around, and we headed along Edgeware rd. to the M25, and I headed south towards Kent, Dawn commented on how nice the country was, and I told her to wait until we went visiting the rellies, and got down to the West Country. We arrived in Sevenoaks at ten am, the funeral was another hour away before starting, so first I drove to the funeral home, and they told me which church was being used for the service, and then where the burial would take place, and after thanking them, I returned to the car and told Dawn that I needed a drink, and she agreed. So I drove to the soldier's arms, and we went in, I noticed a lot of people in the pub dressed in suits, even the sergeant was dressed in going out finery, except for a jacket, and he as he saw me he called attention, and threw a salute, and said "Welcome Colonel, what can I get you and your wife?"

When he brought the drinks, he told me that the wake was going to be held at the pub, and that all drinks during it were on the house, and that Marshy as they knew him was well liked as he spread his arm, saying that everyone was ready to go to the service, and he would be too, while his wife looked after the pub, so we'd have to excuse her, and I told him there was no problem with that. Then at ten to eleven, he announced "Those that's coming, bottoms up, it's time!" As he grabbed his suit jacket from the wall pegs near the bar.

We walked to the church from the pub, and the burial was going to be in the churchyard, at the front of the church the officiating priest stood near the entrance welcoming everyone, and as I was pointed out, he came and introduced himself and shook hands, and asked "Colonel Davis, Father Harris, I am right in assuming that you will be giving the eulogy seeing Mr Marsh was one of your deep friends?" So I told him that I'd thought someone else would be doing, but even though I hadn't written anything down, I'd do one off the cuff if he wanted me to. He told me that Dumper really wasn't known outside of the village, and had only been living there, for the last ten years or so, whereas I'd known him for such a long time. I agreed to deliver the eulogy, and he'd let me know when.

As I looked out at the congregation, when I went up to the front lectern, I was amazed at the number of people in attendance, and I also noted that Hunt and Townley were present, and as I looked down at the coffin bearing the remains of my friend, the opening line for my off the cuff eulogy came to me.

I looked up again, and said "We're all here today to say farewell to John Dumper Marsh, now some of you may not have known him well, but I'm reminded of a line I heard once and it goes, little do any of us know just how many people we touch in our lives in small ways and large ways, or just by offering a friendly hello. And that has never been more evident to me than now, as I look around at all your faces, Dumper probably never guessed that so many of you would have turned out to say farewell to him. You knew him as John Marsh, or Marshy, but to me he will always remain Dumper, one of the most reliable, and loyal soldiers I knew, I know that because we served together for many years and in some hellish places, and he along with his fellow team members stood fast by my side throughout it all. To give you an idea of who Dumper really was, let me tell you how he earned his nickname of Dumper." Then I proceeded to tell them the story, and afterward there was a lot of laughter, so I continued to tell them of some of the highs and lows that we'd shared, and of some of the comical situations, and some of the terrible times.

To close what I had to say, I said "That was the man, comrade, and friend I knew, and I hope that gives you better insight into the man you came to know, and now farewell, to my friend I say, see ya later old mate, you remain with me always in my memories until we meet again! Now if anyone wishes to say anything please come up and be heard, thank you." As I stepped down I lay my hand on Dumpers coffin, and said a private farewell before sitting down beside Dawn, who was misty eyed.

The publican of A Soldiers Arms, whose name I'd found out earlier was Ronny Jessop spoke of Dumper for a little while, and patted the coffin as he finished, and then Father Harris moved forward again and finished the service. The Pallbearers moved forward to lift and take the coffin, as we all filed out of the church, and followed around to the burial site, after Harris gave the burial service and the coffin was lowered into place, I was looked upon by Father Harris to throw the first sod of dirt. I picked up the dirt in my left hand as I moved to the graveside and came to attention and saluted before lowering my hand and throwing the dirt in on top of Dumper, and I did a smart turn and marched out of the way of the other mourners.

Dawn followed close behind me, and we stood off to one side as each person contributed to the soil in the grave and move off towards town, and as some of them passed there was the odd sniffle heard. Father Harris was the last to leave except me and Dawn, he came up to me and shook my hand as he gave his condolences once more before heading toward the church, we stood there for a few minutes, and then with a long sigh, I said "Ok let's go to the pub, it's time for a drink."

We walked into the pub hand in hand, and we were ushered into the dining room, that also had one side of the main bar, as we entered Ronny called attention, and everyone present stood and complied, even the ladies, we were both given a drink by Ronny as we reached the bar, as I turned with my glass in hand and toasted "To Dumper." Everyone murmured the reply and we all drank, and then I was applauded for my eulogy, and Ronny turned on some low music, as his wife helped him refill drinks.

That afternoon the drinks flowed without stop, and I did get a little pissed, so it was Dawn who ended up driving back to the hotel, while I slept some of it off. It was just as well she'd taken notice of the route on the outward trip, anyway next morning I woke with a terrible hangover, but at least we were in the right hotel room.

CHAPTER 25

Well as I said before I was suffering a massive hangover, but did I get any sympathy, as you guessed it, not, even though I felt like remaining in bed all day, and shut the rest of the world out, Dawn wasn't going to let me do that, so I knew that I would receive no piece, and rang room service for breakfast, and I ordered bacon, eggs, sausages and hash browns loaded with Tabasco sauce knowing that if the hot sauce didn't bring me right, and burn out the excess alcohol nothing would. Finally, after ten am, I was in a fit state to go out, the shakes and the pounding in my head had stopped, but to be on the safe side, I swallowed a couple of disprins with my coffee. As I started to wonder, *am I getting too old for this? Did I really drink myself into oblivion just for the hell of it, Christ I was only thirty-three, this sort of thing shouldn't happen to me, it must have been all the mixing of the different drinks that wiped me out. I decided that was my excuse and I was sticking to it. It had nothing to with my age and fitness.*

So eventually we went back to the Tate to try and finish seeing everything, and by mid-afternoon, I was looking forward to afternoon tea and something to eat. That night over dinner in the restaurant, we discussed what we were going to do next, and it was decided that we could still continue the tourist thing, but also combine that with visiting some of my relatives. So next morning I called my Aunt Dorothy to see when it was convenient to call in, she had been expecting the call, and it was arranged that Dawn and I would get there in the afternoon, and stay for a day or so before continuing to visit other members of the family. Dawn enjoyed the trip down, because Peterborough is in a part of the country known as the new forest, (considering it's been there for over eight hundred years), but also Winchester is close by, and she enjoyed looking at the cathedral. That night we went out to dinner, and I explained that we were now running to a timetable to see everyone, so we could only stay the one night, I was going to show Dawn Portsmouth naval base in the morning before heading across country to Uncle Tony's, and then down to Devon to see Uncle Robin on Dartmoor, before going to my home town of Plymouth. On the way I was going to stop at Stonehenge, somewhere during the journey, but we had only a week to do it before having to be back in London. I agreed with Aunt Dorothy when she said that I would be covering a lot of countryside in such a short time, but I knew if we didn't do it now, we wouldn't have a chance later on, plus Dawn wanted to have a look at the northern part of the country, and Yorkshire too.

So that's the way we did it, we travelled the southern and south west country, taking in places like Plymouth, Exeter, Bristol, Stonehenge, Alcott, and then back to London for a couple of days. While we were back at the hotel, I had a call from Hyde-Spiers to inform me that everything in Dumper's will was ready for transferral, so after telling him I'd call him back. I phoned Gabriel Salter's office, and he was out of town for three days, so asked for him to ring me as soon as he was back. After ringing the solicitor back, I told him I'd phone for an appointment as soon as I could get back from Yorkshire, and he told me that would be alright, just in case any further loose ends needed tying up in the meantime. So Dawn and I went and played at being tourists up north for four days.

There was a message from Gabriel waiting for us when we got back, and so I decided to ring him after I'd made an appointment with Hyde-Spiers, which was set for eleven the next day, and then I rang Gabriel asking him to meet us at the solicitor's office the next day at eleven, and gave him the address after he did confirm that he'd be able to do that.

We all arrived within a couple minutes of each other, and joined up in his secretary's office, and then all three of us were shown into Jonathon's office, he stood as we entered, and said "Ah Mr and Mrs Davis how nice to see you again, and this is?"

As I introduced Gabriel Salter to him, Gabriel handed him a business card, as they shook hands. Then once we were seated, Jonathon said "When we spoke last week Mr Davis, I mentioned that I was glad of the extra time for any loose ends, well there was one, and it was finalised yesterday afternoon. You see Mr Marsh had held an insurance policy with the bank as well as his accounts, and it was only a policy that covers accidental death, so they weren't going to pay out the one point five million pounds sum insured, because Mr Marsh's death was by suicide, now my argument to them was that they were unable to prove that it was suicide same as the police, therefore the coroner's decision ruled it death by misadventure, as is stated on the death certificate, so they were obligated to pay the sum insured, because misadventure is the same as being an accident, anyway they finally saw reason and paid the amount into our holding account yesterday. So the good news is that the total of cash assets of the estate are at present three point eight million pounds, and out of that we have to pay out ten thousand pounds to Mr Davis, so here is your cheque, and if you would kindly sign this receipt, also tax, stamp, and death duties, and our fee round out to ninety thousand pound!"

He sat back and looked at us, and handed me an authorization form, as he continued "That leaves you with a grand total of three million seven hundred pounds, plus the late Mr Marsh's property. Now if you would kindly sign that authority, it allows us to draw that sum from your inheritance, and I can then write you a cheque for that amount if you like, or we would have to take a few days to get it in cash, which would you prefer?"

Dawn and I smiled, while Gabriel looked a little stunned, as I signed the authorization form for him, and said "Firstly Mr Salter will tell you how to make the cheque payable to the Red Cross, secondly, I want you to transfer the deed for the property to the Red Cross without charging any duties, call it a charitable contribution shall we?" Gabriel told him that he'd make out a receipt for the amount of the transfer fees, so it could be used for taxation purposes.

Jonathon was shaking his head in disbelief, as he asked "You're giving everything away, are you mad?" I started to laugh and told him, yeah I must be, but I've got enough as it is. Jonathon sighed, and replied "Well if that's what you really want to happen, there's some paperwork that needs to be done and to be signed." With a smile I told him that's why we were all here! After all the paperwork was signed, we all stood to shake hands, and Dawn, Gabriel, and I left his office, and headed to the Red Cross building. Where with another verbal thank you from Gabriel Salter on behalf of the society, and handshakes, we prepared to leave him to go up to his office, as he said "I hope my brother was proud of you Mr Davis, because that would make two of us Salters." I looked at him with a moist eye, and replied "Oh, I'm sure he was Gabriel, and thank you."

When we walked into the hotel, we went towards the restaurant, but the receptionist saw us and called me across to tell me that she had a message for me, and handed me an envelope, I thanked her and then we headed back towards the restaurant for some lunch. We ordered lunch, and I also ordered our drinks, mine being a double shot, and as soon as they arrived, I ordered another double to by brought to me. Dawn wondered what I was doing and asked, so I told her that I was having a couple quick belts to get over the fact that I just gave away nearly five million pounds. She thought for a minute and laughed, and then told me I'd better get her another as well. It was only after four drinks that I decided to look at the message that had come in, and it read: "Urgent call me as soon as you receive this, problems in the Caribbean, must talk as soon as, Callaway, for Gorman!" I instantly sobered up.

After looking at my watch, I did some quick mental time calcula-tion, and passed the message to Dawn, as I did our lunch arrived, so I ordered two more drinks and waited for her response. As she looked at me over our plates, she asked "What's this mean, and what are you going to do?"

I smiled and told her I was going to finish our lunch, and then go back to our suite, and then make the phone call back to

Australia. Back in our room she gave me some privacy to make the call in the lounge, and I reached Callaway after two rings, and waited for the international pips before speaking, and said "This had better be good John, I'm on holiday."

He laughed, and replied "Yeah sorry about that Tiger, also condolences on John Marsh's death we heard about it through our MI5 contacts, and I hope you've had time to fix everything, but your old mate Stein in the DEA has been on the blower to Gorman pleading for your help in another of their operations, he's okayed it, but he has stressed that you're not to take part in any ground activity, you're to advise and observe only that's all, is that understood?"

I nodded to no one, as well as replying "Yeah understood, I can be in L.A. in roughly twenty-six hours, but what do I do with my girlfriend she's on this trip with me?"

I could almost imagine the cogs operating in his brain as he thought that over, as his end of the line was quiet for a while, and then he replied "Well you could send her to Disneyland with the plane crew to look after her." After his non thought out comment I burst out laughing, and told him what I thought of that idea, and that I'd ring Alex Stein direct as soon as we finished talking.

I was smiling as I went into the bedroom to get my satellite phone, and I asked Dawn "How would you like to spend a couple of days at Disneyland on the way home?" She jumped up and told me she'd love it, as I picked up my phone and searched for Alex's number, and as I pressed it, I told her I'd see what I could do, and then went back into the lounge as Alex came on the line, saying he was glad to hear from me, and proceeded to let me know what was happening. After hearing it all, I told him that I could probably be in LA within twenty-six hours, but he needed to provide accommodation, refuelling, transport, and five entries to Disneyland for my girlfriend and crew. He agreed after hearing the whole story, and said "I'll organise for you to be refuelled JFK Airport in New York, (which was originally Idlewild until 1963), and I'll book you all into the Airport Hilton here in LA, I'll ring you back in an hour in regard to the rest."

While I waited for Alex to get back to me, I phoned Ross and informed him that we had a flap on, and that I wanted to know how soon we could be in the air heading for LA. He told me we could be airborne within two hours, all he'd have to do was file a flight plan, and inform everyone, I told him that we'd refuel at JFK, and that I'd ring him as soon as I got an answer back from the DEA. Then I told Dawn to start packing, because we'd probably be leaving in a couple of hours.

Alex was as good as his word, and he rang me back fifty-five minutes later to tell me he'd booked three suites at the Airport Hilton in LA, a hangar and refuelling for the jet, transportation for me, and also the others while we were there, and five VIP passes for Disneyland for the crew and Dawn. After getting off the phone with Alex, I told Dawn we were definitely leaving, and with a laugh she told me everything was packed and ready to go, even my go-bag. I smiled as and thanked her as she handed me a drink, while I phoned Ross, and I let him know everything was a go, and that we'd meet him at the jet within an hour. The next call was to reception to inform them we were checking out, and that I'd need a limo to Heathrow as soon as we came down with our luggage.

An hour later Dawn and I were waiting at the jet hangar for Ross to arrive with the flight number, and while everyone got the plane ready for take-off I called Alex to let him know our flight number, and that we'd be in the air in less than thirty minutes, so he could go ahead and arrange our refuelling at JFK, and that I'd ring him from there. When I got on board, I told everyone what we were doing and that while I was looking after business with the DEA, they would be enjoying themselves at Disneyland, then I gave Jerry a hand to shut and cross lock the door before Ross started to taxi out onto the runway for take-off.

During the flight, the women seemed to be getting on better than the previous flight, and spent a lot of time together discussing what they would do when they got to Disneyland, and after getting some shut eye, I relieved Ross on the flight deck, and climbed into the co-pilot's seat as Jerry took the controls. Eight hours later I was at the controls and Ross was the co-pilot as I started our descent into JFK in New York, once we felt the nose dropping onto the front wheel, we both grabbed the thrust levers and pushed them into reverse thrust as we hurtled down the runway, and then I started to apply the brakes slowly, once off the main runway I followed the instructions to the refuelling spot, and once in the right position indicated by the ground crew, I halted the jet and then we powered down before shutting off the engines.

A maintenance bus took us to the custom and immigration lounge, and once the formalities were over, we split up, Ross and Jerry were going to organise the refuelling, and then join us in the crew cafeteria for some breakfast before we took off on the last leg to California, while the women and I went into the airport concourse for a look around and some shopping, while they were browsing, I went outside and enjoyed a smoke, before going and buying some more booze and smokes.

An hour later we had all had an enjoyable breakfast, and were relaxing with smokes and coffee before going out to the plane for take-off, Ross and I had both worked out that it would take about eight hours after leaving to reach LA. So while we relaxed I phoned Alex and told him to expect us in eight hours, as we would be leaving JFK within half an hour. Then we caught a lift on a maintenance bus out to our plane, and Ross had told me that I could take us into the air while he played co-pilot.

Now I've talked to you before about the exhilaration I feel during that full thrust rush along the runway on take-off, now sitting up front in the pilot's chair is a little different than sitting back in the main cabin, back there you feel the rush straight away, but up front what happens is, that there is a build-up time before you actually get forced back in the seat from the G force. Here's the difference in the pilot's seat as you sit at the end of the runway and once getting the tower clearance to go, the engine thrust is put to full power, and release the holding brakes, nothing seems to be happening, and then you start to roll forward slowly at first, and then increasing, then all of a sudden you get forced back into your seat by the G force, so it seems to take forever to do that, even though you know you put the throttles to full power yourself. It took me a while to work this out, but I finally realised it's all because the engines are so far back from the cockpit in a passenger plane, in the cockpit you don't even hear the engines screaming. However, it's a completely different tune in a fighter jet, because you're actually sitting between the engine intakes, you hear the screaming and feel the power straight away, you put the throttles into full power in one of those babies, you're really forced into the seat through the G force acceleration, and boy is that fun!

After take-off I flew until we were out of the New York area, and then flipped it to auto pilot as Ross complimented me on the take-off as I got up and he climbed into his seat, and Jerry got into the co-pilot's seat, and I left them to it, and went back into the main cabin to join Dawn.

I knew that she'd been dying to ask me something for a while now, so as I sat down, I looked at her and said "Ok I'm sick of waiting for you to bring up whatever it is that you want, so let's hear what you want to ask before I die of old age." She looked at me rather exasperatedly and replied "I'm not even going to bother asking how you knew that, but yes you're right, I've been thinking it over now ever since we were in England. You know how back there everyone just automatically assumed I was your wife, and called me Mrs Davis? Well why don't we make it official, let's just go ahead and get married when we get home, (She laughed and continued smiling as she said), besides it's not as if I'm marrying you for your money, you just gave a whack away!"

In surprise I automatically replied, "Well I'll be fucked!" Dawn jumped back in immediately, and said with a smile and questioningly raised eyebrows "You will be if we adjourn to your office bed." Half an hour later, we were relaxingly lying back in each other's arms on the bed, as she asked "So what do you think?" Knowing exactly what she was asking about but deciding to have a bit of fun I replied "Yeah that wasn't bad, but I've already initiated you into the mile-high club!" My remark got me a punch in the left ribs, as she said "I wasn't talking about that," so I laughed, and replied "Yeah I know, I suppose we could, I'll buy you an engagement ring when we get home, but you'll have to take care of anything to do with the wedding, I'll be too busy."

She seemed to ponder for a while and the agreed that would be ok, but she'd ask me about anything important, to which I agreed, and then she asked "Are you going to wear a wedding ring if I buy you one?" I looked at her and replied "No, I'll switch this one to my other hand, but as for wearing another, no." She grabbed my right hand and looked at Bill Fredrick's company ring a lot closer, and then asked "This ring means a lot to you doesn't it?" I looked her straight in the eye, and said holding up my right hand "This ring means more to me than anything I have now, or could have in the future honey." She nodded and replied, "Then that's your wedding ring, I'll buy you something else as a wedding gift, oh by the way you can swap that onto your wedding finger anytime you feel like doing it, if you need help I'll help you put it there right now if you'd like."

So with that I switched Bill's ring to my left hand, and Dawn theoretically became Mrs Davis number three. *Shit what was I doing, Christ I was only thirty-two, and about to get married for the third time, what the hell was I thinking? To make matters worse, I wasn't sure if I was in love with Dawn or just lust.*

Shari was still uppermost in my mind as the one person I was truly in love with, but she wasn't around anymore, and I wondered if I'd ever feel the way I felt around her again, or had that been ripped away forever in the same hail of bullets. Anyway Dawn seemed to be happy, so I let those thoughts drop, and went back to concentrating on the upcoming task ahead.

When we landed in LA it was thirteen hundred local time, under direction Ross had taxied to a hangar on the far left or the airport, and we stopped at a hangar, where the undercarriage was hooked up to a motorised trolley that backed us into the hangar. When we cracked open the door a stairwell was set in place, and at the bottom of the stairs there were two limousines waiting, one was for me the other was for the others on board. With a kiss good bye, I took my go bag and told Dawn I'd see her later, and then told Ross to look out for my future wife, and then I got into the limo that drove me to the DEA headquarters that I'd visited some years before.

As I arrived I noticed John Mosely waiting for me, and we shook hands and exchanged greetings as we entered the building. We went up to Alex's floor, and as I exited the lift, two plain clothes men stepped forward to stop me going any further, until Mose stepped out of the lift and told them to leave me be. We walked into Alex's office bypassing his secretary, and sat down facing him at his desk. He was on the phone, but hung up soon after we sat down; he looked at us and laughed, and then yelled to his secretary "Marjorie! Coffee and cakes, and I don't wish to be disturbed until further notice!"

He looked at me with a worried frown, and asked "So Tiger, happy to see you man, sorry about dragging you into this, so what's new?" As I was about to start filling them both in on what had been happening in my life, Marjorie came in with a wheeled trolley that had a coffee urn, and Danish's on it, left it beside Alex's desk, and then left the room. So while I was bringing them both up to speed with what had been occurring with my life, we all had coffee, Danish's while I brought them up to speed, and I received the obligatory condolences when I told them about my time in Israel, and then when I reached the end of my story which brought us up to date. Alex opened one of his desk drawers, and pulled out three glasses and a bottle of bourbon, he filled all three glasses, and as he passed them to Mose and myself, he stood, so we followed suit, he picked up his glass, and saluted and said as a toast, "To fallen comrades, and those that a left standing," We all clinked glasses and swallowed down the bourbon in one drink, and replaced them on his desk, their salute to me and SRT was touching.

After some reminiscing about our experiences, because they had both known and been in combat with every member of my team. Before we got down to the business in hand, I had to tell them that I was under express orders not to go into the field myself I was to give advice only. Alex laughed and informed us that he was probably responsible for that, because he'd refused to tell Gorman what the mission was, and that he'd only tell me so I could help plan it. We all chuckled after I told them that would have pissed him off, and then Alex told me that Mose would be the agent in charge on the ground, and it was to be a quick in and out, without informing the Columbian Government about the strike.

I nodded and said, "Ok, before we go further let's go to your operations room, and you can brief me there." The operations room was a down the hall from Alex's office and had a number keypad entry. When we were inside I saw the reason for the security entry, and told them that it was almost the same as my TAC Room back home. Alex told me they called this room MTAC which stood for mission tactical, and that the screen could all have different feeds, be it satellite or computer. Mose moved to one of the keyboards and a map came up on the central monitor, and the screen beside it gave a satellite view of the same area.

Then we got into the briefing, with a laser pointer in hand, Alex pinpointed spots while he gave me the information. There was a small cocaine farm and refinery that was owned by the Montero family, a minor drug cartel until now, when the bigger cartels were being raided and destroyed, however it had been allowed to flourish because the head of the Montero family was also a major minister in the Columbian Government, and the reason for not informing them of the coming destruction.

Alex looked at me, and said "We know where it is, and the opposition forces approximate numbers, we have three assets in country, but we haven't got a way in, because we can't fly in, anything in the air would be picked up on radar, which would seem like an act of war, so that's out, anything we do has to be covert, do any ideas spring into your mind?"

I looked at the map and sat image, then back to Alex and

Mosely, and said "A few, John how many men are you taking, do they look Columbian, and are they parachute qualified, Alex do any of the in country assets have access to a large open boat and a truck?" A very devious and audacious plan was forming in my head, and their answers would hold the key to whether it could work or not.

It would also require some cooperation from the US Coast Guard as well, but I was sure that Alex would be able to arrange that, because I knew that both departments had operated together many times in the past to bring down drug operations.

John Mosely started chuckling, as if he was reading what I had in mind, and answered "Yeah I know you've got something devilish in mind Tiger, I'll have ten men with me, and yeah they look sort of like Columbian natives, all ex marines so they're jump qualified, we'll be using the same stuff we used on the poppy fields in Laos, and you should remember we didn't need much of it to incinerate and ruin the fields, each man will be carrying ten canisters', so we'll have more than enough explosives." I nodded and thanked him, and then looked at Alex.

He looked at me and nodded saying, "One of them works for a local bus operation so transport is not a problem, but about the boat I'll see what I can work out, what have you in mind?" I smiled, and then went to the keyboard and typed into the google search Santa Cruz Del Islote, and as the screen came alive with pictures, I told John that his men would need clothes like them for after the job, and looking at Alex told him that was the type of boat required a large typical Caribbean banana boat.

CHAPTER 26

We left MTAC shortly after that and made our way back to Alex's office, where we all sat down, and then I told them I'd probably have something put together by the following morning, which suited John because he was itching to get going. Then I told them that after the operation, and John was back all three of us would visit Bill and Mary Fredrick, and inform them of the demise of all the SRT, because they both had the right to know, and that Alex was to track down Wild Bill so we could go and see him and Mary.

They both agreed, and Alex said he'd track him down, and because I knew he was as good as his word, I left it there. Then I told him it was possible that we'd need the Coast Guard in on the operation, and he told me that would not be a problem. Then the talk turned to my clearance into the building, and also into MTAC, Alex gave me his code for that, and said he'd arrange all clearances for me. So with that I told them I was going to call it a day and head back to the hotel, to work out a feasible plan for the operation, and that I'd see them at nine back here in Alex's office. Alex said he'd arrange for my driver to be at the basement lifts for me, and to tell him what time I required to be picked up the next day. With a nod to each I stood and made my way to the lifts.

Back at the hotel, I walked into the bar and saw everyone at a table near the corner, so I joined them, and a waitress was close behind me and asked if I'd like a drink, I gave her my order and looked at each of the others to see if they wanted another drinks, and so a fresh round was brought for everyone. While we waited for the drinks, I asked why they weren't still out at Disneyland, and it turned out that they hadn't bothered going out today, because they just wanted to settle in and see what was happening in the way of time being here. So I told them we'd be here for a least a week if not longer, and anything we did was compliments of the DEA, so tomorrow while I was working in the city with Alex, they could go out and enjoy themselves, Jenny said "That doesn't seem right boss, you should get to be having some fun too." I laughed and told her I was going to be getting all the fun I needed with what I was doing for the DEA. The drinks arrived just then, and after I tipped the waitress with a hundred, she made sure we were well looked after, she even went into the restaurant to get us the menus for dinner, and made sure we were served dinner at our table in the bar. Eventually near ten I made my goodnights, and Dawn and I went up to our suite. I told her what I was up to, and she was concerned that I'd be up all night working on a plan; I smiled and told her I'd already roughly worked it out.

We were joined the others for breakfast at zero seven thirty, an early one for all of us because they were going to get an early start to Disneyland, and my driver was picking me up at eight, from the restaurant we all went to the foyer, and our two vehicles were waiting at the entrance, mine being the one in front, so with a kiss goodbye to Dawn and good wishes and a warning not to lose her to the others, I made my way to my car where the back door was being held open by my driver, as soon as he was in the car we started the commute into the city.

At nine I was seated in the office with Alex and John enjoying a freshly brewed coffee and Danish, after that we adjourned to MTAC where I got John to bring up the map, and satellite view of both the map area and a view of the target site. Once they were displayed on screens, I used the laser pointer to pinpoint certain areas as I laid out my mission plan.

John's force would parachute in, and drop into a clearing two miles from the target site which was thirty miles northeast of Cartagena, along the Cartagena Barranquilla road near an unnamed tributary of the Magdalena River. Alex was to have his ground assets in place with transport at the drop zone, and provide landing zone lighting; he knew what I meant so I didn't have to explain the method to him. Mosely was to move his force and the three assets to the target site, and gain control of the site, they weren't to pussyfoot around, they had to kill everyone they encountered, and then destroy the field. Time from landing to the escape I estimated at two hours at the outside. Now the escape route, whichever of the ground assets that had access to the boat would go on ahead of the main group and secure the boat and take it to the main passenger wharves. Then the main group would be driven into Cartagena and the wharves, they were to time their arrival to between three and four in the afternoon, when they would get into the boat and the local asset would leave the harbour in the direction of Santa Cruz del Islote. Somewhere between Santa Cruz and Mucura Island they would rendezvous with a Coast Guard cutter, which they would transfer to, and resupply the local asset with fuel for the return to Cartagena.

That was the mission plan that I'd worked out, and then gave them my things that were needed and also my recommendations to John. The jump was to be done during darkness but close to morning, observe the target site before attacking at probably around midday. Alex was to make sure of the ground assets and the Coast guard cutter, but we would also be watching the operation from start to finish in MTAC and we would be in constant radio contact, via the personal radio sets, in case we saw anything that could threaten our forces.

As I finished, John said to Alex, "See that's why I wanted Tiger's input he's good at this shit boss." Alex smiled and nodded and replied with a smile while looking at me, "Yep, but he costs us a fortune each time he's here." Then we all laughed and I was congratulated for what I'd come up with, and then we went outside for a break before getting into all the timing specifics of the operation, and I was also asked to do the mission briefing for John's force prior to the mission taking place, which I agreed to.

During lunch we arranged that I would give the mission briefing the following morning, and then Mose and the team would leave for the mission soon after that. The rest of the day was spent in contact with the local assets and also with Coast Guard officers to arrange the pickup and transfer of the team back to here. Luckily the Coast Guard had a cutter in Panama that was due to leave port the following day, so they would delay the departure by a further half day, and that way they'd be in the rendezvous area to pick up John and the team during the afternoon of the day after next. Things worked out well and that meant that in three days John would be back, with the mission accomplished, Alex came into the MTAC room where John and I had been making all the final arrangements, and said with a smile "Well I just got off the phone from talking to General Fredrick at Pendleton, yeah Wild Bill's now a general! Mose and I have been invited to a BBQ at his house on Saturday, and I asked if I could bring a couple of friends, without telling him who it was of course, and he was more than happy, so John don't you go getting killed in the next couple of days."

That night at dinner, I told Dawn about the BBQ on Saturday, and why we would be going, and she asked if the work I was doing would be finished by then, and I smiled telling her that when I went in the morning I'd probably spend the next few days running the operation which meant being there overnight, so by the time I came back to the hotel on Friday, the mission would have been completed, and then I'd also be able to tell her when we would be picked up for the Saturday BBQ. She smiled and told me all about her first day at Disneyland, and how big the place was, and said "It's just as well you were able to get us multiday passes, so by Friday we should have seen everything there is to see with a bit of luck, will you be leaving us after breakfast like we did today, or are you leaving earlier?"

I told her that I'd be doing the same as we had that morning, and I'd tell the others about what was going on while we were having breakfast in the morning, and toyed with the idea of heading for home the coming Monday.

When we finished dinner, we went into the bar for a couple of nightcaps, and then went up to our room, where I packed a few things into my go bag while she was having a shower. At breakfast the next morning everyone agreed that they'd be ready to head home on Monday, and I told them about Dawn and I going to see Wild Bill on the Saturday, so they wouldn't have her company at Disneyland that day, and we arranged to all meet up in the bar on Saturday night before we went to dinner. We all left the hotel at the same time as we'd done previously, and I told them I'd see them either Friday or Saturday night as I walked to my car carrying my go bag which I slung on the back seat as I got into the front with the driver.

Alex showed me the briefing room, and I was amazed that it had the same capability screen wise and could give me the computer view that was available in the MTAC, an idea that would cause many discussions between Harry, John, and I at a later date. John Mosely led his team into the room at eleven for what ended up being a two-hour briefing, with the main emphasis on the timing of the attack, most wanted to know why they were attacking in broad daylight as opposed to a night time assault. My answer to them was quite simple in the fact that any noise would be disguised as usual daytime noises; the explosions in the field wouldn't cause as much curiosity from neighbouring farms and haciendas and that they wouldn't have to wait around at their escape point. I explained that the escape window was only available during the late afternoon, and I didn't think they'd like being holed up in a hostile country for hours which gave greater opportunity for them to be discovered, this way they were able to do the job and get out immediately, this point brought nods of agreement from all of them, I finished the briefing by telling them that I would remain in MTAC from then until they were back on US soil in a couple of days, and I wished them good luck and happy hunting, which drew a laugh from them.

After the briefing Alex and I went and had some lunch, and then when we went back into MTAC, Alex showed me a room off to the side which had a bed and on-suite in it, so I picked my go bag up from the table and put it on the bed, back in the main room, Alex introduced me to the MTAC staff and told them that I would

315

be in charge of the coming operation, and that I was to be given their complete cooperation. Once back at the table he explained to me that once an operation was under way, a canteen only for MTAC staff was setup, and that meals could be delivered into the room and showed me the number on the internal building phone, and then he took me to the canteen.

Once I'd been introduced, I grabbed a menu of what was available, as we headed back to MTAC. We were at the table just discussing some finer details, as the room speakers came alive with, "Strike one to MTAC, we're about to board our plane, so I'll be switching off until we are close to the drop zone, over."

Alex whispered in my ear that the internal room mic would pick up my voice normally, so I answered "Copy that John, have a safe trip, I'll be watching, over." John's voice came back, "Roger that Tiger, talk to you when we are ready to hit the silk, over." I smiled and replied "Copy that strike one, MTAC out." Then I asked for the satellite view of the target area without the zoom, that way we'd see the plane as it entered the target area.

Hours later, I was getting some sleep, when I heard a knocking on the door, and someone was telling me that the plane had just entered the target area. I got up and rushed into MTAC coming fully awake as I moved into my seat at the table, a hot coffee was placed beside me as I watched the screen, and asked for it to be zoomed in, then to the right of the plane I discerned three lights blinking in a triangle which meant the ground team was in place and signalling from the landing zone. Next moment I heard John saying, "Strike one to MTAC, back on air and ready for the jump."

I replied "Copy that Strike One, your ground crew are in place, you should be getting the green light any second." I heard John laugh as he answered, "Roger that, we're already getting out of this can will call from the ground." I smiled as I watched each dot come alive on the screen to indicate a team member as they left the plane; I was amazed to see that each dot lit up with a number as they became visible. By this time Alex had entered MTAC and sat beside me, and informed me that each member of the team tracker emitted their team number, so we knew who was who, by name and number, number one of course being Mose. Alex continued talking saying that there were separate colours for different designations, all the team members were coloured green, friendlies were red, and enemy were coloured white, but as yet there were no different colours showing up. Then as team members got closer to the ground I noticed the difference in the colour to the ground crew that were now emitting a red colour, and then John's voice was heard, "Strike One to MTAC, on the ground, all team members A ok, moving to observation post that locals established earlier, for shut eye and observation, over." I smiled as replied "Roger that John, we'll be keeping watch, give me a shout when you're ready to insert, out."

I looked at the clocks on the wall, and estimated that we had roughly seven hours to wait until the attack took place, so I suggested that Alex and I go and have a leisurely breakfast while we waited. After having a leisurely breakfast with Alex, we went back into MTAC, and while he resumed his seat I went to my room to get a little shut eye.

Alex woke me at midday local time, and told me that John and the team were making their preparations, and as I took my seat at the table, I had the communications officer flip the radio on, as I said "MTAC to Strike One leader copy?" Mosely's voice came through, "Copy MTAC, attack has been planned during target observation, about to move on the hacienda, and then the field, over."

Before answering, I had the sat view of the target zoomed in so we could also see what was taking place, there were only half a dozen white dots on the screen, as I said "Ok John, I count six oppositions at present, and will keep watching, over." I heard John mutter back, "I'm glad you're running this show, Tiger you're our guardian angel right now, ok moving in, out." Shortly I was able to see the eleven green dots of the team, as they advanced on the hacienda, and then four enemy dots flashed out, which meant the four on the roof corners had been taken

317

out, now it was just the two interior guards, and these were taken out by team members three, and six at each of the end corners of the L shaped building. Then five of the team entered the house, as number six started moving toward the back of the building, just then a white dot showed coming out from the middle of the building at the back!

Without any thought, I yelled "Six freeze! You have an enemy at ten o'clock to your corner moving toward you." As we watched six's dot was right at the building corner, and then the white flashed out, as a voice said "Thanks, nicely targeted too, Guardian Angel, out." Then we heard John's voice say, "Leader to team, coming out the back of the house, reform on me, and we'll head for the field, three and six out on scout." We watched as if mesmerised at the screen, as the dots for three and six moved off in the direction of the field, while all the other greens gathered at the back of the house, and then headed after the other two.

I had the zoom adjusted to take in the field, and three and six were half way there, and as I look over the site, I was hoping that any guard would be having a siesta in the hut located next to the road that headed toward the main house.

As I watched, I saw a dot come from the hut heading toward the road, and then stay in that position, so I informed both scouts to alert them to his presence, and a couple minutes later the white dot went out. Three moved toward the hut, and next minute we all heard, in a whispered voice "Three to leader, five enemies inside hut all in relaxed posture, three laying on bunks, two playing cards."

Then John's voice spoke, "Copy that three, five and seven moving to reinforce you, then take them all out, main force will head into the field, Jose do you copy?" Another voice answered, saying "Si senor Moseley," John replied "Good man Jose, now in ten minutes you bring the bus into the property and drive to the field where you will pick us up, copy." I almost laughed as I heard Jose reply with "Si senor, will I bring Manuel and Jesus too?" John mumbled something indistinguishable before telling him exasperatedly yes. We all had a chuckle after hearing John's reply, and I must say I felt for him.

The satellite zoom had to be kept on zooming out bit by bit while the strike force was on the site, because to the planets rotation and the satellite position which would work well for us during the escape phase of the operation, as we would be able to see what was taking place, but if they didn't finish soon we would lose being able to see them because of the height of the zoom out. So I decided to find out how close to finishing they were, and as I was about to call them, John's voice came through, saying "Strike one to MTAC, all the explosives are planted, and we're about to set them off, then we'll be making tracks to Cartagena, over." I sighed knowing that that was cutting it real fine as I replied "Copy that John, I was just about to call you, and say that if you didn't hurry we were going to lose sight of you, over." He was laughing as he replied, "Oh yee of little faith, one minute and this place will be ash, out."

After his words, we watched as a fireball erupted over the top of the field, and then saw the bus moving away from the field, onto the main road and heading toward Cartagena. There were cheers and smiles on every face in the room, as I looked at Alex with a smile, with my head cocked to one side and raised enquiring eyebrows, and he replied with a wider smile and a couple of nods. I let the celebrations continue for a little while, and then raised my voice saying, "Alright gentlemen, that's half the job done! Next we have to make sure these boys come home to US soil, so let's get back to work please." Everyone had faced me as I addressed them, and as I finished they all just responded with smiles and a unanimous "Yes Sir!" Then turned their attention back to what they were doing.

I must give points to the person controlling the satellite zoom, because he kept the view fixed on the escape bus as it made its way toward the city. On the outskirts of the city, a red dot appeared from out of the bus, and made its way at a good speed toward a marina, again the zoom controller was spot on as we were able to follow the progress of the bus and the local asset that had gone to get the boat.

John's voice came through as the bus neared the wharves, saying "Strike One to Tiger, all team members are taking out the radios, but our other gear is under our large colourful shirts, so you'll be able to see us but not communicate, I will restore radio contact after we clear the harbour, over."

My reply was immediate, "Tiger to Strike One, copy that John talk to you soon, out." Then the communications went dead, as they switched off the radios. My gaze went immediately to the screen, and we watched as they boarded a banana boat, and slowly left the harbour. I instructed the communications to get me the Coast Guard cutter on the radio, and as he made the connection he turned and nodded, so I said "DEA command to coast guard cutter Texas copy?"

The reply was immediate, "DEA command this is coast guard two nine the Texas captain Jensen speaking, over," as I answered I dropped all formalities, and asked for his current position and ETA to the rendezvous area, and was told that they were only half an hour from the pickup area and that once they had our men aboard they would be heading for their home port of Galveston, and would arrive there around eight the following morning, and then I informed Jensen that our team had just left the harbour, and would be in the area in about an hour, and thanked him, and let him get on with his duties.

When I finished talking to him, I called Mose, who should have turned on the radio by now, and sure enough John answered, so I gave him the call sign of the cutter and the captain's name, and then passed on the fact that as soon as they were aboard the cutter it was going to be heading for Galveston, and that arrangements were being made to have transport for them from there back to LA. While I was talking Alex had got on the phone and arranged an air force plane that would be waiting for them at the coast guard base when they arrived and they would be flown to the base that the DEA used, so with a bit of luck they would be back in the office by fourteen hundred the next day. I decided to save that information until they were aboard the cutter and on the way back to Galveston, so I called the Texas again.

After the calling formalities, I said "Captain this is Colonel Davis speaking again, once my men are settled and you're on your way back, could you please have John Mosely give me a call on your radio." He told me that he'd be happy to do so, and I told him we were observing via satellite imaging and that John would call the ship direct as soon as they were in the area.

While Alex and I were having some coffee a little later, we heard Mose call the cutter and listened to the ensuing conversation as we watched both boats on screen, "Strike One to Charlie Golf two niner, copy?" "Strike one this is two niner copy," "Two niner we have you in sight and heading your way, which side is best for boarding over," "We will lower the boarding steps on the starboard side strike one, two niner out."

The zoom was able to close right in, and we watched as the team made their way up the boarding ladder, and fuel was replenished in the banana boat plus an extra four jerry cans full were placed aboard, and with a wave the local asset untied from the landing platform at the base of the ladder and turned away from the cutter, as it too started to power up to speed in a slow curve to the left away from the islands. Shortly we heard "Strike one to MTAC, we're all aboard US soil and coming home." I spoke over the cheers in the room, informing John of the arrangements and told him we'd still be operating in MTAC until he was aboard the aircraft and ready to leave Galveston.

I told the MTAC staff that they'd done a marvellous job, and that we could now go onto a more relaxed style of operation, but the men weren't all the way home yet so we would still maintain our vigil until the call from Mose to say he was leaving Galveston. We got his call concerning that at zero eight hundred the next morning, and then I officially announced that the mission had been successfully completed, and therefore they could all stand down from operational status. Then Alex and I left MTAC went to the canteen for breakfast, and then went into his office, instead of having coffee, I asked for some strong stuff, and as he looked at me enquiringly, I told him that it was a nightcap, because I was going to get some sleep while everyone waited for John to get back.

Four hours later I woke, and had a long hot shower before getting dressed and packing my gear away into the go bag, and then left the side room and MTAC. I joined Alex in his office and put my bag on the sofa, and we went and had a relaxed lunch, at 1:40pm John strode back into Alex's office with a grin.

We greeted him with handshakes and congratulations, before we all sat down to talk with a few bourbons. Over our drinks we received a debriefing of the mission from John, the overall dead count was twenty, and he had raided the safe and split the money on hand in it between the three local assets, plus the field was completely destroyed, all up the mission was completely successful, which they put down to my exceptional planning abilities, speaking for myself I just did what was natural, I saw the problem, thought it out, and then fixed it.

During our talk that afternoon we arranged that Alex would use a company limo to pick us all up, that way we could drink as much as we wanted to, he and John would be picked up first, and then Dawn and me at twelve thirty, which would get us to Bill's Pendleton house by one fifteen.

After our talks had finished it was decided that both of them would come back to the hotel with me, and have dinner with us that night, and meet Dawn and the rest of the crew. So after another half hour of paperwork and so on, which included me ringing the hotel and leaving a message for everyone, we all headed down to the car to take us to the hotel.

CHAPTER 27

After an exhausting night of catch up, dinner and drinks I awoke the next morning at eight with a slightly fuzzy head, but otherwise alright, but I was famished, so while I waited for Dawn to surface, I ordered a light breakfast of hot bacon, egg, and cheese croissants from room service, but made sure there were two urns of fresh coffee, and orange juice.

While I waited for room service to arrive I had a shower, and that helped, but after having the food that had arrived I was on top of the world. I was relaxing over my second coffee and a smoke on the balcony as I heard Dawn get up, so after finishing my smoke, I took her in a cup of coffee to the bed, and was greeted with a kiss good morning, as she enquired whether the coffee was fresh or instant, after I told her I'd had it sent up from room service, she told me I was wonderful.

When she eventually got up, we decided to have an early meal at the hotel, because I surmised that we probably wouldn't eat much before four, and so we went down to the restaurant at eleven, and had a cross between breakfast and lunch, and finished in time to go to the foyer, and wait for the limo that was picking us up. It drove in right on twelve thirty and as we climbed in we said our hellos to Alex and John, before the driver shut the door, and then started the journey to Pendleton.

The limo pulled up outside Bill's, which was still the same house as the last time I visited, at 1:20pm, and as the door was opened by our driver Alex told him he'd have to wait, which could be a few hours, he nodded and told him that was alright. And then we made our way to the door, and I rang the doorbell then stepped back slightly behind John. Mary answered the door, and shrieked "Tom!" As she spotted me, and pushed past Alex and John, (no mean feat because he was quite big and large), and flew into my arms and hugged and kissed me on the cheek. Bill had joined her at the door, with an inquisitive look on his face, until he saw me. He shook hands with Alex and John, before Mary released me enough for him to say hello and shake, so I took that quick opportunity to introduce Dawn to the both of them, Bill shook her hand, while Mary swept her up in her arms, gave her a kiss on the cheek, and told her she was welcome, and then she seemed to realise that we were all standing at the front door still, and so ushered all of us inside. Mary took Dawn's hand and led her in, as the rest of us followed.

As I was about to pass Bill we embraced like brothers, and then followed the others inside. Once inside, as Bill started pouring drinks, I introduced Mary to Alex and John, and she apologised to them for ignoring them at the door as she shook hands with both of them, when we all had drinks, Bill called a toast to "Friends," as we all called "Cheers" in return. Then after some small talk he announced, "When I got your call Alex, I assumed that you wished to discuss business, so when I invited you and John, I decided not to invite anyone else over, so it's just us, so let's talk about our days in 'Nam together, and then do some catch up while we have some drinks before I fire up the BBQ and we have something to eat.

Over the next few hours, we did just that, and then while Alex was bringing them up to date with what he'd been doing, he told Bill and Mary how it was that I had turned up with them, and the call had been made by him at my insistence so I could fill them in on information that I had for them. So naturally I had to tell them my news straight away, and so I told them how one by one each of the guys that they both knew had died, and that I was the last surviving member of what had been an elite group of men. Bill refreshed everyone's glass, and staying on his feet toasted, "To fallen comrades, and those left standing!" We all stood and repeated the toast and drained our glasses, and held a minutes silence before Bill refilled all of our glasses, and the solemn mood was shaken off slowly, Mary was visibly crying silently until Bill put his arm around her, and she said "I'm sorry, but it just seems like yesterday they were all here laughing and joking," and then Bill reminded her of Lizard squirting her with water with one of the kid's water pistols, and that lightened her mood as she started laughing, pointing out other things they'd done to her as a joke.

Bill wanted to know how John's operation had gone, and because we were all on the same footing security wise, He told them what had happened and how it all been successful, due to my planning, and it was agreed around the table that I was good at what I did, and they all laughed when I told them I'd much rather have been doing the field work. Bill said "Tiger you are definitely a holy terror and good on the ground, but your much better off doing the planning for these types of operation, remember we're not getting any younger." And they all agreed with what he'd said by saying, "Here, here." While the cooking was being done, I had the chance to ask Mary how Moira had taken my departure, and she told me that she got over me eventually, and that they still saw each other from time to time, but that she'd married a doctor upstate.

Then she asked about Dawn, and I told her that we'd probably be married after we got home, and she told me that was good, because I deserved someone good, and then she asked me if Dawn would give her a hand in the kitchen, and after telling her that I was sure she would, I went and asked Dawn to give her a hand, and she jumped at the chance, probably sick of hearing war stories from us lot I guess.

We eventually all left Bill and Mary's around seven that night, all well fed and quite tipsy, and we said our goodbyes with hand-shakes and embraces. Dawn and I were dropped off first, but on the way back I told Alex and John that we'd be making tracks for home on Monday, and both wished us a good trip, and Alex told me just to check out without paying. The hotel knew the bill was being paid by the DEA, so we could leave whenever we wished, so I jokingly told him that if that was the case we'd stay for another month, and we all laughed. At the hotel we said our goodbyes with handshakes, and Dawn and I watched as they pulled away in the limo.

When we went into the hotel, we went to the bar for a couple more drinks before bed, and joined the rest of the crew that were there, and I apologised for missing dinner, and arranged for all of us to have dinner together the next night, as it would be our last night here, because we would leave for home Monday. After a couple more drinks, I called it a night, and we excused ourselves as we went up to bed, but Dawn wanted my body before going to sleep, so I happily lay back and let her take me into her, until exhausted she collapsed onto me, I rolled so she slid sideways so she was beside me, and she fell asleep in my arms.

It was after nine when we both woke slowly, and after lazing in bed for a while I picked up the phone and ordered our breakfast through room service, and fifteen minutes later we were enjoying our breakfast seated on the balcony. Then we had a bit of a lazy day, and in the afternoon we went down to the indoor pool and after a swim I went into the gym for a workout, and then had another swim before we both went into the steam room. Now I don't know if you've ever had sex in a steam room, but believe me you certainly sweat a lot, but not from the steam, she was giggling all the way back to our suite, at the fact that we'd got away with it without being discovered in the act, I thought it rather amusing myself. During dinner that night we arranged when we would leave and the route we would use to get home, and then after a couple of drinks called it a night, because we'd be up early the next morning.

Next morning, we all met in the restaurant for an early breakfast, and then checked out after arranging a limo to take us all to the airport, and after getting everything ready and packed for the flight, this included meals and snacks, drinks, and the most important thing coffee. While we were being provisioned for the flight, Ross had been at air traffic control lodging our flight path, which would put us into Manilla in the Philippine's for refuelling, and then down into Brisbane. We started to taxi, and then came the rush down the runway as we took to the sky, and left LA behind us by nine am on the Monday morning.

We arrived in Brisbane two days later at zero five thirty local time, and by the time the plane was in the hangar refuelled, cleaned, and ready to go again if needed, it was just coming on to six thirty am, Dawn and I drove into the valley to a coffee shop that I knew would be open and we had a wonderful breakfast of toast, bacon and eggs, sausages, tomato and mushrooms, and large cappuccino's. By the time we'd finished our relaxed breakfast, and I'd had a couple of smokes, it was nearly eight, and knowing the person I wanted to see would be at work, I drove to my jewellery maker. Karl was Swiss but instead of being a watchmaker he turned his talents to making jewellery many years ago and was the best I knew at designing things. As I entered the shop with Dawn, Karl greeted me and asked if we'd like a coffee, and we both accepted, and while we were seated drinking them, I told him that I wanted an engagement ring made for Dawn and a wedding ring that matched the engagement ring.

Ideas of what they should look like were thrown around, and eventually he came up with the design of the engagement ring, which ended up looking somewhat like a capital italic D in calligraphy and the centre of the D would be a half carat diamond, and then he showed us how the wedding ring he had in mind would look, and as soon as Dawn saw what they both would look like, she looked at me and nodded, so I told Karl to go ahead, and he started sizing Dawns finger, and then we worked out thick to make them, what grade of gold, and the cut of the diamond for the centre. After all that was worked out, I asked him how long it would take, and he said he'd have the engagement ring ready in two weeks, and the wedding ring another week after that, and then he passed me a slip of paper with the price for doing the job, which was twelve hundred dollars, I scrunched up the note and threw it in his bin, and told him to start work on them and that I'd give him five hundred as a deposit and the rest to be paid on completion. He agreed and told us he start on them that day, he knew how to contact me, which he would do as soon as they were ready.

We left him to it, and as we made our way back to the car, Dawn told me she loved me, and she would start on organising our marriage, when she had her next days off, because she wouldn't have time to do anything else for the rest of the week except get her work gear ready and look after me, and drop in and see her parents before going back to work on the Sunday coming, and she'd have to check on that also for her start time. I apologised for taking on the job in the US which had eaten up the buffer zone time that we would have had, and she told me not to worry about it because we'd virtually had two holidays in one, and besides how many people got to see as much of Disneyland as she did, she loved the whole trip, and thanked me for taking her.

When we arrived home, we sorted out the washing and the unpacking, and both got into very casual gear without wearing any underclothes because by now it was late October, and the weather was starting to heat up, and besides I was going to power up the spa pool so that later we could have our cocktail time naked in the pool, and what we were wearing made it easy to slip out of, and a damn sight easier to touch or caress each other. I phoned into the office and let Janice pass the word that I was back and would be in the following day, and then I rang the dive shop, Robert answered and I told him I'd just got back, and that I'd call in the following day, if I got rid of my jetlag, and he said to take my time, and call in anytime. I wasn't suffering any jetlag because we got plenty of sleep on the plane, and even when I fly commercial on long flights I've never suffered with jetlag the way some people do.

Readers Note: At this point in the book, as I have said earlier, the mid to late eighties was an exceptionally volatile time for dive shop owners, and all tourist operators in general, because it was in late eighty-six that the first round of the Australian pilot's strike started which of course affected a lot of tourist businesses. Also it was building up to some hectic happenings with the job I was doing with ASIS, and as well as things going on in my personal life. So I have had to come to a decision whether to concentrate on my personal and business life as the main structure for the rest of the book, or to concentrate on what was happening in the spying game, I can't do both, otherwise this would become a quadrilogy, if there is such a thing. I can tell you enough about both and that would fill up two books instead of just this one! So here's what I've decided, I'll concentrate on the spy work I was doing with ASIS, because as you know by now, I was doing both and juggling them quite well I might add, so I won't go into too much detail about the other side that was happening at the same time.

For those of you that do want to hear in more detail what was going on in my personal and business life, I will try and convince Tim to write a follow up book that would be an extension of what was happening in my personal and business life during that period from eighty-six to ninety-three, and concentrate on that side, while keeping the ASIS work as a peripheral and not the main theme. So I hope you can bare to go along with the decision I've made, thank you. Anyway let's now get back to the main story.

While I'd been on the phone to both works, Dawn had started a wash with the first load of the dirty clothes, and came and put her arms round my neck to give me a kiss, and as she did, I could feel her nipples hardening against my chest through the flimsy material of her dress, and I think she was able to feel me hardening in my loose shorts, because she pushed hard against me while emitting a low moan, then for the next hour nothing happened apart from the two of us contenting ourselves with each other's bodies, as I took her over the brink of orgasm a number of times before I poured myself into her, and so after we rested and got up from the floor she had to put the dress she'd been wearing into the wash pile along with my shorts, after that we decided to stay naked, to hell with the convention of wearing clothes, there was nothing wrong with either of our bodies that needed hiding.

After that we kept to that idiom of wearing either very loose clothing without underclothes, or none at all whenever we were home alone during the summer months, and this lasted through the better part of our marriage. A little after three, I grabbed a couple of drinks for each other, and then enticed her into the spa pool, and as she settled into the formed seat beside me with a groan of pleasure, she said "But it's not four o'clock yet," to which I replied, "it is somewhere, anyway the sun's over the yardarm, so drink my sweet." She laughed and said with a smile "As the master demands I shall obey as a dutiful wife should." I just looked at her and we both burst out laughing, as I mumbled "Yeah well I knew that was bullshit."

With a few drinks under our belts, that we weren't wearing, I turned to her and asked, "So what has the dutiful wife made for dinner," A look of horror came over her face, as she replied "Oh shit! I'll be back in a minute," as she got out of the pool, reaching for a towel to put around her, and disappeared upstairs, when I heard her coming back, I knew she'd been gone five minutes, and I knew this because that's how long it took for me to smoke a cigarette, and as she sat down into the water, she said "Dinner is twenty minutes away, and you'll like it."

I couldn't resist, so I asked "So she who must be obeyed, what are you serving for dinner?" Knowing full well nothing was being cooked. But she answered with such a straight face I burst out laughing again, as she answered smiling, "Pizza, just the way you like it my love." As I replied, "Ah, delivered!" She laughed and then said, "Yep now you better go put some clothes on and pay for it, come on let's go!"

Next morning, I was in the office at eight thirty, and as I passed Janice at her desk, I told her Business as usual Janice, shortly she came in carrying two coffees and her note pad, and as passed my coffee to me she took a seat, and I looked at her and enquired what had been happening, her reply of business as usual suited me down to the ground, and we got into the routine traffic. I knew that DJ had taken my place during the usual Monday meetings, and asked her if anything unusual had come to light, and she told nothing that she knew of, so closing the book on our usual routine, I asked her to send DJ into me when he arrived, she nodded and left, while I started to go over what had been happening while I'd been away.

I did notice that there was a couple of different reports suggesting that an attack on one of the dive resorts at Jaba near Motupena point in the Gazelle harbour which was owned and staffed by Australians had been made by the BRA (Bougainville Revolutionary Army), which was a group of independents led by one Francis Ona a bouganvillean born half caste that had been educated at Queensland University. His group wanted to succeed from Papua New Guinea control and join with the Solomon Islands.

Now if they'd attacked an Australian enterprise to bring their rebellion to our notice, then they'd really screwed up, because retaliation would be the name of the game, not the political help they'd probably hoped for. However as yet the facts needed to be investigated to determine the true state of affairs. I noticed that one of the reports had come via a dive operation based at Kimbe on New Britain, while the other came as a query from the Foreign Affairs Department in Canberra, so I took it upon myself to take the matter further.

After DJ had come into my office, I had Janice join us with morning tea for us all, which was really only coffee and biscuits, and I asked DJ if anything had been actioned in regard to the Bougainville report. He told they had both come up at the usual Monday meetings but as yet they'd been put onto the back burner, because of other operations taking place in the far north of the state.

I nodded and then told him that I wanted to call an extraordinary meeting of department heads right away, and that he was to organise it, and that we'd meet in the TAC room in half an hour, and I asked him "Aren't you guys aware of how important an issue this could become? There's Australian companies all over Bougainville if one interest has been attacked, which is yet to be determined, then surely the other interests would become targets as well for the BRA, which was led by an Australian educated half caste with a possible axe to grind!"

As he left my office to arrange the meeting, I looked at Janice, and quietly said "When you get back to your desk would you put in a call to Colin Gorman at HQ please?" She nodded, and stood up to leave, ten minutes later her voice came through the phone saying she had Mr Gorman on line one, I thanked her and then pressed the number one button on my phone, and said hello to Gorman. As we discussed the reports, he said he was aware of them, but as yet the facts hadn't been determined, and that I was probably the only well suited agent to find out the truth of the matter, so I pushed him to get me permission to land at the military airfield at Rabaul the capital of New Britain, instead of the civilian one, and I'd do some investigating. He told me he'd get back to me before the day was out, so I told him I was having a meeting of department heads soon so anything he came up with could be taken by Janice, and if there was a problem I'd get back to him, he agreed and rang off. I pressed the intercom switch and asked Janice to come in, when she was sitting opposite me I told her what had taken place during my call with Gorman, and told her that if he rang back while I was otherwise engaged, that she could take the message and pass it on to me when I was available.

She nodded, and told me she would, and then I told her I'd go to the cafeteria for lunch after the meeting, so I was leaving things in her hands. Then we both got up and made our way to the door, while she took a seat at her desk, I carried on to the TAC room for my meeting.

I had just finished making a brew as the others trooped into the room, and they took their seats, as they congratulated me on the Columbian affair, I took the praise and thanked them, and then held up the two reports I wanted them to read, and passed them around. After John, Harry, Tim, and DJ had read them through thoroughly, I asked if any of them had any idea as to what was at stake in Bougainville, and what it could really mean for Australian interests. None of them could answer that, except Tim.

Who with the courage of his convictions stated "Well he's just another piss ant revolutionary with an axe to grind, isn't he?" I smiled and looked at him, and around at each of them, and said "At least Tim is on the right track, so let's have a bit of a history lesson. Then I started giving them the facts about Ona, "He was born in nineteen fifty-three as a half caste bastard between a Dutchman whose name has never been recorded and a Buka Island girl, god knows why they're the blackest and ugliest people to ever set foot on the earth, you can't even tell if they're around even when they smile because their teeth are so black. Anyway somehow she managed to get him educated in Australia, and he earned a master's degree in engineering at Queensland University. When he returned to Bougainville it was as an engineer at the Panguna Mine that was run by Bougainville Copper, he started voicing his concerns with the mine and also with the PNG government that runs Bougainville, and when they took no action he formed the BRA Bougainville Revolutionary Army with the aim of sabotaging the mining equipment and having Bougainville separate from PNG, and join in with the rest of the Solomon group of Islands, any questions so far?"

There weren't any, so I continued, "Now this upstart has had a few successes, and could eventually become a force to be reckoned with, in my view if the PNG army doesn't squash him now, he'll end up running the whole island, and that's what we don't want, so seeing PNG are loath to go against him, if he attacks Australian interests on the island, then we need to deal with him, and kick him in the teeth and show him who's boss when it comes to Australian lives, so yes Tim you were right in a way, and we have to treat him like a piss ant revolutionary, and take care of him like we would a rabid dog. Now I'm planning on taking a team of six agents with me to PNG, and then onto Bougainville to, one, establish the truth-fulness of the attack, and two, if Ona's BRA were involved, meet with him and establish the rules regarding Australian interests, and if they don't fall into line, I'll shoot him, and hope we can get off the island ok, questions?"

John asked, "Who are you going to take with you, boss," I looked at him with a smile, and replied "Apart from myself and DJ, I want you to find me six agents that have had previous military experience, preferably special forces, but that may be asking too much, and I want them in the briefing room at ten tomorrow morning, also the rest of you will be keeping an eye on us from here. So you can see and hear what's happening, this is to be treated like a full on operation, you've watched me handle it, so now it's your turn, John you'll be in charge."

He nodded and asked, "Wouldn't it be easier if we sat in on the briefing tomorrow as well?" I nodded with a smile and told him that was going to be my next suggestion, and then after all the questions were answered, I called an end to the meeting, so they could get on with what needed doing, but I had DJ join me for lunch, and we talked over the operation. He smiled and said, "Well it's true what they say the grass doesn't grow around your feet, you've only just got back from an operation overseas, and you're going again, things certainly happen around you, boss, don't they?" I nodded with a smile, and told him they sure did, whether I liked it or not.

After lunch, I was in my office, and had taken out my MP4 and UZI and were cleaning them as Janice came in and announced that Gorman was on the phone, so I asked her to put it on speaker, as I said "Yes Boss, were you able to get what I wanted?"

His voice replied, "Tiger you're going to be the death of me, but yeah I got what you needed including a helicopter pilot that'll fly you to Jaba from Rabaul, he'll also be at your beck and call for the entire time you're up there, how many men are you taking?"

I replied, "All up there'll be eight of us all fully armed, because if I have to, I'll give Ona a kick in the teeth before he gets too ambitious, by the way do you want to come up and run the TAC room operation?" he laughed and told me my men were more than capable of handling it, and then I told him I'd ring him the next day, to let him know when we were going, and then we both hung up.

CHAPTER 28

After I finished cleaning my weapons, I rang Ross at the hangar and asked "How soon before the plane could be ready for another O/S operation?" He told me that we could take off at a moment's notice, and all that he needed was the destination for a flight plan, and then I told him that he and Jerry had best come into the office the next day, and to be in by nine thirty for a briefing starting at ten, he told me they'd be there, and we both rang off.

My next call was to Rob at the dive shop, telling him I'd leave coming into the shop 'til after I'd got over a bug I must have caught while overseas, and feigned at hacking cough, he told me to take as much time as needed, because there wasn't much going on at present, I thanked him and hung up. Now all I had to do was tell Dawn, hopefully she'd understand. After checking the wardrobe in my office quarters I found that I had four sets of camouflage uniforms, and two pairs of boots there, that was good, so all I needed from home was my knife and pistol.

Dawn wasn't as understanding as I thought she'd be, but after explaining that this was my job she quietened down a bit, besides I pointed out that she would be back at work a day or so after I went, so she wasn't going to have much time with me after that anyway. She asked when I'd be going, and I had to tell her I wasn't sure yet, but probably in a day or so, and added, the sooner I get up there the sooner I get home again. She smiled and told me that it had better not take too long, because her ring would be ready in another week. I smiled and told her that I hadn't forgotten. Then I went about putting some clothes in my go bag along with my knife and pistol, and my shoulder holster, my thigh holster was already at the office, and then took the go bag down and put it in the car ready for the next day.

Next morning, Dawn asked if I'd be home that night, and I told her that I would, unless I rang her, so if she didn't get a call from me, I'd be home for dinner. I had left leaving the house till right at the end of peak hour, and drove into the parking area at nine fifteen. When I got to my office, Janice and I went through our usual routine, and as we were finishing up John stuck his head in the door, and I told him to come in because we'd finished with the routine work, as he took a seat opposite me, I asked "Ok I hope you got me some really good agents for this little jaunt," and he told me that he'd gone through all the agents available personally, and the ones he picked were all ex-service.

"Brilliant, now have you really earned your pay grade, by getting what I wanted?" He smiled, and replied "Tiger all of them are ex commando's, except one, who's like you ex sas, so you've got a good crew." I nodded and laughed, before saying "Good looks like you earned your wage this week, you bloody beauty."

At ten, I made my way to the briefing room flanked by John and Harry, and as we entered DJ, called everyone to order, I noted that Ross and Jerry were seated right at the back, Harry had gone to the computer terminal and next minute Rabaul flashed up on the screen that everyone would be looking at, I knew that he would follow throughout the briefing bringing the right screens up. So as John took a seat off to the side, and as I looked around I noticed some faces that I'd seen before, others I hadn't so I started the briefing.

"Welcome gentlemen, for those of you that don't know me, my name is Tiger Davis, the tactical officer for this branch, now some think I'm not that, but just a glorified field agent, and their right I prefer to be in the field, and that's why you're here, to protect my ass while we go on a mission that I have planned, and that I wanted to be on." I gave a couple of minutes for the laughing to die down, and then continued "We'll be flying out to Rabaul in PNG, and from there transferring to a helo, and then flying to Jaba on Bougainville, and there we'll be investigating whether or not a dive operation run by Australians was attacked by the BRA or not. If it is determined that it was attacked by said faction, I intend to have a meeting with their Commander Francis Ono, and read him the riot act, and if I decide that he hasn't taken any notice of my demands, then it's up to us to give him a big kick in the teeth, so he learns whose boss. Now because we're such a small force, I think they'll underestimate our fighting capabilities, and they'll probably think we're a joke, so all of us on this operation should be prepared to kill, because once we show our resolve the shit will hit the fan, but make no mistake, they may underestimate us, but don't let's make the same mistake ourselves, everyone clear?"

I waited for the nods of accent, before asking if there were any questions, there weren't any, so I continued "Ok dress cams if you have them, greens if not, now weapons, your own or your pick from the armoury, but include a sidearm capable of fitting a silencer, we are going in armed to the teeth, and we will classify this as a wartime mission, take off will be zero six hundred tomorrow morning from our airport hangar, transport will be arranged from here by John Lime, any questions?" Again there weren't any, so I dismissed them.

As everyone started to leave the briefing room, I had Ross and Jerry stop behind, and asked "Ok a quick question, can we fly direct to Rabaul instead of going through Moresby?" Ross looked enquiringly at me, and he asked if we'd be landing at the military field, I nodded, and replied "Yep and a hangar has been arranged and quarters for you guys, as well while we're in Bouganville."

Ross nodded his head, and said "No problem, the strip is long enough, and it's a damned site easier to fly direct than having to go into Moresby first, flying time should be around four hours, so we should be on the ground by ten hundred hours, so unless there's anything else I'll get the flight plan sorted, and we'll have the jet ready for when you get to the hangar." I told them to carry on and I'd see them about five am the next day, as they headed out of the room, I asked John and Harry to join me for lunch, and we headed off to the cafeteria.

On the way we met DJ, so I got him to join us as well, and then when we'd all got our food we started discussing the transport arrangements for the other six agents, it was arranged that DJ would take three with him and John would drive the other three to the hangar, and they would leave the office at five, John would pass onto the agents when they were to be in the office ready to go. Meanwhile Harry was also going to come in early to establish the TAC room personnel, so if I took my gear with me that night I could drive straight to the hangar in the morning.

After lunch I had Janice get Gorman for me, and told him that we were leaving at first light for Rabaul, he told me he'd get in contact with the helicopter pilot whose name was Bruce Davidson, and that he worked for a company called Pacific Helicopters, he would have him meet us at the airfield the next day, and pointed out hopefully he'll be there before you.

I started sorting my gear after getting off the phone with him, I decided to take my UZI instead of the MP4, but I would also have my Ingram as well, and then made sure I had a full complement of ammunition, and just for good measure I put in a couple of grenades. After putting all my weapons and combat gear into a duffle bag, I took it all up to the garage and placed them in the boot of the car, I took my knife out of my go bag, and my pistol from the shoulder holster, which I left on the back seat, and then transferred the knife and pistol into the duffel bag with my field gear. Then I returned to my office and closed up telling Janice she was to look things until I got back, and then I left for the day, as I passed DJ's office, I told him I'd see him at the hangar in the morning.

I got home, and took my go bag upstairs and took out a set of cams to wear in the morning along with a pair of boots, and while I was in the bedroom, I set my alarm for three thirty in the morning, and then got undressed, and put on a pair of shorts before going down to the bar area and fixing a drink.

No sooner had I finished making my drink, when Dawn drove into the garage, so I went to meet her, and close the garage door, and as I did she said "Good you're home early, I've been doing a bit of shopping, and picked up a nice meatloaf from the butcher for dinner, so if you make me one of those I'll go start the dinner going honey." After I'd finished my first drink, I made her another and another for me before she came back downstairs to join me, and while we had our drinks and smokes I told her that I'd be leaving early in the morning while I looked into the thing in PNG, she nodded and asked how long I'd be away, and I told her that I would back in a few days, but I wouldn't be gone longer than a week.

Then she told me that she'd checked her roster, and that for eight out the ten shifts were daytime and then the following were four to midnight, and then three days off, but it meant getting up early on the Sunday for the first one. As I made us both another drink, she asked because the next day was Friday, would I be able to get any work over the weekend, so I told her that what day of the week it was up there didn't matter, as dive resorts worked almost every day, and that they rarely shut down. She laughed, and said "That's good, because I know how cranky you get when you have to wait around to do something," I looked at her sideways, scowling, and mumbled "Yes dear," and she burst out laughing.

While I up pouring us another drink, she said "Oh by the way sweetheart, I was on the phone to my parents earlier today, and I let them know that we were engaged, so we'd better make some time when you're back to go over and see them, and do the family thing." I groaned, and she laughed again, as I brought out the drinks and numbingly told her, if we had to.

Next morning as the alarm went off, she asked if I wanted her to make me some breakfast, and I told her no, I was only going to have a coffee and toast, go back to sleep, and I'll say goodbye before I go. I had left my clothes out in the lounge, and so as I left the bedroom, I turned out the light as I made my way to the kitchen, and put the jug on, prepped a cup with coffee, and headed into the lounge to start getting dressed, I finished dressing as I sipped my coffee, and then made some toast, after that I said my goodbye to Dawn, and left.

On the way across to the airport, I stopped at a bakery that was open and got a dozen croissants, and as I pulled into the hangar Jerry was making coffee, so I told him to make it three, and then we had the warm croissants with our coffee, after that I took my gear aboard, and finished getting dressed, so when the others arrived, I was standing there in cams with pistols strapped to each thigh, and my knife hanging from my belt. Everything was loaded and then, after we were all aboard Jerry signed for the ground crew to take the boarding steps away, as he closed and cross locked the hatch.

After we taxied and took off, I looked over each of the agents, and was pleased to see that they knew what gear they were to bring, one being a sniper, was not about to let anyone near his rifle, which I considered to be thoroughly professional, then the main aspect was comm's and I was glad to see each had the same equipment that DJ and I had, and all comm's were tested and it was with relief that I heard Harry's voice come back through each personal radio set.

We landed in Rabaul five minutes earlier than expected, but as we taxied to the hangar, a bell jet ranger the private equivalent to a military huey was waiting on the tarmac. My first sight of Bruce Davidson was as a brash know it all helicopter pilot lazing in a director's chair as we waited for us to land, he was five eight with brown curly hair, and had an angular face, the knowing smile was wiped off his dial as I approached him armed to the teeth so to speak, his jaw had dropped, and he was staring hard as I introduced myself, he was a little dumbstruck as I told him what he'd be doing, and I think the fact that everyone in my group towered over me in height and weight, but called me boss was awe inspiring and didn't seem to fit with his mental picture of me. However, this was only the first time we met, so he didn't know what to expect, in later years we met many times and he was a lot more respectful, after I won his respect during that first mission that we used him.

Fifteen minutes after being on the ground we took off again in Bruce's helicopter for the two-hour trip to Jaba on Bougainville.

Once we landed again I told him to get the chopper fuelled and be ready to go when I returned, and then I commandeered a truck to take my team to the dive resort that had allegedly been attacked by the BRA. After extensive questioning of the staff and the managers, Charlie and Estelle Richards, I was of the opinion that they had indeed been attacked by the BRA, and planned to talk further with the managers before my team and I did anything more, so I sent the truck back to the airport to bring Bruce to the resort where rooms were arranged for us at short notice.

That night DJ and I held long discussions with the Richards couple, trying to glean as much information out of them as we could, and they both confirmed that it was one of their workers, a kitchen hand, that identified the attackers as BRA, so I gave orders for my men to interrogate the kitchen hand. The interrogation went on all night, and I had my answers by morning, apparently the kitchen hand's cousin was a member of the BRA, and he had told his cousin that the place was susceptible to attack, and that a lot of money was held in the resort safe.

He was made to repeat his claims in front of Charlie Richards, who identified him as someone that demanded he be paid more, and was at times a sort of troublemaker, after hearing that, I had him questioned further, and eventually he volunteered to lead us to his cousin's camp, just outside of Jaba. After quick consultation between DJ and me, we decided that considering there was only a light number in the camp, that we attack them and take as many prisoner as we could, so we timed it all for late afternoon to leave the resort, and attack the camp during the night. The briefing was held at sixteen hundred, and we departed the resort soon after in the truck, when we were close to the camp our prisoner was gaged and we moved silently toward the camp, and were in place before sundown, after full dark, having been in radio contact with our TAC room it was determined that we would be face odds of three to one, however we held the advantage due to our night vision equipment, we took them from all sides just as they were eating, and ended up without a shot being fired, and taking twenty prisoners all up.

After we had secured all the prisoners, and then sat down and finished off their dinner, and as I ate, I said "DJ, this fish is bloody terrible, how about taking one of these for a walk, and bring back some fresh meat." He grinned evilly, nodded and then walked over to the prisoners, and looked at them, before grabbing one and dragging him into the jungle. Five minutes later there came a blood curdling scream, and then silence. All the prisoners were looking jittery as I got up, and placed a large frying pan on the fire, soon after DJ walked into the camp, carrying a few steaks that we'd brought with us, but the prisoners didn't know that, for show he had moistened them with water and appeared to be dripping blood. Then he asked "Which do you prefer arm, or leg?" Catching on, one of the other guys grinning asked for arm, while I went for leg, DJ tossed a so called piece of arm and I caught some leg, and went and threw it in the pan, after letting it cook a bit, I took a bite, and remarked "Hmm black isn't bad."

When I went back to sit with the boys, DJ told us in a murmur than he'd knocked the prisoner out cold and gagged him after he'd made him scream by kicking him in the balls, which made us all laugh, as we chewed on some of the steak that we had cooked. Then I leaned back, and said "I think they'll tell us anything we want to know after that performance we gave, so I guess it's time to start, let's go boys." We all sauntered over to the prisoners, and one of the guys said "I'm still a bit hungry boss." I smiled and told him to pick one, and as he was dragged to his feet, his eyes bugged out, and he started yelling and pleading saying that he'd cooperate with us, and tell us anything we wanted to know.

I smiled as we dragged him away from the others, and asked who was in charge, who had given the order to attack the dive resort, and where was Francis Ona. He told us that their boss man, Ericki had told them they had been given the task to attack the resort, and he'd been told by Ona, and that they were to stir up as much trouble for the whites as they could, so they had come down out of the mountains, last month and began a harassing campaign. He pointed out Ericki for us, and in his pidgin English told us that Ona was still at his base at Mainoki, which was in the middle of the Island, up in the highlands about eighty miles east north east of Panguna.

Ericki soon found himself securely bound to a tree, and after we secured a zip tie around his neck and the tree trunk, he learned not to struggle too hard as soon as we did that, and then all of us escorted the prisoners to the truck, and after they were secured, all but two of my men were going to take the prisoners into town and hand them over to the local law, not that we had much faith in them. Then my two men and I returned to where Ericki was, we had learned that he spoke perfect English, so as soon as he tried to play coy I slapped him across the face, and asked again how he contacted Ona. Eventually he told us about a hidden radio not far off in the scrub, and the starting's of a plan was forming in my head, as I sent my men off to find the radio, making sure that Ericki knew what would happen to him if he lied to them.

The two boys came back with the radio that looked as if it had started its service during World War Two. Apparently there was no set time for calling, so I intended to take Ericki back with us, while I let the plan in my head form solidly. This could be our way of facing off with Ona, and sorting things out, or by taking the shortcut, and kill him while we had the chance, in my mind I knew that this would solve a lot of turmoil in the future for a lot of people.

About an hour later DJ and the rest of the men returned, and DJ gave me a brief rundown on what had happened with the local constabulary, and sure enough it was as we expected, but DJ had got angry and started throwing his weight around, and had finished up by telling them that if these rascals got out of jail before the end the week, he was going to come back here and shoot every officer in the station for treason himself, which had put the fear of god in them, the men and DJ left with assurances that they would not go before a magistrate for two weeks, and until then would remain in the cells.

I smiled and nodded as I listen to the story, and by the time it was finished I was laughing outright. Then I filled them in on the plan that had formed itself in my head, which would hopefully put us face to face with Francis Ona. The plan involved having Ericki calling Ona on the radio first thing, about a soldier wishing to meet him, and if that would be possible, but the meeting was to take place on neutral ground, and Ericki had suggested the ruins of a mission school in the village of Korpei, not all that far from Ona's basecamp, but far enough away to be determined neutral. Bruce could fly us in either an hour or two before the meeting so we could sort out our defensive zone, should it be needed. During the meeting I'd either put Ona on notice, or if I have to, I'll kill him, then we bug out as fast as we can go, if I just put him on notice, then we'll let him leave the area first before we pull out.

The plan worked, at zero six hundred the next morning Ericki made the radio call, DJ and I were right beside listening in, but eventually Ona's curiosity got the better of him and he decided to agree to a meeting, after some persuasion he agreed to meeting at the neutral site at thirteen hundred that afternoon, Ericki told him that I'd only be accompanied by one person beside himself, but that I would be armed, and he laughed, said he'd only bring one other, and also they'd be armed of course, so with the meeting set, I then had to see Bruce to see how long a flight it was to the mission ruin. After some calculating I announced that we'd arrive onsite at midday, so everyone was to get some sleep before departure which would be a ten.

Before leaving the resort, I had a talk with the managing couple, and told them what I was about to do, and that I couldn't do too much to stop the attack on them, the first time round, but I was going to make sure it didn't happen again or to any other Australian operation, and then told them about having caught all the gang responsible, and that if they wished to proceed with charges, they were all in the local lockup, and the local cops would love a charge to pin on them.

Fifteen minutes later we were all aboard the chopper headed for the meeting place, Ericki still bound, was sat on the floor where he could be kept under watch during the flight. When we arrived Bruce dropped us, and then went to a clearing we spotted on the way in, and he would wait there until I called him on the radio to pick us up. Our offense and defense positioning was quickly talked over and arranged, with Steve one of the team that was sniper qualified, electing to climb into one of the trees ten yards away that would give him both all-round vision of the area, and offer him concealment. Then DJ and I grabbed Ericki, and took him into the remains of the building with us and tied his feet and gagged him, and then we waited.

After waiting awhile, Harry's voice came through my earpiece as clear as bell from the office, "Tiger, there's a group of thirty approaching your position, it looks like Ona's reneged on the deal!" Then Steve's voice came through saying, "Boss, they were right, but he's left the main group outside of the area and he and another are approaching on foot toward you." I replied to both the office and Steve, as I ordered "Ok everyone calm down, my team stay concealed and in place, Harry keep an eye on things, and let me know if any of his men move towards us, you too Steve." I got affirmation from both as DJ moved to the door and leaned against it looking out, then he glanced back and nodded.

Then I heard a deep voice from outside asking DJ if he was the man he was meeting, and I smiled and watched as DJ shook his head in a sign of No, and then cock his head toward us as if to say inside, as he moved from the door, and backed inside. Then he was followed in by a man nearly six foot two, ugly as all sin, and just a lighter shade of midnight black in colour, and built like a brick shithouse, Christ he was huge! He looked closer to an ape than a man, with close cropped jet black hair, but his eyes were blue, which I found surprising, and assumed that defect had something to do with his father.

As he and his escort moved into the room, they're eyes fell on

Ericki, who was sitting and looking toward them with his eyes bugged out and trying to say something while his hands were secured behind his back and feet tied. Ona looked around spotted a chair, and went over to it and brought it back to sit in front of me, and said "I take it that you are Colonel Davis, the man I have come to meet, as you can see I and my companion are alone, but as you we are armed, shall we commence our discussion?" His use of proper English was a complete surprise to me, usually a national would occasionally use pidgin, but he didn't, and I had to assume it was because of his time in Australia.

I looked him straight in the eye, so there could be no misunderstandings, and said "Francis, I hope you don't mind me calling you that, my name is Tiger, and yes I'm the man you came to see, as you're already aware I'm from Australia, but let me tell you this, and I can speak for the Australian government, now we really don't give a shit what you do on this island or about your beef with the PNG government, and let's face it, your intentions from the start about what Bougainville Copper and Panguna were doing was right, however starting a rebellion? That's not going to change things, and you know it."

Pausing to let my words sink in, I continued "Now to give this poor shmuck (indicating Ericki), orders to attack an Australian business, well quite frankly that was stupid, surely you knew we'd take action? So here we are, now listen real close, if you attack Australian holdings, I personally am going to come after you, and I won't be satisfied until you are dead and you're so called rebellion put down forever, do you understand!"

As I faced him down, I was reminded of a scene I saw once back in Burundi, of a monkey facing down an ape, that could have swatted the monkey easily, but instead turned and walked away.

CHAPTER 29

He looked at me with a level gaze, and said "Alright I can understand your position Colonel, but where do we go from here?" I told him that as long as he didn't touch any Australian holdings or civilians, I was quite happy, however should he take that extra step, he knew what would happen. He then looked at Ericki, moved to him and drew his gun, which was old British army .38 calibre, and shot him in the head, looked at the body for a second and then went and sat back down, he looked at me, and said "I gave no such orders, for that to happen, however if some of my people take that into their own hands, where do we stand?"

I looked him straight in the eye, dropped my voice to its normal deathly chill, and replied "Then I'm coming back and I'll be after you, and I won't rest until you're dead, do I make myself clear?" He seemed to sit back as if physically pushed, and seemed to think over what I had said, before replying "You have made yourself perfectly clear Colonel, but what if I just kill you now, I wouldn't have to bother about that?"

Smilingly, I answered his question, by saying "Surely you're not that stupid? I have a force of men that are poised ready to strike at the little army you brought with you, but beside that, you'll be dead before you even complete the command to take me out, if you think I'm bluffing, try me, plus everything that has passed between us has been recorded, so it's your move Francis, what do you want to do?"

He looked as if he was a caged lion, and looking around replied "You seem to have me at a disadvantage due to your technology, for the time being I will accept your terms, no man associated with me will harm any Australian, or Australian ventures on this Island, apart from my original grievances with Rio Tinto, the group behind Bougainville Copper, is that fair enough?" I smiled and nodded my head, as I relied "That's sounds fair enough to me, but be warned, you break your word and all hell will break loose upon you, understood?"

Looking around, he sighed and stated "Agreed," as he strode forward to shake my hand to seal the deal we'd made. We shook and I told him to take his rubbish with him, indicating the body of Ericki, so he and his escort, that was never introduced, took an arm each and dragged the body from the building, DJ and I watched them go from the doorway. Harry's voice came into my ear saying, "I'll keep sight of them now they're out of the building."

Thirty minutes later, I was given an all clear by Harry, who'd been watching the area through satellite observation, and then I withdrew my forces, and radioed Bruce to collect us, and we flew to Panguna mine ten minutes flying time away, and there we refuelled the helicopter and then flew directly back to Rabaul from there. During the flight back, DJ asked "Tiger, while we were on Bouganville, you kept referring to your old honorary rank, and may I ask why?"

I smiled as I answered his question, "Sure DJ, it was for two reasons, and I think Ona got them both, one was I wanted him to think we were Australian soldiers, which clearly showed to him that if Australia wanted we would just take over the Island and attack his little army, and to hell with asking permission from the PNG Government. Secondly I wanted him to think that we thought he was important enough to warrant a high ranking officer to perform the negotiating, not a lowly sergeant, if he'd have known that it would have infuriated him beyond measure to think that we didn't consider him important enough, it has a lot to do with the way these guys think I suppose, but it can be a very fine line to tread, also it has a lot to do with the character of the person you're going up against, you have read the type of man, and you either treat him like a piece of shit, or someone you think important. In Ona's case treating him as important stroked his ego, and made him more compliant to negotiation, he was after all raised in Australia."

DJ replied with "You're a real devious bastard, you know that boss." I smiled as I remembered how many times I'd been called that, and by whom over the years. The conversation that DJ and I had started continued most of the flight back to Rabaul and only ended when we came within sight of the airfield just prior to landing. After saying our goodbyes to Bruce, we spent the night in Rabaul, and then returned home to Brisbane the next day, and we hadn't fired a shot in the time we were away, which I thought was pretty spectacular, as we arrived back in Brisbane only four days later. A debriefing was scheduled for ten the following morning for all of us that took place on the mission, in the briefing room at the office, and after saying goodbye to everyone I headed into Newfarm to see if Karl had finished the engagement ring for me.

Not only had he finished the engagement ring, but he had also done the wedding ring that would match it, and after seeing the end products, I was over the moon, and paid him what I owed him for the job, he placed both rings in separate presentation boxes for me, and I left his shop with a smile on my face a yard wide, knowing Dawn was going to love it.

I had decided however not to show her the wedding ring that accompanied the engagement ring, that would be surprise for the wedding. Knowing that she was still on days was great, because that would mean she'd be home that afternoon, so I booked a table at our favourite restaurant in Arana Hills for that night at seven, and I would give her the ring during the meal.

All that went well, and then on the weekend we made the trip to her parents, to announce the engagement, and plans were put into place to marry ASAP, so between Dawn, her mother, and her already married sister they had a few things to organize. Considering that they only had a couple of weeks to organise it, they did damned well, and on Saturday the fifteenth of November eighty-six we were married, she for the first time, and me for the third. Standing at the alter in front of the marriage celebrant, I had to wonder if this one would at least last, and I had hopes that it would. Our honeymoon consisted of a ten-day trip to Vanuatu, that was a diving exploratory freebie organised for dive shops owners to send business to Vanuatu dive operators, when Rob knew that I was getting married to Dawn, a bit hard to miss seeing he was best man, he decided to send us as our wedding present. This suited us both down to the ground, because it gave us both the chance to dive the President Coolidge wreck, truly one of the best wreck dives of post-World War Two, surpassed only by diving the Japanese wrecks in Truk Lagoon, where the yanks surprised the Japanese Pacific Fleet, and innumerable transport ships, in a tit for tat style raid four years after the Pearl Harbour attack.

By the time we returned from our honeymoon, which was something spectacular, mainly because of the diving we got to do and our time together. (All up that year we spent more time with each other twenty four seven, than we did in all the time we were married which unfortunately ended in March of ninety-three, however it was still the longest time that I'd been married in the course of those three marriages). Anyway when we got back, it was almost near the time that most intelligence agencies entered the dead zone, with little or no activity, so I concentrated on my business life, and returned to work at the dive shop, which was still in the process of having the complex and teaching pool built.

Dawn was working varied shifts, and I was taking trips away to the bunker group with students and as a guide for certified divers, but even with that, because I'd taken the trip the year before, it was my time to spend Christmas and New Year with family, which Dawn and I appreciated immensely.

Things progressed at a busy pace during the main tourist season that lasted until the end of January, and then during February because the pilot strike was still going on as a rotational thing, business started to dry up, because we weren't able to cater for tourists from the southern states, that weren't arriving because of the strike. So what we relied on was the repeat business from past students, that either took dive trips with us for pleasure, or taking part in other dive courses available to them. This also meant that I was able to get away to do my mainstay agency work, which was handy because there were a few operations that were getting close to the final stages, and we were also handed a few more alerts from the AFP, that required looking after.

One of those came from Jack McCord in March, as he called and asked me to visit his office, and as I was shown into his office a few minutes later, he rose from his desk, and put out his hand, as he said while we shook "Nice of you to come up, I know you don't like to beat around the bush, so if you take a seat I'll explain why I asked you to come up Tiger." As I sat he passed me a file, and said "As you go through that I'll explain, but first off let me tell you this, it originally started as a request for cooperation from our counterparts across the ditch in New Zealand." Before I opened the file, he went on to explain that the Kiwi's had been keeping tabs on a large eighty-five foot sailing yacht that was owned by an Australian named Matt Harris, who they suspected was running drugs or guns, because he always seemed to have plenty of money, and no way to show how he had earned the money he always had, but no matter how many times he was boarded by Customs, they couldn't find anything.

When he placed an advertisement in the paper looking for crew for an extended voyage, they feared he was going fly the coop, so to speak, so they quickly had one of their best female undercover officers apply for the job as a cook. The boat the Westwind had set sail from Auckland three weeks ago, and hadn't been seen or heard from since, the AFP had drawn a blank in finding it, and he wondered if we could have a go at finding it.

I opened the file, and the first thing I saw was a photo of the Westwind, and it looked marvellous, nice sleek lines, everything in the right position to get the best out of the wind and keep crew members dry as much as possible on a yacht, and I found myself hungering to have control of such a prize. Then came photos of Matt Harris, and also the undercover officer Mia Mahineck, physical descriptions of both, and reports from the New Zealand police, and details of the surveillance they had carried out, and what he was suspected of.

After going through the file folder, in asked Jack if I could have a copy of the file, and he told me I was holding it, so with a smile I told him to leave it with me, and I'd see what I could do. Back in my office, I had Janice ring Harry, and have him come down and see me, and then I started looking at the descriptions of both Matt Harris and Mia Mahineck, for some reason she looked familiar to me, and I requested Janice to get me a complete dossier on her.

Matt Harris was six foot, with curly blonde hair and blue eyed, in his photo it looked as if he was trying to grow a beard, his background was as a NSW vice cop that had been dismissed, due to suspected tampering with evidence, and concealing sizable drug raid hauls, before he was due to be arrested by NSW internal affairs department, he'd quit the force and left NSW on the Westwind, which itself had been seized under the proceeds of crime act in which Harris had been the prime investigator, but charges had been dropped against the perpetrator due to lack of evidence, it was suspected that Harris had hid the incriminating evidence on the Westwind, before leaving the country.

Janice came into the office followed by Harry, and as she dropped a folder on my desk, asked if we wanted coffee, both of us declined, and as she left she closed the door. I looked at Harry, and asked "Let's get straight down to it, is it possible to track a boat after its left port?" Harry's answer actually did astound me, as he said "My word it is as long as it uses GPS for positioning, and the auto helm, we could find it within a radius of four hundred metres, as long as we know which frequency it's using for the GPS."

Looking at him in wonder as if he was the second coming of Jesus, I passed across the file concerning the Westwind, saying "Harry, you take the cake, I need this boat found ASAP, the boat was here in Australia before taking off to New Zealand, find that frequency, and find me that boat please." He smiled and told me that he'd probably have the frequency before the end of the day, and then he'd pass it onto John in communications to find it for me, with a bit of luck, by start of work in the morning, I'd probably have an answer.

For the rest of the day I was tenterhooks, but by the time I'd finished lunch, I had somewhat cooled down, and went back to attending to business as usual, so I looked over the file that Janice had procured for me in regard to Mia Mahineck's background, as I was sifting through her file it became apparent why so was so familiar to me, her cousin Willie was also a New Zealand cop.

I had worked with him before on other matters that resulted in the bringing down of a major drug running family based on the North Island. Even though it had lasted only a week for me, the investigation behind it that Willie had conducted, had taken over six months, and included the use of his cousin Mia as a resource. Just as I was about to leave the office that afternoon, I received a call from Harry, who told me that he'd been able to find out the GPS frequency of the Westwind, and had passed it along to John in communications.

So I put through a call to John, and asked him to make the search for the Westwind a priority, and he told me that he'd pass it onto the night staff that were due to take over the communications watch at four PM, I thanked him, and told him I'd be in my office by nine the next morning. That night Dawn was on an afternoon shift, which meant that she'd left before I got home, and wouldn't be home until after midnight, probably closer to one. Even though I had a couple of drinks during our usual cocktail hour, I still couldn't settle down, and so I ended up going down to the local league's club for a few more drinks and dinner. By the time Dawn made it home, even though I'd gone to bed, I still hadn't settled down, so when she got home and into bed, we ended up making love for an hour or so before I was able to switch off and go to sleep.

The following morning, after making coffee for both of us,

and putting hers in the bedroom, I knew that if a kissed her good morning she'd end up drinking the coffee before drifting off back to sleep after I left. I had breakfast in the cafeteria in the office during these times, it was a little different when we were both on days, and we'd have breaky together. After breakfast, I went to my office and Janice and I would go through our usual routine, the only difference that morning was that, the overnight communications staff had left a message to contact communications as soon as I was in for the day. I smiled, and then frowned, as the phone I was about to pick up rang, but I relaxed as soon as I heard John's voice saying, "I think I better come down and see you," to which I answered, that I'd be waiting.

Five minutes later John was ushered into my office by Janice, who also brought in coffee and a plate of biscuits. John told me that the Westwind had been found in the vicinity of the Galapagos Islands, and was apparently making its way north, with the possibility of heading toward the Panama Canal, after telling him that I wanted to know where it was at all times until further notice, and why. He suggested that I use the contacts I had with the yanks, to make contact with the Kiwi undercover officer aboard should the yacht make port in the region.

When he left my office, I thought it over for a while, and then looked at the clocks on the wall to check the time in LA, and then had Janice make a call to Alex Stein of the DEA. After half an hour on the phone with Alex, he assured me that should the yacht make port anywhere within his region, he'd try and have his agents contact the Kiwi undercover cop, and find out what the story was. He told me that this may end up being a unilateral operation across legal jurisdictions, and should that happen, and then I could be assured of his cooperation, and help if required. He told me that he'd keep my informed on the situation, as it became available.

There really wasn't much more that I could do except wait, and see what happened, and wonder. I knew that I should let Jack McCord know that we'd located the Westwind, and

354

tell him that we were keeping an eye on things, and would continue to track the yacht and the personnel on board, so I rang him instead of going up to his office. That afternoon Harry asked me to join him and John in the TAC room, but only told me it was a surprised when I asked why, curiosity got the better of me, so I followed him to the TAC room, as we entered, I saw straight away that the main screen that usually faced me while I was sitting down was on and showed a map of the South America from the Pacific side covering an area from mid Chile up to Mexico showing latitude and longitudinal lines with each map grid in six inch squares, also there was red dot on the map with dotted tracking lines that came from the Galapagos Islands. The next screen showed the yacht Westwind from a tight zoom coming from one of our satellite feeds.

I smiled as I turned to Harry and John to find them smiling also, as they explained in turn, Harry going first, saying "It was really quite simple to manage once we had the GPS tracking frequency, I asked John how we could see it, and this is what he came up with." John then took over telling us that he had put in a dedicated feed line to the computer that fed the GPS frequency, and then it was a simple case of bringing up a semitransparent global map and enlarging it to cover the region that the boat was in, the only downside being that even though the computer position would be available twenty-four seven, the satellite feed would not be, as a matter of fact we'll lose it in five minutes, as he looked at his watch. I stared at the satellite picture of the yacht cruising along, and was quite envious, it looked graceful as it moved along with the wind filling the sails, and looking at the boats wash I did a quick estimate that it was travelling at close to fifteen knots which was good going in that area.

The winds can prove to be very fickle around the Equator sometimes it was hard to get a breeze, the Westwind was sailing very close to the Equator heading towards the country of Ecuador by the looks of it. *For readers not used to marine terminology, you will find the meaning of GPS, and boat speed in knots on the glossary of terms page.*

As I watched, the screen with the satellite feed went blank, which meant that unless the satellite was retasked to keep watch on that area, we'd lost it until it was due to come around the Earth to that area again. However, as John had said we would have the computer tracking twenty-four seven, so I could come in here and see where it was, I turned to John and told him not to turn this off until further notice, and then asked about what happened if it moved out of the mapping area, and he told us that the map would shift with the boats position, so would always know which part of the world it was in, fan damned tastic I told him laughing.

Back in my office I was still smiling, and thinking, *that it was great to have such loyal co-workers, we worked well as a team, and individually but we always tried to keep each other happy in one way or another, plus it also helped us as a group when we had to make the hard decisions, now with what they'd both done without being asked to bring it about, it would help us all make the right decision if we had to make a move on this one operationally. I wonder if I should invite McCord down to see where his target was.*

Leaning forward I picked up the phone, and dialled Jack, and when he came on the line I asked if he would like to see where the Westwind was, and he told me no, that he'd leave it with me until we knew something concrete about what was going on, and I told him I'd try.

When I walked into the TAC room four days later, it was longer hugging the coast but making a beeline to Panama, quickly glancing at the clocks, if I hurried I'd be able to get hold of Alex before he left his office, so I rushed to my office and quickly told Janice to get Alex Stein for me quick smart, as I went through into my office. I had sat behind my desk as the phone buzzed, and Janice said she had Alex for me so I told her to patch him through. I gave Alex the news about the Westwind, and told him that at her current rate of speed, she would dock in Panama at close to zero nine hundred their time, and asked that one of his agents try to contact Mia and also slip her, a Sat phone with my number programmed in, so she could call me direct.

He laughed, and said "Tiger you don't know how lucky you are, my best agent is in Panama right now sorting a few things out, so I'll get onto John after our call is finished, he still has that Sat phone you slipped him Columbia, so who knows it may eventually make its way back to you one way or another, you take it easy brother, I'll be in touch." Well! That made things a lot easier John Moseley was in Panama, great that meant I could definitely rest easy, because John would go through hell and high water to accomplish something for me. My mind drifted back to our times together since our first meeting those many years ago in Perth, we really didn't get off to a fine start, but our respect for each other grew to the point where we had saved each other's lives a number of times.

It had become my practise to go into the Tac room to check on the Westwind prior to going and having breakfast in the cafeteria, but because to the turn of events my events that morning changed, so after the call to Alex, I let Janice know that I would be in having breaky before I came back, and we went into our usual routine. While I was having a relaxed breakfast, I was also doing some mental calculations in regard the time difference between us on kilo time and the west coast time zone which was on uniform time, and the Romeo time zone where the action would happen. This meant that everything would happen thirty hours behind our time, due to the international dateline, which meant that if the Westwind docked in Panama at zero nine hundred I wouldn't know until fifteen hundred the day after. In other words, I wasn't to expect anything until tomorrow afternoon kilo time, *Confusing, isn't it? This is one of the crosses I had to bear.*

After Janice and I had finished our usual morning routine, she reminded me that I had my usual weekly department head meeting that was due to start in fifteen minutes in the TAC room. *Thank god for secretaries, there're worth every penny they get paid.* So after we finished I made my way to the TAC room.

During our usual Monday meeting, John, Harry and myself, sorted out what operation was going to take priority over any other, one of the ones that was broached during that particular meeting, was a request from Customs about a query they had in regard to the smuggling of gold into the country of late, and they had supplied us with the before and after jumps in statistics, showing an eighty five percent jump, within the last three years, none of us was able to shed any light on this, so unfortunately with hind sight we tended to sort of ignore it, and place it on the back burner, oh stupid that decision was, as time would tell.

So placing the Customs query on the back burner, to be addressed at another time we continued with our meeting. We had two undercover operations that were about to complete, a ship coming from the Philippines, that was carrying two containers of weapons, that was due to dock in Townsville, so we decided to send the necessary information to Customs, they were to arrest our agent along with other crew members, and then quietly he would be set free to return, to us.

The second involved some drug running from Bali to Australia aboard a yacht that was due into Half Moon Bay Marina in Cairns the day after tomorrow, the subject yacht suspected of carrying two kilos of Heroin, and ten kilos of Marijuana, our agent was aboard and could help with the search for the contraband, again we'd passed on the information to the local Customs office, and our agent, after producing sufficient ID was free and able to return to us.

Then it was my turn to fill them in on what was happening with the Westwind, so in told them all that had transpired up until now, and it was decided that I would keep them appraised as to what was happening, I myself thought that we were only trying to find out what was transpiring, and possibly wouldn't require our involvement much further, how wrong I was!

CHAPTER 30

My satellite phone started to ring at four o'clock in the afternoon our time, just as I was ready to leave the office, so I sat down again and tentatively answered, with "Hello?" the next voice I heard, enquired "Am I speaking to Tiger Davis?" I smiled, and then replied "Yes it is, I take it that I'm talking at long last to Willie's cousin Mia?" I had worded my answer so that Mia knew that I was proving my bonafides by remarking about her cousin Willie, and that I could be trusted.

She replied with an offhand remark that had two purposes, one to find out if really knew her cousin, and two to find out what I wanted. So she asked, "So how come you know that fat over-weight pakeha Maori." I immediately knew what she was up to, she wanted to know if I really knew her cousin, because the term pakeha Maori is given to whites that have inter married and produced half breed offspring, so I answered "Am I speaking to the right Mia Mahineck, she of all people should know that her cousin is pure bred, where she on the other hand has white in her family from her grandfather's side, so yes Mia I do know your family quite well, now what the hell is going on? I've been asked by your bosses to find you, and I'm with ASIS."

"Oh thank god," she replied "I was hoping that someone had noticed our disappearance, it happened overnight, and had no way of letting any of my colleagues know what was happening. To put you into the picture Tiger, we've long held suspicions about Harris, but have never been able to prove anything solid, I'm undercover on this trip as the ship's cook, and as far as I have been able to find out the boat hasn't any drugs on board yet, however Harris disappeared a couple of hours ago, saying he was going into Columbia and would return in a few days, now apparently our next port of call is going to be Davao on the Island of Mindanao in the Philippines, and then Benhoa harbour on Bali in Indonesia. After that we could be coming into Australia, what do you need me to do?"

Thinking quickly, I asked if she'd been given a charger for the phone, and I was really amused by her reply, hesitatingly saying "Yes, that bloody great hunk you sent grabbed me off the street, handed the phone and charger saying to ring the programmed number, and speak only to you, Christ he scared the living daylights out of me, I thought I was about to be raped and killed." I laughed, and told her to hide the phone, and only to use it in an emergency.

She was to try and call me from each port of call, but if she found out if any sort of contraband had been loaded onto the boat, it would be great if she was able to give me a heads up, then I told her that my phone would be on twenty-four seven from then to when we finally met, hopefully after the boat had been boarded and seized by Customs in Australia, if not, I'd try to find a way to get her off the yacht somehow, and to hang in there, and not get caught. We both laughed as she told me that getting caught was the furthest thing on her mind.

On the drive home, I decided that during the next day, I needed to know as much about Mia as I could find out, because this could turn into a very lengthy exercise. After I calculated the amount of time required to get from place to place on the itinerary she had supplied to me on the phone, this was quite likely to last six to nine months easily.

Next morning, I rang Willie Mahineck in New Zealand, and found out that it was him that had alerted the AFP to the boat, so I filled him in on what had been taking place since then, he was grateful that it was now under my control, and he gave me all the information that I needed as background on Mia. I asked him to send me a photo of what she looked like for the assignment on the Westwind, and if they had added any criminal charges into her biography for the assignment, and he told me he'd send me a copy of the legend they'd made up for her, that way if I needed to get her off the boat. I could have her arrested, and detained until we could go and get her, but that was going to be, the all else fails plan. At this time, I had someone on board that could tell me when and where the boat was carrying contraband, which would come in handy considering we already had the Westwind under surveillance, and while it was sailing around outside of Australia's international limits, it couldn't be touched, but if it docked anywhere in the country we would have it, and we would have advance warning if that was going to happen, it was a win, win situation.

The information came through from Willie, and I had Janice make copies and start up a file on the Westwind, and to mark it as ongoing. While she was doing that, I started writing up a report at the whole thing, and she typed it up for me making the appropriate number of copies, and these joined the files in my weekly meeting tray. Then I rang John and had him come down and meet me in the TAC room, when I got there his eyes were automatically drawn to the screen, which showed the yacht in the same position it was earlier that day. I explained to him what was happening, and asked that he transfer the image from the main screen, back to one of the other computers, but still keep the tracking.

John nodded his head, and said that it was easy, and went ahead and made the adjustment while he was there, and showed me which computer would keep the tracking going, should we need to see it. While we were there, I brought up a subject that I wanted to put to a vote at the next meeting, I wanted to include DJ in on the Monday meetings as my 2IC, told him that we should think of expanding the department head meeting to include all our respective deputies, as well, in case any of us were absent from the meetings for any reason. He thought my idea was a sound one, and would give it some thought over the days before our usual meeting.

On the Friday of that week in the middle of the afternoon, Harry was in my office, and I was explaining the same idea to him, as my Sat phone started ringing. He cut off what he had been saying as I answered the call, saying "This is Tiger, can I help you?" I heard Mia's voice reply that it was her, and as I replied "Mia! Go right ahead." Harry started to get out of his seat to give me some privacy, but I waved him down again. As I listened to what Mia was telling me, which in essence was that Matt Harris had come back to the boat with a truckload of cocaine, and was in the process of loading it into smuggling compartments on the Westwind, they were going to leave in the morning, and were heading to Davao on Mindanao Island in the Philippines, and from there were going to Benoa on Bali in Indonesia, so I told her to try and call me before they left the Philippines, and I'd have someone try to contact her when they got into Bali.

Harry had been brought up to speed with the state of affairs regarding what was happening with the Westwind, so I filled him on the call from Mia, and told him I'd make sure the file was up to date regarding it. Then we returned to what we'd been talking about with the change I was going to propose, at Monday's meeting. Like John he thought it had merit, and was going to think it over, as it turned out he had in mind replacing his present deputy, with one of his own underlings who he thought was better suited to the job, and I told him it was up to us as the department head to promote, or demote as we saw fit, we weren't ruled by anyone else, even if the Sydney office thought that they could lord it over us, this was our office, therefore we made the rules here not anyone else.

He thanked me for my support, and told me it may come to a showdown between offices, so I informed him I would not tolerate being told how to run my department by an outside source, they could take a flying leap, as far as I was concerned, and I would back anyone who was like minded.

After our meeting, I packed up for the weekend, and as I left, I wished Janice a good weekend, and told her I'd see her on Monday. I took my time driving home because Dawn was still on nights, so I'd be going home to an empty house, and after arriving there, I had a few drinks, and instead of cooking, there was a new player on the pizza delivery scene now, called Dominos, so I decided to give them a try.

On Saturday afternoon, just after Dawn had left, I got a call from Rob at the dive shop to tell me there was going to be a directors meeting that night at seven, at the dive shop, and he asked if I was going to be there, so I told him I would, and that if he got in some pizzas, I'd pick them up on the way, so we arranged to meet at six, and he'd have our pizzas ordered at the pizza hut so I could pick them up. I filled up a hip flask with some of the liqueur that I liked, and popped the flask into the fridge while I had a shower and got changed, retrieved my hip flask just prior to leaving home, and made my way to the dive shop via the pizza hut, where I picked up three pizzas and two garlic breads.

While we had our pizzas, Rob and I discussed what had been going on around the place which wasn't much, but the building was coming along nicely, and I told me that what happened with the building project was one of the items on the agenda that night. After hearing that I had some misgivings, and thought to myself *"Uh oh! What the hell has been going on while I'd been taking time off."*

The only director absent from the meeting was our main Japanese investor Yoshihara Denzo, what was tabled was that due to the increasing building costs, it had been proposed to call a halt to the building until our finances were in a better position, and we had decide whether or not to let go some of the paid staff as well, so it was a fiery type of meeting with tempers getting frayed, but eventually the voting decided that we'd let go two of the dive masters on staff, or they were to be given the choice to work without pay but in lieu of wages, the trips they went on were paid for by the company, and also to halt the building program for the time being until we had more money coming in than outgoing.

After the meeting and everyone else had gone, Rob came back from his car with two bottles of Tequila and a bag of lemons, and the both of us sat on the porch outside of the office, and quietly got well and truly plastered, as he told me about his marriage was about to bite the dust over the fact he hadn't been drawing wages, and she was really peeved about having to support both of them and their daughters, and demanded he sell his shares in the business.

A little after midnight, the dive trip that was over pulled into the yard where Rob and I were passed out lying on the porch asleep, I awoke to see two empty bottles and chewed lemon quarters everywhere, and the salt container on its side. I shook Rob awake, and then went to meet David who'd taken the trip. In the cold air I sobered up pretty damned quick, so was in a reasonably and presentable shape, again after everyone had gone Rob and I tidied up the place, and were sober enough to drive home. I made it home prior to Dawn getting home, so I didn't have to make any excuses, and I was asleep when she got in. The only thing that happened was that when I woke up to make us breakfast, she asked what I'd got up to the previous night, because I smelt like a brewery when she got into bed, so I just passed it off has having too much to drink.

On Monday I headed into the office, and after checking the Westwind position, I went and had breakfast before Janice and I got into our usual routine prior to the Monday Meeting. When we were all seated in our places, each of us with a pile of files in front of us, John was first to start, as we referred to copies of his files, and then we started whittling them down until he was finished with the case files he was dealing with, the files we all dealt with were placed in a different pile. Harry followed, and it didn't take long to dispose of his business, luckily we were all down to five files, which were my concern, and we started to deal with each one in turn.

The last one dealt with the Westwind affair, and apart from the transcribed report I filled in all the bits and pieces, and then continued with the latest being the phone call from Mia, as John was making notes in his folder, he asked "Do you know how much she'd be talking about when she said a truckload?" I told them I wasn't sure of an exact amount, but that I could hazard a guess knowing the type of vehicles used in the country and the state of the roads and conditions, but Mia had said a whole truckload, now they usually use three to five ton trucks, because any bigger truck wouldn't be able to handle the jungle roads and mountains so, as far as I can guess the Westwind is now carrying between three and five tons of cocaine as ballast, and as of this morning they're position was.........so it looks as if she was right when she told me that Davao was the next port of call. Then after all our notes had been jotted down, we started to try to figure out why Davao, did he have a buyer there? Was he going to exchange the drugs? If so for what? If he was doing that, why go to Bali afterwards? I ended the speculation by saying "Well all we can do is wait until Mia contacts me again, hopefully she doesn't get found out."

I then looked at them one by one, and continued "Of course you know what happens if she is sprung, her body will be slung overboard, and they'll be able to deny all knowledge of her, or make up a story about her falling overboard, and not being able to find her, so let's just end the speculation about what they're up to, and wait for her next call, remember I told you this could run into a lengthy investigation, but it's not costing us anything, so it's a given, if it comes off."

We moved onto general business after that, to look after the housekeeping issues, and then it was time for new business, this was where is was going to introduce my idea, and so I said "Ok now you both know roughly what I'm about to propose, and this is a contentious issue, but I think we've grown too big in the last few years for just the three of us to handle everything, so we all have department deputies, so I'm going to propose that are we discuss this issue, that we allow our deputies to take part in these department head meetings, and they could also have their own say when it comes to a vote, however the deciding vote in case of an impasse, will always be mine as station chief, so let's have the discussion on this topic, Harry would you like to start?"

What followed was an invigorating discussion where pros and cons were thrown around, jokes, and arguments, they were both for the idea, but didn't want to come right out and say it, and so after a while things started to go round in circles, so I put an end to it by saying, "Ok we've had our discussions on the subject under proposal, now it's time to vote, show of hands, do our deputies now attend department head meetings, those for yes, (all three hands went up), good voted in the affirmative, right next!"

Eventually our meeting finished after being at it for three and a half hours, so we decided to go to lunch in the cafeteria before going back to our respective offices. Over lunch speculation returned to the Westwind, and I said that during the second world war there was an enormous amount of munitions that had been buried on Mindanao, but I thought that most of it would probably be useless now in this age, but you never know, and I left the sentence hanging.

After lunch, I stopped by DJ's office before continuing into mine and asked him to join me, once we'd sat down I congratulated him, and told him about what had been going on during our meeting, and told him that he was to take his place at my side during the next meeting. He pointed out the fact that I didn't have a deputy department head, so I laughed and then said "You're it."

As I continued, "Didn't you realise that when you agreed to be my 2IC, that you were also becoming this department's deputy headman, anyway just so you know it, that's exactly what happened, even though you didn't have an eight classification before, you have had since you moved into the 2IC spot, it's a wonder you didn't pick it up from your pay level going up, anyway have a drink, and we'll toast your promotion."

During the second week of May, I received another call from Mia, and she told me that they'd docked two days ago, but this had been her first chance to get away. Since arriving about a third of the cocaine had been off loaded, and replaced with weapons and explosives, some of the other crew members had been bragging about suppling arm to Timor rebels, but considering they were headed for Bali, she wasn't so sure, there were as yet no plans to dock anywhere in East Timor. I asked how she was coping, and she told me that she more or less kept her head down and did her job, but Harris had sounded her out about the criminal charges in her legend, which meant he had a source within the New Zealand police force, apparently he had been satisfied with her answers, and was now counted as one of the in the know crew members, that left three so called innocents amongst the rest of the crew. So far the plans for the boat after being in Bali were to head into an Australian port before heading home to New Zealand, after telling her to be careful, I told her we were tracking the boat and I would have someone try to contact her in Bali when they docked.

The next morning, I had Janice retrieve the recording of the conversation from the Sat phone, and write up a transcript of the call. While she was doing that, I placed a call to Willie, and informed him of the latest developments, and I told him about Harris having a source within his department, so he told me he'd track it down and nullify it if possible. I warned him that if didn't, there was a good chance of Harris finding out Mia was an under-cover officer, and if that happened, well I didn't have to spell it out for him, he promised to take care of it. I left it at that without the need to tell him if he didn't, that he'd have one less family member.

On the following Monday, at the Department heads meeting, I brought up the latest with the Westwind affair during our ongoing active operations time, Harry John, and I still had the case folders, but now the deputy heads were privy to the information they held, and it was decided that due to ongoing operations, that it was time for DJ, to check on the current position of the Westwind each day, instead of me doing it every morning and afternoon.

This would leave me free to attend to other matters that may arise, or demand my immediate attention. One such matter came up a couple of weeks later at the start of June, when I had to attend the annual heads of station conference, which meant I was away from my office for ten days. This was the first time I was meeting the heads of different state branch offices, because over the years I was either overseas, or taking part in an operation, whenever the conference came up, but this time Colin Gorman had insisted I be present.

We all assembled at the Sydney headquarters, at the given time of ten AM on Monday the 1st of June. Some of the branch heads I knew, were the ones that hadn't changed from when I did my first induction into ASIS, but there were three new faces for the states of: Tasmania, Western Australia, and the Northern Territory, these I were introduced to as we all got acquainted during the first hour of the conference.

Considering that I would have a lot of contact with Western Aust. And the Territory, I made time to get to know the respective heads, and I think that because we did a lot of frontline types of operations, we seemed to gravitate to each other, in a sort we versus them attitude, and we tended to share our knowledge with each other quite openly, but we were a little more guarded sharing with the other state heads. So I seemed only natural seeing we were staying in the same hotel to tend to talk to each other away from the conference, and over the course of the conference, I gave both of them the heads up on the Westwind affair, and they both gave their recommendations, and agreed to give me any assistance that I may require should I need it.

Colin Gorman spent most of his days with us at the conference, and one day we were to concentrate on the results of the previous year, and I was really pleased that in regard to arrests, operations run, drug and guns seized, it was my office that stood head and shoulders above the rest, and also in revenue raised in asset seizures. He also asked how many ongoing operations were being conducted, and when I announced that five were still active, I was grilled over the fact that I had four that were known of and being funded, so how come I stated I had five ongoing?

So then I had no choice but to disclose the Westwind operation, he asked why I hadn't asked for funding for the operation, and so I told him that it was costing us nothing, and had only cost me a couple of owed favours, and then I went on to disclose the possible outcome. When I stated what the boat was carrying at the present there were intakes of breath, and murmurs from all around the room, so he told me that we'd talk further about it later.

I nodded and assumed that I was going to be hauled over the coals for not disclosing the operation earlier, but when we broke for lunch he came over to me and asked me to join him for lunch, over which the Westwind operation was discussed, and I was congratulated over my handling of the affair, and told to run it as I saw fit, but to keep him informed.

One of the other queries Gorman had was if we'd been able to get anywhere with the inquiry from Customs, about the amount of gold that was finding its way into the country. After I told him that we'd gotten nowhere with it, and were coming up against a blank wall. He nodded and said "Well, I gave your crowd first crack at it, before sending it out as a general enquiry, so I guess I'll send it out to the other branch offices seeing you've been unable to turn anything up, it was worth the try, thanks for having a go."

The day before the conference was due to end; a message was passed to me by Charlie John Callaway's secretary, as I was making my way into the conference room. The message was from John, and passed by DJ informing me that the Westwind would probably dock in Bali within the next twenty-four hours. As we were about to start, I stood and faced Gorman as he was about to speak, and said "Sir I have had some news from my office that I wish to discuss with you and Agent Callaway as soon as we break for morning tea, it's to do with the topic of conversation at lunch the other day, but I must contact my office and leave the conference today I'm afraid."

He looked surprised, nodded, and said "Very well agent Davis, you, me, and agent Callaway will discuss this in his office during the morning break, and thank you for bringing it to our attention." What happened during the next two hours was a bit of a blur, because my mind was ticking over at ten to the dozen thinking of what I needed to get done before leaving the office and my hotel prior to taking a cab to Mascot airport. I also kept looking at the Sat phone, though I knew I wouldn't possibly get a call before morning.

Eventually the session came to an end, and it was time for morning tea, so Gorman, Callaway and I, left the conference room, but not before I had time to shake hands and say my hurried goodbyes to my counterparts in West Australia, and the Territory. After we were seated in Callaway's office, I told them of the message from my office, and my plan to fly straight to Bali and be there when the Westwind docked, so that it was me that Mia saw, and not just some other agent, whom she wouldn't know to trust or not.

They both agreed to the wisdom of what I was saying, and then Callaway told us about the three indigenous agents that we had on the Island, and so it was decided that he would contact them, to let them know I would arrive in Denpasar on a private flight, and they were to meet me and give me every assistance. So I told Callaway that I'd make sure that Ross let me know the flight number we'd use so he could pass it along to the agents on Bali.

Everything was ok for me to leave the conference, and I was asked to keep them both informed on what was happening, and then Gorman asked what I needed to do, I gave him the list of what I needed to do before leaving, and was told not to worry about the hotel bill that was fixed anyway. Then Callaway called Charlie in, and told her that she was to give me everything I needed, and that she was to be at my disposal until I left. After that he looked at his watch turned to Gorman, and said "Boss it's about time we headed back in," then he shook hands with me and wished me good luck, as did Gorman.

CHAPTER 31

The first thing I did was to get hold of Ross, and tell him to prepare the jet for a flight to Denpasar on Bali that afternoon, and he told me that it would be eight hours flying time, and that he'd ring me on the Sat phone as soon as he had a flight number. Next I rang my office, and after speaking to Janice, got her to patch me through to DJ, and I gave him a whole heap of instructions, after I said that I was going to fly straight to Bali to make contact with Mia personally, and I asked him if the Westwind had made any deviations on the way, into East Timor, and he told no that hadn't happened, which meant that the boat was still carrying all the contraband from the Philippines.

I told him that I was carrying my normal earpiece comm's, so when I got to Bali, I would try to make contact, and to ask Harry if they would need to retask a satellite to keep Bali under surveillance for the time I was there. Then I had him transfer me back to Janice, and I gave her the job to find me a decent hotel in Benhoa preferably near the harbour, and told her I'd hopefully be in radio communication as soon as I was on the ground in Bali, any time before that, she could get me on the planes radio frequency. As I was about to leave Callaway's office, the Sat phone rang, it was Ross to give me the flight number, and ask when we were going to leave. I told him that I was going to the hotel, grabbing my gear, and then a cab to head to the airport, and he told me the plane would be ready, fuelled and with food and drink on board by the time I got there. I left the flight number with Charlie to pass onto Callaway and our Indonesian agents, and then told her to ring Janice for the name of the hotel I'd be staying in.

My Sat phone rang as I got into the cab to take me to Mascot, it was Janice to tell me she'd booked me into the Novatel Benhoa, which was a five-minute walk to the major marina in Seclusion

Bay where the Westwind would probably dock, after thanking her I asked her to pass that onto Charlie in the Sydney office, and told her I'd see her when I got back.

We left Sydney at midday, and due to the time difference we would arrive in Bali at zero four hundred (local time) the next day. When I took a turn piloting the plane, I had Ross patch the radio into the office frequency, and called in, and then had the operator put John on and to get DJ up to the comm's floor as well. While I waited for DJ to arrive, John and I talked, and I filled him in as much of the conference as I could remember without looking at my notes.

DJ had checked the position of Westwind before coming up to the radio, he had estimated their position and worked out that due to the speed they were making, it should reach Bali around midday. He also made the suggestion that now that I was on my way to an operation that the office heads go onto tactical mode, which meant that the TAC room would be used, and all communication would take place there, I approved and authorized it, so by the time I landed in Bali the Tac room would be fully functioning. John also told me that the next day we'd have satellite line of sight from ten in the morning until six that evening, unless we asked for a retasking, it considered it for a moment, but decided that would give us ample opportunity to look the Westwind over without actually going near it.

If it required any more than that, well I would be there and the local agents would also be keeping it under observation, before I signed out I told them that I would turn on my earpiece transmitter when we landed, and that I'd be armed the whole time I was there. An hour later Jerry came back into the flight deck, so Ross took over the piloting while I went and had something to eat, and go and get some sleep.

I woke as I felt the change in altitude as Ross or Jerry started the decent into Denpasar, as I walked into the cockpit Jerry was on the radio with air traffic control requesting hangar accommodation for our plane as soon as it was refuelled. Obviously he got what he wanted without too much argument, because he rogered out after a couple of minutes, noticed me standing in the background, and said "Hey boss, they were giving us some stick about parking the plane, we'll offload at the main terminal, and after being refuelled their ground crew will take us to a hangar, also Janice has arranged for us to stay at the Plaza in Denpasar, so we'll be there if you need us."

With a smile, I said "Copy that, so you two are coming up in the world, getting to stay at a swanky hotel like that, don't let go to your heads!" Ross said over his shoulder, "Ahh got to keep up with the boss you know, after all he gives us such wonderful places to stay, so the office has keep up his work, otherwise we'd think of going on strike!" And we all laughed out loud, as I replied "Don't even think of that sort of shit."

Then he stated, "There it is." I looked through the cockpit window at the lighted runway lights, and told them that I'd go take a seat as I noticed the altimeter just under a thousand feet, knowing we'd be wheels down in five minutes if not before.

When we taxied up to the main terminal building, I heard stairs being put into place. I called out Ross that I was about to unlock the door, and then grabbed my go bag, as they came from the cockpit, so I told them to have fun, and I'd call when I was ready, and then walked down the stairs and went into the terminal to start the customs and immigration protocols. Any difficulty I was going to have about wearing a gun was circumvented by my showing my police credentials. After coming out of duty free I saw my name on a placard being held by a local dressed in a cab drivers uniform, so I made my way towards him, and noticed that he wasn't alone, another national was off to my left at a bookstore surreptitiously keeping an eye on me, and the same at the money exchange to the right and behind the driver.

I moved over to him, and as he introduced himself as one of the three agents, I told him we were being watched, and we'd best get going, as we moved off the other two locals started to move also, they kept pace with us but hung back a little as we neared the exit doors to the outside, I saw a ford taxi cab sitting there empty, and assumed that was our vehicle, so I hung back further as my driver moved toward the cab, and then as the first of the other two came out the door, I was in position to drop my bag, turn and strikeout!

Somehow I had given myself away, because as I was about strike my intended victim, took a step backward and raised his hands in front of himself to block the punch that I was about to launch, as he said "Tiger Davis Sir!" The cab driver had shuffled back, picked up my bag, and said "Come Mr Davis he is one of us, and also the man behind him, quick let's go so we don't draw any attention," we all got into the cab the one I nearly hit got in front with the driver, and the other came around the cab and got in beside me on the driver's side.

Once we were clear of the airport the cabbie pulled up, then turned and told me their names, he introduced himself as Kam, beside him was Fong, and Tepi, and was beside me in the back, they'd been told that I would give them their instructions when I got here, but they were to consider themselves at my disposal. So on the drive to my hotel at Benhoa, I filled them in on what was happening, and what I expected from them, the main thing being that Kam would stay close to me as my driver, and Fong and Tepi would keep the boat under surveillance when it docked later in the day, and to follow Harris should he leave the boat at all, and then I showed them the photos of Harris and also Mia, telling them that she was a New Zealand agent, and she was the one I had come to meet.

By the time we got to the hotel I was starting to become daylight, so I told them that I was going to get some sleep and hopefully be awake to watch the Westwind come into the harbour, as I got out of the cab, Kam took off with the other two agents, and I went and checked in. As I did the receptionist told me that the restaurant was open for breakfast from five AM, so arranging for my bag to go to my room, I went to arrange a relaxed and pleasant breakfast. After breakfast on the patio of my room I tried my communication with the office again, because it had not worked when I left the plane, after a couple times of trying I was able to receive a reply, when I enquired what was wrong, I was told that there was an hours lag between overhead satellites, therefore at that time of each day we were without communications. Being none too happy with that state of affairs, but there was nothing we could do about it, and so I hoped that we wouldn't need the comm's between four and five am, and let it go. After that I went had caught up with some sleep.

At midday I woke and after establishing contact with the office, I was informed that the Westwind was probably half an hour from docking, so I went out to the entrance, and saw Kam waiting for me, so I hoped into the cab, he headed toward the marina, and we made it with a bit to spare, because from a vantage point I was to observe the Westwind making its way to the harbour. From my vantage point, I saw a harbour side open bar near the marina confines, which could overlook the way in and out of the marina, so I had Kam take me there, and as he waited with the car, I strolled into the bar and perched on a stool where I could observe the marina entrance.

Roughly twenty minutes later I saw Matt Harris hop into a vacant taxi, and as the taxi moved off, I smiled as I saw Fong follow the cab on a moped. About half an hour after that, I was three women and four men walk into the bar, one of them was Mia! Thinking quickly how best to play this, I walked over to the group, and with my best British Upper Crust imitation, said "I say chaps and ladies, would there be any chance that you are from that wonderful looking schooner that I saw come into the harbour a short time ago." They looked rather blankly at me but a couple of them nodded and said they were, so I pushed it a bit further, saying "Well in that case let me buy you a round of drinks, who's to say you may be able to take me for a short cruise in her sometime." Then one of them said that they weren't doing charters the boat was privately owned, so I replied "Oh what a pity, I'll go get you that round of drinks anyway." Mia being on the end of the table volunteered to help me get them.

As I thanked her in my posh voice, "Oh how helpful, thank you my dear." She replied as she got up, saying "That's ok sir, I know what everyone is drinking anyway." As we moved away from the table toward the bar, I dropped to my normal voice without looking at her, and said "Is there some way you can get away from this lot Mia?" She almost tripped but recovered quickly, and asked "Who are you?" I smiled and replied, "Really? My voice doesn't change that much on the phone." With surprise in her voice hesitatingly asked "Tiger?" I nodded, and we took our time getting the drinks order, as she said "Harris has gone for the rest of the day, at least that's what he told us, I could tell them I'm going off to have a look around."

I told her to give herself half an hour or so after I left, but take note of the cab, I'll send him back here to give you a lift to my hotel where we can talk. When we arrived back at the table both carrying trays, I put mine down, and said in my posh voice again "There we go chaps and lasses, and thank you, kind miss for giving me a hand, enjoy your drinks everyone, but I must go right now, maybe we'll meet again, toodle pip!" I felt Mia's eyes on me as I left, and headed towards Kam and the cab, as soon as I was in the cab I told him to drop me, and then come back and wait for her.

Forty minutes later she walked into the foyer of the hotel, and I got out of the seat I was in waiting for her, and took her by the arm steering her to my room, and as we sat on the patio overlooking the pool with drinks, she filled me in on the goings on aboard the Westwind from the start of the journey after slipping out of New Zealand. After she finished her tale, and took a sip of her drink, I held up a finger for quiet, as I said into the air, "Ok did you get all that report," the earpiece told me they had heard everything and that it had been recorded, as I continued "When the tape is made have Janice transcribe a copy for me to send to New Zealand please, ok now we're going to move on with what is planned next, so Mia what's planned next?"

She told us that while he was here, Harris was going to meet someone who was going to purchase the weapons that had picked up in the Philippines, for a massive amount of Heroin, but the only drawback was that they had to deliver the weapons to East Timor without being sprung by the Indonesian Navy, who kept a very close eye on boats anywhere near East Timor. After that the plan was do some diving on the Great Barrier Reef, go into Cairns for a few days, and then slowly make their way down to Sydney, where according to Harris he had contacts who would buy most of the drugs on board.

As soon as she mentioned the drugs, I immediately had a couple of questions spring to mind. The first being, a deeper explanation of how much was loaded aboard at Panama, Mia said that the truck used was fully loaded and it took most of the night to put all the drugs into the smuggling cavities, the truck had been an oldish Dussenberg. So that meant that five tons of drugs had been placed aboard, if it had been a ford truck, it would have been only three tons, I knew this and explained to the office that it was intel I'd picked up while I was in Columbia, different trucks for different loads. The next question I asked was to do with the location of the smuggling cavities, and Mia told us that all the strengthening bulkheads were hollow, plus also there was a false cap on the keel, and false flooring as well as false ceilings, and that there was a false wall in the nose behind the anchor chain locker, at present the weapons were under the false flooring.

Then I told her what our plan of action was going to be, which was that we'd be keeping tabs on them, and when the Westwind was in Australian Territorial Waters that the boat was going to made to heave to, and it would be boarded by Customs, Navy, and Federal Police, and a search made of the boat, of course we'll find something which will allow us to arrest everyone on board, you included, just so your cover isn't blown, in Cairns you'll be separated from the rest, because a New Zealand police officer will be coming to extradite you. She smiled knowing that was all part of not losing a cover identity, as I asked what name she was using, which was Mia Short, and then asked her if she had any questions, she didn't, so while I talked further to the office, she sat back relaxing with her drink, I finished giving instructions to the office, by telling them I was going off air for a little while, and then removed my earpiece.

While we sat relaxing, I asked "Mia, the last time we spoke on the phone you sounded as if you wanted to get off the boat then, what was happening?" she told me that the engineer on board had been persistently been trying to get into her pants, until she sliced his arm with one of the kitchen knives, when he tried to kiss her in the galley, apparently that ended any further attempts to get her into bed, and as she was talking about it, she said he'd always been big noting himself by say things like we're sailing around with tons of gold, and stupid Matt wanted to do some drug running. So I asked her if she'd ever seen any gold to which she shook her head in the negative, and said "Nah it was all shit, I even asked him to show me some but he never did, just trying to make out he was a big man I guess, I didn't put much store in it when he couldn't show me."

I smiled and nodded, then asked "So you don't think there's anything in it?" She smiled and replied "No, if there had been he'd have shown it to me, just to prove himself, besides who's going to risk going to jail running drugs if they've got millions stashed away somewhere." I smiled and replied "Only an idiot." We both laughed and clinked glasses in a toast as we had another drink.

Eventually it was time for her to go, so I told her that the boat was under twenty four hour surveillance, and that I'd stay in Bali until they headed out again, and she told me that they were supposed to leave in two days, but she'd try and firm that up for me, and then asked if she could visit here again if she had the chance to get away, and I told her she was welcome anytime, I escorted her to the driveway where Kam was waiting, he turned to me and said "Thank you Tiger Davis, you are everything cousin Willie says about you, which is that you're a gentleman with hidden talents, thank you." I nodded and said goodbye to her as she got into the taxi.

After I'd had a sleep in and a relaxed breakfast before a workout in the gym followed by fifty laps of the long pool, it was close to midday when my Sat phone rang, it was Mia asking to meet me at the harbour side bar in an hour, so I told her I'd be there. Then went to see if Kam was in his usual place, which he was, so I went back to my bungalow room, after slipping on my shoulder holster, I changed shirts, and grabbed a light jacket, put my earpiece in and turned it on, and headed to Kam's Taxi. On the way to the harbour I said in my posh accent "Ok Gentlemen it's time to wake up and take note again." I heard DJ say "Oh god, not the bloody Brit accent again!" I laughed out loud and replied "One has to go with the flow dear chap." I laughed out loud again as I heard a strangled AARGH!

As Mia joined me at the bar, I said "Well hello dear girl!" She laughed and told me no one was behind her, and that she was in the midst of going to the on shore toilets, so had to be quick, and told me they were going to slip out on the evening tide that night, I nodded and told her to stay safe, it wouldn't be too long now before she was in safe hands again, we shook hands and she took off, while I headed to the taxi, and I told him where to take me.

While we drove along, I spoke to the office to make sure they heard everything, and told them that I was on my way to see Ross about flying out tonight, I asked Kam what time the high tide was that night and he said it was at five thirty, so I told the office that I'd probably leave about seven, and be on my way home.

When we go to the Plaza I went to reception and asked for Ross's room to be called, it was and he and Jerry joined me in the bar, and we all had a glass of the local beer that was almost entirely water, which was good as I told them last drinks guys, I want to be ready to leave at seven tonight, they acknowledged and told me they'd be ready.

Back at my hotel I had lunch before lazing in the pool, at three I went and had a shower, and started packing, I checked out at four thirty, and on the way to the harbor bar Kam told me that Fong and Tepi had their mopeds nearby, so I told him I was going to send home after the Westwind sailed, but that I'd need him to take me to the airport. When we got to the harbour bar I asked him where Fong and Tepi were watching from, and he pointed out both locations. I strolled over towards Fong's location, and told him what was happening before I left we shook hands and I thanked him for his help, then I made my way to Tepi, and repeated it all, as I moved away from Tepi I noticed some of the crewmen on board Westwind getting her ready to sail. Back at the bar, I ordered a scotch and sat back to watch both the marina and the water to see what the tide was doing.

As soon as I noticed the tide turn, I also saw the Westwind slowly pull away from the marina, Kam had given me a set of field glasses, and as she pulled away I watched her, and saw everyone on deck then start to disperse, as the mainsail started to rise up the mast, that was the signal to me that it was time to go, and as I walked to the cab, I said to the office "Ok she's away, keep an eye on her and I'll be there around three or four in the morning." After that I removed my earpiece and put it in my jacket pocket. I said my goodbyes to Kam at the airport and thanked him for the work, then after finishing with the outgoing immigration protocols, I boarded the jet and we left Denpasar at eighteen fifty-five. I arrived back in the office at zero four hundred, told the TAC room personnel that I was back and that I was going to get some sleep.

Two weeks later, I was aboard the Naval patrol boat Ambush, heading out to sea alongside the Customs Vessel Botany Bay. The day before I had flown to Cairns after we figured that the Westwind would be within Australian waters by midday the next day, after getting away from East Timor without being noticed by the Indonesian navy, so everything had been put into place and I was met by Navy personnel and taken to Cairns navy operations office, where I had a briefing with the commanders of the customs boat and patrol boat that were going to make the intercept together, and also the AFP team that was being headed by Jack McCord who had flown up with me.

We stayed on board the respective boats we would travel on that night, so we could get away early, we had left port an hour before, and once away from land would push up to full speed headed north easterly, by all calculations we would intercept the Westwind forty nautical miles north of Thursday Island. Because I was travelling on the patrol boat the radio communication to the office was easy, they could call us direct, and we could do the same, so I didn't need to wear my earpiece just yet, probably not until I left to board the Westwind.

After I had had breakfast, I was called to the bridge, and told that my office would like to speak to me, as I took a seat beside the commander he passed the radio mic to me and I called "Ambush to TAC room copy?" The answer came swiftly "TAC room to Ambush, Tiger I have picked up Lieutenant Mahineck, and he is now with us in the TAC room, also Janice will take care of him, while he's here, over." I smiled as I replied "Roger that DJ and hello Willie, I've made arrangements for my plane to pick you up and fly you to Cairns as soon as the intercept has taken place, and I'll see you in Cairns when we return, over." DJ 's voice came "Roger that Tac room out."

Due to a last minute change of course by the Westwind, the intercept took place ten nautical miles northwest of Thursday Island, and it was a joy to see how these two commanders that had worked together before played it. The Ambush went up to full speed and went past the Westwind but we were below their radar horizon and then we did a loop to come up on the Westwind from astern, while the Botany Bay moved to cut them off from the front, as the ambush closed to within line of sight the commander called over all frequencies "Westwind, Westwind, this is the navy patrol boat Ambush please heave to, we intend to board you, over." Not receiving any answer, the commander hailed again, by this time I was sure their proximity radar would have picked up the Botany Bay to their immediate front though not yet visible. This time we had a reply to the hail, "Ambush, Ambush, this is Westwind over," "Westwind this is Ambush please heave to, we intend to board you over." The reply came back "Ambush, Westwind, any particular reason, over." The commander turned to me smiling, and said "This is where he either makes a run for it or complies, Ambush to Westwind, we are part of a smuggling task force and we intend to search your vessel under Australian Maritime Law and in accordance with Australian Customs, you can now see Customs Vessel Botany Bay approaching you to search your ship, please have your manifest and passports available, over." As he had been speaking, the Botany Bay had indeed arrived.

That was not all; the gun turret of the Ambush had trained itself on the Westwind! Now Harris surely had to know the jig was up, he could try to bluff it out, or if he decides to cut and run, the Ambush's one hundred and five millimetre gun would turn the Westwind into toothpicks. After a minute or so Harris replied "Westwind to Ambush, more than happy to accede to your request commander, am heaving to." The cheeky shit's going to try to bluff it out, I thought.

There was activity aboard the Westwind as the fore and mainsails were reefed in and furled, and the boat slowed, as the Botany Bay pulled up alongside the port side of the yacht, and lines were thrown and buffers placed as the Westwind was tied fast to the Botany Bay, and we heard the commander of the Botany Bay request that Harris have all crew assembled on the fore deck with their passport handy. I was then put into a rigid inflatable boat (R.I.B) and transferred to the Botany Bay and joined the chief Customs Inspector and Jack McCord as we made our way aboard the Westwind.

While we went towards the bridge of the yacht, the customs officers and AFP went toward the crew and started examining the passports, as we approached Harris the inspector introduced us all, me as being with the AFP, as Harris introduced himself, and then the inspector asked Harris "Are you the Master of this vessel sir?"

Harris then made the biggest mistake of his life as he answered "Yes."

CHAPTER 32

The Customs Inspector then said "Sir this vessel was reported stolen from Sydney three years ago, and I am therefore impounding this vessel and placing you under arrest until such time as this matter can be cleared up in a court of law, and we also intend to search this boat for contraband, do you understand, and do you have any questions?" As Jack moved forward and placed Harris's hands behind his back and handcuffed him.

As we were talking, one of the AFP officers came up to me, and said "Sir there's a wanted fugitive from New Zealand aboard by the name of Mia Short, she claims she's the ship's cook and it isn't her that's wanted." I turned and was about to answer him, when McCord said to Harris, "If this is true you'll also be charged with harbouring a fugitive." Harris had gone white as I turned from him with a smile and said to the AFP Officer, "Show me to this alleged fugitive please."

While two officers stayed with the crew, the rest had moved toward the bridge, I approached Mia and said as I looked at her passport, "Mia Short, I'm arresting you on suspicion of being a wanted fugitive, you will be returned to your home country under an extradition warrant as soon as it can be arranged, officer please cuff the suspect," so as she was cuffed the others gathered around to comfort her. While I went to make an inspection of the boat.

I was about to go below decks as I heard the Customs inspector say to Harris, "Sir we have found a quantity of contraband aboard this vessel and therefore the vessel is subject to seizure, and will be piloted to the nearest port, you and your crew are under arrest, and will be conveyed to the patrol boat Ambush, and incarcerated until we reach port, where you will be transferred to the Cairns police station and watch house for interview, prior to facing a magistrate, do you understand?"

Below decks, I made my own inspection, and I eventually made my way to the engine room, after looking round at the engine and bilges, something didn't seem quite right, but for the life of me I couldn't put a finger on it. Back up on deck, the prisoners were being transferred to the Ambush, while a prize crew of navy personnel were being assembled to sail the Westwind into port. I got into the last RIB going back to the Ambush, as the navy crew started to get the Westwind ready to sail, because the Botany Bay was slower in speed than the Ambush, she would remain in contact with the Westwind on the way to Cairns.

However, the Ambush would make all possible speed back to Cairns where it would off load me and the prisoners, who had been sorted into two different cells, one for the males and the other for the females. As soon as we were on the way back to Cairns I radioed the office, saying "Ambush to TAC room, this is Tiger, copy?" DJ's voice came back, "TAC room to Ambush we copy Tiger, over," so I continued to give them the news that the intercept had gone well, and that DJ was to send Willie to Cairns on the jet, and Ross and Jerry were to remain in Cairns, to bring me home.

Two days later the Westwind made port at eleven am and was immediately taken to the Customs wharf, prior to its arrival however, Willie had arrived in Cairns, with Ross and Jerry, Janice had arranged accommodation for all of us at the usual hotel, the Continental and had booked an extra room for Mia. Willie had arrived at the Cairns police station the previous day, and between us we put on a reasonable performance, as Mia was turned over into his custody, after he had played the big bad kiwi cop around the other prisoners. As soon as we were back at the hotel, she hugged both of us with relief and pleasure, and then I invited them both to dinner with me.

Over drinks and dinner, it was arranged that they would both accompany me aboard the Westwind as soon as it docked prior to the search that would reveal a treasure trove. As I strolled along the deck of the Westwind with something that was nagging at my mind, then I spotted it! Near the bridge doorway there was a scraggly area where the deck looked as if there had been an overspray of grey paint. I asked Mia about it, and she told me that it had been there all the time she'd been on the yacht, so I moved over to one of the inspection officers, and had a word with him. He disappeared below decks, and then came back ten minutes later carrying a grey rectangular piece of metal, and said "I think your wrong sir, this is just a normal ballast block," and passed it to me.

I was a little disappointed, as I put it down on the deck rather dismayed. There was that nagging feeling again as I strolled along the deck, and then everything snapped together in my brain, as I asked the same officer if the ballast block was the usual shape for ballast, he looked at a little closer, and said "Well not really sir, usually they're thicker and not as long." I smiled, and asked him if he had a knife, and he passed me a pocket knife, and then watched as I picked up the bar, and started scraping the bar with the blade of the knife. As the paint started to be scrapped away it was replaced with a glowing shade of yellow, and I smiled as I returned the knife, and remarked "Looks like a gold bar to me."

He looked stunned, and said "Holy shit! There are heaps of them lying around the engine room and bilges, Christ. Hey boss you better come and have a look at this." The head inspector walked over, and bent down to have a look at the bar sitting on its edge resting in my palm, and looked as where I had been scrapping the edge, looked at me, and said "Well that's a cleverly disguised piece of ballast, certainly looks like gold to me, but we'll have to get it examined, and appraised to be sure. Harry, tell the others not to dismiss any of these ballast blocks, there could be more on this yacht than we realize, good catch sir." I asked him how long it would take get an estimate of the value of the bar, and he told me he'd take it to the lab for testing right away, and so as he lifted it, he made comment on the weight of it, saying "This should go close to twenty kilos, and depending on purity, should be worth easily a couple hundred grand at today's prices.

I smiled at Mia and Willie as I got up from the deck, Mia looked stunned, and muttered "So there was gold on board," I laughed and switching accent, said "But of course there was my dear, and it was your comment in Bali that led me to make this discovery, Willie dear chap, I'm afraid that I have inadvertently robbed your government of quite a few million in seizure profits, but too bad what?" Both Mia and Willie were laughing as I finished, and Willie tried to imitate my accent, as he said "Indubitably dear chap," but he couldn't quite pull it off, and we all roared with laughter. As we continued to stroll around the yacht, above and below decks, I was thinking that, *I wouldn't mind owning something like this, but it wouldn't any good for what I'd like, too big, I could probably get something smaller that could be sailed by one person if it had all the right sort of equipment.*

As we were about to leave the Westwind, the customs inspector came back carrying the bar that had now had all the paint removed, and he handed it to me, saying "There you go sir, a paperweight for your desk that weighs twenty kilos, and is pure twenty-four carat gold, worth two hundred and sixty-three thousand dollars." We all looked at it in awe, and as I went to hand it back he smiled, and said "Keep it as a souvenir sir, without you we wouldn't have found this out, and quite frankly with the amount of those on board, I don't think we're going to miss it, enjoy sir." So before he changed his mind I thanked him rather humbly, and as we left the dock area, I was walking smartly towards the car to get the bar out of sight. We stayed in Cairns for another week while the final tally was made of the drugs and gold, and assessment of the Westwind's Value.

During that week Jack and I accompanied Mia and Willie to do most of the tourist things that are available in Cairns, including a day out on the reef at Mikklemas cay, the one day I wasn't going with them, I arranged that they would board the Skyrail in the morning and go up to Kuranda, and come back aboard the train that afternoon, and I'd pick them up at five from the station.

That day Jack and I went to the customs office for a briefing on the final assessment made of the haul aboard the Westwind, and the charges to be laid. All up there had been five tons of Cocaine, two and a half tones of Heroin, two RPG Launchers, twenty RPGs, six high powered rifles, six automatic pistols, and one thousand gold bars. In monetary value the drugs were estimated at between seventy and ninety million dollars' worth that would be destroyed, at market price the gold was estimated to be worth twenty-six and a half million, and that would find its way into the government coffers, the weapons, except for the RPGs and launchers, were going to be auctioned along with Westwind herself and would fetch around another half a million dollars' worth. If we added up all the jail time that Matt Harris was looking at facing from various charges, even with a very good lawyer, he would never be released from jail alive.

Jack took great pleasure in telling Harris that, who definitely wasn't as cocky and self-assured as he was when he was first arrested. He was still a little smug though as he told us, "I can afford the best lawyers out that'll run rings around you lot, so do your worst!" Jack hadn't told him all the charges, and considering I have a vindictive streak as well, and I took great pleasure in telling him, that we'd found all the gold, and he'd be facing charges for the smuggling of it as well, and finished with saying "Now that all the gold has gone, and the Westwind sold under the proceeds of crime act, just how are you going to pay your fancy lawyers dickhead?" the sneer on his face was wiped off with what I told him, and all he could do was defeatedly tell us to leave, which both of us did, while we smiled at him.

The next day we all flew back to Brisbane aboard the jet, and Janice had arranged accommodation for Willie and Mia at the Tower Mill overnight before their return flight to New Zealand the following day, but for the rest of that day they were my guests at the office, and they got to meet all the agents that had taken part in the operation, and as far as I could tell, they had an enjoyable afternoon, and then it was time to say goodbye to both of them, as I wouldn't see them the next day, so we said our farewells before they left the office.

After that things settled down for the next couple of months, and apart from the usual daily routines and the weekly meetings, there wasn't a lot taking place, for some reason all security agencies around the world experienced a period of quiet. Taking advantage of this I would spend more of my time at the dive shop, the only day that I wasn't there was on Mondays, which was when the department heads meeting took place, as for the usual daily routine DJ and Janice managed it well, and there was, only a couple times that I was consulted by Sat phone.

Once I was sprung with the Sat phone while on a call by Robert, who thought I'd been able to get a small mobile phone and wondered where he could get one. So I had to explain to him that it wasn't a mobile phone as such, which really disappointed him, because he was hoping to get a smaller mobile phone. In nineteen eighty-seven there were only two types of mobile phones available, one made by Motorola, and the other by Nokia, but both were big and cumbersome. I had thought that my Sat phone was fairly large until I saw those, and I stopped a lot of my complaining about the size of it, plus with my Sat phone I could speak to anywhere in the world, but these so called mobile phones were only good for around major cities. So a compact mobile phone like my satellite phone wasn't available for another couple of years, and even then they only had limited capabilities. That is probably why I never bought one until after the year two thousand. So at that time, I told him to give it a couple of years and they'd start coming down in size eventually.

During that slow time, I worked at the dive shop most days, and because of this I thought that Dawn and I would become closer in our marriage, but for some reason this didn't happen, and I started to have some doubts creep into my thinking, even when she had the time off to be home, most of the time she wasn't, she was always doing other stuff, so I let it slide for a while. The only time she did join me was for a ten-day trip to North Queensland to dive the reefs off Townsville and the wreck of the Yongala, but even then it wasn't as if we were close like in the first year of being together.

Then in October of that year, we started to get security scares, so it was back to work at the office for me, and by the end of the month there were eight operations on going, six had to do with drug importation, and two were concerned with stolen weapons, not just normal weapons, but high powered, rifles and machine guns, and explosives, and these thefts were committed as acts of piracy, one in New Guinea, and the other in the Solomon Islands.

During one of our meetings, it was decided that DJ would head the investigation and bring about closing down those involved, because it was centered in the Bundaberg area, he would operate out of the office we had there, and the other deputy department heads would assist him. While I concentrated on the weapons thefts, because of the proximity of the attacks, I wondered if Francis Ona and the BRA had anything to do with it, but as it turned out he was innocent this time.

While DJ was away in Bundaberg the TAC room was operational, and one the things I had Harry do was to find out if any of our surveillance satellites had been over the area in question during either of the pirate attacks. Hopefully one would have been, and then all we'd have to do was download all the data for that time and area, and troll through all the footage, it was a bloody thankless task that would take hours if not days, but for the time being it was all we had. After asking him to do that, I started too reread the reports, and then I made a discovery that had my mind whirling, the attack in the Solomon's had taken place prior to the New Guinea attack, then I went to the TAC room and did a computer search for the area map, after marking both sites, I measured the distance between the two, and then had a print made, once I had it I noted the scale onto the printed map, and headed back to my office, asking Janice to bring me a geometry compass set, I sat down and started working, because I was sure I was on to something that had been overlooked!

After three hours' work, a heap of jotted down notes, and a lot of mathematics, I had the beginnings of an idea of what had happened, but I needed confirmation, and looking at the wall clocks, I saw that I wouldn't be able to get that sort of confirmation I needed until the next day. As I resigned myself to the wait, my phone buzzed. It was Harry asking me to join him and John in the TAC room.

When I got there, up on the main screen was a blurred image and on the screen beside it John had done his magic, and had the area up with map coordinates, and as when we followed the progress of the Westwind, he had enlarged these areas. Harry excitedly said, "I've been able to pull out the relevant details of not only the first attack, but also the second attack, and we've been looking at this the wrong way round! The Solomon's attack took place first as the satellite can prove!" I really didn't have the heart to tell him that I'd worked that out hours beforehand, and so kept quiet as he continued, "So with John's help we've been able to construct what really happened, and I thought you'd better see this, so with that in mind let's see what happened with both attacks."

Without saying anything, we all watched while standing in front of our chairs. After John made some adjustments, the main screen became clearer, as Harry explained we were watching the attack on the cargo vessel San Palo, this was the first attack in the Solomon Islands.

As we watched the ship was approached by six RIBs, each obviously heavily armed, we saw two with RPG's trained on the ship, as they pulled alongside a lowered boarding ladder. As they climbed the ladder I asked Harry to zoom in as much as possible, and we discovered al the pirates boarding, were of Asian, or Philippine extraction, the thoughts I was harboring were becoming stronger by the minute, as we watched the rest of the attack, and the passing across of the shipment from within a container to the RIBs and then their withdrawal. I looked again at the statement tendered by the ship's captain, in which he stated that the pirates knew the container number that held what they were after. As the RIBs cleared the area they proceeded in a north westerly direction, and met up with what appeared to be a navy patrol boat, or of similar design, and as we watched the RIBs were hoisted aboard the mother ship one by one, without any of the crew getting out of the RIBs until on deck of the mother ship.

The mother ship then proceeded on a north westerly course out of the area, I looked at both of them, and said "Ok let's adjourn to my office before we look at the next bit of footage, and I'll fill you in on what I may have discovered, and some speculations I have, however before we do, John can you take the bearing that ship is headed on as it moves out of the area please." In my office after orienteering my map correctly, I had John mark in the line of escape from the first attack. Then I marked in a line from the second attack, which intersected John's line, my line however had an end point, after showing them the map, I started telling them of my assumptions, and how I'd arrived at them. Harry looked at me, and said gruffly "You could have told me this earlier, it would have save a lot of work!"

I looked at him rather apologetic, and replied "I'm sorry Harry, but I was working on this at the same time you were, and I knew that where I was only surmising, you'd come up with the right way of it, but there is one thing we've dismissed from both of the reports, and that is that the pirates knew the numbers of the containers they were looking for, and also that they were located amongst the containers on deck, and not in the hold!" John exclaimed "You're right, so they've got someone feeding them information! So what do you think they're up to? Is this for making money, or taking over a country?"

I looked at both of them, and replied "I'm not sure guys, but I hope it's the former, also we have to find out who's supplying the shipment information, and we have to firm up our suspicions first, let's go have a look at the second recording, you've uncovered Harry." As we got up without saying a word, and making our way to the TAC room again.

When we got there however, on the main screen was a view of a raid that DJ was about to commence on a house in river bend. Just down from the mouth of the Burdekin river, watching the screen, we saw that DJ had the whole compliment of the six Bundaberg agents with him on the raid. I asked someone how much opposition he faced and was answered with ten. We took our seats and watched as DJ moved in, and prepared for the assault on the premises. With two agents to cover the sides without access, DJ had the rest ready to swarm in both entrances after throwing in concussion grenades to incapacitate the occupants. Apparently this was the third raid he'd conducted in the area to close down the drug running, and I watched in with pride, and a smile as everything went according to plan, and after the raid was over I raised my voice, and said "Well done DJ, perfect takedown, congratulations." He responded to my comment with, "Thanks boss."

After the raid had wound up, and DJ had thanked everyone for their assistance, Harry commandeered the main screen again, so that we could carry on with our case, and so John and I sat, as Harry was going through the footage on fast forward, and then he found the right spot but had overrun it, and reversed the feed until it was where we wanted it. Then we watched the whole scenario, without saying anything, until it ended with the RIBs making their escape, and meeting up with the mother ship, then we watched to see which way the ship headed, and after following the same course for a while Harry stopped the tape, while John moved to the smaller screen to determine the bearing the mother ship was on. Without saying anything, we looked at each other, and as I nodded Harry stopped the video feed, and we silently walked to my office again.

Once there I pushed the map I'd been using to John, and after orientating it, he started work, and it didn't take long his bearing line and mine were the same, he looked up and first looked at Harry, and then me as he stated "An exact match for the line Tiger had already drawn." Harry looked at John and then me, as he said "Well it looks like our colleague has hit the nail on the head once again, so where do we go from here, seeing we're dealing with the Philippine Territorial Waters?"

I looked at them both before, saying "We'll have to cross that bridge when we get to it, before we do anything else, we have to find out how they are getting the information, and this is where we may be lucky, both ships attacked belong to the Australian Cargo Line, and they only have offices here, so it's a good place to start, there'll be no quick fix on this one I'm afraid."

Luckily ACL's head office was in Brisbane in the old wharf precinct of Newstead, and after obtaining a federal warrant, with Jack McCord's help, it was up to Harry's department posing as AFP officers to troll through the thousands of shipping documents, and who had access to them. After we got cooperation from the General Manager, Harry started on this task in late October, and by the time we entered the dead zone, (1st Dec through to 2nd week of Feb), he'd been able to narrow it down to maybe twenty people, so still had a way to go. During that time two more ships belonging to ACL were attacked by the pirates, one after leaving Palau toward New Guinea, and the first one, between the Solomon's and Nauru. In both cases weapons and explosive materials were stolen, in the case of the former the captain reported seeing a patrol boat just on the visible horizon, but this couldn't be verified.

Something about this whole affair had been nagging at me, and after a weekend away when Dawn and I celebrated our anniversary, instead of that coming Monday night when she had to work, I went into the office and made a call to Willie Mahineck in NZ, and asked him if he could put me in touch with Mia, he told me to hold the line, as he transferred the call. Then I heard "Detective Sergeant Mahineck" in her kiwi accent, I said "Mia, Tom Davis, I need to pick your brains for a couple of minutes."

She replied "Hi Tiger, yeah by all means, what can I help you with?" So I told her about the piracy attacks, and then asked her about her time in Davao when the Westwind was there, and she told me that they actually didn't go all the way to Davao, but stopped at a village in a natural bay on the south western side of the Island just off the coast from Davao. Elaborating she told me that all the men in the village looked hard and mean, and always armed, but it was pretty modern because they had about ten RIBs on the shore with big powerful motors, and she finished, by saying "Also back from us on the wharf, there was a framework covered with tarpaulins so we couldn't see what was in there, but a lot of the men worked in there during the day, being curious a snuck out and looked at night, and it looked as if they had a patrol boat there with a deck gun and all." I thanked her for her information, telling her she'd made my day!

After I hung up the phone, I couldn't help but say out loud, "Bingo! Gotcha you bastards!" Janice rushed in, and asked if I was ok, I nodded yes while smiling and chuckling to myself. Then I lifted the phone again, and dialing internally, asked John if he was doing anything special that required his immediate attention, and after he told me no, I told him I was coming up to see him.

In John's office, I told him I might have a lead on our pirates but it required confirmation, so I asked him to bring a map of the Philippines up on his computer, which he did, and I showed him the area I was interested in, and asked "Do we have any satellites that go over that area?" After pulling down one of the folders on a shelf, he spent a couple of minutes looking it up, and eventually answered, by saying "Yep, but it's at the limit of its range, I suppose you want the whole area photographed?" I nodded yes with a smile, as he continued "Ok I'll get it organized," and after consulting his folder, said "The first pass will be at fourteen hundred, today, now get out of here and let me get this organized, besides you look like a Cheshire cat who swallowed the cream, with that bloody smile on your dial."

CHAPTER 33

During the following Monday's meeting, all the photos taken by the satellite were analysed by everyone, and after picking a few possible' we had them zoomed four of the location shots didn't amount to much, but the fifth and sixth, were zoomed up even more, and the pirate base was discovered. So while we were there John went to the computer, and sent the satellite further instructions, and then told us that on the next pass more zoomed and detailed photos would be taken. Harry's team announced that they'd been able to narrow down the list of suspects to three people that could be the informer. Their plan now was to plant listening devices in their work phones and plant three false shipping instructions virtually word for word except the destination would be different in each case but within the strike range of the pirates. It seemed feasible and was given the green light.

After that meeting I rang the boss in Sydney for his thoughts, after I outlined the case, because my idea was to send SAS or the navy in to destroy the base, but to do that permission from the Philippine government would be required. Now at this time Bob Hawke was the prime minister, and some of the things he had said angered the Philippine government, and the federal labour government didn't help soothe the relations when they cut nearly ten billion off their aid package. Gorman told me we had Buckley's chance of getting any sort of cooperation, and that I'd have to come up with a better way to solve the situation, but if a came up with a suitable plan, he'd put the navy at my disposal.

Two days later, Harry came rushing into my office, saying "We got him!" As I sat him down and tried to calm him I yelled for Janice to make some coffee, after a little while he settled down and the flushed look left his face, and while we drank our coffee, he told me what had happened. His team had set up the fake shipping orders as they'd been approved to do, well only one phoned out after the shipment about the shipping orders, and on the phone he only spoke a Philippian language, and because the call was recorded, they knew they had their man. But twenty-four hours later someone rang this person on the work phone, stating that his information proved false, which resulted in a loss of fuel and time, and they berated him and said for the money he was paid he'd better do better. I smiled as a plan started forming in my brain, and I asked Harry, what if anything had been done to unmask the pirate's contact. He told that nothing had been done as yet, because he wanted to see how I wanted it to play out, and my brain started going ten to the dozen as I processed the information.

I told Harry to sit on the information, and not to do anything until further notice, I would have an answer for him within the hour. Then I made two phone calls, the first to the General Manager of ACL, and the second to Colin Gorman. The call to the General Manager involved finding out the next ship to Nauru, the captains name, and telling the general manager what I had in mind, after that he was amenable to whatever we intended to do, and I asked him to fax me that permission to place in our files, (it really was to cover my own ass, should anything go wrong more than anything else).

Between calls I asked Janice to call a special meeting of department heads in the TAC room within the hour, and then made the call to Gorman. After I informed him of what had happened since we last spoke, and what I'd come up with as workable plan for eliminating the pirates and their base once and for all, which was a two phased attack, he gave me the green light, it was a go! All he wanted from me was the code word for phase two of the attack that would be carried out by a submarine based SAS TAG team, and I smiled as I gave him the code phrase which was the line and title of a Deep Purple song, Smoke on the Water, which seemed appropriate for the mission.

I strolled to the TAC room, with a smile on my face and a spring in my step, I was the last one into the room, and all eyes turned to me as I entered. As I took my place at the head of the table I noticed all the file folders closed in front of each person, the files carried the name Pirates Smoked, which was the name that had been given to the operation. I started speaking for a short time before I had to break for applause, as I said "Gentlemen, we've been given the green light to take these bastards down!"

When the applause and cheers died down, I continued "So here's what going to happen..." Then I went into all aspects of the plan, which meant I was stepping down as the onsite leader, as I told DJ, he had to pick a team of twelve agents that would sail with the vessel Pacific Dancer from Sydney enroute for Nauru, in the meantime Harry's team would have made up a false manifest, that would cross the informants desk only, stating three containers full of arms destined for the Nauru Defence Department containing high powered weapons, machine guns, and explosive devices, everything to make the ship a target for the pirates. In the meantime, DJ would board the navy frigate HMAS Darwin in Cairns and make for the operational area. Once the pirates made the attack the captain would make a mayday call about the attack. It would then be the Darwin's turn to sink the mother ship.

While the team DJ had assembled, sank the RIBs that attacked the Pacific Dancer, once the Mother ship had been sunk, it was the Darwin's job to transmit the code phrase, which would unleash a full on amphibious assault by members of the SAS, their job being to obliterate the pirate base once and for all, before leaving the area aboard the submarine that had taken them to the area.

By the time we had our next Monday meeting, operation Pirates Smoked had been completed, without loss of life on our part, however all hands were lost aboard the mother ship. After they tried to make a fight of it, and then after transmitting the code phrase to the submarine, which would unleash the SAS TAG team to swim ashore, and destroy the base and any other personnel. Once the mother ship had sunk, the Darwin then turned their missiles to the RIBs attacking the Pacific Dancer, between the Darwin's missiles and the accurate fire from DJ's defenders all the RIBs were destroyed and sunk, with only three survivors from the RIBs that were picked out of the sea by one of the Darwin's RIBs that also took off the Pacific Dancers defenders, and she continued on her way, after our thanks to the captain and crew.

My old regiment had also done extensive damage to the base, when they left they left everything ablaze, as well as blowing up the wharf, again no casualties on their side, but nearly twenty pirates that hadn't gone on the raid were dead, or severely wounded. The submarine that was to take them back to base, radioed the mission success, and then started heading south to Bass Strait, and then onto Western Australia.

DJ had made it back in time for the Monday meeting and he was met with the usual cheering and handshakes, and my congratulations, because DJ had now completed two very successful operations on his own, while I remained behind in the TAC room running things. Once everything settled down to business at that meeting, I brought up the fact that now we had to start to find quarters for the agents that would start to arrive from the other branch offices over the coming month, because from that meeting we only had four weeks before Expo eighty-eight was due to start in April. So it's just as well DJ had proven mainly to himself that he could handle things in my absence, I was going to be taking part in every security meeting all that month, also John would be with me during most of the meetings and conferences, so his deputy would also be running the communication department, even after the lead up month, we also had a hectic time during the whole of the six months that the Expo was on, but at least we were able to go to it whenever we wanted.

A couple of times I took Dawn because she wanted to go, so whenever she had time off, we would go and wander around, also I was able to bypass all the waiting ques for the exhibitions because of our security badges, when Dawn was with me I would give her my spare AFP Badge, and we had access to all areas without the wait. Also I learned that the German beer hall was quite popular with our office staff, as a place to eat and drink and

I must say that I frequented it on more than the odd occasion. During the last month of the Expo, because our dive shop was a member of the Queensland Tourist Bureau, we had the opportunity to run a booth in the Queensland pavilion and so some of the time I would also work there joking with visitors, and explaining what our company did. During that time there was a lot of names and addresses taken, and a heap of business cards given out, and the dive shop did have a surge in custom, both during and after the Expo, but it only lasted until the end of the year.

The Expo went off without many hitches, and the security breaches were minor, in the early days as it was being established was the time of most breaches, but a lot of those were due to negligence on the part of the public, and more than one surprised face melted at the fact that they had a gun barrel pointed at them! During the whole six months of the Expo there were only eight hundred odd arrests in the expo precinct altogether, so all in all in was a major success security wise. Then all the security agencies had to deal with the removal of all the extra personnel that had been brought in for the event, that took nearly three weeks to organise agents back to where they'd come from, not only did it affect my office, but the AFP, QLD Police, ASIO and Customs and Immigration.

After the Expo wind down, we started to enter the dead zone again, so I was able to spend more time at the dive shop, not only running courses, but taking trips away also. Luckily though I didn't have any of the over Christmas period trips, Rob was doing them this year, and I passed along six students to him that were all doing the advanced diver course. Dawn and myself had to do the family thing over Christmas, which involved going to the parent's place Christmas day, our place for boxing day lunch, for her family as well as mine, and having New Year's eve at the sister in law's, all of these occasion required the consumption of a lot of alcohol, so we both drifted along in a drunken haze for that week. With the arguments between us centred on who was going to be allowed to drink, and who was going to drive, and we took the easy way out and took it turnabout, it also gave the one not drinking to dry out before the next time that it was time to let go.

However, during this time, due to the fact that I had no reason to want to get alcohol poisoning I was always soberer than I made out. Due to the fact that if it was scotch or rum that I was drinking, only one, in every three glasses would contain alcohol, the beauty of drinking spirits instead of beer. As the end of February approached, the work at the dive shop slowly started to die off again, and though Dawn had drawn closer to me over the Christmas period, she still remained distant, and even though I had asked her what was wrong, she would never give a straight forward answer, so I decided to do something about it, for my own piece of mind.

While I was at the office one morning, I happened to sit across from Tim, the surveillance chief, and during breakfast I broached the subject of keeping tabs on Dawn with him, but it was not to be considered a priority, and he told me that he'd be able to manage it when there wasn't anything on, so I wasn't to expect any quick results, because things like that sometimes took ages before a full picture can be established, I thanked him, and told him that I was the only person to know the results, and he said "As if I'd tell anyone else, don't worry Tiger, leave it with me, I'll take care of it for you."

March eighty-nine almost took off with a bang when another Exxon tanker ship, the Houston ran aground in Hawaii with one hundred and twenty thousand gallons being released into the island waters. The dive shop eventually ended up going into liquidation due to our biggest investor Yoshihara Denzo coming to Australia, and deciding to have a dive shop located on the Gold Coast, with Japanese staff that catered to Japanese tourists and locals. However, Nick Adams, one of the smaller investors in our dive shop, who would manage the dive shop, convinced him that he'd need at least one Australian instructor, and I was approached. Needless to say I was feeling fairly bitter, considering all the time and effort I'd put in at no pay. So I asked for an exorbitant weekly wage, and a place to live, when down the coast, which would only be three days per week, and Yoshi didn't even quibble, he just agreed to what I wanted! I would be on the payroll, as of then, but the dive shop wouldn't be ready for four weeks, so I was effectively paid for doing nothing that first four weeks, but after that I would work from eight to five every Friday, Saturday, and Sunday. So I told Nick I needed the address of where I was going to live while I was down there, because I would arrive on the Thursday night to be ready for work on Fridays. He asked me for a phone number he could get me on, and so I gave him the Sat phone number, and he told me he'd work it out and get back to me.

It was during those four weeks that the shit hit the fan yet again! The usual Monday meeting was taking place, as my phone started buzzing, so calling a halt to the meeting, I had everyone wait while I answered the call, which was from Janice saying that the boss Colin Gorman was on the phone and wanted to speak to the meeting urgently, so I told her to patch him through as I flicked the switch and hung up, there was silence for a little bit, while I said "It's the boss!" Then Gorman's voice came through on the conference line, as I said "This is Tiger, boss I have you on speaker, go ahead please."

Gorman's voice came through, saying "Good Tiger, I'm glad I'm on speaker, good morning gentlemen, I'll keep this as brief as necessary, we've had the management of Ok Tedi mining on the blower most of the morning, jumping up and down, and screaming blue murder, eventually we calmed them down enough to establish that during the weekend, six of their top production personnel were kidnapped by the so called West Irian Republican Army freedom fighters, as yet there have been no demands, but I would assume we're going to get some, and they'll be asking for a lot. So Tiger, your mission is to find them and bring them home. I've already put the SAS on alert, and Tag team two is ready to go, apparently you've had dealings with this crew before, so work your magic, so to you, John and Harry, this is top priority, and no expenses is to be spared, is that understood? Also I'll update you when we receive the ransom demands, ok gentlemen get to it, as I said this takes priority!" And he hung up.

I looked around the table, there were stunned looks on the faces of the deputies, but John and Harry were looking directly at me, waiting for orders. Ignoring the deputies, I said to John only one word and he knew what I wanted in return, satellite? John told us, yes passes over every six hours and records the entire pass. I nodded, and said to John's deputy, "Steve you get together with Harry, I want everything from that satellite for the last seventy-two hours, get on it now!" Both of them left, as I continued, "John I want the SAS TAG team two here in Brisbane yesterday arrange it!" After he'd left the room, I looked at the remainder, which was me, DJ, and Harry's deputy Mike, to them; I said "ok get this room on an operational footing now, DJ let me know when it's done!" As I got up and left the room for my office. When I got there, I had Janice contact home for me, because I knew Dawn was on afternoon shift which was four to midnight, she'd be awake by now, and as I sat down at my desk Janice patched her through, I explained about a flap being on, and that I wouldn't be home.

This really didn't go over too well, and I didn't look forward to telling her about the deal I'd made about the dive shop. I was saved any further dwelling on that by a buzz from Harry, asking me to come up to the Technical department, where he and Steve had gone after leaving the TAC room.

Arriving up on Harry's floor I went straight to the service room where he said they would be, and as I walked in there were images screening on four of the monitors that were on the wall, Harry said "Ahh Tiger, during any one time we have four satellites going over and covering that area, and there is only a half hour gap between passes, so we've got the footage running from all four, at present we're up to the Friday, and we're about to start running the footage of the weekend, would you like to see it raw, or just the relevant bits when we've found what we're looking for?"

I smiled knowing he was asking for the benefit of a third set of eyes, so I said "Yeah I'll watch it raw with you two, but first I've got a couple of calls to make, if you can hang off for ten minutes or so?" Harry nodded, and I moved to a phone on one of the benches, and dialled Janice, and then asked her to get me Major Nabors at SAS HQ, and then I spoke to John asking him what he had gotten up to, and was told that he'd arranged landing clearance at Pearce for the jet and ordered Ross and Jerry there ASAP and to wait for passengers and bring them back as soon as. I said "Good, I've got a call into SAS so I'll tell them to liaise with Pearce on the ETA of our jet.", as I put down the phone it buzzed and Janice told me she had Major Nabors, and I got her to patch him through, and as she did, I said "Carl, Tom Davis ASIS, hope you're good, now I need a favour." I laughed at his reply about my favours always costing him time and effort, and telling me he was good because he'd had a marvellous game of golf the previous day coming in with only four strokes over the course par.

So I told him I wished I could get a game like that sometime, and then continued, saying "Carl the favour I need is the use of TAG team two, Terry Witherspoon's team, for a quick job in New Guinea, now I've sent a plane for them, that'll bring them back over here, and then onto PNG, you'll have to speak to Pearce about when the plane is due, but it's in the air on its way to you as we speak, so quick turn around and back here, so Terry will need to be at Pearce when it arrives." He told me he'd arrange it and then asked what sort of operation, and I told him that it was going to be a rescue from a kidnapping, but to have the men in full kit all the same, which meant full battle gear and weapons, and I was truthful with him telling as yet I was unsure of the opposition forces.

He told me he'd organise the team with a miniscule briefing, telling them that they'll be briefed when they get to Brisbane, anything else that I need to tell them? He asked and I told him to leave their guns and equipment on the plane when they arrived in Brisbane, and there'll be cars to pick them up, after wishing each other a good day, we hung up from each other. Harry was about to start rolling the film, but I held him up with a finger, and dialled John, and asked him to join us.

When John arrived, we all watched the footage from each of the satellites, and the relevant parts of tape marked for later viewing, after the edits had been made that were relevant to our operation, as each satellites footage was viewed we'd jump in say "There!" This is how we progressed through the raw footage and took hours, by the time we were finished, it was almost knock off time, so I told them to get the edits done first thing, and we'd meet in the TAC room the following morning, to view them in detail and sequence. When I arrived back at my office, DJ was talking to Janice, and he told me the TAC room was fully operational, so I told him I was staying in my office that night, and I'd see them both in the morning.

After having a shower and getting into some real casual clothing, I had a very nice and relaxing dinner in the cafeteria, and then made my way back to my office and had a few after dinner drinks with a couple of smokes, and after I caught up on the paperwork that I neglected during the day, I was at a loose end, and so made my way to the TAC room, and asked the comm's guy to link me up with the plane. The speakers came alive with Jerry's voice replying to the call, and I asked "Jerry, Tiger, are you still on the way across, or on the way back, over."

Jerry came back saying that they were on the way back and ETA at the airport was zero six hundred in the morning, so I replied "Roger that, I'll make sure there's another car at the hangar, when you get in, will you and Ross take them somewhere for a good breakfast, and then bring them to the office, or come straight to the office and you all have breakfast here, because I want you and Ross present for the briefing, over."

He replied that they'd come straight to the office and have breakfast there, so I said "Copy that Jerry, ok I'm staying in the office tonight, so I'll see you in the morning in the cafeteria for breakfast, and then we'll sort out where the briefing will take place, most likely in the TAC room, over."

He replied "Copy that boss, we'll see you in the morning, flight JLniner, out." After talking to Jerry I decided to go and get some sleep, and headed back to my office, and into my private living quarters, and after setting the alarm, I lay back and went to sleep.

The next morning, I was awake, dressed, and in the cafeteria as, Ross proceeded the TAG team into the cafeteria, and Jerry entered last. Once they ordered their food Ross, Jerry, and Terry Witherspoon joined me, as we made our hellos, and went through all the usual small talk while we waited for our breakfast orders to arrive, and while we ate I gave them a brief rundown on what had happened and why they were here. I also warned them that information was still coming in, and things could change fairly quickly, and I still had to arrange transport for the team from Moresby to Ok Tedi. The team would spend most of the day in the TAC room and be present as the mission parameters developed.

After breakfast, I left them to relax, while I went to my office, and when Janice came in, I was on the phone to Bruce Davidson at Pacific Helicopters in PNG, He did have what I needed, which was a ten man Huey to take the team to Ok Tedi from Port Moresby, he could refuel there, and due to his time in the Australian army as a helicopter pilot in Vietnam, he was used to dealing with special forces, and he volunteered to take the team into West Irian if need be. He also told me that he was happy to take a more active role in the mission, than I would let him on the last operation when I had to chase down Francis Ona.

Once I finished on the phone with Bruce, things were building up under their own steam; the information that was flowing into the TAC room was also starting to arrive at a rapid pace. As I walked into the room the SAS team were helping the others as much as possible and also answering questions for some of the guys. Everyone had been waiting for me to arrive before we all sat to watch the edited footage from the satellites, and as the first screen came to life, I started to give a running briefing to the SAS team, and also filling in Ross and Jerry on what had taken place, and the object of the mission, which was the freeing of the hostages, and returning them to Australia for debriefing before being allowed to go back to work at Ok Tedi.

As we watched, everyone was able to see how they were abducted, and the number of men that took part in the kidnapping. Also maps were produced, and the direction of travel after the kidnapping studied, as more and more footage was studied, the village where the victims were taken to, was discovered.

Once we went over the footage a couple of times to make sure nothing was overlooked, then Terry started going over the footage and found two possible Landing zones for the chopper, so it would be easy to get in and out without too much trouble.

The hostages were taken to a small village near Agapun in Irian Jaya. So then we started looking into the Irian Jaya freedom fighters, which had claimed responsibility for the kidnapping. They were known to operate around the Senggo region, which was to the south west of Agapun and about two hundred kilometres away. The group we were observing was only twelve men strong, so this could be a troop that were assigned to pull the kidnapping off, and then wait for whatever ransom was demanded.

Terry and his team, had seen and heard enough, and announced that they were ready to go after the hostages, looking at the clock Ross must have read my mind, and told me it would be three hours flying time to Moresby, it was only ten AM so they could fly to Moresby transfer to the chopper for the flight to Ok Tedi, all before dark. So I gave them the go ahead and as they started to leave the TAC room I reminded Terry about the half hour we'd be without sight as the satellites changed.

CHAPTER 34

Once they had left with Ross and Jerry, I buzzed Janice and had her get hold of Bruce Davidson at Pacific helicopters in PNG. I needed to warn him that my people were on their way, and therefore he'd have to meet them at Jackson Airport in Port Moresby, and then I got onto Colin Gorman, asking him to arrange clearance for my jet, and also Pacific helicopters to land and at a predetermined hangar. Where my plane would await the return of Pacific helicopters, transfer all personnel to aboard my plane, which would take off bound for Brisbane, as soon as the passengers were all aboard.

He told me he'd get straight on it, and would call back within the hour, and then I told him that there was to be no compromise, my plane had to get in and out without any bureaucratic red tape, also there was to be no repercussions for Pacific Helicopters for their role in the operation. True to his word, Gorman rang back within twenty-five minutes, and told me the deal had been done, and also that he would make sure there was a consular official waiting at the designated hangar in case of any screw ups, he would be there to facilitate everything going smoothly, and to plan.

After hanging up the phone from his call, I stood and said "Ok gentlemen and ladies, we are now on an operational footing as of zero ten thirty today, please have it registered in the log. I want satellite coverage at all times on the main screen, and yes I know we will have a blackout period, but we won't lose comm's, so the comm's channel is to remain open at all times, if there are no questions, get it done! DJ, you take over while John, Harry and I have a quick talk in my office." Without sitting back down I turned from my chair and headed towards the door, John and Harry were right behind me, and we all made our way to my office, I had

Janice make some coffee, as we sat at my desk to talk things over, as to what we could expect in the coming hours.

I looked at Harry, and asked "Harry, the blackout time between satellites, is that timing correct, from one to the next?" He returned my look with a worried frown, and said "Yes I think so." I did a quick double take, and replied "Harry, this is critical! No guesses, is it thirty minutes of black out, or not?" He looked me straight in the eye, and replied "Yes, give or take a couple of minutes for each different one of the four we've got available." I nodded and said "Fair enough, because we'll have to work our timings out around the blackout times, and let Terry know when we have eyes, and when we don't."

Having a quick gulp of coffee, I continued "Hopefully we can work around the blind spots, but I can tell you from experience, thirty minutes of being left out in the cold during an operation, gives plenty of time for things to go tits up! I don't want to get our guys into that sort of situation, so anything we can do lessens the chances of screw ups, understood." Even though they both looked grim they nodded their understanding. All of us knew though, that if there was a screw up, I would be the one taking the blame, after all it was my operation, and as head of station, the buck stopped with me. Also that didn't take into account, how I'd personally feel if things went wrong and people were killed because of my decisions. We all knew that I wanted everyone back alive and uninjured.

By the time we'd finished in my office, it was twelve thirty, which came as a shock to all of us, because of everything that had happened during the five hours, it seemed like we'd already done a full days' work. So we all went off to the cafeteria for a hardy lunch, before going off to do our own thing, which in my case meant going back to the TAC room and running the operation. After lunch both John and Harry were to go home, and then when they came back at zero six hundred the next morning, it was for the duration of the operation, so it could be a couple of days before they got home again. That's why I was sending them home, there was nothing their deputies couldn't handle during the lead up to the operation, at present it was just wait until our team was in place, and then and only then, would the mission would go into full gear.

When I returned to the TAC room, I asked DJ what had been going on in my absence, and he told me that he'd sent the operational day crew personnel to have lunch while the standby night crew ran the operations in the room, and once the day crew came back from lunch, the night crew were on stand down until twenty hundred hours. I nodded and then told him to take the other two deputy department heads to lunch, and I'd run things until they returned in an hour.

I asked the communications operator to get hold of the plane for me, and as Jerry answered, I asked for an update, and he told me that they were ten minutes out of Moresby and that PNG air traffic control, had already assigned them a hangar to pull up to, and that the connecting helicopter had already arrived, and was waiting near the hangar for the flight to arrive. Jerry also told me that Ross would make sure that the chopper was tuned into the operation frequency, and that the TAG team radioed in when they were on the ground in Ok Tedi.

Just after ending my conversation with Jerry, the phone buzzed, it was Janice telling me that Gorman was on the line, so I had him patched through, but Janice was to stay on the line and record the conversation. As Gorman came on the line, I flicked the switch to take it off speaker, and lifted the handset. Gorman said "Tiger, the mine management received a ransom fax, and copied it before faxing it to us, so I'll fax a copy to your office as we speak, but the gist of it is that they want twelve million, two mill per man. Now I've been talking with the mine management people, and told them to ring the kidnappers, oh yeah, I forgot to tell you that the ransom note, also gave a phone number to ring, getting pretty sophisticated and tech savvy for just run of the mill freedom fighters. Anyway to give you time, I had them ring back and say that the matter was in the hands of head office that would ring them back as soon as they'd been able to raise the money from banks. I've bought you some time so use it well, and keep me informed."

So I told him that the Team were on their way from Moresby to Ok Tedi as we spoke, and that I'd be talking to them once they were on the ground, I assumed that the mine people are expecting them. He told me they were, hence the stalling for time, so I told him to leave it with me, and hung up the phone. Five minutes later, Janice came in with the fax, and told me she'd transcribe the tape and put the transcript in my office. Then I asked for the operating frequency to be put on speaker, as I called "TAC room to Pac Helicopters, copy?" Then I was answered "Pappa Hotel zero three to TAC room, I copy, over."

I smiled as I heard Bruce's voice, and replied "TAC room to papa hotel zero three, good to hear you Bruce, where are you over?" The reply came back almost straight away, "Tac room pappa hotel zero three, left half an hour ago heading to the Western Province and Ok Tedi, it's on the northern fly river, which is a two-hour flight, our ETA is sixteen hundred local time, over." Glancing at the clock I smiled as I replied, "Copy that, have Terry call when you get there, TAC room out."

Looking once more at the clock, *I figured I had an hour to come up with something really good to stall the kidnappers, and while I thought, I was also looking at the satellite screen, and also the one beside it showing the region between Ok Tedi, and where the hostages were being held, and I was doing some multi thinking, one part of my brain was working out roughly how long it would take the team to get there, while the other part worked out what to say.*

I worked out what I could claim, find out again the demands, ask to speak to each hostage for proof of life, and then negotiate on the terms of release, and how the ransom would be paid. As I finally worked it all out, I smiled as I heard an inner voice echoing, "Christ you're an evil devious bastard Tom Davis." I picked up the ransom note, and jotted down the number to ring, and thought. *That was curious the number was for a satellite phone, as I recalled what Gorman had noted, that the so called freedom fighters were rather tech savvy, and sophisticated. The ransom demand looked as if it had been typed, and was phrased rather eloquently, as if an educated white man had written, or rather typed the demand, and then I thought about the kidnapping itself, it was unprecedented, and the execution of the raid was timed to perfection, so I started to wonder, if this had really been an attack by the freedom fighter movement, or a gang of highly educated criminals? I was jotting down a note as the others came back from lunch.*

There was only one sure fire way to find out for sure what we were dealing with, and that was to make the call to the kidnappers, and see what sort of response I got. Before I made the call, I gave DJ, Mike, and Steve, a job, which was to go up to the tech floor troll through the footage again, and try to zoom in on the kidnappers as much as possible, and try to determine the cultural backgrounds of the kidnap soldiers, it was a long shot, but it would be helpful. As they left the room, I called for absolute silence, as I picked up the handset, and dialled the number I'd written down.

The following is a transcript of the call; the answers given to me will be in italics:

Hello, my name is Tom Davis, and I represent the Ok Tedi Mining Company, could I speak to the person in charge please? *You are speaking to him Mr Davis; my name is Joseph Ali.* Well Joseph, I take it I can call you Joseph, you don't sound like the average run of the mill terrorist. (Laughter) *That's because I'm not a terrorist as you call me, I'm a freedom fighter in a cause that I believe in, the independence of Irian Jaya from the oppressive government of Indonesia, and Mr Davis you are right to think that I'm not run of the mill as you call it, I was brought up and educated in Australia, I was an engineer before I came here and witnessed firsthand the atrocities carried out by the Indonesian Army, and now I do all that is in my power to rid the country of this blight upon the land, and if that means killing soldiers, then that is what I'm prepared to do.*

Does that include kidnapping innocent men working in another country to your own Joseph? *Yes, Mr Davis, you see the ransom that you will pay will be used to buy decent weapons, so we don't have to rely on bows and arrows, spears, or homemade rifles.* Speaking of the ransom, what is it that you want? *We have six men here Mr Davis, now I think that they are worth at least two million dollars each to their employer, but I want sixteen million but I am willing to negotiate a little for expediency, and a safe return of our hostages, so to that end, I'm willing to take only fourteen million.* Good god man, you're willing to trade people's lives for guns, so you can kill more people? *Yes, Mr Davis I am, you see, the end justifies the means.* Alright Joseph, but the most we could come up with is six million.

The transcript continues: *Do not treat me like a fool Mr Davis, your company can get that in mere hours with a phone call, but I will free them for thirteen, no less.* Joseph it must have been a long time since you lived here, I couldn't possibly get that much, the best I could probably do would be eight. *No! You will have to do better than that, twelve nothing less, or I could shoot one of them.* No! No don't do that Joseph, look I'll go out on a limb here and say that ten is about all that we can get you. *That is good Mr Davis, I will agree to ten million, as long as you can get it to me quickly, the longer it takes might make me change my mind.* Thank you Joseph, now you know I have to ask this, I need to speak to the hostages, you understand that don't you? *Yes, I do, please give me a minute or two.*

He let me speak to the hostages, and as I spoke to them one by one assuring them that they'd be free in a day or two, as I was doing this I was also working on formulating a better attack plan to suit the circumstances. Then Joseph Ali came back on the phone.

The Transcript continues: *There you see Mr Davis, I'm a man of my word, and now we'll see if you are a man of his word. The ransom money must be delivered to me before sunset tomorrow, if*

not I will kill the hostages and leave this area, do you understand?
Yes, I do Joseph, the money will leave here this afternoon and be
in Port Moresby tomorrow, I will arrange for a helicopter to take
it to Ok Tedi, and then on to your location, I will ring you when
it leaves Port Moresby, can you give me your location please?
(Laughter) *No, I'm not foolish Mr Davis, if I did that you could
have the Indonesians attack us, no I will give you my location
when you tell me the payment is on its way.*

After that he hung up, now all I could do was wait until I heard
from Terry's team when they got to Ok Tedi. So the first thing I
did was look at the clock, and as I did, the three deputy department heads returned to the room, and as I watched DJ, looked at
me and shook his head, so they had no joy, luckily though I was
one up on them, as I said "That's ok boy's it was worth a shot,
now I've spoken to the kidnappers, and I need a full background
check done on one Joseph Ali, he supposedly grew up and was
educated here, and was an engineer before he ended up in Irian
Jaya."

As they started on that, I watched the main screen which was
centred on the Ok Tedi gold mine offices area, and helipad, just
I was about to look away, I saw Bruce's chopper come into view
and land on the helipad, and the team exited the chopper as it
powered down. With a smile I also saw the pilot come around to
one of the team, and I imagined that Terry was being told about
my message. As I watched one of the team put his hand to his
ear, and then the speakers in the room came alive, with "Tag two
to TAC room, Tiger we're on the ground at the mine, and I'm
about to go and meet the head honcho, over." Then the screen
started to break up and then went dark, and that meant that we'd
lost the satellite coverage for the next half hour, as I yelled for a
countdown timer to be activated. Once that was done I answered
the message from Tag Two, saying "TAC room to Tag Two, roger
that Terry, have lost visual, so you go ahead and do what you
need to do, but if you can I need to establish visual with you and
the team, progress has been made while you were in the air, and

I have formulated an attack plan that may be feasible, but will require your input as I give it to you, understood, over?" the reply came back almost immediately, "Roger, copy that Tiger will call soon, Tag Two out."

While I'd been talking to Tag Two, DJ had been able to get the background of our main target, Joseph Ali, and as I came off the radio, he had Ali's face up on the main screen, and gave the background briefing to me, and the rest of the group.

Joseph Ali was born in Sri Lanka in March nineteen fifty-four, his family immigrated to Brisbane Australia in nineteen sixty, he went to primary school at Sandgate, and secondary school in Nundah, and won a scholarship to Qld University, where after five years graduated as an engineer, and went to work for Shell petro-chemical, married in nineteen seventy-nine at age twenty-five, at thirty-one, his wife and family two boys one four the other two were killed.

They were in a traffic accident involving a police car, it was later determined that the police were speeding and took right of way from them for no reason, after recovering from his injuries, he was offered a job with the Ok Tedi mining group which he took up, and then a year later in nineteen eighty six he vanished from the mine, some thought he'd been taken by the PNG nationals and killed because of his colour, taking him for a half breed, which is taboo up there apparently, and that was the last anyone ever heard of him until now.

After thanking him, I sat back and thought about what we'd been told. *Well, that was interesting, so he actually worked at the mine site, no wonder they were able to move around as easily as they did, he would have known where everything was, I only hoped that none of the hostages knew him, or they could all end up dead, if he wanted his identity kept secret, thankfully, it obviously wasn't a problem for him, otherwise he wouldn't have given me his name. Being raised here, he would have known that I could quite easily have gotten the information we now had.*

Then the speakers crackled, "Tag Two, to base, copy?" I

replied "Base to Tag two, copy loud and clear, over." The speakers crackled again, "Roger that base, we have use of a project room, my comm's guys are working on a video feed, shouldn't be long, over." I smiled as I replied "Copy that Terry, make sure nothing can be recorded by mine personnel, and also you will need Bruce in on the briefing, over." As the speakers crackled the reply was quick, "Roger base I will get him, wait five, over." And then we heard "You hear that sparks, you've got five minutes," and another voice said "Roger that boss, it'll be ready."

While waiting for them to call back, the comm's tech placed a camera so that I would be seen from their end if the video came up, then watching the screen I saw a face on the screen, and then the camera track back until I saw the whole room, which held all of the Tag team except Terry Witherspoon, then the door opened and in came Terry and Bruce, as Terry said "Grif, guard the door."

Terry came to centre screen and said "Tag Two to base, copy." I replied "Roger that Terry, now that we can see each other we'll dispense with the proper radio protocol, now first things first. While you were in the air to the mine, there was a fair bit happening back here, so I'll let you know what has taken place, and then you can fill me in on what you've learned, and after that, I'll give you my ideas as to an attack plan, and between us, we'll come up with something that works."

After I asked if there were any questions, which of course there were none, I then told them everything that had transpired while they were inbound to the mine. I played the tape of the ransom negotiations for them, and I saw the team smiling as they listened to the conversation, and once it was finished, Terry said, "That was bloody well done Tiger, you even got his name, and he doesn't know that we know exactly where he is, well done!" Then I had DJ tell them what came up in the background check, and once DJ stopped the report, Terry asked "Is there anything in there, that might say whether he has suicidal tendencies or not?" DJ had to tell him that there wasn't, and that seemed to satisfy him.

Then I said "Terry, it may pay to have a word with management, and see if there's anyone around that remembers him, it may give you more insight into the man, and it also explains how they moved around the buildings so easily having worked there. Now before we move on I need to ask Bruce, from the clearing near the hostages, can you get from there and back to Moresby in one flight?" Bruce answered "Yeah sure Tom, as long as I've got a full tank, I'll top it to the gunwales before leaving here, but I won't be able to do it with sixteen passengers, I can only carry ten." "That's ok" I replied, "How many forty-four gallon drums does it take to fill your tank Bruce?" His answer was quick, "Just a little shy of four why? I smiled, and said I'll get into that when we get to the briefing, but right now I need to know what's new at your end Terry?"

He told us that when they'd got there, that the entire mine hierarchy were giving complete cooperation as much as they could, and had shown Terry the ransom demand. They'd supplied aviation fuel for the helicopter and filled it, and given the pilots and team members quarters to use, and also had given them the use of the building they were now in, to use as a headquarters, and of course they had canteen facilities.

I told them that was great, and then I asked if the team could travel on foot from the furthest LZ that Terry had picked, to the target area at night, and be able to go to ground before sunrise. Terry told me that would be easy because the LZ was only a click (Kilometre) away from the target zone. I laughed, and then said "Good, now you need to have a word with mine management, because you'll need four heavy canvas bags, like the type they use for cash payrolls, or something like it, now Bruce could you fly to that LZ at night without lights, and too much noise?"

He told me that it wasn't a populated area, and not on any air traffic path, so it wouldn't be a problem, as long as it never got out that the flight took place. I nodded, and replied "Yeah I hear you, let's hope your co-pilot's not the squeaky clean type, because you, and him will taking part in the mission briefing, and I want you all to go and have some grub, if you're on the same time as

417

here, it's just after five, we'll reconvene at eighteen hundred for the briefing, and then you'll insert tonight, any questions?" Bruce put his hand up, and told us that it wasn't a question, but wanted to clarify his co-pilot's status, and told us that he'd picked his man because he was ex- military, so we'd have no problems on that score. I thanked him and then sent them all to get some food. After the comm's had been shut down, I said I was going to do the same, and get something to eat, and I left DJ in charge.

At a quarter to six pm I was back in the TAC room, as John and Harry entered, they both went to their seats, and told the deputies they were relieved, and could go home for the night, I also told DJ to do the same, as they all looked at me with disappointment, and then Steve raised his hand, and said "Sir please, you haven't had much rest today, you've been in and out, but not really rested, so I think that you should at least keep DJ here in case you get fatigued, and I myself would really like to stay and hear you're briefing, none of us have any idea what you've come up with sir because you haven't confided in us, so for my own peace of mind, I'd like to stay and hear what you have to say."

Well that started a furore in the room, John started yelling at Steve, saying "Don't you ever have the gall to call into question what our station head has in mind, if it wasn't for him, you wouldn't even be in this room!" Harry was also yelling at Steve, and his deputy Mike, also DJ was shouting at me, telling me that he the right to be there, so all up you could say that chaos erupted in the room at that time, with everyone yelling at everyone else. Looking at the clock, and the shocked faces of the technicians, I decided to put a stop to it, then and there, with a signal to the comm's tech, I signed for the room speakers, not moving from my seat, or standing up and slamming my hand on the table as normally I would have done, I yelled "All of you shut the fuck up!"

Considering the speakers were on, my voice exploded across the room, and everyone shut up mid-sentence in some cases, and with a shocked looked stared in my direction, as I considered the verdict to bring down, the silence was certainly enticing, but I knew it wouldn't last for long.

Besides I had a briefing to deliver to my forces on the ground, in a few minutes, so I was not going to be distracted from that happening, by the squabbling going on within the TAC room over position boundaries. Especially from smartasses that thought it was owed to them, to hear what I had to say, glancing at the technician, I received the nod that told me the speakers were still on.

Then in the silence my voice blared, "Alright, this is what is going to happen, first off the junior dynasty, you may stay to hear the briefing, however, you will remain silent throughout! Once the briefing is over you will knock off, and you will not return to this room, until further notice. After that it will remain up to your department head, whether you retain your present position, or not. There is an exception to that rule where DJ as a level eight clearance, must remain as my deputy!"

Because the room had gone silent, my voice echoed throughout the room, and I attracted the attention of the tech responsible. Who turned down the volume, as I spoke. As I looked at the clock, I said "Now every one of you will shut up, as I deliver this briefing to the men in the field."

CHAPTER 35

Well as the clock ticked down the main screen was blacked out, and then at six PM on the dot the screen came alive, with all of TAG team two, seated and listening, also I was able to see Bruce and his co-pilot sitting in, and as comm's was established, I enquired whether they could see me, or not. After receiving the answer that I could be seen, it was time to deliver my briefing, and so I started with, saying "Well gentlemen I hope you had time to have a relaxed and enjoyable dinner, but now it's time for you to do what you've been trained to do. This briefing is only a guideline, and is only acceptable if your commander, LT Witherspoon agrees, therefore it may be a case of on the spot determination, and that can only be decided by your commander, so with that understood let's get into what I have been able to piece together, as the best attack plan that has a reasonable degree of success."

Looking at the faces waiting for my assessment, I was struck with the idea that I should be the one on the ground, my own team wouldn't even think of questioning what I'd come up with, it was a heavy heart that I came to the realization that apart from myself, they were all dead, and I really did feel alone as I spoke to the next generation of clandestine fighting soldier. And I hate to admit it but I felt old and past it.

Drawing a deep breath, I started the briefing, "Gentlemen, I hope you've had a good meal, and relaxed a bit, now we get down to the business end, this is what's going to happen: Later tonight you will be taking off to fly to LZ two, where you will disembark the chopper and at your commander's discretion you will make for the target area. In the meantime, your pilot and co-pilot will be getting some sleep, because they will not be required until the following afternoon. Now once you are in the vicinity of the target area go to ground, and please have silencers on your weapons, I don't need to tell you to have good line of sight on any target, but no matter how tempted you are, do not kill anyone until absolutely necessary." I took a quick drink of water, as I watched the gathered faces trying to read the reactions, and then I continued.

"At ten AM local time I will call your opposition, now because you're all tied into the radio network, you will hear what I'm saying, which will be that the money will arrive by helicopter at twelve thirty, and because the pilot is not allowed to land, he will throw out the bags containing the ransom, before moving off to a clearing a kilometer away, which will be the LZ that you used."

After another sip of water, I continued, "I will tell the leader of the opposition that it will be his job to take the hostages under escort to the chopper, however it will be your job to kill any of the opposition before that happens. Once the chopper arrives, I hope that most of the opposition will come out to help recover the ransom which hopefully will put them into your killing zone, there maybe one or two of the opposition left to guard the hostages, so Terry you need at least one trooper close to nullify them, once the chopper arrives. Any questions so far?"

Bruce raised his hand, and asked "How are we going to throw out the bags?" I smiled, and replied "You'll have to fly from the LZ to the target buildings without your co-pilot in his seat, and he'll toss the bags out, remember to give them a big heave, the team need them spread out, so they can be taken out. Ok anymore questions?"

There were none so after another sip of water, I continued "Right, now after all the opposition is accounted for, Bruce you will fly to LZ one after Terry has given you the all clear, where all the hostages will board, and you will take them directly back to our hangar at Port Moresby, once they are offloaded, Ross and Jerry will give you a hand to strap in four forty fours of fuel and a hand pump, and refuel you at the same time. Then you will make your way back to the target area and pick up the team, if there are any unforeseen circumstances, you take your orders from Terry, as to extraction. Now Terry your team will be without any extraction for at least five hours, maybe make it six, what happens during that time is at your discretion, but don't forget we will be watching, and if something out of the ordinary takes place, I'll be on the blower straight away. Ok any questions?"

Terry raised his hand, and asked "What about the satellite black out time, and if I want the target buildings demolished?"

I replied "As far as the satellites going dark, I've timed them, and I now know the longest dark time and coverage time that we have available. The longest dark time is thirty-four minutes, so if you count on that as the dark period, you'll know when we're watching again, but don't forget that during that dark time, we will still have radio comm's. Now as far as the rest is concerned, whatever happens during the time you're waiting for extraction, as I said before that is up to your discretion, you do what you think necessary."

I took another sip of water before continuing, and said with a smile "However if it were me I'd booby trap the buildings to explode after a tripwire was snapped, instead of just blowing them up, that way you take more rebels out, but as I said that's your decision."

He smiled, and answered "I think I'll try it your way, it's more devious and sends a subtle warning." Terry's team and Bruce all laughed, and I joined them in the laughter, and then said "Ok any more questions." There were none, and so I said "Right you know what you have to do, lock and load, and good luck!" The team sergeant cocked his MP4, and then the team started to move around, and with comments of thank you and sir, the screen was turned off from their end. As that happened the comm's tech switched from the video feed to the satellite feed, which was coming in at an extreme angle from the right of the mine area, and I surmised that we'd not long had the feed coming in from this particular satellite, so we should be able to see what was transpiring for most of the night.

As I glanced at the clock bank on the wall, I turned to the

deputies, and said, "Well you've heard the briefing, so there's no reason for you to still be here, DJ I'll see you at eight, as for you other two... well that will be up to your respective department heads, but I can promise you one thing, if you're ever allowed back into this room, and I get a repeat performance of what I witnessed a while ago, they won't be making the choice, I will, and I can tell you that I don't screw around, you will be sacked, is that understood!"

DJ was the only one looking at me, the other two stood there with their heads bowed down, not daring to look at me, which was probably just as well, otherwise they would have seen the anger flashing in my eyes. As I threatened them with the sack, they both looked up, and it looked as if Steve was about to say something, but thought better of it and remained silent, again just as well, otherwise I'd have sacked him on the spot, and had him removed from the office because it really doesn't pay to cross me.

After they left the room, I turned back, and looked at Harry and John, and enquired "Well?"

Harry was the first to speak, as he lifted his glasses off his face and rested them on his forehead saying, "I for one think you did the right thing, but threatening the sack went a bit too far, but now you know why we've never had our deputies allowed into the Tac room before, they get too swelled a head."

I looked at John, and he said "I agree with Harry, except I know I intend to keep Steve as my 2IC, because despite his behavior tonight, he's damned good, also I disagree with Harry, and still think we need to have our deputies allowed into this room." I looked back at Harry and asked "Do you feel the same way as John about Mike as your 2IC?" Harry nodded his confirmation, and so I sat back and thought about the next step, as I watched the screen, which showed the chopper taking off from the helipad, circling once, and then heading west towards the border, without any navigation lights showing. Then having come to a decision, I leaned forward with my arms resting out in front of me on the table.

Looking at both of them, I said "Ok, here's what I think should happen, and I'll open it to a vote after I'm finished. I still think our deputies should be allowed access to this room, but because of what took place earlier. I propose that all of them are given an official written reprimand from me, with a copy into their personnel files. After that they can learn to cool their heels for a month or two, before they're let back in here for our usual meetings, or any operation that may come up, this will also apply to DJ, he can run the rest of my department if I'm in here. I won't write the reprimand until after this operation is over, and then I'll give them to you to pass on to them, plus any other advice you may care to give them. So those in favor?"

They both raised their hands, as I did, and I said "Good we're all agreed, now let's get back to the job at hand." Then I said a bit louder "Base to Chopper, copy?' There was no immediate response so I glanced at the technician, and she had turned towards me, saying "Sorry sir, I cut the radio feed just after your briefing while you spoke to the men leaving, I didn't think you'd want that broadcast, and I forgot to switch it back on." As I looked at her worried expression, I couldn't help but smile, and replied "In that case you showed very good initiative, thank you, now can we have it switched back on please?" She smiled and started as she flicked the comm's switch, saying "There you go sir, back online."

I was smiling as I said again "Base to chopper, copy?" This time the reply was immediate, Chopper to Base copy, over," I kept it as brief as I could get their position and ETA at the LZ, and whether or not they'd been able to procure the bags, and passed on that the satellite was directly over the LZ, and that there was nothing moving, even on infra-red no heat signatures had been detected. I was told that they'd been given bank payroll bags.

Great these would do the job nicely, because they were hard to undo and were made of a heavy mesh canvas, that wouldn't fall apart from heavy usage. I laughed as Bruce told me they'd been filled with useless phonebooks. After a flying time of twenty-five minutes, they reached the LZ, as we watched them land, and the

Tag team exit the chopper, they turned their com sets on as they left the chopper, and I heard Terry order for night vision goggles to be put on, and then he asked Bruce if the two of them were going to be ok until morning, and Bruce told him that'd helped themselves to supplies back at the mine. so had plenty of food and coffee, so they'd be right, and then Terry said when I call in I'll use the call sign wolf pack.

Then I watched as they grouped together, and Terry ordered, "Grif you're first scout, time to go for stroll boys, move out." I ordered the screen to tactical mode, to test to see if their locators were working, and all ten were, so I had it switched back to infra-red because it was easier to follow their progress. We were getting the images at an acute angle from the left and I started thinking that we were going to lose the satellite soon, and sure enough before ten minutes passed it had gone dark.

As soon as I saw the screen start to flicker, I said "Base to wolf pack, copy?" And the reply came back from Terry with a breath-less chuckle telling me, he thought I'd catch that, and I replied "Yeah I heard it, just to give you a sitrep the satellite has gone dark so we'll pick you up again in thirty-four minutes, what's your situation, over."

John, Harry and I, all started laughing as his report, of the terrain came over the radio, "Christ this is nothing like what you put us through in Africa a couple of years back, the bloody un-dergrowth is so dense it's not funny, at times we're nearly getting strangled from the vines, I don't know why you're all laughing, I'm serious!" to put him out of his misery, I said "Base to wolf pack, sorry for the laughing guys, but we're all Vietnam veterans in this room at present, and we trained in PNG before going to Vietnam where the jungle was ten times worse!" He didn't answer, but we all heard his comment to his team, "Christ! No wonder the old guard called us pussies." To add insult to injury, I said "We operated in that sort of terrain for up to ten months of the time, and most of that was in the pouring rain! Now quit your bitching and get on with the job." As I ceased transmission, we

425

heard comments like, "Hear you boss, shit they must have been tough mothers, roger that, yeah, yeah ok." I looked around at John and Harry, and they were both smiling.

I laughed, called the comm's tech, and signed to kill the audio, and said to the others, "Well that should give them something to bitch about, while we wait for the next sat feed." And they burst out laughing aloud, and I was not able to stop laughing myself. Then I said I needed something to eat, and some coffee, so I was going to the cafeteria while we waited for the next satellite, John said he'd join me, but Harry said he'd only had dinner before leaving from home so he'd stay.

In the cafeteria, I ordered a round of toasted sandwiches and a cappuccino, and took one of the take away menus with me when I went and sat at a table to wait for my order, and went through some of the things of interest to me that could be ordered while we were in the TAC room, we both received our orders at the same time, and made our way back to the TAC room. I was just about beat; I'd been on the go for nearly twenty-eight hours now without any sleep. I was starting to get more than a little tired, and I was almost on the verge of getting irritable, but had decided to delay sleep until Terry's team were in place and ready to take out the kidnappers when it became necessary, but their movement through the jungle was pretty slow going, and by the time the satellite came online again, they were only half way to the target area.

After another hour, I was flagged right out, and told Harry and John that I was buggered and needed sleep, so I was going to my office quarters to get some kip, and asked that someone wake me at zero six hundred, and also to let Terry know each time the satellite went dark.

Next morning, I figured I'd must have had a good sleep, because I woke at zero five thirty, half an hour before I was due to be woken. Having a quick shower, I got dressed, and then headed to the Tac room. John was there, but Harry was missing, as John explained, we've been taking turns, Harry's sleeping at present, and pointed with his thumb toward the bedroom that was part of the TAC room. He took the first shift and woke me an hour ago, he's set to join us at nine. I nodded my understanding, and then asked for a sitrep. John told me that the team had made it to the target area, and were positioned so that they could take any opposition out from any direction. I looked at the screen and the satellite was still on infra-red, so I was able to see where the team was positioned and the kidnappers. Nodding I asked about the satellite status and John said, we probably had another two hours of this one left before the change, and I did some rough timing calculations. I looked at the comm's tech slumped at her panel, and said loudly, "Comm's up please." She jerked up, and nodded.

Looking at John I smiled, and the said, "Base to wolf pack, if you're going to relieve yourselves and have some breaky now's the time, we've still got two hours of coverage, and the opposition is still asleep as far as I can make out, over."

Terry replied in a whisper, "Wolf pack to base, copy that and thanks, Grif, Max move off and do as you heard the man say, then we'll relay it, and don't forget to keep it quiet, go!" And the two team members moved off to the rear for a hundred yards before having their relief. The rest of the team did the same in relay so by the first stirrings of the kidnappers and hostages, all the team had had food and drink and taken care of the other essentials, and were back in position. I had the screen taken back to tactical, and directed the colour coding for the hostages, who were all apparently in the same area we saw them last, they hadn't moved, so I hoped like hell that I was right with the coding. And then I raised my voice and said, "Ok now we wait!" Then I signed to the comm's tech to flip the radio off speakers.

As I picked up the cafeteria menu, John told me that Harry told him that before they got into the target area the team were all whining about the density of the jungle they were having to go through, and I looked at him and laughed, saying "Well you and I know they're getting it easy, what's the bloody army doing these days, producing a bunch of pussies? anyway I'm going to get some breakfast delivered, you want any?" As I shoved the menu towards him. He was going to have the same as I'd decided on, and I picked up the handset, and dialed the extension of the cafeteria, and ordered two big breakfasts' and two large mugs of cappuccino to be brought in, and while we waited. We discussed the time of making the call to the kidnappers, because I didn't want to make it too early, but also I didn't want the team waiting and sweating for hours on end either. We decided that I make the call at nine, which would mean that it would be eleven thirty, when Bruce was to be over the camp, and by twelve everything will be done and dusted, as I finished in my mind, with the hostages freed and all the kidnappers dead.

The breakfast was welcome and great, I don't know what I enjoyed more the breaky, or the coffee and smoke afterward. At eight DJ arrived in the Tac room, and I told him that because he was part of the previous day's shenanigans, he was also on the punishment list, and that he would be in charge of the rest of the department while I was engaged in the Tac room with the current operation, and therefore he would not be needed in the Tac room until further notice.

His look of disappointment was obvious to see, and then I told him about the letter of reprimand that was coming his way, along with the others when I was free of the current circumstances, and had time to write it up. Watching his expressions, I tend to think he was more disappointed at not being able to continue on with the operation, than the coming letter of reprimand. As I was talking to DJ the shift change from the night to day of room technicians took place.

At eight forty-five am, I had the tech flip the speakers on, and said, "Base to wolf pack and chopper, copy? The answers came rather quickly, "Chopper to base, copy, and Terry whispering "wolf pack to base, copy." And then I said, "Base to both wolf pack and chopper, in fifteen I will make the call to the kidnappers, and will leave the speakers open so you can hear what takes place, under no circumstances make any comment! Bruce you'll have to keep waiting, and wolf pack sorry boys but you know how to handle things, Terry you're the closest to the enclosure if there's a chance to move to cover the hostages when Bruce arrives take it, because I expect them to leave at least one guard on the hostages, and remember don't give these suckers an even break, shoot to kill, no prisoners understood?" the chorus of copy, you got it, understood, and roger came over the speakers, and then the speakers went silent.

As I dialed in the number, I glanced at the satellite image, and at an acute angle made out the buildings, the call was answered by Joseph Ali, and the following is the transcript of the call, as before his responses are in italics: *Mr. Davis is that you?* Yes, Joseph, the chopper is in the air, and heading to Ok Tedi with the money, so if you bring the hostages there you'll be given your money. *No that will not happen you have to have the helicopter fly to us! But Joseph you won't give me your position, so how can the chopper get to you?* The pilot won't know where to go. V*ery well Mr. Davis write this down your helicopter will fly to these coordinates, and as we hear him approach I will let a green smoke canister off, 141 degrees 4minutes long by 5 degrees 10 minutes lat.* Yes, I've got that Joseph, just hang on and I'll radio the chopper.

While he listened I radioed Bruce, and we went through the routine we'd come up with the previous day, where we would refuse to land, and would throw out the bags, and that there should be a clearing close by them where he could land after the hostages were taken there, and the kidnappers had left. He wasn't going to land while the kidnappers were still in the vicinity, and in the end I gave into his demands, and went back on the phone to Joseph.

The transcript continues: Well Joseph you heard him, is there a clearing nearby your position that you could deliver the hostages to? *Very well, yes there is Mr. Davis about three hundred metres, but he is to deliver the ransom to me first, is that agreed?* Yes, it is Joseph, he'll toss the bags out of the chopper where you mark your location, oh just hang on a minute Joseph the pilot is calling (raised voice) yes understood thank you, (normal voice) Joseph the pilot has just advised me that his ETA should be around eleven thirty, so hopefully you will have your money, and I'll have my men back by the early afternoon, and I hope none of them have been harmed in the interim. *They are all still all right, and if your money arrives they will stay that way Mr. Davis, it has been good to have conducted business with you Mr. Davis in such an amicable way, thank you.* Thank you for that Joseph, but don't take this wrongly, but I hope to never hear from you again. (Laughter) *You never know Mr. Davis.*

From the last part of the conversation, I gleaned the knowledge that they were definitely going to try this again, at some later date, and I told John and Harry my conclusions about the end of the call, and they agreed that I was mostly right, because it sounded that way to them also. Then I raised my voice, and said "Base to chopper, well done Bruce great performance, let's just hope they don't hear you starting up."

Terry chimed in, with "Wolf pack to base, the choppers about a click away so the chances of that are minimal at best, and I agree with your assessment that they intend to do this again, but as we all know, if it does happen again, it certainly won't be done by this lot. Tiger I've shifted position where I've got a good visual of the hostages, and the enemy has been rotating the guards, wolf pack out."

Before having the speakers off, I asked "Base to both, is there anything else before I close the conversation, over." Bruce came back, with "Chopper to base, I'll be refueling prior to starting up, so I'll have plenty of fuel to get to Moresby, Terry you'll have to let me know if you hear me start up, but you shouldn't, chopper out." Then I had the speakers turned off, and contemplated what else had to be done, and then I remembered that I still had to get hold of Ross at Moresby. I turned to John and asked him to get hold of Ross for me, and then looking at the screen, I asked Harry how much longer would we have sight of the target base, and we came to the conclusion that we'd lose our sight just before twelve, and I was glad that it would go dark after and not before that, because then we'd be able to watch and oversee the exchange with the enemy.

John got my attention, and I had him put Ross on the speaker, as I asked where he was, and he told me that both he and Jerry had stayed close to the plane, and that he was on the hangar phone. Then I filled him in on what would be taking place, and what I required him and Jerry to do, in the way of arranging fuel for the chopper and so on, and what they were to do when everyone one was back on board the plane.

My next call was to Colin Gorman, and I started by bringing him up to speed on what was going to take place, and then told him that I wanted Ok Tedi Mining to pay for the accommodation I was going to use in Cairns for debriefing the hostages and crew, and he agreed, and told me he'd ring back within the hour. He got back to me less than half an hour later and told me that to book whatever I needed at the Continental under the Porgera Mining account and that the password to be used was reef and sun. Great so they used the same hotel we used that way we knew the layout and it suited me down to the ground, it was perfect for the debriefing because we'd book out the conference room as well.

Smiling I quickly got hold of Janice and had her get onto the Continental, book out the small conference room and I wanted twenty-two rooms booked, preferably all on one floor, or over two, and gave her the information to use the mine account for us all and the password. They were to be booked for early arrival the following day, and that she was to be ready to book three seats for myself, John, and Harry to Cairns at short notice.

CHAPTER 36

After that we waited and also ordered some coffee and Danish's from the cafeteria menu. As the clock slowly made its way to eleven o'clock, all hell broke loose! Two screens flickered and came alive, as the comm's tech, spun his chair around, and yelled "Sir we've got a problem! I've been keeping an ear on what the Indonesians are up to, and the chatter is they've landed a company of soldiers at Sengasse, and are commandeering transport to take them north, and the rebel channel has come alive with movement as well it seems they're sending a force to Agapun from Senggo!" As John jumped up and ran toward the comm's station, the phone started ringing.

I answered the phone and it was Gorman, who told me that he didn't know how they found out, but the Indonesian military were sending troops to Agapun, somehow they'd gotten wind of the kidnapping and where the kidnappers were, and I told him I had already found that out, and I'd call him back. John looked white faced as he looked at me and nodded, in other words what the tech had said was true! I flashed a look at Harry, and asked "Harry, does the satellite have multiple cameras that we control?"

A flash of inspiration came to him as he got up, shouting as he raced to the comm's desk "Yes, but I'll need John and the tech to work with me, and give us a minute!" Harry was shouting instructions to both the tech and John, while I watched what was happening on the screens, and another tech was listening to the radio chatter. First one, and then the other screen started to show picture of different parts of the country, while the main screen still showed the target area. My attention was drawn to the screen beside the main screen, it had been zoomed in and I could see Indonesian troops, stopping trucks and pulling the drivers out, and hijacking the vehicles, so I assumed I was looking at Sengasse.

The other screen came alive, and was zoomed and focused on a poorer part of the country, and activity was taking place within a compound on the outskirts of a town, with the magnification I could see people in non-descript cloths gathering in the centre of the compound carry spears, some bows and arrows, and some lugging homemade guns, that I wouldn't trust after the first round had been fired, and I thought, *Christ if this lot and the army clash, this lot will be slaughtered. No wonder Joseph Ali wanted to buy decent weapons! But I knew from experience that decent weapons still don't mean that they could use them, and act as an army!* However, that wasn't my call, my people were at risk!

As John and Harry joined me, and we watched the screens, John remarked "Oh shit!" and Harry was shaking his head from side to side, saying "Pitiful, if this lot try to go up against the military forces, they'll be murdered!" I nodded in the affirmative, and said "Well that's not our call guys, right now our job is on our people, and getting them out of there in one piece, John distance and ETA's the target area please." With a sorrowful feeling in my voice.

John said "Even with transport the army are six hundred kilometres away, and judging by the look of the roads. It would be late evening tomorrow before they get into the vicinity, the rebels however are only two hundred clicks away, but they seem to moving on foot, so I can't imagine them being able to reinforce the kidnappers before the following evening, so it's going to a race to see who gets there first, but hopefully our force will be out of there and long gone before these two forces converge."

Then from the speakers came Bruce's call, "Chopper to base, refuelled starting main engine now, over." I looked at the screen and was just able to discern the rotors of the chopper start to turn, as I replied Base to chopper, copy out." Then I heard Terry say, "Leader to wolf pack, ok boys you know what to do, I can hear the chopper now, so be ready, leader out." The screen was zoomed down by John, and as we watched men streamed out of the ramshackle building, and we watched as one of them moved off away from the building and a canister was thrown from his hand, that started issuing green smoke, and then we saw the chopper come into view, hover near the smoke that was going straight up, and we saw bags come flying out of the chopper two on each side, and then the chopper moved away from the smoke marker. Because the screen was on tactical as each man had come from the hut a white marker appeared where they were, the team were marked with red and the hostages, as yet not out from the building were assigned green.

While we watched six of the white markers went out almost at the same time, meaning they were dead, one of the red was at the building, and moved inside, I knew this as his marker went out from view, then there were only two whites, and then one, and finally none, and then voices came over the speakers, "Wolf leader all dead outside, do you need help? Then the reply in Terry's voice "No, one down in here about to come out with the hostages." We watched as all the reds concentrated toward the building, and then six green markers emerged along with another red, and we got the call, "Wolf pack to base, everyone alive and safe, heading to rendezvous with chopper, over."

I was one relieved man, to see the line of markers heading towards the chopper in the clearing, and watched as each green went into the cover of the chopper, as I heard Bruce say, "We got them all, about to lift off, see you guys in six hours at the latest Terry, take care, chopper out." As the chopper lifted, I waited until it was out of the screen picture, before I spoke.

"Base to chopper one and wolf pack, well done boys, but the job isn't finished yet, now chopper one your reception committee will be waiting, and it is imperative that you understand that you must get back to pick up the wolf pack on time, is that under-stood, chopper one?" Bruce's voice came back loud and clear, saying "Chopper to base, roger understood!"

Then I listened as Terry said, "Wolf pack to base, that sounded a bit ominous Tiger, let's have it!" I replied "Base to wolf pack, ok here's what's happened, and it's not good news I'm afraid," and then I told them everything that had occurred in the last hour, and finished with saying "So there is going to be plenty of time for you to get out before anyone gets near you, as I said they shouldn't be in the vicinity until late tomorrow afternoon, but to be on the safe side, I want you to get rid of the bodies, find and break that satellite phone, and rig the building to blow, then retreat to the secondary LZ, Terry this is no time to decide to fight, now it's the time to run, you have two opposing forces numbering upwards of a hundred men in each force, even I wasn't that suicidal to go up against that sort of number, the job is done, now it's time to get out, over."

After a few minutes Terry called back, "Wolf pack to base, situation is understood, we'll do as you request, and pull back to the alternate LZ, chopper one do you copy that, over?" "Roger wolf pack, understood alternate LZ, chopper out," Bruce replied. Then Terry called back, "Wolf pack to base, what do we do if there are any forward parties from both armies, over?" I thought quickly before replying, and said "Base to wolf pack, that should not be the case, but if there are and they track you, then I'm afraid you'll have to make a fight of it until you can be extracted, base out." Terry replied "Roger that, wolf pack out." Then he said "Ok guys you heard the man, let's get the area cleared up and then bug out."

I let out a sigh of relief, as we heard none of them complain about not making a stand where they were, as we watched them clean up the building area while we still had the satellite, but were due to lose.

I hoped they could make it back to the other LZ faster than it took them to get to the target area originally, but this time they'd be moving in the daylight and wouldn't have to rely on night vision equipment. As the team started moving back to the alternate LZ was when we lost the satellite, and so I called them, saying "Base to wolf pack, the satellite has just gone dark, will pick you up on the next pass, base out."

Once I'd passed the news on to the team, I looked at John and Harry, and said "Ok it'll be a few hours before they make the LZ, in the meantime, you two had best get your go bags organized, also don't forget we'll need recording gear and equipment. Also on your way to your offices, could you do me a favour and send both DJ and Janice into me please." They nodded and cleaned up their work areas before heading out of the room, and while I waited for Janice and DJ, I looked over the meal menu realising that it had been hours since I'd eaten, and I was getting hungry. When DJ and Janice joined me, I told DJ to take his normal seat, and then asked Janice to stay longer that afternoon, because the flight to Cairns would be made by John, Harry, and me that night. I would buzz her as soon as it was time to do so, and she'd have to adjust the booking for our three rooms at the Continental. She smiled and told me she'd get it all sorted for me, and would stay until I left the TAC room. In an uncharacteristic move, I grabbed her arms, pulled her towards me, and kissed her on the cheek, and told her she was a treasure, and I couldn't do without her.

Looking rather surprised, but smiling, she left the room, as I turned to DJ, and told him that we would need an agent to drive us to the airport when the time came, and he told me he'd organise it shortly, and then I said "Ok now forget about any suspension in regard to this room, I'm aware you got drawn into that other stuff without knowing about it, plus I need you to run things while I'm not here, so give me a minute to order some food, and then I fill you in on what has been happening, and bring you up to date." He nodded, and I picked up the phone and ordered the meal I'd decided on and told them to deliver it into the room, along with a large cappuccino. While I'd been onto the cafeteria, DJ had also been on the phone, and as he hung up, he told me our driver was organised for whenever he was required, so I thanked him, and then started briefing him as to what had been taking place, and what I wanted done once I left for Cairns, during our exchange, my meal arrived, and so I continued while I ate, and after he knew what I wanted done, he remarked that I was forgetting to bring the boss up to date with the operation, I smiled, and said "There's the phone, you do it!"

Just after five PM, we heard through the radio speakers, "Ok guys, defensive arc on the LZ, and grab something to eat; the chopper should be here in thirty." Almost as Terry started giving his instructions, I glanced to the screen, obviously the satellite was still in the east, as the camera was coming in from an angle and the target area couldn't be brought into focus yet. Thirty minutes later I was looking at the target area, and it was empty, hah we'd got out before anyone had arrived in the vicinity! Then we heard "Chopper to wolf pack, five minutes out, what's your situation, over?" Then "Wolf pack to chopper, come straight in LZ is cold no sign of opposition, over." The reply "Chopper to wolf pack, roger that keep an eye out, we'll need to refuel, so we need to be quick, maybe some of your boys can help, chopper out."

Then I decided to let them know they were in the clear, by saying "Base to chopper one and wolf pack, keeping tabs with sight, no opposition to be seen, I repeat no opposition, will be keeping watch, base out." Twenty minutes later, Bruce took off again, and he radioed in "Chopper one to base, have all my passengers, and heading for home, over." Everyone was clapping and smiling, as I said "Congratulations chopper one, and thanks for your help on this one, when you guys get back to Moresby. Ross has dinner laid on at the hotel and drinks are on the house. I'll talk to you sometime next week Bruce, right now I'm about to head for Cairns so I can be at the airport when Ross touches down, thanks again to you and your co-pilot Bruce, base out."

As I reached for the phone I dialled Janice, told her to book us on the next flight, and then got up out of my seat, I told DJ that the driver was needed, and to remember to leave a message for Gorman to say mission completed, and the place is all yours until I get back.

In Cairns that night, the hotel had laid on a limo, and the driver was waiting with a sign displayed with Mr Davis Porgera Mining

Ltd, so that saved a cab ride, not that we had far to go. Next morning, we were back at the airport, to meet the plane which was due in at ten. Ross landed five minutes ahead of schedule, and after he and jerry organised a hangar and refuelling, all four limos from the hotel were filled and we headed back there, so I could start with the debriefing process. After everyone was settled into their rooms, I decided to start with the Tag Team, because that wouldn't take all that long, and I wanted to give the hostages time to rest up before I started questioning them one by one, whereas I could debrief the team in one go as a group.

After the team debriefing, I told them what was next on the agenda, which was that they'd all fly back to Brisbane with us, and then Ross would fly them on to Perth, but they had a couple of days' downtime to relax and have fun, while I questioned the hostages. When we ended the session, Terry told me to focus in on the man named Pedersen, because he'd told Terry that he knew how the smuggled gold was leaving the mine, I looked at him, and asked "What smuggled into Australia?" Terry just looked at me and nodded in the manner of someone saying yes.

Over the next two days, John, Harry and I spent a long time individually with the ex-hostages, and had only talked to two of them that first day, but because we got a lot of information out of the first two, it would make it quicker as we went on. We'd just be confirming things from the first two. That night I got two calls one from Gorman, telling me that when I was ready to pack up I could do so. Apparently the mining company were going to send up some upper management people to look after the executives, during the following day. The second call was from a Dr Carey from Porgera management, who told me he'd arrive on the two PM flight, and would talk to me when he got to the hotel. So I told him that he would have to wait until I was finished with whoever I was talking to first, I was not going to have my debriefing interrupted.

At breakfast the next morning, I asked Terry if I could have a guard placed on the conference room while I was in session, so that there would be no interruptions, and I explained why. One of his team volunteered his services, he wasn't going to go to Green Island with the rest of the team, because he'd already been there, so at least he'd have something to do. I thought that was great and I told him so as I thanked him. On the way to the conference room, John wondered who to grab next, and so I said "Let's start with Pedersen, I want to know more about this smuggling routine that he knows about, and how they're doing it, and I'd rather have that before the Porgera people get here, but we'll make it a side issue. Just follow my lead, when I make the switch, and for Christ sake don't run out of tape!"

They started laughing, because I was referring to the day before when the ex-hostage was saying something important, and the tape ran out. So after getting a spare tape we had to start again from scratch, to keep the flow of information from the hostage going so he didn't leave anything out, or jump over events. John said not to worry he made sure that there was a good supply, and a backup recorder going just in case of problems.

So we started with the routine questions that confirmed a lot of what we already knew, and once we'd done that I conversationally switched track and questions, and asked in a matter of fact manner "Well that's just about it George, oh by the way I suppose you know about the gold smuggling routine as well?"

He laughed and said, "Yeah sure we all know that they're doing it, mind you it's quite ingenious really, and the company doesn't really give a shit anyway. They don't care if the tradies make some money on the side, besides we wouldn't get them up there otherwise."

I agreed and asked, "Yeah I guess you're right, so how come it's so ingenious?"

He replied, "Well if you think about it going to all the trouble of making perfect moulds so that if they were inspected they'd work like any tool of its kind. I guess the company policy tends to help them do it, because when a tradie travels for us we pay for an extra seat beside him for his tools to go on. His tools are his living, if they go missing from the cargo bay he's up shit street as far as his job is concerned, mind you we've built up quite a store of tools left behind after a tradie heads back to Aus. So we turn a blind eye to the couple hundred grand of gold he takes with him, and good luck to him if he doesn't get caught by customs."

I was smiling, as I enquired "Yeah but don't you try to discourage that sort of thing, especially if everyone knows it's going on surely?"

He smiled, and replied "Yeah of course we do, well at least we try to warn them that if they get caught by the company, they'll lose their job, and if customs catch them they could end up being jailed, but because we know it goes on, and turn a blind eye, what more can we do? Once we had one of the company executives arrive at the mine site, and he caught one of the tradies doing a pour into a mould, and was going to sack him, that guy still works for us off and on, but the exec, well his ute was found at the bottom of a ravine two weeks after the incident, his body was still inside without a mark on it, I've got a wife and kids, and this job is paying my home off, next year I'll be debt free, so I'm not about to rock the boat, and most of us that know are in the same sort of boat, nah, we'll keep quiet, take our money, and we can't get into trouble."

I smiled and laughed, before saying "Well what about searching the men before they leave the job, wouldn't that put an end to the smuggling and stealing? Surely if they knew they were going to be searched, they'd think about it."

He really started laughing, and said "Oh come on! That's against the law, the unions would close us down pretty fast if the company tried that, and then where would we be?"

I shrugged my shoulders, and replied "Yeah I guess you're right, well that's about it George, of course I'm asking each of you not to say anything to the others about the questions we've asked, because most of it helps us build a better picture of how to protect you guys, but if everyone knows what we ask, then it's a wasted exercise isn't it? You've probably all talked to each other about it anyway, but I'm asking again, please don't divulge what we've asked; it may save your life, as we've already done, ok?

He answered me straight away, saying "Yeah we've talked and tried to find out what you asked, but no one's talking, and rest assured I'll do the same, is that it?"

Smiling I said, "Yes, thanks George you have a good day, and maybe we'll see you before we go, John can you escort George out please." I stayed silent until the door closed after he left, and John took his seat, and then said "Well it looks like we've found the way that customs wanted the answers for, shit say a couple of dozen tradies, tossing their tools, and having gold replicas of them in a toolbox, now my toolbox weighs in at nearly thirty kilos, imagine what a tradies toolbox weighs in at? They're certainly making more than a couple hundred grand, and no frigging wonder customs are missing it. It's right under their bloody noses!"

Harry asked "So what are they doing to get away with it?" I started laughing, and enquired "You don't know?" Harry shook his head, and John was sort of looking a little blank, so I said "Let me tell you a story…." I told them both of a time I hire a boat to take an exploratory dive on a wreck I knew of in amongst the Indonesian islands, and how I found a gold bar on the wreck, and after I brought it up, how I melted it into dive weights from a mould I usually carried, before I came back into Australia, I had stopped in Madang in PNG, and bought some dark grey paint, and as I sailed back I painted each piece so it looked like a divers weight. Once they were dry after a couple of coats, some I put on a dive belt, and some of the others I left lying around the boat. When I reached Cairns here I was boarded by customs and immigration, and naturally they didn't even think to scratch the surface of the weights lying around, and so found nothing to interest them, and I was cleared to continue my trip.

As a matter of fact, some of my dive weights are still gold under the paint! And I finished my story, with saying "So does that tell you how they got away with it Harry?" He was laughing, and replied "Gosh yes, how simple? Now what I want to know is have you been back to the wreck and where is it?" I shook my head, and replied "Well I'm certainly not going to tell you, I'm the only one with the location, and no, I haven't been back yet, I've been too bloody busy and I'll need four people that I can trust implicitly to go with me, there's quite a bit there."

John was laughing, and said "Put me down I'll be in it, joking, course you know what we've done here, we've cracked the customs case that the boss has been getting a hard time over, and rescued six Australian ex pats, all in one operation, shit Tiger! You've done it again! Made our office number one yet again."

I mockingly replied as I shrugged my shoulders and with false modesty, said "Well one but tries. But we will need to verify this story of course so let's get the next one in, and see if he has anything to add."

Well we got more or less the same thing from the others when we broached the subject, and by the end of the day, we'd finished with taking the statements from all six, so we could think about returning to Brisbane the next day, I for one had some making up time to my wife, I hadn't been home for five nights, and that was going to take some soothing over.

That night at dinner, our operations group, was joined by the Porgera mining people, and I announced that we were finished with gathering statements, and that our group would be heading back to Brisbane the next day, facing the senior mining person, told him that a copy of the report concerning the operation would no doubt be passed on to the company chief executive officer by my boss. During drinks in the bar later, I told my people to have a bit of a sleep in but I wanted to be headed for Brisbane by midday, and looking pointedly at Ross, he acknowledged with a nod. I would tell him later during the flight home about taking Terry's team back to Perth, after we were dropped in Brisbane.

Before leaving the hotel in Cairns, I made a call to the office, and told DJ that I would need a driver to bring us in from the airport, and asked him to arrange it, and then on the trip home told Ross about having to continue on to Perth, so Jerry arranged to have the plane refuelled at our hangar, before they would take off again bound for Perth to drop the team and then return

By thirteen thirty, I was walking into my office, and dropped my go bag on the sofa, as I made my way to my desk. Janice had followed me in, and told me that Gorman wanted me to call him as soon as I was back. So I wearily nodded, and as I sat down, I pulled open the middle drawer of the desk and pulled out a bottle of scotch, and poured a generous bit into a glass, took a sip and lit up a smoke, as I sighed with pleasure and then lifted the handset of the phone.

We were on the phone for quite some time, as I filled him in with every detail regarding the operation, both here in Australia, and what took place in PNG. Luckily I had remembered to hit the record button, because this would make writing the mission report easier later. Then I told him about the possibility of being able to get the customs office off his back, due to having found out a source of gold smuggling into Australia.

This news really got him excited, and he wanted to know how soon it could be, before I was able to report to him in the treasury offices in Canberra, so I told him I'd sent Ross and the jet to Perth to drop off the TAG team, so I could probably get there the day after next. He was happy with that and told me he'd see me then.

CHAPTER 37

Well when I finally got home that evening, I assumed that Dawn was on afternoon shift, seeing she wasn't home, so I'd make myself some dinner and relax by watching some TV, while I waited for her to get home. By two am she still hadn't arrived home so I rang her ward at work, and she answered. I asked what shift she was on, and she told me night shift, and then I said I thought she was on an afternoon shift, because she hadn't been home when I got there. The slight panic tone in her voice, as she told me she'd been at friend's place and went straight from there to work, put me on alert, and I made a mental note to have a word with Tim in the morning, and told her that I'd most likely be in Canberra for the following day or so but would ring the house as soon as I was back in Brisbane.

So I decided to have a shower and change clothes and then go back into the office, and if I got tired I'd sleep there. While I was having a nice hot shower, I started to feel like a shit, because of my suspicious mind, after all she could have been telling the truth, and I might have been imagining something that wasn't there. Then I realised that she still didn't know about the times I'd be spending down the coast yet, and I wanted to talk to her about that as soon as possible, after all I was supposed to start down there in two weeks.

In the office I caught up on everything outstanding, and after a couple of hours my inbox was empty again, so I didn't forget, I jotted down a couple of reminders, and a note to Janice telling her I required three copies of the recorded interview with George Pedersen, and three copies of the mission report, by Midday, and to put Ross and Jerry on standby for a flight to Canberra at thirteen hundred that day, and to arrange hotel accommodation for us. Then I went to sleep on the couch in the office, instead of going into the living quarters.

When Janice came in at seven thirty, she saw me and then went about what I'd left her, but she woke me carefully, so I could go and have breakfast, and when I came back she the coffee all made and sat waiting with the daily signals, and we went through our usual routine. This took a little longer due to the fact that DJ had not bothered with this part of the department routine, because he knew it was not for him to bother about. Mental note: *teach DJ everything that has to be done, and cleared each day, even if there is an operation taking place, these must be handled by whoever is running the department at that time.*

After I asked Janice about this, she said she had tried to get him to do it, but was under the misapprehension, that if I hadn't showed him, then it didn't need to be done. So I wrote down to get him into the routine of getting this sort of thing done and out of the way. I asked Janice to send him into my office as soon as he came in, and I would sort out what he had to do, and what not to worry about. She also told me that Ross and Jerry knew about the standby, and that we'd been booked into the Crown Plaza, after I thanked her she left my office to continue her work.

Ten minutes later, DJ came into my office, and I asked him to call Janice in with the usual stuff, and she came in with a handful of the paperwork we'd attended to earlier, and between the both of us, he soon learnt the routine. After that I told Janice she could carry on with her work, and as she left, I turned to him and said "Right, now every now and then you'll come across stuff that I haven't showed you, so in that case Janice will let you know and help you do it, she knows the whole routine, so learn to be guided by her, understood?" He nodded and told me that he got the point.

Once he'd left, I went to the outer office and told Janice what I'd said to him, and she smiled, and I asked her to have Tim come and see me. He entered the office twenty minutes later and closed the door before he came and sat down. Having shut the door didn't go unnoticed, and I sighed and prepared myself for some answers that I really didn't want to hear. Looking at him, I said "By your closing of the door, I take it that means you have something for me?" He nodded rather hesitantly, as he replied "Yeah, sure do boss, would you like me to go on?"

I nodded my head and told him to get on with it, and he started telling me that she'd been seeing another bloke for the last four weeks off and on. Very rarely did she go back to our house in between her shifts. The other guy was a single doctor, that lived in the Herston area which is close to the hospital where they both worked. He gave me the guys address, and I asked him to keep someone on her until the end of the week, and then call it quits, but I needed to know where she was when I got back from Canberra. As he got up he turned on his way out, and said "I'm really sorry boss, but you said you wanted to know for sure, and I'll keep my people on her, as you've asked until Saturday, the radio call sign for my people on your missus is SV two, just in case you'd like to know boss." I got up from behind my desk, walked towards him, and shook his hand and thanked him for getting it done without anyone knowing.

Then I went back to my desk, and did some thinking about what I was going to do about the situation, and that was only interrupted at ten by Janice, who brought me in a coffee and some biscuits, and told me that she had everything that I wanted done, and we had our smoko together making small talk, and when I was finished, I asked her to bring the stuff in, and packed it all into an attaché case in the order I wanted to use it, and then I told her to let Ross know I'd be at the hangar at midday.

After packing my go bag, and having a shower, I changed and then went to the cafeteria and had a decent meal, before going back to my office, and on the way through I asked Janice to get DJ and then both of them were to come in. I was strapping on my shoulder holster, and putting my gun into place when they came into the office, and I informed them that I'd be down in Canberra for probably a couple of days, and that I wanted things to run smoothly while I was away, and as I put my jacket on, and picked up my go bag and case, I walked out of my office with them, they went to their own desks while I headed up to the car park, and my car.

As soon as we arrived and checked in, I rang Colin Gorman from my room and told him I was in town at the plaza. He told me to wait because he was sending a car for me. Twenty minutes later I was standing in the foyer of the Foreign Affairs Department, alongside two security guards waiting for Gorman to come down and vouch for me, just because I'd forgotten my gun, and it set off the metal detector. When Gorman came out of the lift, and came striding forward, he said "Why didn't you just show them you're ID?"

Sarcastically I replied "I did and they refused to accept it, and they've still got my gun."

Well that was like waving a red flag at a bull, Gorman proceeded to tear strips off these guys for not accepting my ID, and told me to come with him, but before I did, I went to the senior guard that had my gun in his belt, and reefed it out of his belt, and with a deadly whisper said, "Next time you'll learn to listen you bloody turkey!" Leaving him white faced, I walked away following my boss Colin Gorman, who'd shown himself to be a bit of rebel after his tirade that he focused on the guards, my case in one hand, and gun in the other and replacing it in its holster. Up in Gorman's office, he asked for everything I had in relation to the gold smuggling, and after he'd read the file, I played him the interview tape, and he remarked "Oh Tiger this is priceless."

He started laughing, and then continued, "Tomorrow we're meeting with the head of Customs and I'd like you to brief him on what you uncovered, so I'll need you here at ten, so the car will pick you up at nine thirty ok?" I nodded with a smile on my face, and then he carried on "Right now let's go over everything to do with the operation, while you sit I'll probably ask you questions as I'm reading these reports, then we'll figure out what to pass onto the mining company heads.

The following morning, I arrived back at the Foreign Affairs building and this time as the detector went off all I had to do was show my ID, and I didn't have any problems. I found out later that following the incident with the guards the preceding day, a scathing fax had been sent to their head office by Gorman soon after I left, obviously it had the desired effect. We all met in the conference room on Gorman's floor, and I delivered my briefing for the next hour, and finished with using the interview tape, to say that the Customs head was astonished was putting it mildly, and he asked Gorman if he could have a transcript of the report and tape, and then the question was directed to me, and I answered "Sir in front of you in that folder is everything you've just asked for and a little more, that you haven't asked about yet, it's all there and in order, and I hope I've been able to anticipate everything you'll need, thank you."

Once the briefing had been done, I just had a few minor things to talk to Gorman about before leaving, and then after lunch at the hotel the three of us checked out, and we landed back in Brisbane by three thirty in the afternoon. Instead of going to the office, I pulled the radio from the glove box and called, "Davis to sierra victor two, copy over?" the reply came back "Sierra victor two to Davis copy, over." I asked "Sierra victor two, where is your target right now please, suburb will do, over." The reply was quick "Sierra victor two to Davis Herston, over." I fired back "Copy that sierra victor two, Davis out!"

So I drove to the address I'd been given by Tim, and sure enough her car was there, after knocking on the door, it was opened by a guy that had much the same height and build as I did, but not as broad shouldered, with blond hair. He asked if he could help me, and I replied "Sure you can, you can tell me if my wife Dawn is here?" I held my jacket open so he could see my gun and his face went sickly white as it drained of colour, so I said "Look turkey I'm not going to hurt either of you yet, but you tell Dawn that her husband Tom expects to see her at home over the weekend, if not, then someone will get hurt, now stop pissing yourself go tell her, and get the hell out of my sight!"

Then I got back into my car, and drove off towards the office,

I would stay at the office overnight, and as the following day was Friday. I'd do some work in the morning and then go home for the rest of the day and weekend. I made good use of the time I was at home, before Dawn finally put in an appearance, by packing most of my gear into the car and also retrieving all the hidden US and Australian notes that Lisa had helped me hide some years ago. I counted it all as I packed it into my old go bag, and found out I still had over two hundred thousand in US currency, and seventy-eight in Australian dollars after placing some sets of clothes on top of all the cash I closed it and put I small padlock on the zipper, and then put it in a safe place in the car.

Dawn came to the house at about midday on the Saturday, and instead of letting my temper flare, we had a sort of calm discussion over the matter, with me asking a few questions to start with. The first being of course "Ok whatever possessed you to end things that way, you know that what you did is my main pet hates, you're lucky that the both of you aren't dead. Which was the way I was feeling when I got back from Canberra the other night, but your so called boyfriend was shitting himself before I even let him see the gun! You also know that I could have shot you both then and there, and I would have got away with it, are you stupid, crazy or what?"

Her answer was "I really don't know Tom, I was stupid enough to let his flirting with me go this far, which it shouldn't have, but I was lonely, and you weren't here, and of course I don't know if you're coming back, I was missing you, and I guess I had a few drinks too many, but I still love you and want you, and in a way I guess I'm crazy enough to have fallen in love with him also. I really don't know what to do.

I stared at her as I answered "Well, I don't share, you're going to have to make your mind up, it's me or him, and if it's me, please be aware that I'll always be wondering whether I can trust you again. You know how to get hold of me, but also this is not an open invitation forever, it has time limits. Now I've packed all my gear, you can have use of the house, because this is what's happening…" and I told her everything about what was happening down the coast, when I'd be there and when and where I'd be when in town, which was I would take most of my stuff to the office, and stay there when not down the coast. I told her that I wasn't giving her the house, it was still mine, and I would always have a set of keys, however she could still live there if she wanted to, and she could also tell her parents about the split, I wasn't going to bother.

She was responsible for the split and I expected her to tell them the truth, she would have to carry the blame, for her not me, even though to some extent I was. By the time she left, I hadn't offered her any dinner or drinks, and even thought she intimated she'd like to spend the night with me, I wasn't having any of it, saying angrily "Look you only want to be laid by me again, just to remind yourself what you're missing, sorry no deal, besides who knows what diseases you've pick up, I don't play second fiddle to anyone, now go if you're going! I'll be out of here Monday morning, after that it's all yours, just do both of us a favour and piss off!"

After she departed, I took off down the road to the leagues club, had some dinner and then proceeded to get rather inebriated before driving home, and going to bed. The next morning, I slept in, and once awake I couldn't face getting out of bed and just dozed for a time, but in the end my mind started going ten to the dozen, so I eventually got up, and made some breakfast. Once I'd eaten I was about to do the washing up, and then thought bugger it why bother, and left the dirty dishes in the sink, fortunately for whoever did the cleaning up, I was out for lunch and dinner, so only a couple of glasses from drinks joined the dishes in the sink.

Early Monday morning, after making a few trips up and down from the car to my office, everything I'd packed was put away in my living quarters, except the dive gear which was going down the coast with me and my golf clubs. Janice was at her desk when I came back from having breakfast at the cafeteria, and we got down to our usual routine about ten minutes later. Amongst the reports and correspondence that we were going through was a packet from the boss Colin Gorman which contained a copy of a request that he had sent to customs asking for an official thank you to all of those involved in getting the information about the gold smuggling for them, and how it was being carried out, a copy of the report sent to the mining company, and a congratula-tionary letter to be read to all staff involved in the hostage release operation, from the Foreign Affairs Minister at the time Senator Gareth Evans, also a certificate of appreciation to the Queensland Branch of ASIS from the same minister. All of these I put into the Monday Heads of Dept. meeting tray to take with me later.

When we were finished with all the incoming signals and reports, and Janice had her little pile in front of her to take care of. I told her that I would be spending any of my after-hours time in my office quarters from then on, and also why, so not to be surprised at seeing me, and she gave me her commiserations.

At the heads of dept. meeting, everything was running smoothly and we took care of business at a faster rate, because after the last operation, we didn't have too many investigations going on. Our individual piles were all completed, except for two extra items I had from the morning routine with Janice, and I had decided to leave them until last so they could be discussed at length. The first file I pulled out was all the stuff from Gorman, and we joked about what we thought of Gareth Evans' congratulationary letter, and debated where we would put the Certificate of Appreciation. My suggestion of the rubbish bin was a popular choice but that really wouldn't do just in case he ever took into his head to visit our branch office, like he'd done in Sydney, much to John Callaway's annoyance. It was finally decided to hang it in the cafeteria.

We discussed the report that had been sent to the mining company after the hostage drama, and we all hoped they'd beef up their security flaws that had been identified by us. The last file contained an intelligence report confirming that the BRA in Bougainville, had gone on the offensive, and was threatening the stability of the government of the island. So far Francis Ona had kept his word and not attacked any Australian owned enterprise, except for Bougainville Copper which I wasn't worried about at the time I spoke to him. We discussed the report for quite a while, and agreed that it looked like one way or the other Australian troops could be dragged into this thing, so we drafted a complex recommendation that would be sent to the boss, and we'd leave it up to him, and the other side of his department to deal with.

Later that week I talked to Nick Adams about whether the accommodation would be ready by the following week, he assured me it would be, and asked if I could to be at Mariners Cove Marina on the spit at Main Beach the next Thursday just before the close of business hours, and after telling him I would, he laughed and chuckled saying that I was really going to love my new place, and after he'd showed it to me, he'd introduce me to the regulars at the local bar and grill. I must admit what he had to say intrigued me, and I wondered whether I'd made the right choice in accepting the deal, but I had, and I would honour it, after all it was just another adventure to come my way, and who knows I could probably end up enjoying it. After all a lot of the entrepreneurial set hung out around the Mariners Cove area, especially Keith Williams whose claim to fame was the building of SeaWorld and across the road was the Gold Coast Hyatt that Chris Skase had built. Apparently Nick and Yoshi had been able to make a deal that gave the dive shop use of the Hyatt's pool for training.

So I guess in some respects I couldn't wait to get down there to see what was what, as the days passed before I was due to go down there for the first time. Eventually Thursday arrived and I was on tenterhooks most of the morning, but I settled a bit by the time I had decided to leave the office, which was at three, and so after wishing Janice a good weekend, and telling her I'd see her on Monday, I took my go bag up to the car, and I headed for the freeway south and the Gold Coast.

I arrived a little after four, and parked in the Marina parking area, and then made my way along the concrete jetty to the C/D arm where the dive shop was located, and I saw its sign before I was even ten yards out on the jetty, which was as wider than two cars side by side. When I reached the A/B arm, I stopped and lit up while I made an all over scan of the area, and then watched the dive shop to see what I could see. As I observed, I saw Nick come out of the double door dive shop and start talking to a greyish blonde headed bloke who was washing the side of the game boat "Gamestriker", he'd obviously not been in dock long.

Stubbing out my smoke and putting the butt in the bin, I continued to move toward the dive shop, which was really a shop built onto wide twin pontoons easily each ten feet wide the shop covered an area roughly sixty feet long by forty-foot wide, at first thought I assumed that it would be fairly flimsy, but on closer examination it looked to be very sturdy and strongly built. Finally, Nick spotted me, and called me down onto the floating arm, He introduced me to Ray Bailler the greyish headed bloke, who was the skipper of "Gamestriker", and then after promising to catch up later, he took me across the walkway to the dive shop and inside. Taking everything in at a glance, there was a foyer type area with a couple of round tables and chairs. At one of them three Japanese were seated talking two females and the other male, then there were counters with dive gear and regulator sets, a stand with masks on it and behind that pegboard that had pairs of fins hanging from the pegs in the board. Behind that two desks one each side of the shop, and mobile separating panels behind the chairs at each desk. Behind that was another two desks, and again the separating panels, then a big space each side before a walled off section, that had a fixed door as an entry/exit which was in line with the passageway down the length of the shop area. Nick introduced me to the Japanese staff Fatami, was one of the females, and roughly a little younger than me and about six inches shorter, with long black straight hair, and Nagi, the male was almost the same height as me.

He was about the same age, and had short black hair, and like me had flecks of grey as well. The other female was kiomi, a divemaster, she was about twenty-five and about five foot, and had grey eyes and her short hair had been dyed blonde. All of them were lean, but the girl's features and breasts did look as if proportionate to their height. They talked in English slowly and disjointedly, except Nagi who spoke very good English. After we'd been introduced, Nick gave me the tour of the facility. Behind the second lot of desks, the one on the starboard side being mine, the one in front of mine was Nick's and Nagi's was opposite his, while Fatami's was opposite mine. Anyway behind the partition panels on each side were sort of longish lunch tables and chairs, also in the same area each side was a chained off area, that had a set of steps going down into the hull pontoons about halfway down the building.

Nick told me that these areas could be used for either an eating area or for theory class sessions, and each had a big whiteboard fixed to the separating wall, we went into the back section, there were two showers each with their own fixed doorways and on the opposite side two toilets with fixed doors, beside the showers was a large fridge and cooking area, and there was a big air compressor set down into a soundproof area of the pontoon, beside the toilets. The cover for this area was open, but attached hinges and at the front by rope so it could be lowered over the compressor room, beside that was a service area with a bench and stool, above the bench was a shelf with compartment boxes that Nick said were stocked with range of spares for most makes of gear, and a large toolbox full of scuba maintenance gear was sitting open on the bench.

After the service, and cooking area was another fixed structural wall that had two sliding doors in the middle that led out onto the rear roofed patio type area. At the end of the shop there were two boat tying cleats, and Nick told me that the dive boat tied up here when it was in use for the day, other times it was in the berth two up from the shop. The railing that went around the shop each side joined the short back rail each side of the back but left plenty of open room to fall into the water. So I suggested a chain to go across the space, as I looked around after he asked if there could be anymore improvements, I saw a metal container that had four dive tanks in it and above them were air lines from the compressor into four gauges that had a line out which went to each dive tank, but while the tanks were empty they leaned against each other, and so I suggested separate round stand for each tank. Then I looked for the fresh air feed for the compressor and found it went up around the guttering of the roof.

I put that in obeisance for a while, and suggested hanging rods be attached to the ceiling at the back and along the sides so wetsuits could be hung to dry, he smiled and nodded, and then going back through the shop, I walked up the gangway until I could see the fresh air inlet, when the tubing curled around the guttering it went to a pole and was fixed to the pole, but it was open at the top! If it rained or got water into the pipe the compressor would be drawing in moisture which would then be transferred to the dive tanks reducing their life span. After talking to Nick about it, he said he'd get everything I'd brought up rectified over the next day or two, and then he asked if I wanted to see my accommodation, and I replied that I would, and he told me to follow him.

He led me back into the shop, and into the class area and un-clipping the chain across the railing, on the starboard side looked at me and, told me with a smile "follow me," curiosity was killing me, so I followed him down the ten steps, at the base of the stairs there was a blank wall on one side, and a doorway on the other, he smilingly opened the door and let me past. Inside was a purpose built room, on the port side was a big wardrobe, beside that a writing table and chair, at the end of the room was a queen sized bed with room to walk down each side, up on the wall each side was a set of speakers, and at the door end of the bed was a couch facing the door. Wondering why, I turned and saw a large TV mounted on the wall with two shelfs underneath, one held a VCR and the other had a cassette deck and radio combination there were more speakers on the wall as well, I was dumb founded, and stood there with my mouth agape taking it all in, As Nick said "The phone on the desk is an extension of the phone on your desk

above, but what do you think? Welcome to the Gold Coast's best
waterbed!"

CHAPTER 38

To say I was amazed was an understatement, but eventually my thoughts returned to practical matters, and I had him show me the lighting switches, throughout the entire shop, not only for the after hour areas. Then I had him show me how to use the cooking facilities, heating oven, microwave, and I asked what could go in what, and so on, then he showed me how to relight the gas hot water system outside on the starboard wall, just in case it ever went out or if the four large gas bottles ever ran out, but he told me that the empties were to be replaced every week. After we came back inside he locked the back doors, and as we moved through the shop, because the Jap staff had already gone he only left the front interior light on, explaining that it was on a timer and shut off at ten pm. After locking up the main glass sliders and the fly mesh security screens, he handed me the set of keys, saying "They're all in order of front to back starting with the security screen doors, you'll get used to they're order soon enough, now let's go up to the local hangout, and I'll introduce you around."

I will come back to that shortly, but first I'll give all the non-local readers a history of how the spit area on the Gold Coast developed, when Keith Williams decided to start building SeaWorld, he needed a base area, and so built a group of buildings he called Fisherman's Wharf because it was right beside where all the fishing boats and trawlers used to tie up at the markets, it has undergone a few facelifts since the original was built. When Chris Skase built the Hyatt Mirage, he also bought the land opposite the hotel, and developed a marina and shopping complex called Marina Mirage, but to moor a boat there was very expensive. Because another building group wanted a less expensive mooring area, and the yacht club had extended as much as it could at that time and was full, it was decided to build the Mariner's Cove complex and marina which became home to nearly five hundred boats.

The local hangout was called Gypsy's, and that night I met a few of the regular people that either owned a shop in the complex, or lived aboard some of the boats. In the time I worked at Mariner's Cove both before and after being in PNG, I became well known and I got to know all of them well.

That first three days I was there was quite hectic, organising my room to the way I wanted it, also doing the same to my work area, and overseeing the tradesmen Nick had called into do the jobs that eventually made life easier.

I also met the dive boat owner, and after we went for a spin in the Broadwater and out through the seaway, he also showed me all of the dive sites used on the GPS plotter, and instead of being numbered, he'd actually programmed the dive site names into the plotter. After our spin I parked the boat at the back of the dive shop and he told me he was happy to let me skipper the boat anytime I was free and wished to do so, the keys to the boat were always left at the dive shop, and he showed me where to find them.

Each morning I was at the shop I would dive off the back of the shop and then swim the length of the arm and a back doing thirty laps, and then climb out using the stainless steel ladder that had been made, and fixed to the side of the shop near the rear. Have a hot shower and have breakfast before opening the shop doors prior to Nagi or Fatami getting there. Most mornings I'd be having a coffee and smoke while talking to Ray as they arrived, or if Ray was out on a charter, I'd be sitting on the portside walkway in the sun. Fatami was teaching me Japanese as I helped her with her English, and because I was good at languages I picked it up fairly quickly, and could easily translate what they'd be saying to each other at times during the day.

As time went on I got used to going between the office and the dive shop, and near the end of August Nick took off on an exploratory trip with travel agents and other dive shop proprietors to Lae in PNG for ten days. During that time, I heard from Dawn, asking if we could get back together now and again, as she'd decided I was better for her than the other bloke, and I agreed to her request, so when I was back in Brisbane, I would spend at least one night at home with her, if she was on the right shift.

Not being all that trusting, I called on Tim's services again, and found out that she was still seeing the other guy at the same time as me, and once I found that out I was furious, but I was getting laid every now and then, and when I did bring up the subject to her, I was none too kind or gentle in the way I did, and told her she was nothing but a useless whore, and a stupid one at that because she didn't charge for the service, and I stopped seeing her again.

Anyway after Nick was back, we were at Gypsy's one night and he asked me if I'd like to do a stint in PNG running the dive operation where he'd been? I was intrigued about this and so had him tell me more. It turned out that the owner of the business was finding it hard to get a full time instructor, and was looking for someone that could run his entire business and also skipper the boat.

I asked Nick how long it was for and he said "Well usually the base contract is for three years, but you get housing, a house person that looks after it for you and cooks the pay is equivalent to a thousand dollars a week Australian, and a percentage on sales made, plus you'd still have your job back here when you finished, you interested?" So I told him I might be, but I'd have to think it over.

The Monday following that conversation, after all the usual meetings and lunch, I phoned Colin Gorman, and we got into a discussion that lasted nearly two hours. The upshot of the conversation was that he wanted me to take the position, which would give him access to a freelance agent in PNG, this was something we'd talked about every now saying how good that would be, so in the end I ended up saying that I'd try it, and he told me to call him if I had any problems with paperwork or anything else.

The next time I was down the coast, I told Nick that I'd thought it over, and decided to give it a go, as long as there would be a job for me back at the shop when my contract was finished. He gave me that assurance and then we started to make a few calls, also that weekend, Fatami and I spent a lot of our spare time with each other, and during my next time down there I had overheard her conversation with Kiomi about wanting to go to bed with me, because she thought I was a wonderfully kind person, and she liked me a lot. With a smile on my dial I quietly moved back into the shop, and then headed out the back again this time a little louder so they both knew I was coming.

It was close to days' end and as usual, I was doing last minute checks on everything and while I was out on the back porch area, checking the tanks that had been filled, I called out in Japanese "Fatami could you give me a hand please," and so she came outside, and as we undid the filled tanks, I asked her "Would you like to have dinner with me tonight, but not as friends which we are, but as a proper date?" She looked at my trying to search for hidden motives in my eyes, and finding none, said "Hai, I would like that very much Tom." We made arrangements to have dinner together at the upmarket and upstairs restaurant Gretel Two which was part of the Mariners Bar in the Marina complex at seven thirty that night, she would go home with the others and then after she was ready would meet me at the entrance to the restaurant. So after a few after work drinks with Nick, and the rest of the locals, I begged off any further drinks by saying I had a date that I needed to get ready for. Which in turn started a lot of questions and debate that I didn't answer. I went back to the shop and had a shower and got ready for my date with Fatami.

Our date was perfect, except for one thing, Nick had decided to keep tabs on what I was up to, and while Fatami and I had dinner in the restaurant, Nick had gone to the bar area for a drink, and because I was used to spotting a tail, I was able to see when he came in, luckily I had a table where Fatami's back was to the bar area. So making an excuse I left our table, went to the bar area and in no uncertain terms told him to fuck off! Which he did without discovering who I was having dinner with. After dinner and a few drinks, Fatami and I were walking beside each other with my arm around her out on to the pier, and when we were close to the dive shop, she turned and drew my face down to hers and kissed me full on the lips, at the same time as placing her arms around me and drawing me in close to her body.

That was all the encouragement I needed, and our embraces got longer and longer until she was actually moaning in ecstasy as we kissed. We did eventually make our way to my room in the shop, which she had no idea about, and after making love for the first time together, we slept. She joined me for my morning swim, and after showering together she went to her car that was in the car park, and came back with a change of clothes, which she put on for the day. After that whenever I was down the coast she would hardly leave my side, and during a talking session after an intense couple of hours making love to each other, she told me in Japanese that she would always be mine and would do as I commanded until the end of days, because I was her lord and master.

Well that was a compliment and then some, and I told her about going to PNG for the following three years, and I didn't want her wasting her life on someone that had just gone to bed with her, and her reply was, even though we weren't promised to each other, no other person could come close to fulfilling her sexually as I had, and she had had a few lovers in her time, as far as she was concerned, she was my woman and would be at my beck and call forever.

Shit! *What was I going to do now? Christ, Fatami was great in bed, but hell it was only sex? How the hell was I going to be able to let her down gently? And then I hit on it as I searched my memory, she was married back in Japan, that was my out!* So I brought up the fact that she and I were married to other people, and even though we liked each other we could never ever be together. So we reached a compromise that suited both of us. Which was that while I had time left we would spend at least a couple nights with each other, while I was at the dive shop, and after that we would see each other when we could, without putting each other's marriage at risk, after all we both were grown adults.

Eventually everything was in place for me to leave Australia on the Pacific airways flight into Port Moresby on the morning of November twenty-seven, and once I was finished in customs I would transfer on board the PNG airways flight to Nadzab, which was the airport into Lae, which was sixteen miles outside the city.

On Wednesday the fifteenth of November, I had a phone call from Dawn inviting me to have dinner with her the following night for our anniversary. This did come as a surprise but I accepted, and we arranged to meet at the Top of the State restaurant in the SGIO building in the city at seven. She had booked the table under our married name of Davis, something she rarely used, preferring to use her maiden name most of the time.

Prior to the meeting, I wouldn't have been me, if I hadn't wondered, what the hell is she up to? But time would tell. So the next day being Thursday during that afternoon I phoned Nick at the dive shop to tell him I would be down that night, but it would be late, so I'd see him in the morning. I did this mainly because he would usually wait at the shop for me, and then we'd go up to Gypsy's, and he bring me up to speed as to what had been happening while I was away in Brisbane over a few drinks before he went home. That evening after work I had a shower, and dressed a little up market from my usual casual gear, and the after I put my holster on, my dinner jacket was the last thing I put on, and I grabbed my go bag and took it up to the car, and placed it in, before I relocked the car, because I had decided to walk, and that way I wouldn't have the hassle of parking.

Dawn was already seated as the maître'd took me to the table, and asked if I'd like a drink, so I ordered a rum and coke, having switched my drink preference about a month ago, my choice of drink made Dawn's eyebrows lift. She enquired about my choice of drink, once he had left, I told her, probably like I'd change again from time to time. I must admit that my temper had flared at seeing her again, and I wasn't in the mood for playing nice after I'd caught her out twice. I let her do most of the talking and questioning because of that, I would only answer whenever I needed to. The wine waiter came and asked if we'd like anything to drink with dinner, and she looked at me and asked, "Well it's our anniversary after all, shall we have champagne, you pick a good one I'm paying tonight." Oh, she shouldn't have said that, now I was going to be a real asshole, she was going to pay alright! After looking at the list I looked up at him and ordered a nineteen thirty-eight Rothschild, and another rum.

Then as I was just finishing my look at the menu after reappraising my order, the food waiter came up to take our order, she ordered a rib eye fillet with salad, and then I ordered a seafood basket with a smile, because I'd been calculating with the champagne at two hundred and ten, and my meal at fifty-two, she was going to out of pocket two hundred and sixty-two dollars alone, without the rums, her meal, and the scotch she was drinking, she was paying alright. I looked up at her with a smile, and then took a sip of my drink as I scanned the room, in the bar area, I saw I face I recognised, it was one of Tim's people!

Great! I thought, the shadow team hasn't been taken off her yet, so if I question her about what she's been up to, I had a ready source of information at hand that can tell me for sure whether she was lying to me or not, because in her case, the last time she told me she was through with the doctor, I would have sworn that she wasn't lying. Now it was my time to go on the offensive, and find out for sure.

The champagne came and as I tested it, I thought it was divine, and gave the go ahead for it to be poured. We left it to sit, and after the waiter left, I asked her about why she lied to me about the doctor last time, and she said "I really wasn't lying I had done with him, but he told a couple of days after we were back together, that I'd left some stuff at his place, and to come and get it. Well when I was there he really turned on the charm and before I knew it he was undressing me, he wanted me, but you don't seem to need anyone, and I need to be wanted and needed, and I felt terrible that I'd cheated on you again, but the only time you really told me that you loved me was when you called me that terrible name, and since then I've thought about it, you were right, and it also told me you cared for me. Oh, Tom I was so wrong, and I'm so, so, sorry, but you can trust me when I say, I haven't seen him since except at work, and I've stayed clear of him as much as possible." I thought for a minute, and replied "So you haven't seen him at all since?" She shook her head in the negative.

She seemed to be telling me the truth, though she'd blown my trust already, but I had a ready source of information at hand, so I looked at her, and said "Excuse me for a minute," and I got up and went to the bar, and talked to the agent and he exchanged all the surveillance knowledge with me, and I told him he could go home, and tell Tim in the morning that the operation is over as of then, and then I went back to the table, and she asked who I'd been talking to, and I replied "That was one of the people that have been keeping you under surveillance at my orders, he just confirmed everything you've just told me."

Just then the food arrived, but I could see she was angry, her eyes blazed, but then focused again, and by the time the food had been served, she'd calmed, but not entirely, once the waiters were gone, she asked "You've had me followed, why, don't you trust me?"

I laughed, and replied "I did once, but you blew that didn't you?"

She bowed her head, and then lifted it again and when she did she had tears in her eyes, and answered quietly, "Tom, you've always been honest with me, that's how I know you're not lying, but I have, I've lied to you, and to myself, and I'm as sorry as I can be, but please believe me when I say, I love you, and I want to be with you, and I would like to try again please? Then to hide her sniffles she grabbed the champagne flute and had a drink, and said "Oh god that's good, you sure can pick them, please tell me we have a chance, please? It's our anniversary after all, let's make a fresh start?"

Looking at her I continued to eat the fish I was eating, and after I finished it, I lifted my flute and proposed a happy anniversary, and after we'd drank, we both went back to eating, but I could see she was on tenterhooks waiting for me to say something, and after a couple of lovely scallops. I did, I told her about being down the coast and dividing my time between both jobs, and then I continued to eat some more squid, and then as she was cutting some more steak, I said "Dawn I think you left your run too late, because in two weeks I'm leaving to go to PNG for the next three years, to run a dive operation there and act as a freelance agent for the other crowd, if you wish to wait until I come back...Well that's up to you, I can't tell you how I'll feel in three years, and therefore I'm not making any promises, but I promise I won't make any moves towards a divorce until we speak after I come back, and while I'm away, I will call from time to time if you want me to, but I will always call you for our anniversary, and you know I won't forget, so that's it, the ball's in your court." As I picked up another prawn and started eating again.

To say she was shocked would have been right because the colour drained from her face, and she grabbed the flute and took a long drink while she composed herself, before she stammered, saying "Wwould you ttake me with you, I I could quit mmy job anand come with you, oh god what a mess!" I shook my head slowly from side to side, and replied "No afraid not, I wouldn't take a woman up there, no everything's sorted, and to work up there you must have a contract, so no go I'm afraid, you'll have to wait until I come back."

I took a drink of the champagne, and then refilled the flutes from the bottle in the ice bucket beside the table, and then continued with what I was saying, "But I'm telling you honestly that since you played around the first time, I've since considered myself a free agent, and I'm not likely to change that unless we get back together again, and if you remember what I said then, that you had lost my trust, and that will take some regaining on your part. I thank you for a lovely dinner, and I'm going to finish this glass, and then leave, I'm driving down to the coast tonight to be there in the morning, but for the next three anniversaries I'm not going to be here, so don't feel like you have to celebrate them, if you don't wish to."

She started to say, "You could come home with m..." But stopped as I shook my head from side to side, instead she asked, "Can you ring me when you're back from the coast please?" And I told her I would, and then got up, kissed her on the forehead and left her and the table. As the lift travelled down the thirty floors and I arrived on the ground floor, and started walking up to the office carpark. I was thinking what to do, and came to the conclusion it was too late to change my mind now, and I'd have to see how I felt about her three years from   then, but at least I'd told her I considered myself a free agent, and she knew what I meant by that.

The plane I was on arrived at Nadzab airport at three PM Saturday the second of December, and was met by Ronald Pearce, who was the owner of the diving operation, and as we drove into Lae he told me that my house was ready for me and that the vehicle that I would have would be the one he was driving. Which was a dual cab Toyota four-wheel drive, but all that would have to wait we were heading for the yacht club, where he had another of his boats ready to take us across the Huon gulf to Salamoa were his resort house was.

When we got to the yacht club we loaded what I'd brought with me into a five metre tinny which had the name Gypsy Joker painted on it, I had only brought one suitcase and my go bag in the way of clothing, and the other two plastic tubs were full of my dive gear, and my stripped down forty-five pistol and my UZI submachine gun, plus ammo, looking at the tubs Ron enquired if they had weight belts in them, and I told him one did the other held some ammo, and he just looked at me with a smile. As I climbed in and he got the outboard started, and as we moved slowly out of the yacht club, he told me we were heading to Salamoa, which was fifty miles across the gulf and to hold on because it sometimes got a bit rough going across, and I asked how rough.

He looked at me, and told me sometimes they got up to half a metre swell, I burst out laughing, and told him that was considered calm from where I came from, considering we could get up to three metre waves plus in Moreton Bay. That seemed to deflate him a little, and then he asked if I could handle boats, and I told him that I held Skipper's tickets for foreign going vessels, so I had no problems skippering any boat, and then I suggested he open the motor up a bit more, and that would take the bounce out. He didn't look too happy about my suggestion, so I asked him to swap seats and I'd take it for a while, so as he powered down we swapped seats, and the I told him to hang on as I opened the throttle wide, and then I said to him "See how much quieter, and less bouncy it is now," as we skimmed over the waves, I calculated that I was going about four maybe five knots faster than he was.

The headland of the peninsula grew in size and he tried to tell me where to go, and I told him, I know where I'm going, all you'll have to do is which wharf you use as opposed to Jack Pearce's one. He stared at me and asked if I knew Jack Pearce, and I replied, "No, but I've stayed at his house before, I came here with an SAS team once in nineteen seventy, and Tom Leahy told us who owned the place." He started laughing and said "Head for Jacks place, he was my father, I'll be buggered, I knew about that team while I was at school in Australia, from what I'd heard that was a very special unit," I nodded my head and agreed that it was. Then he started to tell me that he had a group of Swedish tourists staying until the end of the weekend, and then we'd be going back to Lae, I've also got a couple of my buddies that are divemasters looking after them at the moment, and then spotting a boat, told me that was the Barbarian his boat so they were back from the afternoon dive.

As I reduced speed across the millpond like water, I came in slowly to the other side of the jetty where two men were waiting to tie us up, one of them looked familiar, and as we came in closer and tied up, I glanced up and was right. Ron called hey fellas, as he tossed the forward line, while I tossed the rear line to the other.

When we were up on the jetty, Ron started to introduce me as the new diving instructor, first to the man at the rear whose name was David Penhaligan, and as we shook hands, the other one said, "Ron you don't have to introduce us, Tiger and I have met and worked together before," as we shook hands and embraced. As we moved off the jetty with all the gear, Ron tried to find out how Bruce and I knew each other, and I said, "Well it's something that infringes the secrets act."

"Oh," was all he could say, then he turned to me and remarked "So there's more to you than I'll ever know I guess?" I smiled and just nodded my head slowly, and he asked then you weren't kidding when you said ammo? And my grin got wider as I smiled and shook my head.

Once we were all inside and all the introductions had been made, Ron didn't move too far away from me as I opened my dive bins, and as everyone was out of eyesight, except Bruce and Rod, I started pulling out the stripped down parts of the weapons in the bin onto the double bed, and then I started putting the guns together. Rod was taken by my forty-five, he'd never seen combat grips on one before. As I passed it to him, he also marked on the smoothness of the action, but I really blew his mind as I put together the UZI, and as I finished assembling it, he and Bruce asked what it was, as I said with a smile, "That gentlemen is an Israeli UZI assault rifle!"

CHAPTER 39

After the weekend while I skippered the Barbarian back to Lae Ron told me what I'd be doing and where I'd be living, the house was just near the side of the golf course, at the end of the runway for the military airfield, which I knew fairly well, the house itself had six bedrooms, and the master suite had an on suite and walk through robe, he'd employed a house Mary for me by the name of Wanna, and she could speak good English. Her wage per week was twenty kinas which was equivalent to ten dollars Australian.

During the time I was in residence, I increased Wanna's wage to thirty kinas a week, which was unheard of, and didn't the expat community come down on me for that, but it also bought her loyalty, and that of her family. I never had any trouble with any of the rascal gangs that plagued Lae, or anyone I was associated with. Over the Christmas period of that first year, I met Christine, the expat wife of a sales rep that had been sleeping with every female he could in Lae, both white and black, but he had been recalled by his company to Australia. While Christine, an accountant worked for a British packaging company just outside of town, both of us were ostracized by the local expat community, she because of her husband, and me because of my not towing the line with the way things were done. She had two youngsters one of each the youngest being Krystal who was only four years old, her asshole of a husband had not only left her to fend for herself, but the kids as well. Now because we both hung out at the yacht club, me because most of my work was out of there, and she because she was an avid diver.

It was inevitable that we met, mainly because we were both the town pariahs as far as the expat community was concerned. She was good looking, slim with mid length blondish hair, and blue eyes, about an inch shorter than me, and a year younger, her build was proportionate to her body, and she had really nice perky breasts. On the Friday night just before Christmas, we were both at the haus win (Pidgin English for outside) bar at the yacht club, and she shouted me a drink after learning who I was, and then someone about six-foot odd started giving her a hard time, saying that her husband, his mate had left her behind for him, at the top of his voice, and that he was going to have her that night, grabbing hold of one of her breasts. Well for those that know me that wasn't going to wash with me, and so I intervened, I won't bother with what he said to me, about her and me, suffice to say that I struck three times, with the result of him being carted off in an ambulance, and no one daring to offend me further.

After thanking me, and buying me another drink, which by the way had now changed to Canadian Club whiskey, because trying to get Bundy rum was like hen's teeth, she told me that I hadn't won any friends with what I'd done rescuing her, and I started laughing, and replied, "Well I don't have any friends anyway, (as I raised my voice deliberately), because I pay my haus Mary a decent wage."

She started laughing, and said "Oh, so you're the one are you?" and I nodded my head, as she said "Well I'm pleased to meet you my name is Christine Renoldi, what's yours? I laughed and replied "Tom Davis, most people call me Tiger, but I answer to both, Chris, I take it I can call you that." As she nodded. Then a young boy came up to her and asked, if they could eat yet, and as she said they could, she introduced him to me as Clinton, and said she was going inside to get him and his younger sister fed, and so I said I'd join her. As we all moved inside to eat, it really didn't take much to note the hostility from the rest of the whites as we went about getting some dinner for her kids, and ourselves.

As we sat down to eat, I could feel all the eyes us, and I mentioned it to her, and she told me not to worry about it, because come the next day, we'll have been lovers since I arrived, and she would be the town bike if she wasn't already. I dropped my fork, and exclaimed, "What!" as she continued telling me, oh, yes, they'll look down on you and me, mind you they have what's like a bit like the kettle calling the saucepan black. There's only one couple in this town, beside you and me that aren't screwing everybody else, see that guy over there at the bar? I nodded as she kept telling me he's Jane's husband (Jane was a female divemaster that worked with Ron), but as you know she and Ron are together, even when he's around, but he's not worried he's having it off with his boss's wife and the woman next door in their complex. Oh this is a regular Peyton Place is good old Lae, which sort of fits you know?

I burst out laughing, and asked, "Are you being straight up, not trying to pull my leg?" She told me she wasn't and in pidgin said "Tru Tok" literally meaning true talk. We did become friends after that night, mainly because each other was the only person we could have a half way decent conversation with, and she also called it right in her prediction, about talk around town the next day. Ron hadn't been at the yacht club the night before, him and Jane had spent the night at home at his place, but that didn't stop him calling me into to his office the next day, and he congratulated me on getting further than he ever did with the Renoldi woman, so he tried it on her too it seems.

What he had to say next however, nearly ended up with me getting ready to punch him, (and which would probably cost me my job if it hadn't been for the fact, that he would have had to pay thousands to the government in compensation for not keeping my employment up for the full term of the contract, I later learned this from Christine while we had a drink after work at the usual place). Anyway, he told me that I had made quite a few enemies the previous night, and that he was banning me from seeing and socialising with Christine again, and that's when I blew my top, and put him in his place.

I stayed quiet for all of thirty seconds, then hit the roof, and I think everyone in the place heard me, as I exclaimed, "Just who the fuck, do you think you are? No one, no one tells me who or who I can't see or talk to, least of all you, you can't talk you're screwing a married woman, and from what I've just heard you even tried it on with Christine Renoldi and got nowhere, was this before or after you started laying Jane? Well he was furious, as I watched his face getting redder and redder, until he bounded up out of his chair, and as he stood there glaring at me, I continued, "What are you going to be so stupid as to try to take me on? Obviously you weren't listening when I told you what I was doing the first time I went to Salamoa, if you wish to join that idiot that had a go at Christine last night, come on try and take me!" When he didn't move, I smiled a malicious grin, and said, "I thought not, you piece of shit, I quit." And then I walked out, as I got in the car, I saw Jane rush into his office, I started the car and drove to the yacht club.

Twenty minutes later while I was sitting at the haus win bar nursing a Canadian club and dry, I watched as Ron drove in, hop out of his car, and walk toward me and take the bar stool next to mine, and face me. After ordering a drink, he said, "Tom I'm sorry, I admit I was out of line telling you who you could see. I don't want you to quit, I need you here to run the place and turn it into a professional business, and run dive classes, and in time get the divemasters up to instructor status, and conduct an instructor's course and examination at Salamoa." I turned to him and remarked "I can't pass instructors, I'd have to get an examiner from Australia for that," as he replied "See that's the sort of thing I mean you know all this and who to talk to, I don't please consider staying on." I thought it over as I replied "Ok, but I'll see whoever the hell I feel like and if someone doesn't like it tough shit." He told me he agreed and said that my private life was mine to deal with, and he'd no longer poke his nose in, and then said "By the way the guy you put in hospital, he's the General Manager of the Mazda dealership."

I smiled and turned to him, saying "I never have like Mazda's," he laughed and told me give him a Toyota anytime, and so things were smoothed over, Christine, the kids and I all had Christmas lunch together, and she invited me to stay with them for the New Year's Eve Gala Dance, that took place at the Lae International each year, she'd already booked rooms which were always booked three to six months prior to the event, and so I accepted, and asked if she would like me to pay for my accommodation, but she told me not to worry about that, because they had been paid for with company petty cash.

Life settled down a bit after that, and the other expats had stopped treating the both of us like pariahs after they got used to the both of us being seen together, and we really didn't care if they thought we were having it off, we at least knew the truth about our friendship. Then one night in around the middle of January, somehow a national got over the six-foot fence that was topped with razor wire, and when I was alerted to his presence, he was on the back patio trying to break in, so I didn't muck about, my gun was in my hand and I shot him through the glass door. I didn't need to examine him to know he was dead, because I had shot to kill, and I usually don't miss. Now I had a problem, what did I do now, get rid of the body, report the shooting, and to whom? So I rang Chris's place and of course I woke her up considering it was two am, and once she was fully awake, I told her what had happened, and asked her what she would do, and after talking for ten minutes we hung up from each other, and I started to put her advice to use. I next phoned the police, and after demanding to speak with a senior expat officer reported the shooting, and after that I rang Ron Pearce while I was waiting for the police to arrive.

The police arrived followed soon after by Ron, the body was removed and no blame was laid at my feet, nothing was said in regard to the gun, after I had grabbed the senior cop when he arrived, and flashed my AFP badge, and the incident was virtually swept under the carpet, but the next day I was being considered one of the town heroes. It was during this time that I got a call from Colin Gorman in Australia about the latest antics involving Francis Ona, and what the BRA had been up to, apparently the PNG Government had now asked for army troops from Australia to quell the BRA, without the PNG government using their own defence force. Gorman was sending a SAS TAG team to Rabaul, and I was to join them and go after Ona, and take him out of the picture. I disagreed with what Gorman was asking, and I told him why, and after he had listened to my point of view, he agreed to what I wished to do with Ona.

If I couldn't get word to Ona, to come to me, I would need the TAG team to help me get to him on Bougainville. That evening being Friday Christine made a habit of bringing the kids down to the yacht club, so we could all have dinner together, and while we had a couple of drinks at the haus win bar, the kids played, these days' no one was looking down their noses at us, and none of the men tried to get too friendly with Chris, and were extremely polite around her.

We chatted about what had happened during the week, and she said that she had expected them to make a fuss about the gun at least, and thought I was real lucky for nothing to have happened to me in the way of charges, so I told her that having the gun wasn't an issue with me because I could get away with that. The thing that had worried me was that I had shot to kill and given no warning. As she was about to ask me something, I spotted Bruce, and asked for her to excuse me for a moment, I needed to see someone, without waiting for an answer I attracted Bruce's attention, and as he moved toward me drink in hand, I grabbed my glass and steered him toward the launching ramp, where we sat to talk away from everyone else.

I didn't beat around as soon as we were sitting, I asked "Do you know anyone who can contact Francis Ona for me?" He looked at me in surprise, and asked "Are you up to your old games again? Yes, as a matter of fact I do, when do you want me to get hold of them?" I smiled and said "As soon as you can, I need to meet with Ona next week in Rabaul if possible, so the sooner the better." Bruce nodded his head, and told me to leave it with him he'd get hold of me when the meeting was set. I thanked him and we both moved back to the bar and he told me that I'd made a good catch with Chris on the way back. I agreed with him and told him I had, as I moved back to her side and ordered another drink. Then my satellite phone rang, and Christine's eyebrows shot up in surprise as I pulled out and answered the phone, and I said "Colin old man how are you?" He got the gist that I was with people so he told me what was going on no matter what I said, but he needed to know where to have the TAG team meet me, and how they would know me and what word to use, as I said, "Yes well the Rabaul hotel is good, oh yes I'll know them but you know the code for tiger don't you, I thought you might, thanks old boy, I'll catch up later, cheers." Chris looked at me with inquisitive eyes, as she said, "Tom don't take this the wrong way, but I think there's a lot about you that you haven't told me, first off you get away with something you shouldn't have, you carry a satellite phone, not many people have them, and it looks as if you've had it for some time."

She took a quick sip of her drink, and continued, "You seem to have known the owner of Pacific helicopters for some time, and I mean longer than you've been here, and for some reason he defers to you, which he won't do for anyone else, don't get me wrong. I'm not holding any of that against you, but I would like to know the truth, now I know you won't talk to me here with a lot of people in earshot, so here's what I propose, after we have dinner you follow us back to my house, and we talk about this at home, is that fair?" I smiled weakly and nodded my head as I replied, "Nothing would give me greater pleasure, but you may not like what you hear, and may change your mind about me." She threw her head laughing, and with a smile replied, "I think I'm pretty right about you, you don't mean me or my family any harm, so please give me the benefit of the doubt." I smiled and we both clinked glasses and after finishing our drinks, I said, "Fair enough, I'll follow you home, beside the whole town thinks we're sleeping together, this'll just give them more fuel to gossip, hope you're up to it." We both laughed out loud as I ordered two more drinks.

That night we arrived back at Christine's house about nine PM, and as I made coffee she got the kids ready for bed, Krystal wanted a good night hug from me before she would settle down, and then from ten until early daylight Christine and I talked and I smoked, and we drank coffee as I filled her in on the life and times of Tom 'Tiger' Davis. We would go off at tangents now and again as she asked questions, but eventually she got most of the picture, I refrained from telling her about my involvement with Shari, because I still considered that as private. Once the light of day started to filter through the windows, she said, "Well it's coming onto daylight, I think we both deserve to get some sleep, come on the bedroom's this way," taking my hand in hers. We both stopped at the toilet on way the main bedroom, and as she finished, we both embraced and shared a long passionate kiss, before I went to the toilet. As we reached the bedroom, she said, "I sleep without anything on, I hope you don't mind," as I smiled and said "Ditto."

During the early hours of that Saturday morning, we made love for the first time, I tried to be gentle and considerate, but after her first orgasm, that went out the window, as she let her hunger devour her. I almost lost count of the number of times she orgasmed, because sometimes she would have two or three at once, until the sheets were soaking wet, and we still kept going and eventually with her scream ringing in my ear I poured my seed into her, and even as she tried to back away, I grabbed her ass and pulled her closer into me.

Even though I was as far inside of her as I could get, we still tried for further, and exhausted we finally slept, in the mess of the bed we'd made. She was wrapped in my arms with both of my hands supporting her breasts, which was just as well, because Krystle finally came to wake us at one in the afternoon, because she was hungry and wanted breakfast. Our lower bodies were all wrapped up in sheets, but our uppers were bare, which is just as well Christine's breasts could each be covered by my hand. That weekend the only time we left each other was to do only whatever we had to, and I have to admit it was a wrench come Monday morning when we both had to go to work.

During our time in bed together that weekend, I had told her that I was expected to go to Rabaul and try to broker a peace deal with Francis Ona, during that week, but couldn't say when, but we made the promise to meet up each evening at the yacht club. In at work I told Ron that I might have to take off to Rabaul during the week, and he told me to take as much time as I needed. The following day, Bruce took me to see his contact, the contact went off to relay my message to Ona, and came back two hours later with an answer, which was that Ona would meet me the following Wednesday, in the front bar of the Rabaul hotel at eleven am, but only me. I agreed, and then I made arrangements for Bruce to transfer me to Rabaul the day before. When I rang the hotel in Rabaul to confirm my arrival and make a booking, I was told my booking was already made, and they only needed to know when I was arriving, and so the hotel was told I'd be there at on the following Tuesday. I was to meet Bruce at Pacific helicopters at eight am on the Tuesday, and he would transfer me over and back.

My meeting with Francis Ona the following week went off without a hitch, and this time I deigned to shake hands with him, as we moved from the bar area to the pool area, where we had less chance of being overheard. However, my earpiece was in and I knew the conversation was being taped in at least the Brisbane office. The upshot of the meeting was to get him to back off on BRA campaign to kill the opposition to his agenda but to take prisoners and try to persuade them with reasoning, not intimidation, to change sides, and if he did that Australia wouldn't send in its troops, he'd only face the PNG Defence force, and we both knew they weren't really all that good the BRA would be able to run rings around them. Our agreement was sealed, and eventually Bougainville won the right to become independent from PNG rule, and then aligned itself with the Solomon Islands.

After I gave the game away some years later, Francis Ona was gunned down by one of his trusted lieutenants in July two thousand and five. He had been a rebel yes, but he believed in what he had been fighting for, which was the betterment of his people, from the poisoning of the soil by Bougainville Copper which was a subsidiary of Rio Tinto, without any thought of help or compensation to the local villagers. He was a big ugly brute of a man, but his heart was in the right place most of the time, and he had won my respect.

Apart from that the only hiccup to the years I spent in PNG, came the following year when Australia and other United Nations countries went to war against Saddam Hussein and Iraq. I'd had a call from Colin Gorman back in August of ninety, telling me of the build-up of arms and men in operation Desert Shield, this lasted until the eighteenth of January nineteen ninety-one. Australia and the others went to war in operation Desert Storm which lasted until the first of March ninety-one. Christine and I were asleep, wrapped up in each other's arms when my Sat phone shrilled loudly in the quiet night, when I answered it, John in Brisbane replied, "Its two Am local time and the first missiles have been fired into Baghdad, it's on Tiger! The boss says as of now you're on standby." I told him I understood, and let Chris know what was happening, and then we both went back to sleep.

All through the duration of Desert Storm which lasted until Feb twenty-eight, I was on standby but nothing ever came of it. The lifestyle in Lae was great, and Chris and I became more involved, I kept my promise to Dawn, and called her each anniversary, and I had also told her about Christine, as well as the other way round, so she was aware that she wasn't number one anymore. As time went by it was soon nineteen ninety-two, and then before I knew it half the year had gone, and it was time to start thinking about what I was going to do, considering the fact that my contract would end in November that year, one of the things I did was to check out what was happening back at the dive shop, and so I rang

Nick to confirm that I still had a job, which I did. He told me that the only staff member I would know now was Nagi, because of a staff rollover and turn around in staffing at Yoshi's Japan dive shop. I also rang the Brisbane ASIS office and spoke to Janice to let her know I'd be back in November, and she told me everyone was waiting for me to return.

Eventually Christine and I had to discuss what we were going to do, her contract was due to end in Feb ninety-three, which was only a few months after mine, but we had to make the decision to stay on, or go back to Australia.

She was more inclined to go back, because she'd had enough of PNG, and then we had to decide if we were going to stay together or not. I told her that I'd be telling Dawn that I was going to get a divorce, but I'd probably just give her the house, so I'd have to find another place for us to live, which was fine by her, as long as we were together, that's all that mattered to her. I finished at the dive operation a week before my contract expired, and spent that last week at Chris's house, and she and the kids drove me out to the airport, I would be staying in Moresby overnight, at the Jackson International just up from the airport before catching the ten am flight on Sunday.

I landed back in Brisbane, at fourteen hundred, and I had to flash my ID at immigration and customs, because naturally when ex-rayed my dive bins showed the broken down weapons components. After seeing my ID, the customs officer asked if I'd come in on the PNG flight, and I nodded, and he gave a knowing grin, and let me go. As I entered the terminal from customs, with my booze and smokes packed into my go bag, I was surprised to see Janice there waiting for me as she explained that she'd come to pick me up, I smiled and with a mischievous grin said, "Not literally I hope." She laughed and told me, of course not boss, but it's always nice if someone picks you up isn't it, and I had to agree.

Janice asked if we were going to the office or my place, and I looked at her, and she said ok the office it is boss, her car, my ex mustang was standing in the no standing zone with a security guard standing beside it, and as I approached with the luggage trolley, she said thank you so much Derek, and he walked away as I started loading my luggage into the boot. When the car was loaded she started it while I got rid of the trolley, and as I hopped in. I looked at her as she broke into laughter as she told me, this one I didn't even have to boss around, he volunteered to look after the car when I showed him my ID. I smiled as she started to move off quickly punching me back into the seat.

In the office carpark, I put my dive bins into the boot of my car, after pulling out all the weapon components, and relocked the car, she had put them in a bag that she carried, and I took my suitcase and go bag as we took the lift down to our department. In the lift I asked why she wasn't off enjoying the weekend with her boyfriend, and that's when she told me she'd dumped him, and said he'd tried to hit her when he was in a bad mood. As she saw my reaction, she told me not to worry, he tried I said, then I broke his arm, and we both smiled as she told me, and then she said, those defence courses paid off nicely.

I was trying to keep a straight face, but I just had to burst out laughing, and she joined me as she glanced up at me. She placed all the gun components onto the coffee table in front of the sofa, and told me that the cafeteria had changed the food menu and that if there was nothing else, she'd head home and see me in the morning. I told her I was fine, and thanked her.

Has anyone ever noticed how easy it is to get back into the swing of things in natural surroundings, even after you've been away for years? That's what it was like for me, after three years of being away, I was able to pick up my old life within an hour of being in my office, which I even considered my home, all my stuff was there except for gear I'd left in my room at the dive shop down the coast. I think realistically the only things that had changed were some of the TV shows, what really got up my skin was this so called reality shows that were starting to make an appearance, and after watching one for about five minutes that first night home, I wondered what brain dead moron was likely to watch that crap, guess what? Just about everybody but me! Over a cooking show? Christ let's get real for Christ's sake!

CHAPTER 40

*W*ell I have finally persuaded Timothy to write a companion book to this Trilogy, so instead of talking about my personal and business life, this chapter is a condensed version of what happened in my number one job. So during this chapter we will discuss nearly eight years of my life that really didn't mean much at all, except one, and it is one that I feel most guilty about.

After returning from PNG and having dinner in the cafeteria, even though other people were at their jobs, I felt alone, as if I had separated myself from what I was supposed to be doing, some of the doubts that started going through my mind while I was still a soldier, had started to creep back again, was I doing the right thing, or had I just become a cog in a big wheel. On the other hand, at the meeting the following morning, I felt absolutely useless, and I had to wonder, not for the first time, was I getting to old for this bullshit? As I looked at John and Harry, trying to remember if we were ever young, it seemed as if we'd been doing this for ages, and I was struck by the fact that we'd known each other for so long, and yet we never knew anything about each other.

I had had my talk with Dawn quite amicably over the state of our marriage, and because she was aware of Christine being in the picture, she probably realised that our marriage wasn't going to survive her initial indiscretion, and so all we talked about really was the division of the spoils, and she was amazed when I informed her I was prepared to give her the house, as long as she made no further claims on me. Which she agreed to, so we then discussed that if I went ahead with the divorce application, I told her that I was going to back date, our official separation, and she agreed not to contest whatever dates I used on the dissolution of marriage application.

When I put in the application, I had left the marriage home in nineteen eighty-nine, which was the truth, and therefore we'd been estranged since then. So I ended up with a decree of absolution of marriage, that became effective as of January nineteen ninety-three. It became absolute a week after Bill Clinton was sworn in as the President of the US, pretty ironic actually.

Two other major events happened in February of ninety-three, apart from the one I was interested in, first off some of the drug lords in Columbia decided to hit back after the pressure that was being directed against them by the US DEA and the Columbian government, by bombing government buildings, the DEA offices, and the US consulate, and I was happy that no one I knew was hurt.

The second thing that none of us really gave a shit about, was the ousting of Carmen Lawrence, in an election in Western Australia, but at that time her main claim was that she was the first ever elected female and female party leader in Australia. In the last week of February Chris and the kids arrived from PNG, and I was so glad to finally have them here. I had rented an apartment in Enoggera, and while I was concentrating on work and business, Chris took care of establishing the kids into school, and so on. When I returned on the Monday from the Gold Coast, not only did we go looking for a car to buy for her, but also she wanted to enroll in a couple of courses out at Griffith Uni, and so we spent part of that day out at the Upper Mt Gravatt campus.

My time was still being split between the coast and Brisbane, but my main role as station head was starting to change, as more toward a figure head, than an operative. John found the same and he would complain as our field agent roster kept getting reduced due to the leaps in technology, but Harry was as happy as a pig in mud, he was in his element, until the stirrings of words like retirement started to be aimed in his direction from head office. I was nearly forty, and both John and Harry were older than me, but in Harry's case he was over, the first electable agency retirement age of forty-five, but normally that was for field agents, fifty was the next electable age, but at Fifty-five, retirement was mandatory. All of this we discussed one morning, after our normal Monday meeting, and once we'd dismissed our respective 2IC's, because at least what we discussed in the TAC room was private, and amongst ourselves. Harry told us that he only had four more years before reaching the mandatory age, and he hoped to stay in the job until then, but if head office had their way, he'd be shuffled off before that, and so I told him I'd fight tooth and nail to keep him, and the same went for John, but I did warn both of them that unless anything happened to the contrary I was going to pull the pin after we went into the two thousands, I'll be forty six by then, so I could take early retirement because I'd be past the forty five mark.

John asked me why I'd decided to go so early, and I replied as I looked at both of them "Surely you two haven't forgotten! Remember how old I was during my first mission in Vietnam, so come two thousand, I'll have been doing this sort of stuff for over thirty years, and look at it realistically what have I got out of it, but a lot of loneliness and heartbreak, three marriages down the chute, and a lot of affairs, all because I have a warped sense of duty and honour, I gave my word and I honor my word, but I'm out ASAP, we're all too old for this shit."

The following month, the only thing of any interest to us was the IRA bombing in London, the bastards had rigged a car with fourteen hundred pounds of explosives, and killed thirty-eight innocent people, so obviously they still didn't have the balls to take on anyone that could fight back face to face.

During this time my work down the Gold Coast was starting to dry up, and I Warned Nick that I could see the writing on the wall, business had dropped dramatically, on both sides the Japanese as well as the English, and therefore I spent a lot of my time with Ray on Gamestriker whenever he had a charter, and so I learned a lot about game fishing and deep sea fishing, and I have since used that knowledge in other positions. As far as the office was concerned, we were just going through the motions more than anything, and my private life? Well it went on day to day, but Chris started spending more and more time at the Uni on courses, and we split the time of picking up the kids, and eventually one of the other mothers would take them home when she picked her kids up, and I would get them after work.

So nineteen ninety-three ended more with a whimper than a bang, and ninety-four really didn't announce itself with a fanfare either. However, my demons would come back to haunt me in April of that year, which lead me to many sleepless nights prowling around in the TAC room, wanting to go back into action again, and put things right!

This is what happened, some of you may recall the incidents, but not the cause, in late March Juve, the man I had installed as president for life was coming back from a political meeting with the then prime minister of Burundi when his plane was shot down by rebels, killing both countries leaders. Juve's right hand man Benjamin Bahtu then went apeshit, installed himself as president and started a reign of terror in retaliation for Juve's death, so said he, but I have had my reservations about him, and I wondered just how much he was behind Juve's death, he never struck me as the wait in the wings type of guy. Anyway the presidential guard in retaliation started an ethnic cleansing of the country of tutsi tribe members, and it started with twelve hundred tutsi Christians chopped to death in a church in Kigali. The next day seven thousand were slaughtered, each day's reports brought more and more atrocities, and as report came in I felt more helpless and dare I say it, old!

As the days passed, and with no involvement by Australia I was getting more and more than frustrated beyond relief, as my staff knew, in no uncertain terms.

Finally, three months later the French had decided enough was enough, no one else was doing anything, so they may as well. (Go the Frogs!). By the time any semblance of peace was restored, over three million people had been murdered. It was sheer genocide in its purest form! At least Adolf was civilized, sort of, he tried to disguise it. Whereas that bloody monkey Bahtu deserved the hanging that came to him.

Beside myself others have asked how do you live with something like that on your conscience, and my only answer is, I do, and have to that's all there is to it, but in the end when all is said and done. I'm my only accuser, it's not as if I personally took part in the atrocities, I only placed things in the hands of fate. Many have said that I shouldn't blame myself, but who do you blame? After all that's said and done, who wears the blame? I smiled as I thought about that question, and then realized with grim satisfaction, that I had killed the person who had sent me on that mission.

Then later in the year I got a call from Robert Ballzinger, asking what I was up to, and I told him that I was still down the coast, but things were starting to peter out, and he told me he'd lucked onto a project that may be up our alley, and asked if we could meet up. We met at a boatyard up near the mouth of the Brisbane River at Hemmant, and from the shore at the boatyard he showed me a boat with the name of the Venus Portsmouth, and told me the story about it, and what the owner wanted to do with it, but it required a complete refit, and brought up to USL code specifications to turn it into a charter vessel, that would be based in either Gladstone working the Capricorn Bunker group, or out of Cairns working the northern ribbon reefs and island cays. If I took part in the venture, I would become the 1st mate, while Rob would end up as skipper of the boat, when the refit was finished, and we would be employed on a contractual yearly basis to run the boat and any charters, plus teach the odd dive courses.

I was told that if I joined the team, I'd start on a wage of six hundred a week plus a ten percent part of the company. After looking it over Rob and I worked out that the refit was going to take at least three years, to bring it up to code, and would cost on hell of a lot of cash, he told me he'd need to know if I was in by the end of the following week, and if I was he'd arrange a meeting with the boat's owner. Driving home, I figured that I could move back as a freelance agent, as I did in PNG, but because I was in Brisbane, I could also look after my other work if I needed to, plus I wasn't far from the office, so I guess in a way I was talking myself into it, but the end result could be great for me and Rob.

That night I talked it over with Christine, she had at least another year and a half before she finished the legal course that she was doing, and with me being in Brisbane full time, it would make things easier on her. So that weekend we went for a drive to Hemmant so I could show her the boat, and she asked what was going to be done, so I started rattling off a list of the stuff that would need doing, and as I went on, I could see she was getting bored, so I stated, "So as you can see there's a lot to be done, but we've also got a lot of time to do it in."

During the following week, Rob and I met the boat owner Patrick, who was in his sixties, and he was an ex real estate salesman, he'd picked up the Venus a couple of years before, as payment for a debt, and since then he'd done nothing with it, but with the intention to turn it into an exclusive style charter boat. I was hired and went onto the payroll, and as we left his Hamilton mansion, I asked Rob how much he was estimated we'd need, and I told him I disagreed with his estimate of two million, saying it would more likely be about five, if it was going to be done the right way. Three years later in mid ninety-seven, those words came back to haunt both of us as the money dried up without the Venus being completed, and it was eventually sold for scrap. Rob and I were out of a job again, but this time we weren't out of pocket, but during the work happening with Venus, we both ended up with broken relationships, deciding to go our own ways again, I ended up down the coast again, and I later learned he'd gone north.

My new job as a charter boat skipper allowed me the flexibility to work part time, so I could spend some of my time in Brisbane at the office. At the end of August ninety-seven the world was rocked with the news that Diana Spencer had been killed in a car crash, along with her boyfriend Dodi Al Fayed, and I don't think there were too many who didn't watch her funeral.

Ninety-eight wasn't much of a year for news, we went about our normal business, and even though we had perfected ways of infiltrating the drug running gangs, and due to the information that was supplied by our undercover agents, not many shipments made it to their intended end user, but no matter how many we stopped, they still kept trying, and at times it felt like we were beating our heads up against a brick wall. Eventually I came to realize that no matter what we tried to stem the flow, it was always going to be there, and just keep coming. Even if we stemmed the flow completely, people would try to make their own drugs using chemicals instead of the usual organic sources, so really it became just another war we couldn't win.

Sometimes I even wondered why we even bothered, if people wanted to kill themselves with drugs why not just let them? Oh I know why; the governments of the day weren't making any money out of it! I also voiced these thoughts out loud during discussions, John, Harry, Janice, and I would have in my office, after our usual Monday meetings. The powers that be had stopped putting pressure on Harry to quit, after I came down hard with my viewpoint to Colin Gorman, and after he intervened everything stopped.

There were only really two significant events in ninety-nine, the first was early in the year while we were still in the dead zone for intelligence agencies, and we were put on standby when an Australian missionary and his two sons were burned alive while they were sleeping in their car by radical Hindus in eastern India, but the Indian police force did arrest all the sect members and they were jailed, so we stood down and went about business as usual.

During one of our philosophical Monday discussions, I was so peeved off with a signal from head office earlier in the morning, wanting us to step up our antidrug importation campaign that I let my thoughts concentrate on that stupid and ridiculous request, and I made my thoughts known, saying "Just what the hell do they think we do all the time? Sit on our asses, you know sometimes I don't think we make a scrap of difference, and to tell you the truth it feels as if we've achieved nothing, I don't know maybe they're right."

Harry made the observation that no matter how well one did the job, the powers that be would always expect more, and this started us off into a whole new train of thought and discussion, our sessions in my office were never taken seriously by us, it was just our way of venting our frustrations and bitching in general. As the incumbent department heads, we had seen staff come and go, and this was why Janice was included, the four of us had been here longer than anyone, we were all old school, some of this new idea of so called political correctness, was all bullshit as far as we were concerned. Controls were being taken away from parents not just in little things, but even in the way kids were disciplined, Christ they were trying to make it illegal to punish kids for any misdemeanors, and trying to take away the rights of a parent, well that would only lead to one thing, which would be a breakdown in respect to people and property, couldn't the bleeding heart radicals understand that? Of course not, they were too full of their own ideas and importance, they couldn't think beyond the tips of their noses, mind you that was if they had any brains to start with! Worst of all they wanted to push their ideas onto others, and expected others to tow their line.

It was a major pity that you couldn't just take them quietly out back and beat the living shit out of them, because most of those idiots deserved it. I was becoming more and more disillusioned about what we were doing, but after a couple of raids where the AFP found guns as well as drugs, and cash, not only was a sizable amount of drugs were taken off the market, but we also learned the whereabouts of three drug labs that were used to make chemical drugs. Unfortunately, the largest of the three labs exploded as the occupants tried to make a fight of it instead of facing arrest, three out of the six offenders were killed when the place exploded, but luckily none of the Feds or police were injured.

Then during one of our bitch sessions about half way through the year, as I asked if anyone had anything to bring up, Janice said, "Remember earlier in the year we were all saying how you all thought you've achieved nothing, well I for one didn't really agree with that, and so I did some research and have come up with the following facts."

She took a sip of her coffee as we all looked at her and waited for her to continue, and eventually after finishing a biscuit she smiled, and continued as she looked at me, "Since you became the head of station seventeen years ago boss, we have not lost an agent to anything but accident in all those years, a coupled wounded yes, but not killed!" The other two were smiling and gave quiet applause, and I rocked my head in appreciation.

Janice then continued, saying, "In that time you have personally overseen or taken part in Six thousand nine hundred and fifty six operations of varying duration and size, the results of those operations, are over eighty tons of cocaine, and fifty-six and a half tons of heroin, and copious quantities of hashish, and hemp, and other drug paraphernalia, eighteen tons of weapons being recovered or destroyed, five ton of smuggled gold, and millions in cash being seized before it reached its intended destination, and five hundred and sixty three people being charged with various offences, so boss, as long as I have served at your side and continue to do so, I congratulate you for all the nothing that you think you have achieved, and of course you had the help of all of us in this room doing nothing, and if we've really done nothing, we've had a hell of a busy time not doing it."

All of us were dumfounded, and we just sat there staring at Janice in awe, for a couple of reasons, one, she never really talked much, this was the longest we'd ever heard her speak, and two, she must have spent a long time researching all those figures, and where did she get them in the first place?

Eventually she couldn't keep her face straight, and burst out laughing, as she told us we should have seen our faces, and then we all started laughing, and congratulating her on her facts, and asking where she got it all from. She told us it wasn't easy tracing everything, and that's why it had taken her so long to put her answer together in regard to my non achievement comment.

That year I turned forty-five, so now I was eligible to take retirement and leave the service, but I had made up my mind to wait until the year two thousand before I did, after all it was a mark that I thought I would never live long enough to see, also we had a new threat to contend with.

The so called YtwoK computer bug, was going to make it presence felt when all computers in the world would throw the world into chaos, because no one knew what would happen when computers found a zero, zero, date, so there was a lot of doomsayers out there saying the world would end, we'd end up back in the stone age, no electrical appliance would work, airplanes would fall out of the sky, you know the stuff. All that usual doomsayer mumbo jumbo bullshit! The laughable thing about this, is some people are stupid enough to believe them, but what happens after you front them and question them about their rantings. Ok let's look at it, if you question them before the event and don't believe them? You're a non-believer that is going to learn bigtime, but if you question them after the so called event didn't happen, well their calculations were a little out, but it is still going to happen? I mean really how gullible are people, you figure it out.

Near the end of the year, Rob Ballzinger and I got together again, his mother was living down the coast, and usually we'd play golf together on a Saturday morning, and during our game we'd be coming up with schemes where we would end up being financial enough to live the way we wished, and do what we wanted to do without any restrictions. It was his job to come up with a scheme, and it was my job to tear it to shreds. One morning he outlined, the one   something, that no matter how hard I tried, it couldn't be faulted! Yes, it would take a lot of hard work, but nothing we weren't capable of, it could work!

491

I had the initial amount of capital available to start things off, and so we talked about equal shares, and we'd put everything into a company trust, which allowed no one apart from Rob and myself to have a say in the running of the company.

As things progressed in the office it was left to Rob to find what we were looking for, a production based ship yard.

Part one of our scheme involved the building of our own boat, and once the company was going full ahead, we'd build more than the one. Part two involved talking to TV companies, because we were going to produce our own show.

When we came out of the dead zone time in two thousand, I had Janice call John and Harry to my office, and to join them as well when they arrived. After ten minutes, they all trooped into my office, I had to smile as I saw the little bump in Janice's tummy, she'd finally meet a bloke that made her happy and they had been married a year ago, so now she was about three months into having her first child. I waved them all to seats, and then said, "As you three know you're my dearest friends, so along with that you know I've voiced it on more than one occasion, its two thousand, so shortly I'm going to be ringing Gorman to resign, and please don't try to dissuade me, as you know I've been doing this shit for over thirty years, I'm tired and old, and quite frankly, I just don't give a shit anymore, but I have to say it's been an honour and privilege to serve with you all for the last nineteen years, but it's time I was moving on, time to do my own thing."

On Monday the eighth of May two thousand, I sat through my last Monday meeting, the following day DJ would take over as head of department and station, I took only my belongings, gun holster and the forty five I'd been issued with so long ago now, I was sorry to see my satellite phone go, but I was issued with a new apple mobile phone that had features that no one else's had, but don't expect me to elaborate on those features, what you don't know can't hurt you!

EPILOGUE.

I was approached twice during the next twelve months to come back into the ASIS fold, in July of the following year two thousand and one, I almost succumbed to temptation, because my interpretation was need on radio chatter that had been picked up in Afghanistan, I said no, and kicked myself ever since. On September eleven that year the radical Islamic terrorist group, Al-Qaede which was led by Osama Bin-Laden, hijacked four seven four seven jets, and we all know what the end result was.

In two thousand and five ASIS still wanted to bring me back into the fold, and to date I have resisted the urge to get back into the game!

In twenty ten I travelled back to my old SAS barracks at Swanbourne in Perth for a week that celebrated, the commemoration of fifty years of service as a regiment for the S.A.S. when I arrived all dressed in a suit and tie with my old service beret on, I stopped at the commemoration rock, and stared at the names on it, there were a lot more names on it by then. I looked and found all the names I knew, as I stood there I remembered the faces of each and every one of them, and the times we had together. In respect to them, I came to attention, and saluted all of my old comrades in arms.

As I stood there in salute, I was joined by my old commander Mark Ryan, as I dropped my salute, we shook hands, as we looked at each other, we had both grown a lot older than when we first met, and now our hair colour was the same shade of grey and we remarked on how each of us looked, and then smiled, and then we both turned back to the rock, and he said "Tiger, isn't it amazing, the number of names has grown, and still with the amount of wars going on during the intervening years, the number of troopers actually Killed In Action, is still minute compared to those killed in training, and death by accident."

I looked at him, and replied "That's because of the training, and the fact that we didn't want to let anyone down boss." As we both chuckled over that one, he enquired whether I was still a spook, and seemed pleased when I told him I'd given it away.

During the rest of that week I saw Mark, quite a few times, and some of the old regimental commanders I had during my time with the regiment, which I had considered as short, I was with the regiment for twelve of the thirteen years that I was in the army, and when I first enlisted I thought I'd stay in the green machine for at least until the twenty-year mark, but as all things in life, that changed, and as you've read, I had ended up as a spook for eighteen years before actually quitting.

On the last day of the commemorative week, Mark and I, two people who'd formed a bond forty years beforehand, sat drinking together knowing this would be the last time we saw each other. As I told him I thought my time had been short with the regiment, but I'd met guys at the commemoration that had only been with the regiment in some cases as short as two years, he looked at me and smiled, saying "You can take the man out of the regiment, but you can't take the regiment out of the man, Tiger, you should know that!" I learned later from his family that Mark died peacefully in his sleep, at the age of eighty-six. I considered it a privilege to attend his funeral and say goodbye.

AUTHORS NOTE:

To you my readers, I hope you have enjoyed following Tom's adventurous saga as he made his way through life the only way he knew how, by taking the gambles that some of us hold back on, but who can tell what's around the next corner?

Even Tom admits he did some outrageous things, and took some enormous risks at times, but as he has said many times, *"Back in those days one could get away with the things that I did, but now because of all these new laws and this so called political correctness, what I was able to do then, would be near to impossible nowadays. You ask me if I had regrets, and the answer is yes, would I have changed my life if it had been possible. No, because then I wouldn't be the man I am today."*

I can only wish that you were pleased with the "Catalyst Trilogy" and hope you look forward to more Timothy Diamond novels in the future. Remember that Tom hasn't told us everything that was happening to him in his personal and business life during the years from nineteen eighty-six to ninety-three, and from what he's told me that sounds quite interesting, so my next book will deal with those issues, and I've given it the provisional title of: The Other Side of the Coin and will be a companion book to the Catalyst Trilogy. Also Tom may have had some other adventures that we haven't heard about yet.

Until we meet again with my next novel my thanks for reading

Timothy Diamond.